Dear Reader,

Welcome to t g as the year 2000 is t throughout th

In Duets #17 C ous BEST OF THE WEST story in *The Cowboy Finds a Bride.* These three Best brothers sure are learning there's something *better* than being single. Then new author Isabel Sharpe makes her debut in Duets with *The Way We Weren't,* a charming and original tale of revenge, mayhem and love. No matter how the heroine tries to ruin the hero's life, it only keeps getting better and better. Maybe fate is trying to tell her something….

In Duets #18 Jennifer Drew is back with *Baby Lessons,* a fun, delightful story about a woman who gives baby lessons to the hero, but learns a lesson about love herself. Then Kate Thomas, well-known to readers of Silhouette Romance, writes an entertaining and quirky story of a hero who has too much good luck, while the heroine is cursed with bad luck. Together, they kind of even out the luck thing…but what about love?

Wishing lots of love and luck,

Malle Vallik
Senior Editor

The Cowboy Finds a Bride

"Why don't you show me how much you want to see those dusty old family papers," Cord murmured seductively.

"What do you mean?" Hailey said.

"I mean…" He closed the space between them, until there were only a few inches separating them. "What are you willing to do?"

"This."

When she tried to stomp on his feet, he pinned her legs between his. Suddenly he was struck by the most overwhelming urge to kiss her. So he did.

Hailey couldn't believe Cord was kissing her. Just like that.

And just like that she was going up in flames. Cord made her melt. He made her tremble. He made her crazy.

She was attracted to him. *Again.* Dammit!

For more, turn to page 9

The Way We Weren't

Lance was going to kiss her.

Amber closed her eyes, lost in the exhilarating familiarity of the moment.

He ended the kiss and looked down at her, his breathing uneven, his eyes showing equal measures of desire and uncertainty. Then, in their mesmerizing blue depths, came a flicker of smug satisfaction.

Amber recoiled. What had she just done? What had happened to Amber the Warrior Princess?

Maybe he was about to tell her she could expect her design fee to be paid with sexual favors. *"Care to examine my antique sheet collection?"* he'd ask.

Instead, he said, "I apologize. That was way out of line." The smug look was gone. "It won't happen again."

Amber nodded, and something that felt like disappointment sank like a boulder into her stomach.

"Though I was just thinking—"

The weight in Amber's stomach rose slightly.

He smiled devilishly. "It's a good thing we both had the spicy garlic chicken."

For more, turn to page 197

HARLEQUIN DUETS

ISBN 0-373-44083-9

This edition published by arrangement with Harlequin Books S.A.

Visit us at www.romance.net

Printed in U.S.A.

CATHIE LINZ

The Cowboy Finds a Bride

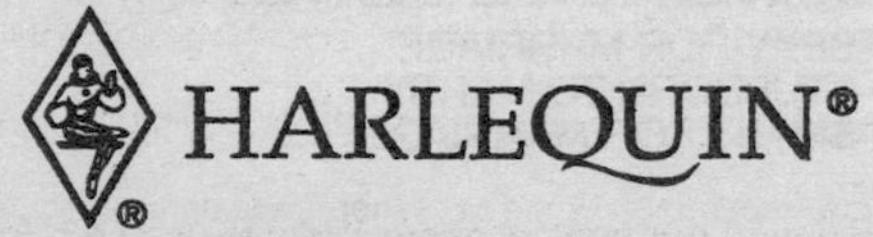

TORONTO • NEW YORK • LONDON
AMSTERDAM • PARIS • SYDNEY • HAMBURG
STOCKHOLM • ATHENS • TOKYO • MILAN • MADRID
PRAGUE • WARSAW • BUDAPEST • AUCKLAND

Dear Reader,

I spent several summers in Colorado and I'll never forget my first visit to a ghost town. It wasn't famous and it had weeds encroaching on the ramshackle buildings. But, oh, the pull of the past was so powerful there…. It was almost as if you could still hear the voices of those long gone.

In this book, my heroine shares my special fondness for the history of the Old West. She also shares my weakness for loners, like Cord, a man who communicates through his work, in this case by making Western furniture. I had a lot of fun putting my own twist on the loner legend, teaming him up with the nuisance next door.

Happy reading,

Cathie Linz

P.S. I wish I owned Cord's rustic mountain cabin, especially if it came fully furnished with Cord and the Western furniture he makes!

Books by Cathie Linz

HARLEQUIN LOVE & LAUGHTER

39—TOO SEXY FOR MARRIAGE
45—TOO STUBBORN TO MARRY
51—TOO SMART FOR MARRIAGE

For my Windy City Romance Writers group with hugs of thanks. You guys are simply the best, constantly awing me with your creative energy and big hearts. With special thanks to Haley for having such a great name even if it isn't spelled right <g>.

BEST
OF THE
WEST

1

"I DON'T TRUST HER. She's up to something." Cord Best shoved a hand through his long dark hair and glared at his older brother, Zane.

"Who are we talking about?" Zane inquired distractedly, his attention on the spreadsheet displaying this year's cattle production stats on the computer monitor in front of him.

"Hailey Hughes. I'm telling you, she's up to something. Coming back here to Bliss and asking all kinds of questions about the legend of Cockeyed Curly's lost gold." Cord started pacing back and forth in the small confines of the den, the only room in the ranch house not yet redecorated by Zane's new wife, Tracy. "She's definitely up to something. I can't help but be suspicious of why she wants that kind of information."

"You can't help being suspicious, period," Zane replied. "Especially where Hailey is concerned. The truth is that she's come home for the summer...you've heard that she's a history professor at the University of Colorado now? Anyway, she's come home to research a book on Cockeyed Curly's treasure."

"There is no treasure. Just like there's no Easter

bun— Oof!'' Cord grunted as Zane elbowed him in the stomach.

''The twins see all and hear all,'' Zane reminded him with a meaningful nod at the open doorway.

''Fight, fight!'' Rusty yelled before jumping into the den from the hallway where he'd been hiding.

''Son of a buck,'' Cord's dad exclaimed as he hurried into the room to give his two grown sons a disapproving look. ''Aren't you two old enough to settle your differences peacefullike?''

''We were talking about Hailey Hughes,'' Cord said in his own defense, sure his dad would take his side.

Sure enough, Buck's expression darkened. ''Tadpole Hughes's daughter?''

''I don't believe that's his given name,'' Zane replied dryly.

''It's the name I've given him. Lucky for him it's not worse.'' Buck's voice reflected his agitation. ''What can you call a low-down, gizzard-sucking coyote who steals the best fish from your own river?''

''I know, I know,'' Rusty interrupted, eagerly jumping up and down. ''You can call them a ba—''

Zane covered his son's mouth with his hand before reminding his father, ''Troublesome Creek borders their land as well as ours.''

''Bah,'' Buck scoffed.

''Hailey is coming back to research one of your favorite topics—Cockeyed Curly,'' Zane said in a clear attempt to head off his dad.

Buck's blue eyes narrowed. "She's coming home? She always was a cute little thing as I recall."

"Cute, hah! She was hell-on-wheels," Cord vehemently declared. "She left a permanent mark on me." He held out his right hand, where a faint scar was still evident on the base of his thumb.

Buck and Rusty both squinted to take a look. Buck shook his head. "Hard to tell with all those other nicks and dings you got on your hands."

"Comes from working with wood." Cord shrugged. "One of the dangers of the trade."

"Carpenters work with wood. You, boy, have a God-given talent." Buck thumped him on the back in a paternal show of pride.

"Yeah, well, talent or not, I'm not looking forward to running into Hailey again," Cord said. "She made my life miserable by trailing after me like a lovesick calf for years. You remember how she used to dog me, no matter how I tried to get rid of her. She had this crush on me the size of Texas." Seeing Zane's frantic hand movements, Cord said, "There's no use denying it, I'm not exaggerating. She was a hellion who wouldn't leave me alone, literally gluing my butt to my seat in high school. Even in the summer, I couldn't turn around without bumping into her...." Finally recognizing his brother's expression, Cord said in a resigned voice, "She's standing right behind me now, isn't she."

"Yes, she is," a woman's clear voice replied. "And I assure you that you have nothing to fear from little ol' me." Her tart voice dripped with sarcasm.

"Son of a buck," Buck exclaimed, looking as if

butter wouldn't melt in his mouth. "You boys sure need some training in how to act when there's a lady around, even if she is an offspring of our no-good coyote of a neighbor, Tadpole Hughes."

Hailey sighed. "I can tell this isn't going to be easy, is it."

"Nothing worthwhile ever is," Buck assured her with a grin.

HAILEY HUGHES HADN'T stepped foot on the Best ranch in almost a decade, but it was as if time had stood still. The stuffed armadillo still stood sentry atop the gunmetal gray file cabinet, and Cord was still complaining that she was a nuisance. Some things never changed.

But she'd changed. She was no longer that tomboyish adolescent with a crush on the boy next door. The boy who'd grown into a man who continued to defy the rules. Instead of going into his family's ranching business like his older brother, he'd made his own way, first as a carpenter and then as a furniture builder and woodworker.

In the intervening time, her father and Buck Best had continued to have their spats. They were usually confined to the fishing rights of Troublesome Creek, so rightly named, but also concerned who had the better ranch.

Her time away in Boulder had given her the emotional distance she needed to return here and encounter Cord. So what if she'd had a momentary lapse and had briefly wanted to strangle him just now when he'd said she'd made his life miserable. *His* life, hah! That was nothing compared to what he'd done to *her* fragile teenage heart. But now all she felt was the slightest sting to her pride that he continued to think of her in such an uncomplimentary way.

She deliberately kept her eyes on him, waiting for him to turn and face her, noting the way he dismissed her with a mocking smile. His dark hair was longer than she'd ever seen it, falling around his shoulders as if he didn't care that he needed a haircut. Like his brother, he was wearing jeans and a denim shirt. But unlike Zane, Cord projected a dark impatience and the aura of a died-in-the-wool loner.

Her father had told her that Cord had made a few comments around town about her turning into a dried-up bookworm. She could tell by the gleam in his riveting ultra-blue eyes that he thought her suit was something a bookworm would wear. She'd come here today as an associate professor of history, and she'd dressed the part as much to remind herself of her identity as anything else. The gold wire-rimmed glasses she wore contributed to her serious look, and her chin-length, dark brown hair was styled in a smooth cut meant to convey she was nobody's fool.

Ignoring Cord, she addressed her comments to the head of the family, Buck. "Look, I realize you and my father have had this feud going for years—"

"—about who has the better ranch," Buck finished for her. "And I'll tell you what I tell everyone else, that the answer is in our name. Ours is the Best ranch."

"Yes, well...." She shoved her glasses up the

bridge of her nose, a nervous habit she was trying to break. "I didn't come here to discuss that. I came here to make a proposition."

"My pa propositioned my new mom," Rusty piped up.

"So, Button, did you come here to talk marriage?" Cord asked Hailey with a mocking tilt to his dark eyebrows that she recognized all too well. Ditto for his nickname of her. It was a nickname old-time cowboys used for a kid. As a chubby teenager, she'd been convinced Cord had used it simply to make fun of her. Buttons were round and so was she. "Did you come here to propose?"

"The best Best brother is already taken," she replied. "Congratulations on your marriage, Zane."

"Thanks."

She could tell by Zane's smile that he was delighted to see someone getting the best of his brother, but she wasn't about to get into a verbal joust with Cord. Returning her attention to Buck, she said, "The only thing I came here to propose is in regard to the book I'm writing on Colorado outlaws, including Cockeyed Curly. As you know, legend has it that he had to stash the gold coins from his last and largest heist somewhere in the area because he was being chased by a posse and the gold was slowing him down."

Buck nodded. "That's right. And legend also has it that my great-great-granddaddy saved Curly's hide in a barroom fight over in Leadville. To repay Jedidiah, Curly drew him a map supposedly showing where he'd buried his treasure. Then Curly went to eat that fateful steak dinner where he choked and died.''

''You could say he was a victim of the pre-Heimlich era,'' Cord drawled.

''Son of a buck, that's a good one,'' Buck chortled, slapping his hand on his knee.

''I'd love to see any paperwork you have regarding Cockeyed Curly,'' Hailey said, determined to keep the conversation on track.

''By paperwork, she means the treasure map,'' Cord said. ''Which we have no proof ever really existed.''

Hailey gave him a look that could sizzle bacon. ''I mean any paperwork, any letters, any references in a diary. Anything that would give me an idea of what kind of man he was.''

''The kind who robs banks and leaves silly poems behind,'' Cord replied.

''Hey, don't you go insulting Curly's poems,'' Buck declared in an affronted voice. ''The man was a genius! And I think it's about time someone wrote a book about him. You're welcome to look at any historical papers we've got, Hailey. There are three old trunks filled with them up at the homesteading cabin.''

''So you would be willing to allow me to see those papers?'' Hailey eagerly asked.

''Those family papers are irreplaceable,'' Cord answered on his father's behalf. ''We're not letting them out of that cabin.''

''That's okay with me,'' Hailey said.

''But I'm living in that cabin!'' Cord protested.

"A huge drawback," Hailey admitted, "but one I'm willing to live with in the name of historical research."

"And what if I'm not willing to live with it?" Cord asked.

"You don't have to live with her," Buck said. "You just have to keep an eye on Hailey here while she does her research, since you're so fired up on protecting those old papers." He paused to fix his son with a challenging look. "Unless you think the job's too much for you?"

Cord scowled at Hailey as if holding her personally responsible for everything that had ever frustrated him on this earth. "I've got better things to do than baby-sit a bookworm."

"Then do them and let me do my job," Hailey shot back, her look equally infuriated.

"Fight, fight!" Rusty gleefully exclaimed.

"Where, where?" his twin sister, Lucky, demanded as she skidded into the room.

"Nowhere," their father, Zane, replied. "I thought the two of you were going to help your mother make brownies."

"It's more fun in here," Rusty declared.

"Hey, kids," a woman's voice called from down the hall. "I'm thinking of adding broccoli to the brownies."

A horrified look came over the twins' faces as they shrieked "No!" and raced out of the room.

"Tracy's clever, I'll give her that," Cord noted.

"She's brilliant," Zane proudly declared.

"And to think she married you anyway." Cord shook his head with fraternal amazement.

"Cute, bro. Very cute," Zane said. "Now, where were we? Ah, yes. You were making a horse's ass of yourself while Hailey here was standing up for herself. Feel free to continue."

2

CORD DIDN'T APPRECIATE his brother taking Hailey's side instead of his. "There comes a time when family need to stand together," he growled with a meaningful look in Zane's direction.

"Not when you're standing on shaky ground," Zane said.

"The ground I'm standing on is rock hard," Cord objected. "And those papers aren't leaving my cabin."

"I've already agreed to those terms," Hailey said. Solemnly placing her hand over her heart, she vowed, "I promise not to take any of the Best family papers from the cabin and only read them on site."

Feeling outnumbered, Cord knew when to cut his losses. That didn't mean he had to be happy about it. Turning to Hailey, he said, "Be at my place tomorrow morning, then. Eight a.m. would be convenient for me." He left the room without waiting to hear if it would be convenient for her. The truth was that Hailey Hughes and convenient had never gone together in the same sentence before, let alone the same breath.

But that had been years ago. He needed some time alone to figure out why he'd reacted so strongly to her after all these years. Heck, he'd reacted even *before* seeing her.

And seeing her had…what? Changed his mind? No.

He still felt she was a nuisance.

He wasn't a man who liked company, who liked people getting in the way of his routine. That's why he lived up in the homesteading cabin instead of down here at the ranch. Because he liked being on his own.

If Hailey had shown up just to say a friendly howdy, he probably wouldn't have gotten all hot around the collar. But no, she'd come to shake things up by plunking herself right in the middle of his life and disturbing his plans.

She'd grown some since he'd seen her last. She was all woman now, without any sign of the baby fat she'd had as a kid. But her eyes still had fire in them, even if her clothes screamed bookworm. Not that he was any expert on women's fashion by any stretch of the imagination. But even he could tell that she looked like a prim and proper academic who was only passionate about one thing—her research.

While she'd been filling her head with historical information at the University of Colorado at Boulder, he'd been traveling the West and apprenticing with carpenters and woodworkers instead of attending college as both his brothers had. He'd been living life instead of reading about it in some book.

Cord had never claimed to be the brains in the family. He'd never done well in school and had seemed to struggle twice as hard as his brothers to do half as well.

But he'd always been good with his hands, always felt drawn to wood from the moment he'd been knee-high to a grasshopper and had collected branches and logs from fallen trees and dead bushes to build his own fort.

Later he'd taken up whittling and made his own toys—animals he'd seen around the ranch. Beavers, elk, deer. He'd carved a particularly fine elk with ten-point antlers, only to have Hailey smash it a few months later when he'd had it on display at school.

As he'd tried to tell his father and brother, Hailey had been the nuisance next door for all his formative years. There was no reason for him to think that things would be any different now.

"I'M SORRY ABOUT MY SON'S reaction," Buck told Hailey with a rueful shake of his white-haired head. "Cord always did have his own way of doing things and never has taken kindly to being told what to do."

"I didn't mean to cause trouble," Hailey assured him. Even if Buck and her father had a feud going, she'd never participated in it and had always had a soft spot for the elder Best and his wild stories of the old days. Her own father's stories were limited to fishing tales, but Buck had fed her love for the Old West with his storytelling skills.

"I know that," Buck replied. "And Cord will know that too, once he has time to reflect on it."

As if on cue, Cord strode back into the room. "I left my hat," he explained, his voice curt.

A second later the soft sound of Hailey's aunt Alicia drifted in from the doorway. "I'm sorry to interrupt, Hailey, but we should be going."

"I didn't realize you were here, Alicia," Buck said, straightening his shoulders before frowning at his two sons. "Stand up when a lady enters the room," he ordered Zane, then smacked Cord on the back. "And, you, straighten up when you speak to a lady!"

"I didn't say a word," Cord muttered. Nonetheless, he stood ramrod straight.

Alicia blushed at all the attention.

Frankly, Hailey was surprised by Buck's reaction to her aunt. He hadn't reprimanded his sons about their posture while Hailey was in the room, which meant that Buck mustn't consider Hailey to be a "lady," or else he wanted to impress Alicia. Either option seemed hard to accept.

And then there was her aunt's blush. Granted, Alicia was as soft-spoken and shy a woman as you'd find in the entire state. But that didn't mean she was given to bouts of flushed cheeks. She'd always had her feet on the ground, and had helped raise Hailey after her mother had died when she was seven.

"We'd better be going," Hailey said.

"So soon?" Buck asked with a strange look in Alicia's direction. "Where have you been all this time?"

"In the kitchen with Tracy and the twins," Alicia quietly replied. "I gave her my double-chocolate brownie recipe."

Buck raised one bushy eyebrow and looked like a kid on Christmas Eve, filled with eager anticipation. "You mean the one that won first prize at the fair?" When Alicia nodded, he added, "That was mighty generous of you. Wasn't it, boys?"

Zane and Cord both nodded even while they looked at their father as if he weren't quite right in the head.

"It was nothing." Alicia's blush deepened. "I was just being neighborly."

Hailey was grateful Cord didn't point out that the Best family and the Hughes family had never been on good terms in the past.

"Yes, well, we'd better be going," Hailey repeated. "I'll see you in the morning, Cord." This time she was the one to walk out first. As she did so, she decided that it felt better being the "leaver" than the "leavee."

Once she and her aunt were in the blue pickup truck Hailey had brought with her from Boulder, Hailey couldn't contain her curiosity any longer. "Why were you so flustered back there when Buck spoke to you?"

Lifting her chin, Alicia feigned ignorance. "What are you talking about?"

"Your cheeks were all flushed."

"That's because I was baking in the kitchen. Leaning over a hot oven will do that to you." Alicia quickly changed the subject. "What does your father have to say about your plans to research the Best family history?"

"I'm not really researching their history," Hailey replied. "It's all part of the history of Colorado's outlaws that I'm interested in."

"You're interested in history, period," Alicia said affectionately.

Hailey laughed. "True enough."

"So I'll ask you again, what does your father have to say about all this?"

"Nothing. Because I haven't told him yet."

Alicia gave her a commiserating glance and patted her on the shoulder before saying, "Better you than me."

HAILEY PLANNED ON WAITING until her father had eaten one of Alicia's delicious dinners before approaching him on the subject that evening.

For the first few days after her return, it had seemed strange being back at the ranch house where she'd grown up after living on her own in Boulder for so many years. She'd subletted her condo there to a visiting professor for the summer and had brought her laptop computer and research materials, along with a couple of suitcases filled with clothes to the ranch.

While Alicia had reupholstered the furniture in the living room and made a few other improvements over the intervening years, Hailey's old room was pretty much as she'd left it, with her honor roll society plaques from high school still on the wall. As a teenager she'd loved the English-cottage floral wallpaper in shades of pinks and greens, and her tastes remained the same.

Another thing that hadn't altered was her father's inherent ability to ferret out information. "Where were you all afternoon?" he asked Hailey, his brown eyes focusing on her with the I-know-you've-been-up-to-something look that only a parent can perfect.

Even after all these years, she had to resist the urge to guiltily squirm in her seat.

"I was doing some preliminary groundwork for the research I need to do for my new book," she replied. "You remember, I told you about it. I'm writing a book on Colorado outlaws."

He nodded as if he knew what she was talking about, although she suspected that once she mentioned research, most of what she said after that went in one ear and out the other.

Although she knew her father loved her, too much sometimes, he didn't share her passion for history. His passion was fishing, something she had no interest in, so she couldn't blame his lack of enthusiasm. She knew she looked just as glassy-eyed after he launched into a discussion about some new fly-fishing technique.

She also knew that she couldn't put off telling him about her visit to the Best ranch forever. But she waited until dessert before going into the details.

"Anyway, I got the permission I needed to continue my research about Cockeyed Curly Mahoney," she said.

"Cockeyed Curly?" Tad repeated suspiciously, his eyes relentlessly pinning her with yet another parental stare. "You don't mean that desperado that wacky Buck Best is always frothing at the mouth about, do you?"

Hailey nodded. "The one and only."

"One Buck Best is one coyote too many," Tad growled.

"He says the same about you."

"I know, but I'm the one who's right. He's the one that's crazy."

"Well, crazy or not, he's given me permission to

go through his family's records for any information about Curly.''

Her father glanced up from the cherry pie he was devouring to fix her with a disapproving look. ''You better not be telling me that you're going to be spending time at that rundown ranch next door.''

''I'm not telling you that, no.''

''Good thing. Because I'd have to put my foot down and say no to that lame idea.''

''I'll be spending time up at their homesteader's cabin. That's where the papers are stored.''

''Wait a minute here!'' Tad dropped his fork. ''Isn't that where Cord is living?''

''Yes. That is a drawback, but I'm sure we can work around it.''

''Not in this lifetime!'' Tad's roar rattled the glasses in the sideboard. Knowing that his bark was much worse than his bite, and accustomed to his temper tantrums, Hailey smiled reassuringly at her aunt, who rolled her eyes in an I-told-you-so kind of way.

''It was bad enough that you kept sneaking off to go over there when you were a teenager,'' Tad raved. ''I'm not having you disgrace our good name by hanging out with a man like Cord. He doesn't even have a decent job.''

''I believe he's made quite a name for himself as a woodworker and furniture maker.''

''That's what I mean. What kind of job is that for a grown man?''

''A good-paying one, most likely. Western-style furniture is very popular right now, and people are willing to pay top dollar for good workmanship.''

''Humph.'' Tad broke off a piece of piecrust and

slipped it to his pug, Belch, so named because of his bad habit of burping.

Her father's other dog, Lurch, didn't approve of Belch getting something he didn't, and made his disapproval known. And when a Great Dane wasn't happy, no one in the household was, either. So Lurch got a piece of piecrust, too. A *big* piece.

"You're just a pair of lop-eared pot lickers," he said, grinning down at them.

Watching her father with his two pets, Hailey couldn't help fondly reflecting that her father had the pugnacious nature and round face of the pug, while his large build resembled the Great Dane. It was said that you started looking like your pets after a while. Or maybe Tad just molded the two dogs to his own character. She found that more likely.

Her father had that effect on people and animals, bending them to his will through the sheer force of his personality. But it didn't work on her.

He'd always been a benevolent dictator, some days more dictator than benevolent, some days more indulgent parent than dictator. But she'd always been able to stand up to him, not in a disrespectful way, but in her own way.

"I don't approve of you consorting with those no-good Texans next door," he was saying, his voice a low bellow now.

"Dad, the Best family settled here over a hundred years ago."

"Doesn't change the fact that they came from Texas."

"And we originally came from Scotland," she replied.

"So what?"

"So we have a long line of ancestors and a sterling reputation. Why don't you research our family instead of theirs?"

So that was what bothered her father. Well, one of the things, anyway. He'd been after her to do a detailed family tree for years, and it was on her list of things to do when she had more time. For now they had names and dates of births and deaths in the family Bible, and that was enough for her, but her dad really wanted her to write a book dedicated entirely to the Hughes family.

"I'm not researching their family," she quickly corrected him. "I'm only researching the legend of Cockeyed Curly and his outlaw ways."

Her dad's brown eyes lit up with a sudden memory. "Isn't he the one who supposedly buried his treasure around here?"

"That's right."

Suddenly her father was all smiles. "So that's what you're doing. You're going to find out where this guy hid his treasure and then steal it right out from under old Bucko's nose."

"I wouldn't do any such thing," she indignantly denied. "My aunt raised me better than that."

"Thank you, dear," Alicia said with a fond smile.

"Sure, sure, you can't admit it yet. Don't want to count your chickens before they're hatched. I can understand that." Tad nodded and winked at Hailey before reaching for his fork. "I'll pretend I didn't figure things out. No one will learn the truth from me, I can promise you that."

Rolling her eyes, Hailey gave up. Her father had

always been a person who chose not to be confused with facts, preferring his own view of the world. And she knew from past experience that once he'd put his own spin on things, there was no budging him.

WHEN HAILEY ARRIVED at the cabin the next morning, the sun's rays filtered through the pine trees, creating a medley of light and shadow. The top of Bear Tooth Mountain peeked through the treetops like a flirtatious woman, disappearing as Hailey came closer. The meadow all around her shimmered with frost. As she climbed the steps to the cabin door, Hailey could see her breath, an unnecessary reminder that the mornings were colder up here in the higher elevation than down in the valley. Out of the corner of her eye, she caught sight of a rabbit, its nose quivering nervously.

Hailey shoved her glasses up the bridge of her own nose before taking them off completely and sticking them in a case in her backpack, where she had her laptop computer stashed. She hadn't dressed the part of an associate professor today. Instead she'd dressed like a woman who wanted to knock a man's socks off.

Not that she was wearing black lace and showing bare skin. That wasn't her style. But while a junior in college, she had actually worked as a catalog model for a regional mail-order company that had specialized in western attire and had advertised on the University of Colorado campus for models. By then Hailey had shed the extra pounds she'd had as a teenager but she was by no means thin. Even so, on a dare, Hailey had gone for an interview, and to her astonishment had been hired. They had told her she had a healthy, outdoorsy look they'd liked. They hadn't been looking for thin waifs but for real women.

Granted, that had been eight years ago now, but the experience had taught her a lot, and the extra money had come in handy paying for her college expenses.

She knew she looked her best in the jeans and matching denim jacket she wore. Her chambray shirt was open at the throat, showing just a hint of cleavage—a whisper rather than a shout. Her sterling silver choker and matching dangle earrings lit up her face, while the rosy shade of her lipstick made her mouth stand out. Her appearance was that of a capable woman—capable of what, she wasn't quite sure yet.

She knocked on the cabin's front door twice before Cord deigned to answer. His dark hair was damp and ruffled, as if he'd just come out of the shower. Thank heavens he was fully dressed, although the buttons on his shirt were still undone. He was doing them up even as he spoke to her.

"You're late," he grumbled, not really looking at her as he turned to make a beeline for a coffeepot on the kitchen counter.

So much for her making an impression, she noted wryly, before removing her gaze from his sexy denim-covered backside to her surroundings. The rustic cabin had an open plan, without interior walls between the kitchen and living room. A large fieldstone fireplace took up most of one outer wall, and the remaining rough-hewn log walls conveyed the frontier life-style of a bygone age. And out back was an addition with what appeared to be a spacious woodworking shop. She saw a tiny bathroom tucked away beneath the staircase, which led up to what she presumed was the loft's sleeping area.

The few and scattered furnishings matched the cabin in texture and design. She wondered if Cord had made the large cabinet in the corner with its meticulously carved inset of a bear, or the wonderfully whimsical bookcase of contorted lodgepole uprights beyond the fireplace. If these were samples of his work, then she could see why he was so popular. Or why his *work* was so popular.

Given his grizzly-bear personality and loner tendencies, Cord had never been the popular one in his family. That label had fallen to Reno, who was now the town sheriff. A perfect job for a person who liked working with people.

She suspected that Cord preferred working with wood. She already knew that he didn't welcome her company. But then she hadn't been the genius who suggested working at his cabin. That brilliantly stupid idea had been all his.

When her gaze returned to Cord, she realized that he'd paused in his coffee sipping to study her, surprise flickering in his deep blue eyes. Surprise...and was that male appreciation she saw? Just for a second?

CORD COULDN'T BELIEVE what a difference a day made. The woman standing before him bore little resemblance to the one he'd seen at the ranch last night. Oh, she had the same silky mahogany hair and flashing eyes. But those eyes seemed bluer today. And her body was a work of art—hips that tempted a man to test their softness. And cleavage…jeez, Hailey had cleavage! When had that happened?

He blinked. She was still there, and so were her breasts, thrusting out as she removed her denim jacket.

"What are you doing?" he croaked.

She smiled at him as if knowing the effect she had on him. Had her mouth been that lush yesterday? He could have sworn it was thin and prim. He was wrong. About some things. But not about others. Hailey wanted to rattle him, he saw it in her expression. And she was pleased that she'd succeeded.

Two could play that game.

"I'm taking off my coat," she answered him. "If that's okay with you?"

He gave her a very slow once-over that lingered on her feminine attributes. "You can take off as many clothes as you want."

She frowned at him, but she seemed uncertain rather than outraged. In fact, she looked as if she couldn't possibly have heard him correctly.

Good. Let her be the one shaken up for a change. She'd made a fool of him by dressing up the way she had yesterday, pretending to be something she wasn't. Or was she pretending today? Who knew? Setting down his coffee mug, he moved closer.

"In fact, why don't you show me how much you want to see those dusty old family papers," he murmured seductively.

Her uncertainty grew. "What do you mean?"

"I mean…" He closed the space between them

until there were only a few inches between his body and hers. "What's it worth to you to look at the Best family papers?"

"The research possibilities are endless," she replied.

Was her voice breathless? He sure hoped so. "I like endless possibilities." He reached out to brush the backs of his fingers across her cheek as she stared at him with the open eyes of a startled doe. "What are you willing to do?"

"Do?" Now she was the one whose voice croaked.

"Yeah, do. To make sure I let you see what you want to see."

"This." A second later, without so much as a warning flash of her eyes, she elbowed him in the stomach. She ignored his startled "oof" as she planted her hands on her hips and read him the riot act. "How dare you make such an outrageous suggestion! Your father would tan your hide if he knew what you just said to me!"

As the firebrand in her came out, Cord knew he'd been had. She was no bookworm. There was nothing prim or proper about her. She was still as hell-on-wheels as ever.

"I've got a good mind to go down to the ranch and tell him what a slug he has for a son." She socked Cord's arm for good measure.

"Hey there, calm down for a minute, would you? I was just teasing you."

His words seemed to inflame her even more. "Tease me? What an idiotic, cruel thing to do, you jerk!" She socked his other arm.

"Stop hitting me!" he growled, slipping his arms around her for his own protection and pinning her arms to her side.

When she tried to stomp on his feet, he captured her legs between his. Holding her this way, he was suddenly struck by the most overwhelming urge to kiss her. So he did.

HAILEY COULDN'T BELIEVE Cord was kissing her. Just like that. One second he was growling at her and the next his lips were on hers. Just like that.

And just like that she was going up in flames.

Her anger had already gotten her blood boiling, but now it was fired by another emotion—desire. Passion. It wasn't a teasing kiss. Had it even started out that way? She couldn't remember. She only knew that he tasted like hot coffee and forbidden sex.

Her eyes were closed, her mouth open. He'd caught her midword, but he made the most of the moment by swirling his tongue across her lower lip with seductive passion. She heard his startled breath as she greeted his tongue with her own. She'd waited her entire life for him to kiss her—wondered about it, fantasized and dreamed about it. And now the moment was here.

This heavenly…terrifying…blissful moment.

A moment that had the power to change everything, unlocking the secrets of her heart and send them tumbling out without protection.

He made her melt. He made her tremble. He made her crazy.

She was attracted to him again.

Dammit!

3

DAMMIT! CORD COULDN'T BELIEVE he was kissing Hailey or that she was kissing him back. He felt as if he'd been hit by lightning. Or a locomotive. Or both.

Talk about sizzle! This was more than sizzle. This was a branding of the soul.

Cattle were branded. Not cowboys. Not him.

He was kissing the nuisance next door, who'd always ended up getting him into some kind of trouble. Tangling with her always resulted with him getting physically injured somehow, someway.

Seemingly on cue, Hailey gasped, as if only now realizing she was kissing him. She shoved him away from her with an unexpected suddenness that sent him stumbling backward, resulting in him smacking his lower calf against the sharp corner of one of the old steamer trunks that stored the family papers.

His curses turned the air blue. Sinking to the trunk, he grabbed his throbbing leg and eyed her warily. "Why is it that whenever I'm around you, I end up as one of the walking wounded?"

She showed no signs of remorse. Instead she wrapped her arms around her middle and lifted her chin to haughtily inform him, "You shouldn't have kissed me."

"Tell me something I don't know," he said. Cord had always prided himself on his ability to remain aloof, but Hailey still had the ability to push his buttons. She got under his skin, even after her long absence. She'd made him lose his temper the first time he'd seen her yesterday.

And today...well, today she'd made him lose his mind and kiss her.

This had to stop. He never lost his temper. And he was always in control.

He had to get away from her. Regain some perspective. Get some distance.

Standing up, he gingerly tested his weight on his bruised leg. He suspected his pride was injured as much as his body, but he had no doubt he'd have a heck of a black-and-blue bruise by tonight, proving that once again Hailey had left her mark on him. The important thing was not to let her leave her mark on his heart.

"Don't take the papers out of this room," he told her. "I'm going out to get some air. But I'll be back."

HAILEY SAGGED like a rag doll into a chair the moment he left. Danger! Danger! The warning screamed in her mind, but it came too late. All her old feelings for Cord had resurfaced with a vengeance.

This was why she'd never been able to fully commit to another man. Because no other man had ever affected her as strongly as Cord did.

There had been other men in her life. She'd even made love with two of them—one, Rob, had been a fellow college student when she was twenty, and the other, Ben, had been a landscape architect who'd wanted to marry her two years ago. But she'd said no to Ben's proposal because deep in her heart she hadn't felt that he was the right man for her.

There was no logical way she could say that Cord was right for her. But she was dealing with emotions here, with feelings that refused to be thwarted by good sense. And after that kiss, there was no use pretending to herself any longer. Something inside of her had clicked, like the tumbler on a safe as it fell into place with the right combination. She'd never felt this way before, all hot and bothered, all churned up as if she had champagne bubbles in her veins.

How had this happened? Who knew that his kiss would be so earth-shattering? Okay, so maybe the earth beneath her feet hadn't actually moved, but it sure as heck had shifted.

Her work. She needed to focus on her work. Not the steamy memory of his lips on hers. She needed to concentrate on the stories of the past enclosed in that trunk.

As she knelt before it, she couldn't help feeling like Pandora opening that box and letting all kinds of trouble out. And once they were out, there was no stuffing them back.

Why had Cord kissed her? What had he been hoping to achieve? Had he just been toying with her? If that had been the case, it had backfired, because he sure hadn't been immune to the delicious fire.

Unlike the last time. She'd only been fifteen, wanting her first kiss to be from Cord and no other. She'd finally cornered him behind the Best barn on a rainy

Sunday afternoon in May and had asked him to kiss her.

He'd looked at her as if she'd asked him to eat cow dung. Then he'd laughed in her face. She'd been so embarrassed and humiliated that she'd wanted to slink off and find a hole to hide in. Even now, the memory still made her cringe.

Like a devil perched on her shoulder, an inner voice urged her to teach Cord a lesson for treating her so badly all those years ago, destroying her fragile self-confidence. Not to mention his bad behavior today. It would serve him right if she gave him a dose of his own medicine.

What if she tried to make him fall for her? Could she do it?

Much as he might try to hide it, she knew their kiss had shaken him as much as it had her. He hadn't been immune to her. He might have tried to dismiss her, but beneath that had been something powerful.

How could it hurt to turn the tables on him? For years he'd teased her mercilessly, calling her Button, making fun of her weight. Now it was her turn to be in a position of influence. And it would serve him right if she "influenced" him to regard her as an attractive woman instead of the nuisance next door.

Besides, it wouldn't do her damaged self-esteem any harm, either. Providing she was successful. And if she wasn't, she'd know soon enough and forget about it. But if she had her way, Cord Best wouldn't know what hit him.

Meanwhile, she had work to do.

By the time Cord returned thirty minutes later, she was already engrossed in the contents of the trunk, which she carefully inventoried as she read through each paper. It was slow going, but she loved the meticulous work.

Her laptop computer made things easier as she entered each new document she found, along with its date and an annotation of its contents. She deliberately immersed herself in the past, ignoring Cord, who was busy doing something noisy in his spacious workshop at the back of the cabin.

But that didn't mean she was able to toss him out of her thoughts. How should she go about making him fall for her? It wasn't as if she'd had much experience in the femme fatale department.

Well, she wasn't about to sit there brooding about it. The point was for her to disturb Cord, not the other way around. And she'd start her plan tomorrow. For today, she'd surround herself with Colorado's past.

The journal was about a third of the way down the trunk, beneath a pile of newspapers and ranch records circa World War I. But the journal was much older than that. She knew that the minute she held it in her hands.

Opening the cover confirmed it. In a formal feminine hand was written the date of the first entry.

June 12, 1880

I leave for Colorado tomorrow morning. My brother Jedidiah has finally come to get me. While I love Aunt Augusta, I'm so glad to be going on this adventure. Jedidiah has finished building a big ranch house and I cannot wait to see the mountains he talks so glowingly about.

Jedidiah tells me it is much colder for much longer up in Colorado than it is here in Texas, but I do not mind. I just know that life will be better there.

Hailey's hands trembled. Jedidiah Best was the homesteader who'd built this cabin, a contemporary of Cockeyed Curly's. And this journal was written by his sister, Rebecca. What a find!

She was tempted to tell Cord, but she doubted he'd appreciate the interruption. Besides, he might not regard a woman's diary as something worthy of such excitement, but Hailey loved viewing the past from a female perspective.

For so many years, history had mainly been the record of men's accomplishments. Now women's history had come into its own. Once she was done with this book on Colorado outlaws, she hoped to do a book about Colorado women.

But first things first. She knew that Jedidiah Best was the one who'd supposedly saved Cockeyed Curly's life in a saloon brawl. Which is why Curly had shown his appreciation by drawing a map indicating where a portion of his treasure was buried. Or so the legend went.

Rebecca's journal was important since it was the first document Hailey had run across from that period. Who knew what Rebecca might have written? The hours sped by as she read each page, becoming thoroughly immersed in Rebecca's life.

She vaguely heard Cord asking her if she'd brought her own lunch. She shook her head and waved him away as she continued to read on.

With her glasses once more perched on her nose, and her nose stuck in a book, Cord was struck anew by how little they had in common. The differences between them hit home for him big time. They might have grown up next door to each other, but she'd gone on to college while he'd gone to work on a construction crew after high school. He was a man who worked with his hands, not his mind. She'd become a woman who worked with her mind, his complete opposite.

So why had her mouth fit so perfectly with his?

HAILEY COULDN'T WAIT to return to the cabin the next morning. She tried telling herself it was because of the discovery of Rebecca's journal, but there was no denying it was also because of the discovery of Cord's Achilles' heel. For all intents and purposes, the man liked kissing her. And she'd certainly liked kissing him.

Not that there would be any kissing going on today. No way. Today she aimed on doing a little flirting. If she didn't chicken out.

It did not go well. To begin with, Cord barely acknowledged her presence after letting her into the cabin. He grabbed his coffee and headed straight for his workshop.

The girl she'd been would have given up. The overweight ''Button'' would have thrown in the towel. Or glued Cord's butt to his seat as she'd done in high school.

But she was a woman now, a woman on a mission. So she brought Cord a thick slice of Alicia's special cinnamon coffee cake and practically waved it under his nose before he noticed her...or more accurately, noticed the food.

"Is this for me?" He sounded surprised.

Surprised was good, she decided. "Yes. I thought you might be hungry."

"Mmm-taks."

She translated that as "Mmm, thanks," but since his mouth was full of coffee cake, she couldn't be certain.

When she perched on the corner of his huge worktable, he finally paid attention to her. She practiced the kind of classically flirtatious look that Liz Taylor would have given Richard Burton—part sideways glance, part sweeping dark lashes.

"Have you got something in your eyes?" Cord said. "You look funny."

So much for that. Apparently you needed Liz's violet eyes to get away with that move. Okay, on to plan B. Which gave her the false impression that she'd actually had a game plan.

When the phone near his work bench rang, she couldn't help thinking, *Ah, saved by the bell.* The phone call would give her a few minutes to get her strategy perfected.

"What?" Cord practically growled into the receiver. "Very funny, Zane. You called to correct my phone manners? Dinner? Tonight? Can't. Gotta go." He hung up without further ado.

So much for having a few minutes to think.

Maybe she should ask him about his work. That usually went over big with the men she'd known. Hopping down from the table, she moved closer to lean toward him, giving him a whiff of her subtle perfume. No use knocking him out with some strong scent. She needed to be a whisper, not a shout. She also needed to be subtle, not sappy. "What are you working on?"

Cord knew she was up to something, he just wasn't sure what. The only thing he was sure of was that he was getting treated to a great look at the curve of her breasts, thanks to the way she was leaning forward. Her open shirt, the same pink as her lips, had gaped alarmingly and was generously displaying an ample amount of creamy skin. And since when had she started smelling so good? Or was that the cinnamon coffee cake?

Hunger prowled through his system but it wasn't for food. It was for her. Man to woman, mouth to mouth, naked body to naked body. Damn, he was horny for the nuisance next door. How had that happened?

She had one hand braced on his worktable, her slender fingers looking even more delicate next to his large capable hands. Yet another sign of how different their lives had become. "Why do you care what I'm working on?" His voice was deliberately curt.

"Because you're such a sexy hunk." Her grin was downright saucy.

Eyeing her suspiciously, he said, "Are you flirting with me?"

Instead of denying it or laughing at him, she astonished him by saying, "What would you do if I was? Run screaming to the nearest hills?"

"The nearest hills are right outside my door," he said with a wry nod toward the window and the mountains visible through it. "Do I seem the type to run screaming from anything?"

"Screaming at, maybe," she said with a rueful smile. "Not screaming from."

He was incredibly tempted by the curve of her mouth. What was wrong with him? He should have been amused or annoyed by her temptress routine, not aroused. The woman was a menace! "You haven't said if you're flirting with me."

"If I were flirting, I'd hardly admit it, would I? That would defeat the purpose."

"Which is?" he said impatiently, never one to play games.

"You'll have to figure that out."

"I haven't been able to figure you out since you smashed my elk," he muttered.

She stared at him blankly. "Huh?"

He felt stupid bringing it up now, but since she'd heard him, there was no going back. "That ten-point elk I carved when we were in grade school. It was my first really good piece of work and I brought it to school so they could put it in the display case. But you smashed it before it got there."

"I would never do something that mean!"

"What about gluing my butt to the chair when I was in high school?"

She waved his words away. "You deserved that. You made fun of me in front of my entire gym class. As for your carving, that was an accident."

"Sure it was," he mocked her. "An accident that happens a lot whenever I'm around you."

It was true. She'd always been awkward when she'd been around him. As for the carving, she'd been jockeying to get a better look at it when she'd accidentally bumped into it. She remembered putting her hands out to catch it, but the elk had fallen to the floor and its antlers had broken. Her nine-year-old heart had broken, too, as the other kids had made fun of her, calling her a clumsy cow.

Those days were gone. Now she had something to prove to Cord. That she wasn't the overweight nuisance next door who smashed things he cared about. That she was an attractive, intelligent woman. Okay, so he'd already indicated that he thought she was intelligent by calling her a bookworm. That meant she needed to concentrate on the attractive part.

And then there was the guilt. She felt badly that she'd caused him trouble in the past, and there was a part of her that wanted to make it up to him. Anyone could see that the man needed a keeper. He didn't take good care of himself. When he worked, he lost complete track of time. She did the same thing. But even she wasn't as bad as he was. She'd taken a quick peek in his fridge and it was pitifully empty.

The next day, after undoing another button on her shirt, she brought along the fixings for a meal fit for a king. Well, fit for a hungry cowboy, anyway. The soup was a specialty of hers and the bread was homemade.

By noon the cabin was filled with the tantalizing smell of simmering vegetables and beef while the bread warmed in the oven. Cord actually abandoned his workshop to track down the source of all this good stuff.

Of course, being Cord, he had to be curt about it. "What's going on in here?"

"I got tired of eating a cold sandwich for lunch and felt like whipping up a little something more substantial. I hope you don't mind that I used your kitchen. There's plenty here to share." As she spoke, she gathered up a bowl and ladled a lumberjack-size portion of the thick soup into it before setting it on the pine table along with a spoon. "I don't know how to make this recipe any smaller and there's enough for an army here." She snagged the bread and butter and added that, along with her own bowl of soup, to the table.

"Go ahead and dig in," she invited him with a casualness intended to tell him that it made no difference to her whether he stayed or left.

He stayed. He ate. She conquered.

If she'd known the way to his heart was through his stomach, she'd have tried it earlier.

Three helpings and half a loaf of bread later, Cord leaned back with a satisfied smile and patted his lean stomach. Dressed in worn jeans and a black T-shirt, he was a work of art. She wished she had the talent to draw him, all poetic sensibility and animal magnetism. But she had no talent that way, which was why she was awed by his ability to create something beautiful out of wood. Sure she could write, but he could create. To her there was a difference.

Catching her staring at him, he said, "If I didn't know better, I'd say that you were trying to seduce me with all this great food."

"What makes you think you know better?" she asked.

Cord appeared stunned by her reply for a second, then his incredibly blue eyes narrowed. "What are you up to?"

"Five foot six," she teasingly replied. "What are you up to? Six foot two?"

"Are you making fun of me?"

She gazed at him with wide-eyed innocence. "Would I do a thing like that?"

"Because I don't appreciate being made fun of," he warned her.

She nodded solemnly. "I can tell."

The laughter in her eyes gave her away. Cord could tell she was not taking him seriously. Everyone took him seriously. He was that kind of a guy. "Listen, you, I don't know what you hope to accomplish here, but you're messing with trouble."

"Is that so? Well, according to you, trouble is something I'm drawn to."

He moved closer. "Is that your way of saying you're drawn to me?"

"Are you trouble?"

"With a capital *T*," he whispered, inches from her lips.

"I've always liked capitals," she whispered right back, not blinking an eye.

His gaze was searching, hers challenging. The fire she saw smoldering in the blue depths of his eyes captured her heart and gave her the courage to meet the intensity of his stare with a fierce need of her own.

"You're different," he noted.

Her smile reflected her approval. "You finally noticed."

"Oh, I noticed all right," he murmured, reaching out to tuck a loose strand of her dark hair behind her left ear.

"Really?"

"Really," he confirmed with a nod.

"You never said anything."

"I'm not saying anything now," he pointed out.

"Not with your words, maybe, but your eyes are talking plenty, cowboy."

Her grin caught him off guard.

This was way too much fun—exchanging tempting glances and provocative phrases. Yes, Hailey thought, she could get used to this real fast.

Cord slowly leaned back. "Never trust a cowboy's eyes," he advised her.

"I'll keep that in mind." Not that she had much of a mind at the moment. Coming in such close contact with him had left her entire body humming with desire.

"You do that." He got up and gathered his dirty dishes. "And while you're at it, remember that playing with fire will get you burned."

"Yeah, but what a way to go," she murmured huskily, remembering how her skin had sung with joy when he'd brushed her cheek to smooth her hair.

Returning from the kitchen, Cord picked up her coffee mug and sniffed her tea suspiciously. "Have you been drinking?"

"Yes."

"I thought so. What did you do, pour a little whiskey into your tea for courage?" He took a sip of her tea, made a face and then hurried over to the sink to spit it out. "Yuck! What was that?"

"Earl Grey tea," she replied.

He frowned at her. "There was no alcohol in there."

She nodded. "That's right."

"But you said you were drinking."

"I was." She gathered her dishes and took them into the kitchen. "I was drinking *tea.*"

"You think you're so clever?" He followed her into the kitchen. "I warned you about making fun of me. I told you that you were playing with fire. What if I were to do this?" He scooted her up against the refrigerator door and planted his hands on either side of her, hemming her in. "What would you do?"

"Stand back and enjoy it," she said, boldly grinning at him.

Cord didn't get it. He was trying to scare her off the way he'd done the first day she'd come to his cabin, but she was not cooperating here. Instead of getting mad or backing off, she was giving as good as she got.

He hated to admit it, but he was impressed...and confused. "That's not what you're supposed to say."

"Oh?" She raised an eyebrow at him. "I didn't realize there was a script."

"The first time I kissed you, you nearly broke my leg," he reminded her.

"You stumbled into the trunk," she observed.

"I didn't stumble." His voice reflected his male outrage at her comment. "I never stumble. You pushed me."

"I'm not pushing you now," she murmured.

"And I'm wondering why."

"You're a smart man. You'll figure it out, eventually.'' She patted his cheek. ''Now I've got to get back to work.''

She ducked under his arm and headed back to the corner of the living room where she was working. She could feel him watching her and couldn't resist looking over her shoulder to see. Sure enough, he was watching her. He was impressed...and attracted. She could tell that much before she walked smack into the corner of the pine coffee table.

4

FEELING LIKE A FOOL, Hailey shouted, ''I am not clumsy!'' before Cord could say a word to make fun of her.

Shoot, she'd been doing so well. Then she had to go and ruin the effect by practically falling on her face, not to mention banging her knee, which was throbbing like nobody's business.

''Did you hurt yourself?'' Cord demanded, his expression one of concern rather than mockery. ''Here, let me see.'' He hustled her over to the sofa and knelt in front of her to take a good look at her injured knee.

When she'd opted to wear khaki walking shorts today, she'd had no idea that Cord would end up on his knees before her, playing doctor. She wasn't sure she wanted him that close to her thighs. She'd wanted him to admire her from afar. Or close-up was good, like the time his body was pressed against hers in front of the fridge. But his current position gave him a much-too-revealing look at a part of her anatomy she wasn't the most confident about. Which was why she hadn't worn cutoff shorts. But sitting on the couch the way she was, the moderate hem of her walking shorts had scooted up.

Not that Cord appeared to notice. He was too engrossed testing her kneecap with his incredible fingers. She was enjoying this *way* too much! She had to say something or she'd start purring and then he'd really think she was a basket case. And it had to be something intelligent, not something sappy. She had some ground to make up for here.

His work. She'd read up on it last night. "Did you make that table I smacked into?"

"Why?"

His caution made her wonder if he thought she planned on smashing the table, and that made her feel like a slug. Scooting away from him, she said, "It's a lovely piece. I hope I didn't hurt it."

"You didn't hurt it." He scooted right after her. "You're the one that's hurt." Reaching behind him, he grabbed some tissues from the aforementioned table and wiped away the thin trail of blood on her knee. "And yes, I did make that table. It's one of the first pieces I made."

"It looks like a Thomas Molesworth design."

He gave her a startled look. "You know about Thomas Molesworth?"

She nodded, eager to show off her newfound knowledge. "He was the leader of the western furniture and style movement in the thirties and forties. He created interiors that were a western fantasy of burls, bright leather and Navajo blankets. He was born in Kansas and studied at the Chicago Art Institute before fighting in World War I. During his career, he ended up furnishing some of the largest hotels here in the West, plus doing a commission for President Eisenhower. But when he first started out in Cody, Wyoming, he made caskets as well as furniture."

"An example of starting from the ground on down," Cord murmured with a smile. "At least I didn't have to start out that way."

His smile tugged at her heart. It was like seeing the sun after a long cold winter. She felt as if she might melt in a puddle right there on his rugged leather couch.

"Do you know how much a real Molesworth piece would be worth these days?" Cord asked.

She shook her head. She didn't even know her own name at the moment.

"Anywhere from five to twenty-five hundred dollars and up," he said. "Not that this table is a real Molesworth, because as I said, I made it. It's a piece inspired by his work."

She was inspired by Cord's work, his work on her knee. On her entire leg actually, as he absently ran his hands from her knee down to her ankle and back up again.

He had the ability to make her shiver and burn at the same time. As if able to read her thoughts, Cord lifted his gaze to her face. She nervously licked her lips.

Fearful that she might do something rash, like pin him to the couch and kiss him, she deliberately forced herself to concentrate on something else. History. Furniture. The bridge between her world and his.

"The early settlers around here had a rough life and house interiors were sparse. There wasn't much time to decorate because they were busy tending the cattle and coping with the hazards of living in the Wild West. In those days, the best way to get furniture was to make it."

"It's still the best way," Cord maintained, before standing up. "I don't think you'll need a bandage for that knee, but I can get you one if you'd like."

What she'd like was him kissing her.

"I'll be fine. I found a Sears Roebuck catalog in with your family's papers." She pointed to it on the coffee table. "With the coming of the railroads, the more affluent families were able to order furniture from catalogs like that. You could get a chair for thirty-four cents, or their finest sideboard for twenty-four dollars. But that Victorian-style oak furniture was heavy to ship and didn't suit the life-style of a cowboy who wanted to put his feet up after a long day."

Cord knew what he wanted. Her. And he knew that she was up to something—cooking for him, fluttering her eyelashes at him, reciting furniture history for him. He just didn't know what her plan was yet, didn't know if it had something to do with that treasure map she was so fired up about. But he'd find out. Until then, he'd be wise to keep his distance from the nuisance next door, who was turning into a seductive temptress before his very eyes and beneath his very hands.

Trouble was that Cord never did the wise thing. And so it was that he found himself back in the living room a few hours later instead of working on that commission for a new lodge over in Jackson Hole, Wyoming. Truth was that he had so much work, he now had the luxury of selecting which jobs he'd accept. And he'd accepted the lodge job because they wanted him to make a pair of liquor cabinets like the one he had in his cabin.

Not that any two pieces of furniture he made were alike. He'd already hand selected the lodgepole pine for these new pieces, but he just couldn't seem to concentrate on the meticulous work of piecing the poles together into a mosaic for the front of the cabinets.

And the reason he couldn't concentrate was sitting on his couch like a seductive pixie, her feet curled beneath her, her nose in a book. She showed no signs of suffering from the same affliction he had of not being able to concentrate. Her mahogany hair slid forward over her cheek, creating a silky curtain that framed her face.

"What are you reading so intently?" he asked gruffly. "You didn't find any treasure map or anything, did you?"

"No. And according to Buck, you don't believe that Cockeyed Curly left a treasure map. But then you're not a man who believes in much, are you?"

He'd learned at an early age that believing was for fools. He'd believed that his mother would get well again. He'd been wrong. But he was a person who learned by his mistakes. He hadn't believed again.

"I know that on the off chance there is a map, I don't aim on letting you wander off with it," he replied. "So what are you reading?"

"A journal written by Jedidiah Best's sister."

"And you think she'll have a map in there?"

"It's even better than that." Hailey's face was lit with excitement. "Did you know she was in love with Rafael, who was a sheepherder? They were star-crossed lovers from feuding families.''

Cord grimaced. ''It seems a little weird to be reading about dead people's love affairs.''

She tossed a throw pillow from the couch at him. ''You have no heart.''

''Hey, I've been telling you that for years.''

She did not appear to be impressed by his claim, instead going on about her latest find. ''I already knew that problems between cattlemen and sheepherders took place over a longer period of time here in Colorado than anywhere else out west. And a majority of those conflicts took place here in the Northwestern section of the state. As I recall, the feud between my family and yours started because the Bests were cattlemen and my family raised sheep.

''How do you know this Rafael guy isn't from your family?''

She frowned. ''I don't remember seeing anything about a Rafael Hughes.'' She scanned the next page in the leather-bound journal. ''Oh-oh, listen to this.''

> Jedidiah does not know about my journal. I am sure that he would never understand what is in my heart. But there is much I can write about, much that fills my heart. From the first moment I saw Rafael H. from the ranch next door, I knew that this man would change my life. Suffice it to say that all the details will be recorded here at a later time. For now, I can only say that I am so relieved to have a place to confide my secrets. And I shall do so with great alacrity in the future, but for now I hear Jedidiah calling

me and I must not let him find me writing.

"Rafael H. has to be Rafael Hughes," Hailey murmured. "It's the only surname that would fit. Strange that I never heard anything about a possible link between our two families."

"You mean we could be related?"

He looked a tad horrified and Hailey wasn't sure if she should take that as an insult or not. "As I said, I don't recall a Rafael Hughes being listed in my family tree at all, but I'll check that out." She paused to write a note on the pad of paper beside her computer. "Even if they did marry, he was my great-great-great-great-uncle. There's a chance we could be distant cousins, but it would be real distant. I just meant that Rebecca's diaries offer a wealth of information about what life was really like at that time."

"By writing about all that girlie emotional stuff?" he scoffed. "Seems like a waste of time to me."

His words irritated her. "I'll have you know that women have a much better perspective on the important things in life than men do. If it weren't for women keeping journals like this, we wouldn't know how families lived, how they managed to build homes here, what they filled them with, how they raised children, how they kept them healthy, how they fought to stay alive. There are some incredible women in Colorado's history. One of the most famous is the Unsinkable Molly Brown, who went through several fortunes in her lifetime and survived the sinking of the Titanic. But did you know about Julia Archibald Homes, the first woman to climb Pike's Peak back in 1858? Or Ellen Jack, a female prospector in the 1870s who was half owner of the Black Queen mine? Or Sally Ray, a young widow who used her profits as a washerwoman in Leadville to buy up property and rent it out, making her a wealthy woman and enabling her to live in high style in Denver. I'll bet you didn't hear about them back in high school.''

''Unless they were on the girls cheerleading squad, I didn't know any female's name,'' Cord said. ''I didn't exactly stand out in school.''

''I wouldn't say that,'' she murmured with a naughty grin, remembering how good he'd looked in high school.

''I meant academically.''

''Oh, I see. Maybe not, but you were successful in other areas. You won several track awards as I recall.''

Cord nodded. ''Yeah, I'm good at running.'' A few women from his past had angrily told him that he was especially good at running away from emotion, from involvement, from love. They were right, but he had his reasons.

''And you're good with wood,'' Hailey was saying. ''I heard in town that you've been given a commission to do something for the Bliss Founders Day event.''

He shrugged a tad self-consciously. ''Yeah, well, I haven't decided what to make yet. A wooden sculpture of some kind, maybe. You wait long enough, the wood tells you what secrets it's keeping.''

''That must take a bit of patience.''

''Yeah, it does.''

She smiled. "Funny, I never figured you to be a patient man."

"I can be when I'm going after something I want," he said with a meaningful look in her direction.

"I'll keep that in mind," she promised, her heartbeat accelerating at the riveting intensity of his gaze.

"You do that." Now his voice was equally tempting.

"I, too, can be patient when going after something I want," she told him.

"Like the treasure map?" he asked, sitting down next to her.

"Like Cockeyed Curly's story," she corrected him, unable to confess that she'd been patiently waiting for Cord for years, whether she'd realized it at the time or not.

"Is that so? Who would have guessed that the little firebrand next door would grow up to be so..."

"Yes?" she prompted with bated breath.

"So...patient." He teasingly tapped his lean index finger on the tip of her nose.

She refused to let him dismiss her. She was determined to prove she could give as good as she got. So she cupped the palm of her hand against his cheek as she murmured, "And who would have guessed that the loner next door would grow up to be so..."

"Yes?"

"So...talented."

He placed his hand atop hers, pressing it against his face. "And who would have guessed that the two of us could be in one room together without..."

"Without what?" she whispered, imagining any

number of erotic scenarios. Kissing, making out, making love until the cows came home.

"Without doing this." Moving slowly, giving her plenty of time to say no, he lowered his lips to hers.

Cord had wondered if he'd blown their last kiss out of proportion. But the second her soft mouth bloomed beneath his, that theory went out the window. So did his common sense.

Tilting his head in the opposite direction, he targeted her mouth again. It was even better this way. Her lips parted and he eagerly accepted her invitation, his tongue sliding against hers in a slick reunion that set him on fire. Her hunger seemed to match his appetite as he pulled her to him so that her body was pressed against his.

Her fingers slid into the thickness of his hair as she held him closer, leaning into the kiss like a woman intent on drowning. She wasn't the only one going down for the third time.

"This isn't a good idea," he whispered against her mouth.

"Mmm," she murmured, whether in agreement or disagreement, he couldn't tell.

"We should stop."

"Mmm." Again he couldn't tell if she was agreeing with him or not.

Abruptly, he pulled away from her. "I've got to get back to work."

As he walked away, he thought he heard her mutter, "You can run, cowboy, but you can't hide."

5

"YOO-HOO, HAILEY!" Geraldine Winters, the postmistress in Bliss, waved her hand through the open window of the small brick building that served as both the post office and the chamber of commerce. Not that there was all that much commerce in the two blocks between First and Third Streets that made up downtown Bliss. There were maybe a dozen or so businesses.

Since most folks in the area had to go to the post office to pick up their mail, it was the one place where everyone showed up at one time or another. And when they did, Geraldine was ready to pounce on them. She knew just about everything that was going on in Bliss. She'd been the postmistress for as long as Hailey could remember. The vivacious older woman, with her short hair dyed Lucille Ball red, wasn't about to give up her duties despite the fact that she was past retirement age.

Geraldine vowed to die on the job. Some days Hailey felt she would die waiting in line for Geraldine to finish a gabfest with every single person who came to the counter.

Need stamps? Expect that to take at least fifteen minutes. And that was after you got waited on. Forget your postbox key? Expect that to take half an hour, depending on what mail you'd received, which Geraldine reviewed before handing over, one envelope at a time.

And then there was Geraldine's chatty parrot, who also took his time calling out postal sayings. Yes, the Bliss post office was a true twilight zone.

"Yoo-hoo, Hailey!" Geraldine shouted and waved again. "You get yourself in here, girl, and tell me what you've been up to!"

Hailey had a feeling Geraldine probably already knew as much about Hailey's life as she did. Once inside the post office, Geraldine ordered her to the front of the line. With an apologetic look at the other two people in line, Hailey did as she was ordered. No one disobeyed the mighty Geraldine.

"I've got your family's mail all ready for you here," Geraldine told Hailey. "Let's see, your dad's new *Fly Fishing* magazine came in. And here's your aunt's *Country Woman.* They have a great recipe in here for rhubarb pie, you tell her I said so. Junk mail, junk mail." Geraldine slapped two more envelopes into Hailey's hand before examining the next one. "Phone bill. Did I tell you that Sandy Bush's son got transferred to Japan from California? He's in computers. And Sandy says that her phone bills have gone through the roof, calling Japan the way she does. I always did say that she kept that boy too close to her apron strings. Ah, here's a letter for you." Geraldine's dark birdlike eyes flitted to the return address. "It's from the university. I hope there isn't anything wrong with your job there?"

"There's nothing wrong," Hailey hastily assured her, knowing how quickly rumors got started in

Bliss. "I'm taking a year's sabbatical to write a book."

"A book!" Geraldine put down the mail. "Why, that's wonderful. I hope you'll write a mystery about a red-haired postmistress in a small town and a grizzly serial killer who mutilates his victims. I just love a gory mystery, don't you?"

"Actually I prefer a good romance novel, like an Amanda Quick book."

"So you're writing a romance novel. Well, no doubt you've heard about the romance between Zane Best and his city wife, Tracy. She came out west from Chicago to be his housekeeper, and ended up falling in love with him. They were married last fall. Everyone in Bliss attended the wedding, except your dad of course. And those devil twins of Zane's were on their best behavior. You should hear some of the pranks they've pulled. Oh, and here's a postcard for you, from Hawaii. Nice beach. I had a cousin who went to Hawaii once. She said she hated it because of all the sand."

"I'm not writing a romance," Hailey said the moment Geraldine paused a second to draw a breath. "I'm writing a nonfiction book about Colorado outlaws of the Old West."

"Is that so?" Geraldine leaned closer confidingly. "Well, my daddy was a bona fide cowboy, you know. This is the one part of the state where cowboys and sheepherders still outnumber skiers and tourists. But I don't have to tell you that, do I? Not with your family's history of being sheepherders living next door to cattle ranchers. It's no wonder your daddy and Buck Best don't get along. As for outlaws,

Butch Cassidy and his Wild Bunch used to hole up over yonder in Brown's Park to escape the law. Legend has it that they had a lookout atop the Canyon of Lodore where they could see for miles and watch for pursuers. And of course you know how Butch got his nickname, from butchering all those people." Geraldine's dark eyes gleamed.

"Actually he got his nickname while making an honest living working as a butcher, and he didn't kill anyone throughout his train-and bank-robbing years," Hailey said. "Not until he was on the run down in Bolivia did he kill anyone, and that was in his final encounter with the law."

"Well, I thought that Paul Newman did a wonderful job in that movie. He has the most incredible eyes," Geraldine added dreamily. "Reminds me of the blue eyes those Best boys have."

"Cord's eyes are a little darker than that," Hailey said. "More intense."

"That so?" The older woman instantly zoomed in on her remark. "And I suppose you'd be the expert, what with you spending so much time with him and all. Not to mention you having such a big crush on him in your younger years."

"I'd rather you didn't mention that," Hailey replied.

"Not that I'm one to gossip," Geraldine said. "Why, if someone tells me something in confidence, then my lips are sealed and no amount of torture would make me reveal my secrets. Unless they tickled me beneath my big toe. I have to confess that I can't stand when someone does that. Why, when my husband, George, was alive, God bless his soul, he only had to wiggle his fingers and me with my shoes still on, and I'd laugh so hard that I near as likely wet my pants. Not that I have a bladder control problem. That rumor is *not* true and if I find out who started it, I can tell you they'll be in a heap of trouble for sure. My kidneys are made of steel!"

Hailey blinked at this unexpected turn of the conversation and started edging toward the exit. "Yes, well..."

"But getting back to those outlaws, what about the legend of Cockeyed Curly and his gold? If you're researching outlaws, you must be checking out Curly."

"I'm checking out a number of things," Hailey said noncommittally.

"Like the color of Cord's eyes?" Geraldine's bark of laughter was enough to waken her colorful parrot in the corner. "Address unknown, address unknown!" the bird screeched.

"I'm still trying to get those Guinness world record folks to come out here and see Dispatch," Geraldine said with a proud look at her pet. "I keep writing them that he's the only bird in the world who speaks postal speak. But they haven't answered me yet. Those Guinness folks, I mean. Not Dispatch. He always answers. Right, fella?"

"Return to sender, *awk,* return to sender!"

IN THE DARK AND SMOKY INTERIOR of the Bliss Bar, Tad Hughes was perched on a bar stool, his drink untouched as he drew out his fishing tale as only a seasoned storyteller could.

"I saw the wink of that trout's mouth opening

underwater, but that devil was determined to chase and not eat. I'm telling you, that trout was a hog.''

''Still talking about the one that got away?'' Buck inquired as he moseyed up to the bar and ordered a bottle of Coors from Floyd the bartender. ''All talk and no action make for a poor fisherman.''

''What would you know?'' Tad scoffed. ''You hold a rod like a girl.''

''This from a man who hasn't caught anything bigger than a tadpole in years. If you fellas want to hear a real fishing story, you should take a gander at this here picture of the monster I caught yesterday morning.'' Buck proudly pulled the photo from his pocket. ''Made me wish for the good old days when you kept your catch instead of having to release it. I'm telling you, he made my armadillo look like an ant.''

Seeing his audience's attention slipping away, Tad loudly said, ''This is a private conversation, Bucko. Go fill some other bar with your hot air and touched-up photos.''

''Make me,'' Buck retorted.

When Hailey walked into the bar to meet her dad, she found him standing toe-to-toe with Buck, both men bristling like a pair of roosters on the verge of a fight.

''Hey!'' Stepping between them, she quickly put a restraining hand on each man's chest. ''What's going on in here?''

''Buckeroo here was butting in where he isn't wanted,'' Tad shouted.

''Hah!'' Buck scoffed, his bushy white eyebrows lowering. ''The truth is that Tadpole here was telling tall tales again.''

Her father's face was suffused with angry color. "You wouldn't know the truth if it came up and bit you on the behind."

"I'm not the one so hard of hearing that he has to bellow loud enough to be heard over in the next county," Buck retorted. "No wonder you can't catch any fish. They can hear you shouting a mile away."

"I am not deaf!" Tad bellowed.

"Didn't say you were," Buck replied with a taunting smile. "You must not have heard me rightly. Wonder why that is."

Tad's stuck his chin forward pugnaciously. "You itchin' for a fight, Buckeroo? Well, the last laugh will be on you and yours, you just wait and see."

"What in Sam Hill are you babbling on about now?" Buck demanded.

"That's for me to know," Tad said with a meaningful glance in Hailey's direction, "and you to worry about."

Buck was not impressed. "Hah! As if I'd ever worry about anything you could cook up in that lame brain of yours."

Furious that Buck wasn't taking him seriously, Tad said, "I'm not the one who is making sissy barbecue sauce. Cooking is woman's work. The entire town is laughing at you behind your back."

"Another fisherman's exaggeration, otherwise known as a lie. As for laughing, I'm laughing all the way to the bank," Buck stated proudly. "My barbecue sauce is selling like hotcakes. And there's no way it's for sissies. It may be for tenderfeet, at least the milder sauce, but it ain't for sissies. Not like sheepherding. That's something Bo-peep does."

"Those are fighting words," Tad growled. "You better hightail it out of here while the going is good."

"You don't own this bar and you sure as heck don't own Troublesome Creek."

The two men were toe-to-toe again when Hailey rang the large brass bell at the end of the bar, thereby getting everyone's attention. Legend had it that the bell, stamped with the date 1880, had once been used by the fire brigade in Leadville in its heyday, and it still had a clarity of sound guaranteed to rouse men from blocks away.

"Okay, the show's over for today, folks," Hailey announced. Taking her dad's arm, she said, "Come on, Dad, Alicia is waiting for us over at the Cut 'n' Curl."

"Give her my regards," Buck told Hailey.

"You stay away from my sister!" Tad said loudly.

"A pleasure talking to ya," Buck called out as Hailey dragged her father out of the bar. "You all come back again soon, ya hear?"

"WHY DO YOU LET HIM get to you that way?" Hailey demanded in exasperation as she pulled her dad along Main Street. "You know he's only teasing you because you respond the way you do."

"As I recall, that never stopped you from pounding lumps on Cord when he made fun of you in grade school," Tad replied. "I used to tell you that he was only teasing you because you responded the way you do."

"The way I did. Past tense. I've grown up since then." She deliberately shoved aside the much more recent memory of socking Cord after he'd kissed her for the first time several days ago.

Seeing her aunt waiting inside the beauty shop, Hailey opened the door just as Tad proclaimed, "I'll never be too old to detest Buckeroo."

Alicia looked up in distress at Tad's words, which he'd just stated in his customary thunderous voice so that everyone in the beauty shop could hear him, even above the drone of hair dryers.

"Shush now," Alicia said as she took his free arm and hustled him outside. With a woman on each side, Tad stared in confusion first at Hailey, then Alicia. "What's with you girls? I'm not a bale of hay to be hauled along the street."

"You're embarrassing me," Alicia hissed, smiling and nodding to a couple getting out of their pickup truck.

"Well, that's your fault, not mine," Tad stated self-righteously.

"How do you figure that?" Alicia demanded.

Tad frowned. "Because I'm just standing here and you're the one being embarrassed. You've got no cause to be treating me like some kind of lop-eared pot licker."

Hailey ignored their bickering, instead noticing that Alicia had a new hairstyle. Besides the new cut, she'd also had highlights added to the strands around her face. Interesting. Could it be that Hailey wasn't the only Hughes woman interested in attracting a Best man?

By the time Hailey had left her aunt and dad behind and headed off to Cord's cabin to get some work done, she'd decided that she was making a mountain out of molehill. She was probably projecting her own thoughts onto her aunt. She had romance on her mind, thanks in part to reading Rebecca Best's diary. And then there was Cord's most recent kiss.

That would get you to thinking about romance.

The truth was that her flirting with Cord was proving to be more enjoyable than she'd anticipated. And more successful.

She was making progress with Cord. She knew it. She'd felt it in his kiss. And while it was true that he'd still walked off in the end, he'd noticed her.

And she couldn't wait to see him again. Plus, there was her work. The diary had captured her attention and her imagination in a way she hadn't anticipated, strengthening her determination to write a book on Colorado women once she finished this book on Colorado outlaws.

When she arrived at the cabin, Cord was already working out in his shop. The day that had started out warm and sunny down in Bliss had turned cool and cloudy up here in the mountains. Her khaki shorts and pink T-shirt were no protection against the chilly bite in the air, and she was shivering by the time she entered the cabin.

Cord usually had a fire burning in the large stone fireplace, but today it was in danger of going out, so she hurriedly grabbed some wood sitting on the hearth and tossed it into the waning flames to take the chill out of the air.

As she did so, Cord walked into the room. "What the hell are you doing?" he yelled at her, running toward her at a full sprint.

6

"DOING?" SHE REPEATED, stunned by his reaction. "I was just putting some wood on the fire." Then it hit her. "Oh, no."

"Oh, yes. You just scorched the wood for my Founders Day project!" He yanked it out of the fireplace and away from the hungry flames about to engulf it.

"I'm so sorry. I had no idea. The wood was right next to the woodpile and I just thought...is it okay?"

"It's okay," he grudgingly admitted as he searched for damage. "From now on, don't touch any wood, no matter what it is. If you want more firewood, you ask me first."

"Are you sure it's okay?" She leaned over his shoulder to anxiously appraise the damage the fire may have done. She wanted to lean on his back and weep. She'd screwed up again and almost demolished his work.

"Yes, I'm sure it's okay."

She sagged with relief. It would have been so easy to slip into the old negative image of the nuisance next door who screwed up. But no, not this time. She wasn't going to take all the blame this time. She smacked his arm with enough force to get his attention but not enough to hurt him. "What's the idea of leaving an important piece of wood right in front of the fireplace?"

"I just set it there for a few hours..." Cord began defensively, before catching himself. "Hey, it's my cabin. I can put my wood wherever I want to."

"You're right." She sank onto the couch and rested her bowed head on her hands. Getting angry hadn't lessened her guilt. "It's just that I feel so badly about what happened."

"What almost happened."

She nodded, nervously nibbling her bottom lip.

"Hey." He lifted her head so he could see her clearly. "You were just living up to your reputation," he said in a teasing voice.

"Don't."

He stared at the big fat tear rolling down her cheek in dismay. "No, you don't. Don't you dare cry! You never cry. Not even when you broke your big toe chasing me out in our barn. Aw, come on." He sat next to her and patted her shoulder awkwardly. "Ask anyone who's been around the outhouse more than once and they'll tell you that I'm no good with weepy women. I'm no good with people, period."

"I'm sorry." She sniffed and angrily wiped the tear away, only to have another take its place. "It's just that you thought I tried to break your elk back in grade school, and now here I am, trying to burn up your work for Founders Day."

"I don't believe you deliberately broke my elk anymore. Or that you deliberately tried to make this project go up in flames."

"But you still think I'm trouble."

He wiped her tears away and smiled at her. "Maybe I'm starting to like trouble."

She sniffed. "Now you're just being nice."

"Hey, watch who you're calling nice," he said in a deliberately affronted voice. "You're gonna ruin my reputation."

She laughed. "You mean your loner-don't-mess-with-me reputation?"

He nodded. "That's the one."

"Your secret is safe with me."

"Which secret?"

"That you may have a heart underneath your rough exterior after all."

"Yeah, well, don't go telling anyone else."

"I won't. And I won't touch any more of your wood, I promise."

"I probably shouldn't have put it there without saying something to you," he noted gruffly. "I've been saving that piece to do a special carving for Founders Day and I was waiting for it to talk to me."

"And when it did talk to you, it was shrieking, *Save me, save me, I'm burning up!*" She raised her voice to a dramatic falsetto.

He grinned. "At least I heard it and saved it in time."

"Thank heavens." She heaved a huge sigh of relief. "I hate to think what would have happened otherwise, ruining a commissioned piece of art for the town's one hundred and twenty-fifth anniversary. I wouldn't have been able to show my face, which would be tough since I've been asked to make a presentation at the event about Bliss's history."

"Including Cockeyed Curly and his gold?"

"Not necessarily."

"Good, because we don't want a bunch of wild-eyed treasure hunters going off the deep end and digging up the countryside."

"That's not something I want, either."

"I'm glad to hear that. Well, I'd best get back to work." Reaching down, he lifted the chunk of wood to take with him.

Despite his words, Hailey continued to feel badly about what she'd done. She desperately wanted to make it up to him but she wasn't sure how.

The thing that had worked the best so far was feeding him, but she'd already done that several times. She needed to do something more for him. His cabin was already clean so she couldn't help him there. Maybe she should get him out into the fresh air. He'd been working so hard that he was practically tied to that workbench of his. The summer would be over before he even knew it, and with it the beautiful weather they'd been enjoying.

She knew he liked being alone, but this was getting ridiculous. He was completely cutting himself off from the rest of the world. Just the other day, after he'd turned down that invitation for dinner from Zane, she'd heard him tersely refuse a furniture gallery's request that he appear for a showing of his work. He rarely left the cabin. The man had no life.

Yes, he needed to get out and relax. A picnic would be good. That way she'd be killing two birds with one stone—feeding him and at the same time helping him relax.

But she knew better than to simply invite him. He'd say no, he was too busy for something as frivolous as a picnic. He'd probably also be suspicious of her motives.

No, she'd have to couch the invitation as a way of checking out something to do with Cockeyed Curly. The problem with that idea was that she hadn't found anything to do with the poet bandit yet. Which left her with Rebecca's journal.

She renewed her reading with increased determination to make headway. And she hit pay dirt a few days later when she found this reference in Rebecca's journal.

> Raphael tells me I must be careful, for there is talk in town that the outlaw Cockeyed Curly may be using the area around Oh-Be-Joyful Falls for his nefarious activities.

Her shout of victory sent Cord racing into the living room. "What's wrong?"

"Nothing."

"Then why did you scream like that?"

"Because I found a reference to Curly in Rebecca's journal." She read him the passage and then casually added, "I thought I'd go up to Oh-Be-Joyful Falls tomorrow and check things out."

"In that case, I'm going with you," Cord said, just as she'd hoped he would.

He'd taken the bait hook, line and sinker. Maybe she'd picked up some of her father's fishing skills after all!

"And before you start throwing a fit about it, you should know that it won't make any difference," Cord told her. "I'm going with you and that's final.

Just to keep you honest, in case you find something up there."

"I thought you were the one who didn't believe in the legend about Cockeyed Curly's treasure."

"I don't. Not really. But Better Safe Than Sorry, that's my motto."

That used to be her motto, too. Not anymore. Now her motto was She Who Hesitates Is Lost.

"BASHFUL, YOU'RE STILL as bold as ever, I see," Hailey noted with a rueful laugh as the horse in the Best barn butted her arm with his head. "You remember me, huh, boy? The way I'd bring you goodies like a fresh carrot or a sugar cube?"

Cord thought Hailey looked like a goody herself. He'd seen her dressed in jeans and a denim shirt more times than he could count. But having her here in the barn brought back memories of her grinning up at him after she'd lost her front tooth.

"And, Rusty, you old lech." She smoothed her hand over the forehead of another horse. "Still copping a feel for a female behind, hmm?"

Cord was feeling like a lech himself, noting how Hailey's jeans conformed to her lush bottom.

"I missed you guys."

Had she missed him? Cord wondered. All those years she'd been in Boulder at the university, had she ever thought of him?

"I brought you a little something." She reached into her shirt pocket, the one curved over her left breast, to remove some sugar cubes. "You know I've got a soft spot for you."

She was all soft spots. The rise of her breasts, the

inward curve of her waist, the supple length of her legs. The shell-like shape of her ear as she smoothed her hair away from her face, the warm hollow at the base of her throat where a turquoise-and-silver locket rested. All these spots were small studies of perfection.

"So, are you ready?" Hailey asked him.

He was just about ready to explode, and now he had to sit in a saddle. The nuisance next door had made him horny again. He had to stall for a few minutes, let his body recover, or he'd do himself permanent harm.

"Give me a few minutes."

"I brought some food for lunch. Thought we might as well eat while we're up there."

She couldn't tell by his grunt if this news pleased him or not. He'd been eyeing her strangely ever since she'd walked into the barn. Was he remembering the time she'd chased him all around the barn after he'd called her Button when she'd ordered him not to? Or the time she'd jumped him from the hayloft above and flattened him after he'd told his brother Zane that she was nothing but a nuisance?

Ah, yes, this barn had been the site of several of her least favorite memories. Including her teenage request that he kiss her.

But that was a long time ago and she was another person now. At least on the outside. But how much could she really claim to have changed when here she was, all these years later, still wearing her heart on her sleeve where Cord was concerned.

"I think I'll wait for you outside," she said.

Once she was back in the sunshine and away from

Cord's tempting presence, she was able to regain her confidence. It was a beautiful day, the sky an intense cobalt blue you only got here in the mountains. Boulder was great, but it was a city after all. Here there was nothing between her and the sky but the kind of billowy clouds that angels were rumored to play on.

She'd brought her favorite horse, Ginseng, in a horse trailer from her father's ranch. The bay mare had spirit and speed.

Hailey was already mounted on her horse when Cord came out of the barn riding Bashful. Cord was at home on a horse, as was she, though it had been a while since she'd ridden. Only now did she realize how much she'd missed it—the freedom, the movement.

She also realized how good Cord looked in jeans and a light blue denim shirt that had been washed to a soft color that made his eyes come alive.

Not giving herself time to admire him further, she shouted, "I'll race you! Last one to the base of Bear Tooth Mountain is a lop-eared pot licker." With that she headed off at a gallop toward the mountains.

Half an hour later they reached the finish line, but Hailey and Ginseng crossed it first.

"I let you win," Cord said.

"Huh!" She wasn't about to let him get away with that claim. "Not in this lifetime. You never let me win."

"Maybe I've turned over a new leaf," he suggested.

"That'll be the day," she scoffed with a grin.

The rest of the trip to Oh-Be-Joyful Falls was at a much slower pace since the path became steeper as it curved up the mountainside. To say the waterfall was off the beaten track was an understatement. Only locals knew about the scenic spot and they liked keeping it that way. Besides, it was on private property, Best property.

Here the path was only wide enough to travel single file. Cord had taken the lead with the natural authority of a man accustomed to having his own way.

The wild grace of a soaring hawk caught her eye. She loved these mountains and all the wildlife that resided here—from the graceful lines of an elk testing the frosty morning air to the flash of color of a pheasant shooting out from its cover and on up to the sky. She could see why the Ute Indians had called this "the land of shining mountains."

When they got close to the falls, Hailey suggested they dismount and check the area by foot for signs of human habitation in the past. It was an hour later before Hailey almost tripped over something in the dirt.

Cord's quick action saved her from falling flat on her face.

"I know, I know," he quickly said, his grin like a flash of sunlight. "You're not clumsy."

"That's right." Leaning down, she studied the ground more closely, willing her heartbeat to return to the normal range from the bolt of electricity generated by Cord's touch. "This log looks like it's been finished in some way. It's not just a fallen log. Take a look."

Cord hunkered down beside her and ran his hand

along the weathered wood. “You're right. It could have been fencing.”

“Why would someone build a fence way up here?”

“Well, it wasn't my family. As far as I know, we never built anything up here. In fact, the family has a thing about it.”

“So it could have been Curly who built this fence. But why? Why just a fence and no cabin? There's no sign of a foundation nearby.”

“Doesn't mean that there might not have been a shack up here. Or it could just have been a corral.”

“A fenced corral wouldn't protect his treasure.”

“He'd want to protect his horses. Most thieves kept extra horses strategically stashed to make get-aways or to spell off a tired mount if they were on the run.”

“You're right!”

“That's gotta be a first. You telling me I'm right.”

“Don't let it go to your head,” she mockingly warned him.

“Starvation is going to my head and making me light-headed,” he said, standing up and wiping his hands. “When are we going to eat?”

“Right now. Or as soon as we can walk to the falls.”

Within ten minutes she had everything spread out from the saddlebags, where she'd stored their food. The vinyl tablecloth was a traditional red-and-white check and the plates were paper.

As waterfalls went, this one wasn't huge or even on the big side. In fact, some might describe it as downright "puny," as Buck had put it in the past. But it was perfect in its entirety.

The No Name Creek began even higher up in the mountains and took its time meandering on down to this point, where it casually spilled over a tumble of boulders before dropping twenty feet from the edge of a precipice to continue its journey down. At the base of the falls, a natural pool had been created.

Cord was already nibbling on a fried chicken leg by the time she got the rest of the meal laid out.

"I've never seen pink potato salad before," Cord noted.

"My aunt used to tell me that it was made with pink potatoes, but actually beets give it the pink color."

He took a cautious bite. "It tastes good."

"You don't have to sound so surprised."

"Everyone knows your aunt is a great cook but I didn't realize she'd passed her skills on to you."

"My aunt has taught me a lot over the years, including how to make the flakiest crust on the Western Slope for a cherry pie that is to die for."

When she waved the dessert beneath his nose tantalizingly, he groaned with anticipation. She decided then and there that he looked incredibly sexy when he was craving something.

If she wasn't careful, she'd have the same avid look on her face—only for him, not cherry pie.

She scrambled to find a distraction, something she could say that would take her mind off Cord's body. "You know that legend has it that the falls got their name from Jedidiah Best, but I ran across an entry in the journal I'm reading at your cabin indicating that Rebecca Best was actually the one who chose the name, as a reprimand to her moody brother."

"Moody? The Bests are never moody."

"Yeah, right."

"What are you doing?" he demanded as she scooted away from him.

"Getting out of the way in case you're hit by lightning for telling such a huge whopper." Her grin was contagious.

"Superstitious little thing, aren't you?" Cord grinned and shook his head. "I would have thought that a professor would be more intellectual."

"I am intellectual about some things. In other areas I trust my...instincts." Having made that proclamation, she proceeded to daintily lick the brown sugar from the plump strawberry she held to her lips.

Cord couldn't tear his gaze away from her mouth, as red and ripe as the fruit she was eating with the seductiveness of Delilah. "Is it getting warm or is it just me?" he muttered, rolling up his shirtsleeves.

"You're right, it is getting warm." She did more than just roll up her shirtsleeves, she took her shirt off entirely.

"What are you doing?" he croaked.

"What does it look like I'm doing?"

"Stripping."

She tossed him a reprimanding look. "As if I'd ever do such a thing."

"Then what are you doing?"

"Taking off my clothes."

She peeled off her shirt to reveal the black tank top beneath. It wasn't until she'd undone the zip on her jeans and shimmied out of them that Cord realized she was wearing a black bathing suit. The top resembled a tank top but the bottom showed off her long legs. For a one-piece, it was as sexy as anything he'd seen on the cover of that sports magazine.

It wasn't that Hailey was revealing lots of flesh, quite the opposite. The suit was almost demure. Now, there was a word he didn't hear much these days. And never one he'd have applied to hell-on-wheels Hailey.

Hailey was aware of his eyes on her as she folded her clothes before making her way over to the stream at the base of the waterfall to test the water. Dipping her toe in, she discovered that the afternoon sun had warmed the water to a bearable temperature. Besides, she could use some cooling down.

It had taken more than a bit of courage for her to strip in front of Cord. Doubts from her adolescence about being chubby still ran around in her head, but she needed to replace them with more positive thoughts. And the hungry look in his eyes helped her to do that. Cord had stared at her as if she were really beautiful, as if she were a true work of art.

Cord watched her slip into the water and couldn't help thinking how much the nuisance next door had grown up. Even so, she still had the ability to give him headaches…and aches in other parts of his anatomy.

"The water is great," she called out. "Don't you want to join me?"

Oh, he wanted, all right. Plenty. Her naked beneath him with nothing but rippling water between them as he made her his.

He shifted, his arousal making his present position downright uncomfortable.

"What's the matter?" she taunted him. "Afraid to jump in the deep end of the pool?"

"I'm fine right where I am."

She shrugged. "Your choice, your loss."

She then proceeded to do a back float across the large pool.

Hailey always had been a self-reliant little thing as a kid and Cord was glad to see that hadn't changed any. It suddenly hit him that it was something the two of them had in common. They both had the ability to amuse themselves without being dependent on others. But that didn't alter the fact that she was smart and he wasn't.

Not that she made him feel stupid. No, she made him feel that what he did was important. She'd gone out of her way to find out about what he did, researching the history of his craft. But then history was her thing.

Like the way she'd talked about those historical women. She'd been talking about her passion, and whenever she did that, her entire face lit up, her eyes glowing with excitement and her voice filled with anticipation.

What would it be like making love with her? Would she show equal passion when having sex?

Cord was indulging in a heated fantasy about that very subject when, out of the corner of his eye, he saw something that had him yanking off his boots and running into the water with his clothes still on.

7

"WHAT ARE YOU DOING?" Hailey cried when Cord rushed into the pool as if the hounds of hell were nipping at his ankles.

Once the water reached his waist, Cord paused and tried to make it look as if it were the most natural thing in the world for him to take a dip fully clothed. "Doing?" he repeated with a who-me? look on his angular face. "I'm not doing anything. I just thought I'd take you up on your invitation for a swim."

"With all your clothes on?"

"Hey, I took my boots off," he pointed out.

"But not your hat."

He hung it on an overhanging branch before diving beneath the water and stretching into a back float. To add more drama to the moment, he spewed a stream of water out of his mouth as if he were a whale.

He was a sight to see, his wet shirt clinging to his wide chest, his arms beneath his head as if he didn't have a care in the world. The man was even whistling.

He'd either lost his mind or…Hailey started laughing as the reason for Cord's uncharacteristic behavior suddenly became clear. There was a porcupine munching away on the remains of their lunch.

"So that's it!" she cried. "I can't believe a prickly man like you is afraid of a porcupine. I'd think the two of you would have a bond."

"Hey, I was stung by porcupine quills when I was a kid," Cord said, standing up to skim his large hands across the water's surface and splash Hailey. "I've got reason to be cautious."

She splashed him right back. "Cautious maybe, but dashing in the water that way was downright cowardly."

"Them there is fighting words, woman," Cord growled, reaching out to grab her in his arms.

"Fighting words, hmm? You know," she said conversationally, "that reminds me of the case of Colorado outlaw Ike Clodfelter—"

"Oh, no, you don't," Cord interrupted her. "You're not talking your way out of this one."

He no sooner finished speaking when she splashed him with enough water to stop his words.

Sputtering, he wiped the water from his face and gazed at her with the devil in his intense blue eyes.

"Uh-oh," she said in a small voice, quickly back-pedaling away from him. But moving quickly was hard to do when you were laughing and kept losing your footing. He caught her in no time.

"Gotcha!" he cried triumphantly. "Now what do you have to say for yourself?"

"That despite his fighting words, Ike Clodfelter got caught in the end and spent three and a half years in the state penitentiary. And to think his troubles all began over a con to sell watches for three dollars. After his victims sent in the money through the mail, all they received were bags of sawdust. Mail fraud is a federal offense, you know."

"When I asked you what you had to say for yourself, I was looking more for something along the lines of 'uncle' or 'I surrender, Cord.'"

"Really?" She made her voice all breathy and husky as she looked up at him as if he were God's gift to women. "You really want me to?"

Caught up in her seductive gaze, Cord momentarily looked as if he'd been poleaxed.

It was all she needed to slip out of his grip. "Tough 'tatoes!" she crowed as she swam to the opposite side of the pool near the waterfall.

"No one says tough 'tatoes to me and lives to tell the tale." Cord took off after her.

He caught her right before she tried to slip behind the waterfall. "I've got you now!" he growled.

"You did that dastardly villain voice pretty well," she congratulated him. "All you need is a waxed mustache to twirl."

"Maybe I'm just the big bad wolf come to nibble Goldilocks."

"They're not even in the same fairy tale. I believe the big bad wolf was going after Little Red Riding Hood."

He splashed her, dousing her with water as she'd done to him. "First rule of combat, never argue with your captor. If I say the big bag wolf nibbled Goldilocks, then you say that's right."

She retaliated by drenching him with a tidal wave of water. The battle was on. A few moments later he had her in his arms again, but this time she was laughing so hard she had to hang onto him to remain upright.

She turned her face to his, only to find his mouth a mere half inch from hers. The water droplets on his eyelashes sparkled in the sun as beads of moisture clung to the sensual curve of his lips. Laughter was instantly replaced with hunger and passion.

She didn't know if he lowered his mouth to hers or if she raised hers to his. She only knew that their mouths meshed as if designed for this purpose and no other.

It was an engulfing kiss, a turbulent seeking of tongues and souls. She savored the heady tastes and textures—a combination of cherry pie and rough heat. He made her want him with a desperation and hunger that shocked her. Reckless waves of desire washed over her, drowning out the voice of logic.

Linking her arms around his neck, she melted against him. His belt buckle pressed against her stomach, and the stretchy material of her swimsuit provided scant protection, allowing her to feel the thrust of his arousal. He had one hand placed against the small of her back and the other on her bottom to pull her even closer.

Still wearing his jeans, he insinuated one denim-clad knee between her legs and then lifted her against him. The abrasive roughness of the denim against her feminine core created flashes of fierce pleasure as he let her slide down, only to lift her again. His hands were making themselves familiar with all her curves and valleys, from the hollow of her throat all the way down beneath the surface of the water to her bare thighs. His fingers were straying tantalizingly close to slipping below the confines of her swimsuit to the aching juncture that longed for his intimate touch.

Closer, closer...

Her groan of pleasure was interrupted by the sound of rustling in the underbrush near the stream, as if a herd of elephants were coming through. Cord heard it, too, and pulled away from her.

"What was that?" she gasped, more startled than afraid.

Cord immediately sought out the whereabouts of the porcupine. "Uh-oh," he said.

"I don't like the sound of that."

"And I don't like the look of that." He inclined his head toward their abandoned picnic site, where the prickly porcupine had now been joined by a skunk. The porcupine wasn't pleased by this new interloper and the two animals circled each other warily.

In the end both animals retreated, but only after the skunk had sprayed the clothes Hailey had left on the bank.

"Phew!" Holding her nose, she got out of the water and stared in dismay at her ruined clothes. "I don't believe this!"

"At least they didn't bother with my hat," Cord noted in relief, snagging it in one hand as he strode out of the water after her.

"Now what am I supposed to do?" She looked and sounded totally frustrated.

Cord tried to be helpful. "They say if you wash your clothes out with tomato juice you can get rid of the smell."

"Forget it." She took a step back and shook her

head, making sure she wasn't standing downwind of the pile of clothes. "I'm not taking this stuff back now, smelling like that."

"What are you going to do? Leave it up here for some nosy historian to find a hundred years from now and wonder what was going on up here? Who knows what they might think?"

"They'd think I was nuts to be fooling around with you while a skunk was threatening my clothing," she said.

Ever practical, Cord pointed out, "You should be counting your blessings that you weren't in your clothes at the time. That would have been much worse."

"Speaking of skunks and clothes, do you remember the time Jodie Cornell got that fancy dress for her stint as...what was she? Cow queen?"

"Cattle queen," he corrected her.

"Right. And she lorded it over everyone at the Fourth of July celebrations until someone's pet skunk got loose and sprayed her and her dress."

"I remember that." Cord smiled fondly at the recollection. "We were hoping to get her out of that dress when we borrowed that skunk."

Hailey's eyebrows rose, as did her voice. "You mean *you* were behind that?"

"Not me alone, no," he said modestly. "You might say it was a group effort."

"In the end, she didn't take off her dress, so your plan backfired on you."

"As I recall, the skunk did all the backfiring with perfect aim at that dress."

"And at Jodie. She left the park screaming her head off."

Cord nodded solemnly. "That's when I decided Jodie wasn't the girl for me."

Hailey wondered who was the girl for him, but lacked the courage to ask. After all, this was the first time they'd shared stories about their youth without reference to her being the nuisance next door, and she didn't want to jeopardize this newfound camaraderie with him.

She quickly packed up what was left of their picnic that hadn't been messed up by the porcupine or sprayed by the skunk. Meanwhile, Cord went through his saddlebags searching for a large plastic bag to put her clothing in.

"I thought I still had this in here." He handed her the bag.

She used a stout stick to stuff the clothes in the thick bag before fastening it securely. After rinsing her hands in the water, she tried to figure out what to do next.

Cord was in better shape. Although his cloths were wet, at least they didn't reek and he could continue to wear them.

"I can't ride all the way back to your dad's ranch in my swimsuit." She wasn't being modest, she was being practical. Without protection on her legs, her inner thighs would be rubbed raw and bruised by the time they got to their destination.

"We could walk to my cabin," he suggested. "It's not as far as the ranch. Then we could call to borrow some clothes from my sister-in-law. Or you could call your aunt."

"That would go over well, I'm sure," she said mockingly. "For me to call home from your cabin and ask for some clothes. My dad would come after you with a shotgun."

Cord shrugged. "He's threatened to come after us with a shotgun before."

This was news to Hailey. "He has? When?"

"Whenever someone in my family fishes in Troublesome Creek."

Hailey sighed. "My dad does love his fly-fishing."

"So does my dad. And I can respect that. There's something to be said for the craft involved in tempting a trout with nothing more than a fly or lure. Respect for your prey is integral to the catch-and-release concept."

"Now, if only our respective fathers could respect each other, we'd be in great shape," Hailey said.

BUCK KNEW that staying low was the key. What a trout could see in its limited view of the world determined its behavior. Buck also knew that sound traveled quicker and farther underwater. He'd tried standing on the bank but hadn't had any luck casting from there.

So he got into the water. His waders protected his lower body while his fishing vest with its many pockets held everything from his box of lures to a squashed sandwich for his lunch.

And, of course, there was his lucky fishing hat. His new daughter-in-law had almost thrown it out, claiming it stank, which it probably did. But there was no way he was going without his lucky fishing hat.

As Buck slowly waded to his position, he was careful not to create any waves. Elsewhere along Troublesome Creek, the rapids could hide a man's movements, but here the waters were calmer in the bend pools that held large trout. They just loved juicy undercut banks.

Buck knew this river like the back of his hand, had learned how to read the bends, the stream flows and feeding lines. He'd learned the currents that carried food on and beneath the water's surface.

Yes, it would be fair to say that he was a doggone expert on this particular stretch of water. And today he was a man on a mission. The fish were calling to him and he was going to answer their siren call.

TAD LOVED HIS DAUGHTER but he still thought there was nothing that touched his heart quite like swimming a Woolly Bugger through a juicy pocket and seeing it disappear into the mouth of a trout. Ah, fly-fishing. This was his idea of heaven. Not that the fish had actually bitten yet. But he had high hopes.

Today was the day, he felt it in his bones. The day he'd finally catch the one that kept getting away.

The sun filtered through the apple green leaves like the glow of one of those old-time stained glass windows, creating freckled shadows on the water.

Trout were extremely wise and wary. Not like Buckeroo, who wouldn't know a floater from a shooting-taper line. The man had bad casting habits and always had been a show off from the time they'd both been pups.

As if conjured up by his thoughts, Buck suddenly came into view upstream from Tad. But not upstream enough. The man was trying to steal Tad's thunder by getting to the fish first!

"Get off my property you low-down, gizzard-sucking coyote!" Tad bellowed.

"Holy buckets, you're scaring the fish!" Buck bellowed right back. "Shut up! Besides, low-down, gizzard-sucking coyote is my description of you. You can't go stealing my words. You're already trying to steal my fish. Now just shut up and get back to your own side of the bank."

"Don't you tell me to shut up!" Tad battled his way upstream until he was only a few yards from his nemesis. "This part of Troublesome Creek is mine. Git!" Tad leaned forward threateningly.

Buck didn't move. "Son of a buck, I'm not goin' anywhere. This is my property and you're the one who's trespassing. So you can just git!"

"I'm warning you..." Tad growled.

"And I'm warning you that you'd better get back to your own side of the creek before I give you the boot."

"The boot, huh!" Tad was not impressed. "You can't even tie your own fly anymore, and I'm not talking about fishing lures."

"Why, you..."

Reno heard the shouting first. Then it escalated to splashing and cursing and what sounded like a sharp crack.

As the sheriff of Bliss, it was his job to see what was going on, even if it was his day off and he was trying to get some fishing in.

It was hard to hurry in knee-deep water, he thought as he plodded around the bend in the creek to find his dad and Tad Hughes sitting in the creek, their bent rods and entangled lines imprisoning them.

Reno had to bite his tongue to stop himself from laughing out loud. His voice was the model of control as he said, "Excuse me, gentlemen, but I was under the impression that the number one fishing maxim you should never overlook is this—if you scare the fish, you can't catch them."

"Tell that to this old geezer," Buck said with a sharp jerk of his head toward Tad.

"I'll show you who's an old geezer," Tad growled, trying to move but restrained by the fishing line.

"You taught me that once you discover where the fish are and what your presentation is, all you have to do is catch 'em," Reno told his father. "You didn't warn me to watch out for crazy old coots who seem hell bent on making trouble."

"Is that any way to speak to your father?" Buck demanded in an affronted voice.

"Forget about catching trout, you can't even control your own kids," Tad scoffed.

"Hey, I don't see you keeping tabs on your daughter, either," Buck said.

Tad glared. "You keep Hailey out of this."

"Listen, you two, knock it off or I'll take you in for disorderly conduct," Reno warned them.

"Your idiot father broke my new fishing rod," Tad declared. "I want him arrested!"

"My rod is better and more expensive than yours," Buck retorted. "And you're the one who broke my rod, so you're the one who's going to be arrested.''

''Am not!''

''Are so.''

The two men tried to duke it out, but they were restricted by the fishing lines.

Reno shook his head in amazement and irritation. ''I should just leave you both sitting here in the middle of Troublesome Creek until you come to your senses.''

''Fine.'' Buck's voice crackled with anger. ''You stay out of it. When the day comes that I can't take care of a low-down, gizzard-sucking coyote like Tadpole here with one hand tied behind my back, then you should just get out the shovel and bury me on the spot.''

''I'll bury you,'' Tad bellowed.

''That's it,'' Reno said. ''I've had it with you two. I'm taking you both in.''

WHEN CORD AND HAILEY REACHED his cabin, it was late afternoon. The skunk had miraculously missed spraying Hailey's boots, which she'd kicked away from her clothing, so she'd been able to wear them on the walk home. Not that wearing a swimsuit with western-style leather boots was exactly a great fashion statement.

But that didn't seem to matter to her. She didn't feel awkward or self-conscious around Cord and that had to be a first.

The time had passed quickly on their downward descent, with Cord doing more talking than he had since she'd returned home. He didn't say anything earth-shattering, like "I love you, Hailey." He spoke about his work, about the ranch, about his dad, about some of the trees they saw, about all kinds of things, really. And in doing so, she grew to appreciate the cadence of his voice.

It had a low rich sound, not as mellow as his older brother's or as fun-filled as his younger brother's. No, Cord's voice reflected his quietly fierce independence.

When they reached Cord's cabin, he phoned his brother Zane to borrow some clothes instead of Hailey calling her family. She could only imagine what Zane's reaction to this unusual request was, since it was Cord's side of the conversation she could hear.

"You heard me right. We need some clothes for Hailey. A skunk messed up hers. While we were up at Oh-Be-Joyful Falls. No, she wasn't wearing them at the time. Get your mind out of the gutter and put your wife on. She's the intelligent one in the family. Yeah, Tracy, listen…oh, you heard on the extension, huh? Well, I need someone to drive up some clothes. What's she wearing now? A black swimsuit. Why? So the clothes you pick won't clash? I don't think she's going to care at this point. Just grab a pair of jeans and a T-shirt. I'd give her mine but the pants would be too big to ride in. What color T-shirt should you bring?" Cord imagined city-girl Tracy taking the rest of the day to choose just the right color. He prided himself on his self-control, but he didn't think he could go much longer staring at Hailey in her black swimsuit without peeling it from her lush body and making her his.

Talk about getting under his skin. She'd done that big time.

And the only cure he could come up with to get her out of his system was to make love to her. Sort of like using snake venom as an antidote for snakebites. Not that he thought of her as something nasty like a snakebite. Not at all. But he wasn't looking for any emotional entanglements. He aimed on telling her that, as soon as he got her dressed.

"Never mind the T-shirt," he told Tracy over the phone, "I'll loan her one of mine. Just bring the jeans, would you? And fast. Thanks."

Hanging up the phone, Cord turned to Hailey. "She'll be up here within half an hour. If you're chilled, maybe you should take a hot shower."

"No, I'm not chilled."

He frowned. "Even so, you should wear something more..."

She wasn't sure what his hand gesture was meant to convey, but he headed up to the loft and came back with a white T-shirt. "Here, put this on." He held open the neck hole for her as if she were his niece and nephew's age, tugging it over her head and then pulling it down. The hem went to mid-thigh.

"You know what this reminds me of?" she said.

He gave her a wry smile. "Some outlaw who dressed in borrowed T-shirts?"

"Well, there was the case of Black Bart in California who was caught because of his shirt, or to be more precise, because of a laundry marking from the collar on his shirt. They tracked it down to a Chinese laundry in San Francisco. Like Cockeyed Curly, Black Bart was a poet."

"So Cockeyed Curly was nothing but a copycat, huh?"

"I suppose that's one way of looking at it. But I prefer to think of Curly as a sort of free spirit."

"Yeah, freeing other people of their money," he noted dryly. "What made you want to write a book about outlaws, anyway? It doesn't seem like the right subject for—"

"For what?" she said defensively, having heard this comment before. "For a *girl*?"

"I just meant that you seemed so passionate about the history of the women of the West that I thought you'd write a book about that."

"I hope to, one day. But for now my publisher needs a book about Colorado outlaws. And it's been interesting to find out about Curly's life as well as other outlaws', including famous ones like Doc Holliday of Tombstone fame, who died of tuberculosis in Colorado and is buried in Glenwood Springs. And the not-so-famous ones—"

"Like Ike Clodfelter," he inserted.

She looked impressed. "So you do pay attention."

Oh, he paid attention, all right. To just about everything she said and did. That was the problem. He just wasn't sure how to tell her that he wanted no part of emotional ties. He wasn't smooth about these things the way Reno was. But even he was pretty sure that it wouldn't do to simply blurt it out.

So how should he break it to her? Hell, he was no good at this human relationship stuff. Give him a block of wood and he was a happy camper. He knew how to make a dovetail joint or hone his ax to a razor's edge, but he was plain no good with people.

Not that he was complaining. He liked his life the way it was. Without complications. Like love. Love was like that beetle that killed trees, weakening them from the inside out. Cord had warned God when he was thirteen that if He let his mother die, he'd never open his heart that way again. A childish vow maybe, but one that suited his temperament and loner ways and one that he wasn't about to break at this late date. It left you too vulnerable.

None of which told him how to talk to Hailey about this emotional entanglement thing.

Maybe he should just be direct.

Yeah, right. Like that would work.

Hailey wished she knew what he was thinking. He wasn't an easy man to read. For all she knew he could be contemplating that commission he was doing for Founders Day or he could be thinking that she looked incredibly desirable in his T-shirt.

Okay, odds were that he was thinking about his work, not her. And he was an incredibly talented woodworker. Some of his pieces had a whimsy she wouldn't have expected from someone with his intensity. Like the contorted lodgepole pine bookcase near the stone fireplace. The gnarled supports left to their own devices to twist and turn gave the piece a magical feel. "Have I told you yet that your bookcase looks like it comes from an enchanted forest?"

"It would have to be an enchanted forest filled with cowboys," he said.

"Snow White and the seven cowboys." She grinned at the concept. "I like the sound of that." And she liked the sound of his voice when it held that rich humor. He displayed it rarely, but when he did, it was all the more captivating.

"I like working with woods native to the West," he admitted. "And I like imperfections."

She was glad to hear that, since she considered herself to be filled with imperfections.

He went on to say, "A lot of the wood I use in my work is hand-peeled."

She imagined him hand-peeling her shirt away. Then he'd start on her bra, hand-peeling that, too. "I imagine you're pretty good at that," she murmured.

"It's all in the hands."

She sighed. "I'm sure it is."

She'd noticed before how he ran his hands over the wood while he worked on it, as if testing the feel of it. He was a very tactile person, she realized. A man who appreciated the differences in texture and composition. A man who noticed details. One who could create powerful magic with the simplest touch...

"Is it just me or is it getting warm in here?" she muttered, tugging on the neckline of the white T-shirt he'd insisted she borrow.

"Don't take it off." He sounded panic-stricken at the idea, which didn't help her ego any.

Then she caught the glow of passionate hunger in his deep blue eyes. That wasn't the look of a man unmoved by her.

A quick knock announced the arrival of Tracy, who entered the cabin with a big grin on her face and a pair of jeans in her hands. "The twins were dying to come up here and see the naked lady you're keeping in your cabin, Cord, but I told them they were too young to see such things.''

''Very funny,'' he muttered. ''If they start blabbing that wild story all over Bliss, who knows what will happen?''

''I can tell you what would happen,'' Hailey said.

Cord cut her off. ''You don't have to. I already know it involves your dad and a shotgun.''

''Speaking of your dad, Hailey, a call came in right before I left the ranch,'' Tracy told her. ''It seems that your dad is in jail.''

''What?'' The news shocked Hailey. ''Why? What happened?''

Tracy held up her hands. ''Whoa, one question at a time. I'm not sure what happened. All I know is that there was some trouble at Troublesome Creek and Reno arrested him.''

''I'm not surprised,'' Cord said.

''I wouldn't look so high-and-mighty, Cord,'' Tracy told him ''Reno arrested *your* dad, too.''

Cord's stunned look matched the one Hailey knew she'd had on her face a few seconds ago.

''I've got to go see my dad,'' she said.

Tracy nodded her understanding. ''I drove up your truck with the horse trailer so that you could load your horse and drop me off at the ranch on your way into town.''

''Thanks.'' Not even bothering to go into the bathroom to get dressed, Hailey quickly tugged the jeans over her swimsuit. Cord automatically reached out to cup her elbow and help her balance as she hopped from one leg to the other. A second later she was zipping up the borrowed pants. "Thanks." She directed those words to Cord. "I'm ready to go now."

Hailey wasn't prepared to find her aunt raising cain at the sheriff's office an hour later. Alicia wasn't angry with Reno for arresting Hailey's father. No, the older woman was raking her brother, Tad, over the coals. "How could you! How could you do such a thing?"

"You're in trouble now, Tadpole," Buck chortled.

Alicia immediately turned on Buck. "And you're no better. Grown men, acting like a pair of spoiled children and coming up with ridiculous excuses."

As Alicia continued her furious dressing-down, both men stood there, behind bars, staring at her with a stunned look that only the male of the species could manage. It was as if a barn kitten had suddenly turned into a snarling mountain lion and attacked them.

Hailey was impressed by her aunt's behavior. While Hailey's dad had always been loud and blustery, her aunt had been the soft-spoken and relatively shy one in the family. Hailey could understand her dad's and Buck's surprise at Alicia's uncharacteristic behavior.

Catching sight of Hailey, Tad said, "Thank heavens you're here. Your aunt has gone off the deep end."

"I support everything she said," Hailey replied.

"Sure, sure." Tad placated her without really listening. "Now pay the fine and get me out of here."

"Reno tells me that we can't do anything until the paperwork clears," Hailey replied.

"And when will that be?"

"Tomorrow morning."

"Tomorrow morning?" Tad's bellow made the windowpanes rattle. "I'm not staying in here overnight."

"Maybe that will make you think twice before doing something like this again." She sent him a reprimanding look worthy of any he'd given her over her lifetime. "I mean, if Cord and I can kiss and make up, I don't see why the two of you can't put this feud behind you."

"Wait a minute here!" Tad shouted. "Back up. What's this about you and Cord kissing?"

"I was using the phrase 'kiss and make up' as a way of indicating a lack of hostility," Hailey hastily explained.

Tad nodded and lowered his voice conspiratorially. "I get it. Part of your plan. No need to say anything more until we can talk someplace private." He scowled at Buck, who had been obviously eavesdropping, as was Opal from the reception desk out front.

Hailey wasn't sure how it happened, but by the time she reached the post office, Geraldine came sprinting out of the building to block Hailey's progress on the sidewalk. "So what's this I hear about you and Cord making out?"

8

HAILEY FEARED she'd been out in the sun too long. Surely she couldn't have heard Geraldine correctly. "Excuse me?"

"No, I won't excuse me." The older woman placed her hands on her hips and gave her a reprimanding look. "How could you tell something like this to Opal at the sheriff's office and not to me? Why, even Floyd over at the Bliss Bar knew about it before I did. I think you've got some explaining to do, missy."

Noticing the nosy looks they were getting from passersby, Hailey said, "Can we at least go inside?"

"Sure thing." As if not trusting her not to take off, Geraldine put her arm around Hailey to escort her inside the empty post office.

"*Awk*, return to sender, return to sender!" the colorful parrot squawked.

"Shush now, Dispatch. I'm on a fact-finding mission here." Geraldine turned over the Back In Five Minutes sign and locked the door. Returning her attention to Hailey, she said, "Now, what's this about you and Cord?"

"I fail to see how it's anyone's business," Hailey felt compelled to say.

Geraldine was not impressed. "That may be the

case in the big city of Boulder, but here in Bliss we keep tabs on such things."

"Well, you shouldn't." Hailey's exasperation was evident.

"Don't you be trying to change the subject," Geraldine scolded.

"I'm not changing the subject. I'm just saying that there must be more interesting things for the people of Bliss to talk about."

"Sure there are," Geraldine agreed. "Like the fact that the historical society was broken into last night and the small portrait of Cockeyed Curly was stolen. Then there's the rumor that you may even be close to finding Curly's treasure. But at the moment I'm more interested in the talk in town about you and Cord. Floyd and Opal are counting on me to get the facts, knowing as they do how folks are eager to talk to me on account of my people skills."

Personally Hailey thought it was more due to Geraldine's interrogation techniques, which would do the Spanish Inquisition proud.

"Don't give me that sour-lemon face," Geraldine reprimanded her. "If you'd wanted to keep this affair private, then you shouldn't have announced it in front of Opal, which is tantamount to announcing it to the world."

"All I said was that since Cord and I had kissed and made up, I didn't see why my dad and Buck couldn't put their feud behind them."

"Kissed and made out?"

"Kissed and made *up*," Hailey corrected her, louder this time, just in case Geraldine hadn't turned up her hearing aid. "And I didn't announce it to the world, I was speaking to my father."

The older woman gave her a skeptical look. "Hmm, your story sounds mighty suspicious to me."

"What's more suspicious is this break-in at the historical society. When did that happen?"

"They just found out this afternoon when Betty went to go open it. You know the place is closed Tuesday mornings on account of Betty having to go visit her sister over in Hayden. You'd never know it by looking at them now, but those two girls were the best-dressed students I ever saw. But that was back in the fifties and Betty has let her herself go since then. I've told her—"

Hailey interrupted her. "Can we get back to the break-in at the historical society, please?"

"Oh, right. Well, when Betty got there, the door had been jimmied open and anything pertaining to Cockeyed Curly had been stolen, which means the portrait, because there isn't much else in there about Curly. And then this morning, Floyd comes to pick up his mail—you know, his girlie magazines come in this time every month—and...well, he tells me that there were two strange men in the bar last night asking questions about the legendary gold that was supposed to be buried in these parts."

Hailey's heart dropped. "What did Floyd say to them?"

"That there were lots of legends about lost gold all over the Rockies and precious few folks finding anything."

She nodded. "Good answer."

Geraldine smiled fondly. "That's Floyd for you, always fast on his feet."

Since Floyd was an octogenarian who moved at a shuffle, and only when in a rush, Hailey had to smile, too. "Yeah, that's Floyd all right. So do they think those two strange men broke into the historical society?"

"Opal says that Reno is still investigating the case. Well, actually, today was his day off and he was fishing in Troublesome Creek. That's how come he arrested your dad and his dad, too. Because they disturbed his fishing."

"I don't think that's an arrestable offense."

Geraldine shrugged. "Well, it was something about disturbing the peace. Which means that Reno's deputy was doing the investigating on the break-in at the historical society, and you know how Barney is. I told his mama she shouldn't drink coffee when she was pregnant with him, but did she listen to me? Heck no."

Hailey resisted the temptation to roll her eyes in frustration.

"Anyway," Geraldine continued without missing a beat, "as I was saying, the perpetrators are still on the loose. You know, I read a mystery with a similar crime in it and it turned out that the villain was the mayor's estranged sister."

Hailey frowned in confusion. "The mayor doesn't have a sister."

"Well, we wouldn't know her if she was estranged from the mayor. Or was it the deranged sister? I can't recall now. Well, in the book the woman was either deranged or estranged. I'll have to go back and re-

read it now. If I can find it. I never forget a plot but I can't always remember the book titles."

When Geraldine paused to inhale, Hailey seized the opportunity to speak. "Listen, I've got to go, but before I do I want to make it perfectly clear that there is no indication that Cockeyed Curly's legendary gold ever existed. In all my research, I haven't found one shred of evidence to support that claim."

"*Awk,* kiss and make out, kiss and make out!"

Hailey shot a horrified look at the parrot. "I thought he only repeated postal terms."

"I guess Dispatch has a romantic soul. I confess I'm glad to hear about you and Cord. You deserve happiness." Geraldine patted her hand. "Have you set a date yet?"

Hailey blinked. "A date for what?"

"For your wedding."

"We're not getting married!"

Geraldine did not look pleased with this news. "Well, the two of you can't continue having an affair and not expect your daddy to get riled up about things. Is that why he and Buck got into a gun fight?"

"There were no guns involved, just fishing rods. And no, that's not why they fought."

"Well, it's not bound to help matters any," Geraldine declared. "Now, you listen to me, the sooner you and Cord tie the knot, the sooner things in this town will get back to normal."

At the moment, Hailey doubted that Bliss would ever return to normal. In fact, she was beginning to wonder if it ever had been normal.

One thing was for sure, she needed to warn Cord

about the gossip as well as the talk about the treasure. It wouldn't do for him to walk into town unsuspecting and get hit with either bit of news. Neither was bound to please him.

HE WAS BENT OVER his worktable, head down and engrossed in the intricate carving of what looked like a bear. Hailey knew from the piece in the living room that this would end up being on the door of a cabinet. She also knew that announcing her arrival might startle him, and who knew what damage he could do with a sharp carving tool? On her for interrupting him or on the piece.

She sighed. When had her life gotten so complicated? It had seemed like such a simple idea back in Boulder. Spend the summer in Bliss doing research while she subletted her apartment at a profit. Then return to Boulder and continue working on her book.

But then Cord had walked back into her life and screwed up those plans. And after he'd kissed her, she'd come up with a new plan, to prove to him that she was a woman and not just the chubby nuisance from next door. But on the drive up here it had hit her. Well, not hit her exactly, not like a bolt from the blue or anything. No, it had been more like a soft rain washing over her—she had deep feelings for Cord. Really, really deep feelings. As in she loved him.

So much for her showing him who was emotionally in charge. Hah! Her femme fatale plans had pretty much gone out the window.

She should have noticed the signs earlier. If revenge was the only thing on her mind, she would never have worried that he wasn't eating or taking care of himself.

Some Delilah she was.

Deciding she could use a fortifying cup of tea before having to face Cord with the latest news from Bliss, she returned to the kitchen and put the battered teapot on to boil. She kept a small stash of her favorite tea—Earl Grey—in one of his empty kitchen drawers. Like most men, Cord didn't have the best-stocked kitchen. In fact, half the cabinets and drawers, while beautifully made by him, were still empty. The man definitely needed a keeper.

"I didn't expect you back today," Cord said as he wandered into the kitchen a few minutes later. "How was your dad?"

"The same as yours," she replied. "Ticked off at being in jail."

"You didn't get him out?"

"No." She blew on her hot tea to cool it down so she could drink it. "Aunt Alicia convinced me it would do both my dad and yours some good to sit there and stew overnight. Reno thought the same thing and I trust his judgment."

Cord didn't know why her words stung, but they did. So she trusted Reno's judgment, did she? Cord doubted she'd say the same thing about him. But then Reno always had been the smart one in the family, the outgoing one. And the most successful one where women were concerned.

He wasn't sure how to warn Hailey off his brother without sounding as if he were jealous, which of course he wasn't.

Okay, so maybe he was. So shoot him.

Cord had been feeling out of sorts ever since that kiss he and Hailey had shared up at Oh-Be-Joyful Falls.

Kiss was an understatement. They'd practically been making love standing up. Or as close to it as you could get with him still fully dressed. He'd had his hands all over her. Heck, the woman had actually purred. She made him want to get naked with her, and that bothered the heck out of him. Or maybe it was just sexual frustration gnawing at him.

She sure had a way of making a man painfully aware of her. He had only to look at her to get his blood pumping, his juices flowing...and bingo, he was fully aroused. She was more potent than Viagra. His jeans hadn't fit right since the first time she'd kissed him.

And he still hadn't figured out how to approach her about curing this powerful hankering he had for her.

"Um..." She nervously ran her index finger around the lip of her teacup. She had nice fingers, fingers that knew how to make a man feel pleasure. He shifted uncomfortably, the constriction in his jeans shouting *Ready for takeoff!* Maybe he'd be better off wearing a pair of baggy overalls when she was in the vicinity.

"I think we need to talk," she said.

Could she read his mind? Was she feeling a similar urgency? Was she going to tell him that she wanted to jump him and tear all his clothes off? How would he respond if she did say that? Shouting "Glory hallelujah" and getting naked ASAP sounded good.

Instead she said, "While I was in Bliss I found out that the historical society was broken into last night and that Cockeyed Curly's portrait was stolen. Floyd reported two suspicious men in his bar last night, asking a lot of questions about Curly and his buried treasure."

The news squelched Cord's overactive sex drive. This was one of his worst fears, that a bunch of troublemaking treasure hunters would take hold of the legend and dig up the countryside, causing all kinds of problems in his beloved mountains. Instead of enjoying his seclusion up here, he'd have to deal with greedy gold diggers after fast riches. No doubt they'd soon start scrambling all over these hills, looking under every unturned rock, seeing dollar signs in every likely hiding space.

Hailey could tell by the look on Cord's face that he was not pleased with this news and she had the feeling that he held her at least partly to blame for it.

She wasn't even sure she could fault him for that, because she was feeling more than a tad responsible herself.

"I knew this would happen." Sure enough his voice sounded like the grizzly growl of a bear. He was not a happy camper.

"I assured Geraldine that I hadn't found anything to indicate that Cockeyed Curly's gold was anything but a legend," Hailey quickly said. "And having told her, I'm sure it will get around the entire town in a matter of minutes."

"It's not the townspeople I'm worried about."

"Well, maybe you should be, because there's something else they're talking about."

"Like what?"

"Like you and me." Seeing his expression darken, she defensively added, "It wasn't my fault."

"What did you say?"

"What do you think I said? That we were making out up at Oh-Be-Joyful Falls until we were interrupted by a skunk? Stop looking at me like that." Her voice reflected her exasperation. She had to take a calming sip of tea before she could continue. "I didn't say anything except that I didn't see why, since you and I had kissed and made up, that our fathers couldn't drop their feud."

"You told your father I kissed you?" Cord sounded horrified.

"I wasn't speaking literally. It was merely a figure of speech."

"Well, do me a favor and don't go using my name in any more of your figures of speech from now on."

"I told you..."

He interrupted her. "I know what you told me, but the bottom line is that folks in town are talking about us."

"They're doing more than just talking," she admitted reluctantly. "They're expecting us to get married."

"Like that's gonna happen."

His words stung. Did he have to dismiss her that way? She hated being ridiculed. It was a surefire way to get her riled up. He wasn't the only one that could make marriage between the two of them sound as appealing as a dip in a skunk bath. "That's what I told Geraldine. That there was no way you and I were an item or were getting married. If that's not enough, I'll go back to town tomorrow and tell her again. I'll say that you're the last man on the face of the earth that I'd want to be tied to,'' she said tartly. ''Would that make you happy?''

''No. I mean yes. Heck, I don't know what I mean,'' he muttered, jabbing a hand through his dark hair and further tousling it.

Even though she was feeling totally annoyed with him, there was a part of her that still wanted to gobble him up. He looked both adorable and incredibly sexy standing there, a mutinous set to his chin and a hell-for-leather gleam in his deep, deep eyes.

Hailey sighed. ''Look, I'm sorry all this happened but I can assure you I didn't deliberately say or do anything to give anyone the idea that you and I...you know.''

Now he was the one who sighed. ''I know.''

''And while I denied the rumors about us, I'm not sure Geraldine completely believed me.'' She paused a moment to take another sip of tea before his direct gaze had the words spilling out of her. ''Okay, the truth is that basically she didn't believe a word I said on that subject, okay? But I did try. And I feel confident that I was more successful in spreading the word that there was no real treasure map for Curly's gold. I just didn't want you walking into town without being forewarned about them trying to marry us off.''

''You wanted to protect me from having a heart attack should Geraldine corner me and ask me when you and I are getting hitched, right?''

She nodded. ''Exactly. Forewarned is forearmed.''

''In my book being forearmed means staying away from Bliss until they've got something else to yap about.''

''It will probably blow over in a few days.'' At least she hoped so.

''It better,'' he said darkly.

''I CAN'T BELIEVE they left us in here,'' Buck muttered from his jail cell.

Tad raised his head. ''Did you say something?''

Buck spoke again, louder this time. ''I said, I can't believe they left us in here.''

''Me, neither,'' Tad admitted, sinking onto the cot next to the bars separating his cell from Buck's.

Buck likewise sat on his cot so the two men were only a few feet apart. ''Your sister sure seemed riled up today,'' he noted.

''I don't know what got into her,'' Tad replied with a baffled shake of his head. ''She's always been so levelheaded and quiet in the past. She had no cause to be yelling at us that way.''

Buck went on to think that Alicia was a mighty fine looking woman when she was in a temper, and he wondered why he hadn't noticed that before. Well, he had noticed her now that he thought on it. He'd gotten more than a little nervous when she'd come to the ranch with Hailey. He seemed to recall slapping his boys on their backs and making them stand up straight. He'd wanted to make a good impression.

A gentle woman like Alicia needed looking after, like fine china. But she hadn't been gentle today.

He knew his daughter-in-law, Tracy, had a temper that could turn a blizzard around and send it south with a suntan, but he'd never realized that mild-mannered Alicia harbored a similar temper beneath her sweet exterior. He'd always been the kind of man who liked some spice in his life.

He truly regretted angering Alicia, even though he had enjoyed watching the color flood her face as she'd hollered at them. Maybe she was right, maybe it was time he and Tad mended a few fences.

"Guess we both missed out on some pretty good fishing today," Buck said. "You know, I've often thought that a big trout approaches a streamer the way my eight-year-old grandkids approach ice cream—quickly, directly, and with little mind for manners."

Tad chuckled.

"My favorite pattern is a Spring Creek Bugger," Buck said.

Tad perked up. "Isn't that similar to the Lucky Leech?"

"Yep."

"I prefer a Woolly Bugger with a rabbit-strip tail," Tad said. "The rabbit strip has a motion similar to conventional marabou, but it's more durable and maintains bulk better in the water."

Buck nodded his agreement. "What about a small Clouser Minnow?"

"That's another good pattern," Tad said.

"Think they'll let us out early enough to get some fishing done tomorrow?" Buck asked hopefully.

Tad just shrugged and looked morose again. "Who knows?"

As Hailey returned to her family's ranch house, she couldn't help thinking the place looked more somber than usual. Her childhood home was big and bulky, like her dad. There was no gay gingerbread trim to soften the lines of the high-gabled roof. Even the dark brown color was serious.

While the ranch house's outside appearance was no nonsense, the inside of the home had always been big and friendly. Maybe that had taught her early on not to judge by outward appearances, like Cord's tough exterior. Over the past week she'd seen glimpses of another man who, while perhaps not exuberantly friendly, did have an inner core of warmth and compassion.

A man as unbending as an oak, yet one who hated to see her cry. A loner who kissed her as if she held the key to keeping his inner demons at bay. A cowboy who expressed himself by pouring his deeply held emotions into his wood carving while guarding his inner thoughts as zealously as he did his family's archives.

Yeah, she was definitely in love with the lug.

But she'd no more picked him to fall in love with than she'd picked this house to grow up in. Both were part of her destiny.

The moment Hailey stepped inside the front door, she found Alicia anxiously waiting for her. Belch and Lurch were also right by the door, looking for Hailey's dad and whining softly when they didn't see him with her.

"They've been getting underfoot all afternoon," Alicia said.

"They probably miss Dad."

As if on cue, Belch burped and Lurch barked sharply.

Alicia was not swayed by their canine antics. "I don't care how soulfully these dogs look at me, I'm not in favor of letting your father out of jail until he's learned his lesson, and I don't think that will happen until he spends the night there."

"I agree with you."

"I appreciate that." Alicia smiled gratefully.

Eyeing the mournful dogs, Hailey said, "It's not easy, though, is it."

Alicia sighed and wandered into the front parlor, where she sank onto the blue-and-white-striped couch. "No, it's not." She absently rubbed Lurch's left ear as the Great Dane sat on the floor near her. "Did you want something to eat?"

Following her into the room, Hailey shook her head. "Maybe later."

"I already gave most of my late lunch to these two lop-eared pot lickers here."

"It sounds funny when you say it."

Alicia smiled. "Perhaps because I lack your father's ability to bellow."

"Oh, I don't know," Hailey teased her. "I think you held your own at the sheriff's office today."

Alicia blushed. "I know it's not ladylike to shout that way, but it was the only way I could get through to your father. I've tried reasoning with him until I'm blue in the face. He just pats my head and tells me not to worry, he has everything under control."

"I think he'll pay more attention to what you say after this incident."

"Where did you go after leaving the sheriff's office? And what happened to your clothes? Now that I think on it, those jeans are tight and that T-shirt is huge on you."

"I had a run-in with a skunk up by Oh-Be-Joyful Falls and my clothes are in the garbage. I borrowed these from Cord and his family earlier today."

"I see."

Hailey wondered about the satisfied look on her aunt's face. Wondered and worried. What was behind that smile? Why would she be pleased that Hailey was wearing borrowed clothing? Maybe she was getting paranoid after her run-in with Geraldine.

"To answer your other question, after leaving the sheriff's office, I was waylaid by Geraldine demanding the details of my supposed affair with Cord."

"And you spoke to her before you spoke to me?" Alicia looked hurt.

"I didn't have much of a choice. You know how things can get totally blown out of proportion in Bliss. Just because I told Dad how Cord and I had kissed and made up, figuratively speaking of course, it got all over town that Cord and I were an item. From just that one misquoted line."

"Well, I don't think that's the only reason for the speculation about you and Cord. I mean, after all, the two of you are working together."

"We're both working, yes, but not together. He's working on his furniture and on that special commission for Founders Day, and I'm working on my research."

"You must be a specialist on researching Cord by now. I mean, after spending so much time with him and knowing him as well as you do."

Hailey just shrugged. "Cord is a hard man to get to know."

"Granted, but then you were never one to give up easily."

"Cord knows that about me." She smiled. "I think he first guessed that when I was six and chased him through the barn in a game of tag."

"But the two of you have been getting along so much better these days, right?"

"Well," Hailey said, rubbing Lurch's ear, "I haven't hit him lately."

"I should hope not! Now sit down and tell me how things between you and Cord are truly going." She patted the couch invitingly.

Belch thought the invitation was meant for him and he jumped up, or tried to. He needed some assistance and Alicia didn't have the heart to turn him away.

Hailey curled up in the opposite corner of the couch, with Lurch's chin on her lap. "Things between Cord and I are going okay."

Alicia looked concerned. "Just okay?"

"He wasn't real pleased when I told him there were rumors about us going around town."

"Why did you tell him that?"

"Because I thought it only fair to prepare him for Geraldine asking him if he's set a date for our wedding yet."

"And have you?"

"Aunt Alicia!" She stared at her in surprise. "You're kidding, right?"

Alicia blinked at her guilelessly. "Now, Hailey,

I've known that you loved Cord from the time you were twelve."

"Yes, but that was an adolescent crush. Now Cord and I are just friends."

"I think you're more than just friends. Unless you're honestly telling me that Cord hasn't kissed you? Is that what you're saying? I'm right, aren't I!" she said triumphantly, having spotted the blush Hailey felt coloring her cheeks. "You and Cord have kissed."

Hailey never had been any good at lying to her aunt. The older woman had always had a way of getting to the truth. When she'd been accused of gluing Cord's butt to his seat in high school, it had only taken one look from her aunt in the principal's office to have her confessing. It didn't matter that Hailey was nearly thirty now, some things never changed—her love for Cord and her inability to lie to Aunt Alicia. It made her feel so predictable.

Not that she'd planned on loving Cord. The opposite was true. She'd hoped to prove that she was over him completely. And to prove to him that she was a capable and attractive woman. Well, she may have hit pay dirt on that last one, if his actions up at the falls were any indication.

He'd certainly acted like a man smitten. She loved that term and had always secretly wished to have a blue-eyed loner with expressive hands become smitten with her. But only one blue-eyed loner would do—Cord.

"Why are you so interested in what Cord and I are doing?" she asked her aunt. "You've never interrogated me about my love life before."

"Because I knew the two of you would get together. I told Betty so."

"You mean Betty from the historical society?"

Alicia nodded. "That's right."

The idea that her aunt had been out there fanning the flames of the rumor mill concerning her and Cord getting together took Hailey aback. "Why would you do something like that?"

"You know that Betty and I are friends."

That was no explanation. "Who else did you talk to about Cord and me?"

"A few people at the Cut 'n' Curl." Rather than appearing chastened, Alicia seemed rather proud of what she'd done.

Hailey didn't get it. "You've never been the gossipy type before. Why would you suddenly start talking to people in town about my private life? Is that what Geraldine meant when she said there was talk in town about Cord and me? That it was going on even before the comment I made at the sheriff's office this afternoon?"

"No one was saying anything disrespectful."

"That's not the point."

"Then what is the point?" Alicia blinked at her innocently.

"That I don't appreciate people speculating about my private life." Hailey's voice reflected her increasing agitation. "And I can't understand how you could betray my trust by talking about me."

"I didn't betray your trust. I only want what's best for you." Then her eyes filled with tears. "No, that's not the entire truth. I also wanted what was best for me."

Hailey didn't understand. "How could spreading rumors about Cord and me be good for you?"

"Because I thought if the two of you got together it would stop the family feud."

Hailey scooted closer to hug her aunt. "That was very noble of you."

"No, it wasn't." Alicia sniffed even as Belch whined his concern at her tears and tried to take a swipe at her chin with his pink tongue.

"Sure it was." Hailey gently pushed Belch aside while giving her aunt an encouraging look. "You only wanted what was best for your family."

"I wanted what was best for *me*," Alicia said, her voice rising emotionally as the truth came tumbling out. "Don't you see? For years now, I've had a soft spot in my heart for Buck!"

9

HAILEY WAS SO STARTLED she almost fell off the couch. As it was she knocked her elbow into Lurch's head. The Great Dane yelped his displeasure.

"Buck?" Hailey repeated in disbelief, automatically rubbing the dog's ear as a sign of apology. "You've got a soft spot for Buck?" Sure, she'd had some suspicions, but even so, hearing her aunt's words threw her.

"That's right."

"For years?"

Alicia nodded.

"And you've never done anything about it?" Hailey said. "Why not?"

Alicia's tone was defensive when she replied. "You know how your father gets whenever Buck's name is brought up. I didn't have the spunk to defy my brother and to hurt him by seeing Buck. I just kept hoping that the feud would wear itself out. And then when you came home and got involved with Cord, I figured that would break the ice. Your marriage to Cord would end the feud and then maybe I could see Buck, if he was so inclined."

Remembering Buck's unusual behavior when her aunt had accompanied Hailey to the Best ranch, Hailey figured that Buck would be "so inclined" to see Alicia. Actually, this explained a lot. She supposed she shouldn't have been so stunned to hear her aunt voice what Hailey had begun to suspect. It was just that it had been an unsettling day, to put it mildly, what with Cord kissing her up by the falls and her dad ending up in the slammer.

"Are you angry with me?" Alicia asked in an unsteady voice.

"Not at all." Hailey hugged her. "Although I would appreciate it if you'd stop the talk about Cord and me. It's not as if he's on the brink of proposing. Not even remotely close. Half the time I'm not even sure he likes me."

"Oh, he likes you all right," Alicia quickly assured her. "Otherwise he'd just ignore you the way he ignores most of the girls around here."

"He hasn't gotten seriously involved with anyone?"

"Not that I know of. You know Cord always was the intense one in the family, and he's so caught up in his work these days."

"What about while I was gone?" Hailey hoped her question didn't sound like that of a woman desperate to hear about the love life of the man she had a thing for.

"Well, he's a good-looking man. There were women who went after him. But he's not an easy one to pin down."

"Tell me about it," she muttered.

"He'll come around in the end."

Hailey wasn't even sure yet what she wanted him to come around to—loving her, making love to her, marrying her? What did she want from Cord? "I don't know." The answer was as much a reply to her own questions as it was to Alicia's statement.

"Men can be stubborner than a mule, but they come around if you give them enough time."

"Well, let's hope Dad and Buck reach that conclusion after their night in jail."

"I'M SO HUNGRY I could chew sticks," Buck declared.

"Me, too." Tad sighed before restlessly pacing his cell. "You know, my dogs love chewing sticks. Table legs, too, for that matter. Sure hope my sister remembers to feed Belch and Lurch tonight."

"You named your dog Belch?"

Rather than get defensive, Tad just shrugged and plopped on the cot. "Seemed the right thing to do at the time."

"I know how that goes." Buck shrugged right back before plopping on the cot in his cell. "Plenty of things seem like the right thing to do at the time, only to come back and bite you later."

"My dogs don't bite."

"I wasn't talking about your dogs. I was talking metaphysically. Or metamorphically. Metasomethingly. Son of a buck." He slammed his hand against the cot frame. "I hate that."

"Hate what?"

"When I can't remember words. It's right on the tip of my tongue… Metaphorically!" Buck said triumphantly. "That was the word."

"Since I don't know what it means, it makes no never mind to me," Tad replied. "But I do know what you mean about forgetting words. And names.

You know, they say that growing old isn't for sissies, and by golly they're right! Sometimes, you start running out of gas before the day is three-quarters gone."

Buck nodded his understanding. "Like you're running on empty."

"And sometimes when I'm tying lures, it's like cobwebs are covering my eyes."

Again, Buck nodded. "I hear you."

"Speaking of hearing, no one has good diction these days. Young folks are forever slurring their vowels, have you noticed that?"

"Sure have," Buck said. "I hate slurred vowels. And tripping. I never used to trip."

"I'm dropping things," Tad confessed.

"And I'm losing things," Buck admitted. "Almost lost my lucky fishing hat. Do you believe my new daughter-in-law actually wanted to throw it out?"

Tad looked suitably horrified. "I'm telling you, young folks today have no idea of the way of things."

"She's from Chicago," Buck said by way of explanation.

Tad nodded. "I'd heard that."

"She's settling in here real good, though, I'll give her that. And she's bright as a penny. Recognized my barbecue sauce would be a big success."

Tad groaned. "Don't mention food. I think my ribs are sticking to my spine right about now."

"You boys ready for some chow?" Geraldine shouted out as she walked into the holding area bearing a large tray.

"We were ready two hours ago," Buck grumbled.

"Well, hold on to your britches," Geraldine said. "Help is on the way."

"Meaning we're getting out?" Buck asked hopefully.

"No," Geraldine replied, "meaning your dinner is here. I cooked this stew myself."

Buck eyed the cutlery on the tray. "I'm surprised my son the lawman is allowing you to bring in forks and knives. Isn't he afraid we'll try and use them to break out of this hoosegow?"

"I heard that," Reno called out from the other room.

"I meant you to," Buck called back.

"There's no need to use a knife with my stew," Geraldine proudly proclaimed. "It's so tender you could cut it with a fork." She handed each man a generous bowl of stew along with thick chunk of homemade bread slathered with butter. "And I'll tell you what else is tender. The romance between your two kids."

Tad almost spit out his stew. "What?" he bellowed, rattling his bowl and fork.

"Cord and Hailey sitting in a tree. K-i-s-s-i-n-g," Geraldine sang off-key.

"What is this, the second grade?" Buck retorted, before eating another generous mouthful of stew. "We sang that ditty back when we were still wet behind the ears."

"Folks are placing bets right now over at Floyd's bar about the wedding date." Geraldine appeared pleased to be the one to bring them this bit of news.

"Last time I checked, the odds were two to one on an August wedding."

"But that's next month!" Tad exclaimed.

"My boys do have a habit of moving quick once they make up their minds," Buck acknowledged.

"What do you know about this?" Tad demanded.

"No more than you do, probably."

"Hah! I wouldn't put it past you to have plotted this," Tad accused Buck.

"If you believe that," Buck retorted, "then you've been sitting under the wrong end of a well-fed bull."

Tad glared at him. "I'll bet you let my daughter look at your useless old papers because you wanted her and Cord to get together."

"You think I can control what Cord does?" Buck said. His voice lowered as he quietly confessed, "I haven't been able to do that since his mother died."

"Same here," Tad admitted with a sigh. "Once her mother died, I just couldn't seem to get Hailey to behave."

Buck took another bite of stew before reflecting, "You know, I never thought of that as something the two of them have in common, losing their mothers at a young age the way they both did."

Tad was surprised by the similarity. "Yeah, I guess that's right."

"Of course that's right," Geraldine said in exasperation. "I'm surprised you two boys didn't realize that before now." Geraldine was one of the few in town who had the seniority to refer to Buck and Tad as boys. Floyd the bartender was the only other one. "Now, you enjoy that stew of yours and I'll be back with your breakfast in the morning."

"This stew does have a fine flavor," Tad said as he picked up the bowl to resume eating.

"There's something extra in it I can't quite put my finger on," Buck noted. "Gives it quite a kick."

Tad nodded. "I do believe I'll have seconds."

It wasn't until later that Reno discovered that Geraldine had generously spiked her stew with booze. By then the two had started singing bawdy cowboy songs with enough gusto to make his ears ring.

> "First came the miners to work in the mine,
> Then came the ladies who lived on the line
> And together they had a fine ol' time."

Reno had the feeling it was going to be a very long night.

HAILEY HAD MANAGED to sleep well while her father was in jail. She felt more than a few pangs of guilt as a result. But they were offset by the memory of the wonderful dream she'd just had.

She and Cord had been back up at Oh-Be-Joyful Falls, only this time he was in the water without his clothes and he'd practiced his hand-peeling techniques on her swimsuit, peeling it from her body inch by inch. The water had been warm, but his hands had been warmer as he'd seduced her with wicked promises, celebrating her with sinfully blissful strokes that had left her glowing with satisfaction.

She almost hated getting out of bed, wanting instead to bask in the afterglow created by the erotic dream. She knew she had a duty to her father. She'd slept in Cord's T-shirt last night. It smelled like him somehow and now it smelled like her, too. After tugging it off, she buried her nose in the warm cotton before reverently folding it and putting it beneath her pillow.

Oh, yeah, she had it real bad for him.

The realization should have panicked her, but other than a few butterflies in her stomach, she weathered it pretty well. After taking a hot shower, she quickly dressed in her own jeans and a soft powder-blue sweater with buttons down the front. Feeling decadent and sensual, she omitted wearing a bra after reassuring herself that the sweater's thick weave hid that fact from others.

While she brushed her hair, it occurred to her that she'd need a trim fairly soon. She loved the carefree swish her hairstylist back in Boulder had captured and had her doubts about anyone at the Cut 'n' Curl being able to re-create the look. She certainly didn't appear as smooth and serious as she had when she'd first visited the Best ranch. Now freckles were showing up on her nose, and her bangs teased her eyes rather than falling in perfect precision.

She had no time to do more than add a coating of lip gloss before hurrying downstairs. Hairstyles be damned, she had bigger worries to concern her. Like her dad in jail.

Hailey and Alicia arrived at the sheriff's office by nine, only to find her dad sitting on his cot, his head in his hands as he groaned.

"Heavens above, what did you do to him?" Alicia demanded of Reno.

"I didn't do anything to him."

An echoing groan came from Buck's cell, where

he, too, was sitting on the cot with his bent head in his hands.

"What did you do to Buck?" Alicia demanded.

"Nothing," Reno denied. "Tell them, Dad."

Buck cautiously raised his head to glare at them with bloodshot eyes, their light blue color a stark contrast to the pinkish whites of his eyes. "Son of a buck, do you folks have to yell so early in the morning? It's bad enough that the sun is shining in the window bright enough to blind a man."

"Our dads tied one on last night," Reno said. "And I'm not talking about fishing lures."

Hailey was not amused. "You gave them alcohol?"

"I didn't, Geraldine did. In the stew she brought them last night. You don't have to look so worried, ladies. These roustabout cowboys spent a lovely evening serenading the stars with off-color cowboy songs."

"What'd you expect us to sing, Broadway show tunes?" Buck growled with a fierce glare in his son's direction.

"No respect," Tad grumbled, "that's the problem with today's youth. Picking on a man when he's down."

"As if it's not enough that we've been humiliated by our own families," Buck added.

"Hey, you managed the humiliating part all by yourselves by fighting in the middle of Troublesome Creek," Reno said.

"Can we take my father home now?" Hailey asked.

"Sure thing." Reno nodded. "Pay his fine at the

front desk before you leave. The paperwork is all ready."

"Fine?" Tad bellowed before groaning at the sound of his own raised voice. "There's a fine?"

"They want their pound of flesh," Buck said, lowering his head back to his hands.

Alicia fixed both men with a reprimanding look. "I hope you two have learned your lesson."

Buck peered at her through his fingers before sighing and standing up. "Yes, ma'am, we learned a great deal."

"Had some great talks," Tad concurred.

Buck nodded cautiously. "Found out we both agree that starting out fly-fishing on the water encourages poor habits."

"Poor habits like fighting?" Reno asked, tongue-in-cheek.

Tad ignored his comment, instead giving him the lofty look of an expert addressing a novice. "Any good fisherman knows that casting on the lawn is the best place to learn. Buck and I both agree on that."

"I hope you both also agreed not to fight," Alicia said.

Buck nodded slowly. "We agreed not to fight anything but trout."

Tad fixed them all with a look of total disapproval. "And now if you're done with your blasted interrogation, we'd like to get out of here."

"Go right ahead," Reno replied with a grin. "The cell door's unlocked."

AFTER SEEING HER FATHER settled at home, Hailey returned to Cord's cabin to resume working on Rebecca's journals. Deciphering the flowery handwriting wasn't always easy. There were three slim volumes in all and she was currently starting on the final one. The journals were the only things she'd found, other than ranch records, from the time period when Cockeyed Curly was active.

She tried not to be disappointed that Cord was gone. At least he'd left her a note saying that he had business to attend to up in Cheyenne and would be gone most of the day. She couldn't help wondering if the gossip in Bliss had driven him out of town. Not that Cord was a man who ran from much, aside from porcupines. He was much more likely to simply ignore whatever bothered him and immerse himself in work.

She tended to do the same herself. Turning on her laptop computer, she reviewed her notes on what she knew so far of Rebecca and Rafael's story. She'd checked the family Bible at home and been surprised to find no record of Rafael in her own family tree. Instead there had been a line crossed through what looked to be the name of the youngest of six sons.

Earlier, she'd asked Cord if he'd heard any reference to Rebecca in his family's records, but he'd just shrugged and said that his father was the expert on those things. She planned on asking Buck about it, but given his hungover state this morning, she didn't feel it was the most opportune moment to question him about his family tree.

As she resumed reading the journal, there was no doubt that Rebecca had fallen in love with Rafael, although in this volume she'd taken to referring to him as "R," as if afraid of having someone discover her journals and use her words against her.

But every now and then she forgot herself and the words seemed to pour out of her, the handwriting swift and almost illegible at times.

> I have found the other half of my heart. How cruel of fate to make that man the son of my brother's enemy. What do I care of battles over sheep and cattle? When I say this to Jedidiah, he replies that I would care soon enough if there was no roof over my head or food on my table because the sheep had grazed the land and left nothing for the cattle. But he is wrong. I would not care if there was no roof over my head, because my home is in R's arms. We can no longer meet by the falls and have had to limit our time together because of the increased hostilities between our families.

A few days later she'd written another entry.

> I am no longer sure I know my own brother, he has become such a stranger to me. He blames all that is wrong in the world on the neighboring Hughes family, and yet they are no better, blaming the Bests for all that is wrong in their world. But their world is not mine, nor is it R's. He says we should run away together, and go east to stay with his mother's widowed sister. This aunt in Chicago has invited him to come work in her store. I cannot see my western hero in the big city, but surely that would be better than

the life we have now, which is no life at all, hiding and sneaking when we should be celebrating our love.

Hailey could feel Rebecca's frustration growing with every entry she read.

There is talk in town that R and I are secretly meeting. I think it was started by that awful Agnes Crowell, who flirted with R shamelessly at the ice-cream social last month. But my beloved gave her short shrift and only had eyes for me. Now I fear our secret will come to light with disastrous results for us all.

Two days later she wrote again.

I have contacted R and told him that we must meet, that I could not survive a day longer without seeing him. It has been so long. So we met at the falls. And, oh, what happened there...I scarcely know where to begin. We were set up by Agnes and her brother and were in danger of being found out when someone came to our rescue. He was gentlemanly in his appearance and had a kind expression. He led R and myself into his hiding place, a cave in the side of the mountain invisible to all except one who knew of its existence. Agnes and her brother did not find us. The man did not identify himself, despite our requests that he do so in order for us to properly express our appreciation. I confess that the tension was such that I confided our troubles to the man. He offered to help us get away. My R was cautious, not wanting to place his trust in someone he did not know. But I sensed this man would not betray us. And when he later, after much renewed coaxing on our part, told us his name, we realized he had secrets, as well. For this courteous and soft-spoken man was none other than Mr. Curly M.

"Curly," Hailey said aloud, her heart pounding with excitement. "She's just met Curly!"

There was no one to share her excitement. She was alone in the cabin, yet accompanied by the vibrant voices of the past. She eagerly continued reading Rebecca's words.

His ways were not well schooled and he lacked the polish of many, but there are many tales being told by others of the good he has done to help the downtrodden. He has a way with rhymes. His brown eyes—the left of which stares off to the right somewhat—sparkle with humor as he spins his tales of stagecoach and bank robberies. He was proud of the fact that he had never shot anyone and did not steal from passengers when robbing stagecoaches. He showed us one of the poems he'd recently completed, which I have enclosed here. He works hard at them and selects a new poem for each of his "unauthorized bank withdrawals" as he describes them.

Sure enough, folded over and inserted in the journal was a piece of paper, and on it was roughly written a poem she'd never seen before. Having read all the available poems he'd written, she recognized Curly's "voice" right away.

Hey, folks, don't blame me,
My pa schooled me in robbery.
But you can be sure the money I took,
Won't be used to buyin' books.

Chuckling, she returned her attention to Rebecca's journal.

I would never have taken Mr. M to be an outlaw from his appearance or manner. I do not know what my brother would do if he discovered I was consorting with outlaws.

Hailey wondered if Curly had met Jedidiah by then or not. According to written accounts in Leadville, Jedidiah and Curly had not met prior to the barroom brawl where Jedidiah saved Curly's life but she had no firm date on that event, or even any confirmation that it had happened, aside from a brief newspaper account. And in that, there had been no mention of a treasure map, only that Jedidiah had helped Curly. She continued reading.

No doubt Jedidiah would send me off to that convent school in Boston he threatens me with if he knew the direction of my thoughts. I am a grown woman of eighteen years and I know my own heart, but it is no good telling my brother these things. It is best that he not know the truth yet. But soon, surely it will happen soon. Yet even now I am afraid to write my intentions, as if doing so may bring bad luck to my endeavors to be with my beloved.

A week went by before Rebecca's next entry.

The situation here is worsening by the hour. There is talk of a full-blown range war between my brother and the Hugheses. When Jedidiah heard the rumor in town that R had stared at me too long at the ice-cream social, he threatened to take his shotgun to him immediately. It was all I could do to calm him down and prevent him from storming over to the Hughes ranch with a posse of cowboys. This cannot continue. R and I must leave this place and quickly.

Then this short and final entry.

Met Mr. M by the falls, one of several meetings, and made final arrangements to accept his offer of help. I will write nothing further here for fear of jeopardizing our plans. We can take nothing but the clothes on our back, but R and I will have a future together in the East. I know we can be happy there. I pray to heaven that all will be well.

Jeez, talk about a cliff-hanger ending. Had Rebecca and her Rafael made it away safely?

Unable to stand the suspense, she decided to use

her laptop computer to hunt down more information. She had the maiden name of Rafael's mother, Maria. From there, Hailey's branch of the family tree descended from the second oldest brother, Alistair Hughes, and split off in another direction.

She was able to track down Maria's sister using some genealogical sites on the Internet. And a search of a Chicago-based historical database provided her with a detailed bio of the woman, Caroline Jessen, and the businesses she ran, a chain of Chicago drugstores. Caroline had no children of her own and, when she died, left everything to her nephew….Rafael! Bingo!

But he'd changed his surname from Hughes to Jessen.

A while later she'd tracked down Rafael's lengthy bio in the same database, discovering that he'd gone on to become a doctor. He was an advocate for the rights of underprivileged children. And there it was, his wife…Rebecca. He died in his sleep in 1949 at the age of eighty-eight. His wife passed on a year later. They had three adopted children.

So Rebecca had been able to elope with her soul mate after all. Her family and his had subsequently disowned them for their actions.

Hailey didn't even realize that tears were running down her face until one plopped onto her fingers on the keyboard.

She needed chocolate after a story like that. Reaching blindly into her backpack, she tugged out a large Nestlé Crunch bar.

Rachel and her true love had made it away safely, presumably with Curly's help in whisking them out of the area to the train headed for Chicago. If they'd had to flee in the middle of the night, with only the clothes on their backs, that explained why Rebecca had left her journals behind.

Hailey had gone through all three trunks and found one journal in each, stashed there amid a bunch of other papers as if someone had simply dumped the contents of an office or desk into the trunk without bothering to go through the material beforehand.

She wondered what Jedidiah thought about his sister's defection. She had no doubt he'd consider it that way—a defection.

She knew the type. Western men had a habit of seeing things in black and white, leaving it up to the women of the West to deal with all the infinite shades of gray that life provided.

Digging in her backpack, she grabbed a handful of facial tissues to blow her nose and wipe away her tears. Even though she rarely cried, she'd never been one to cry daintily. Invariably her nose turned red and dripped, making her feel like Rudolph the Red-Nosed Reindeer. She didn't blow her nose daintily, either, though she didn't do it as loudly as her father did.

Come to think of it, her dad had always wanted a doctor in the family. Now he had one, Rafael Hughes. Even if it had been a hundred years ago.

Grinning, she used another facial tissue to make one final blow of her nose, only to have the used tissue drop in the bottom of the empty third trunk. Awkwardly reaching inside to get the balled-up tissue, she lost her balance and had to brace her hand on the bottom of the trunk to maintain it.

When the bottom gave way, for one horrified moment she thought she'd broken the antique trunk. Then she realized that part of the bottom had clicked open, revealing a small storage area.

She'd heard of chests with false bottoms, but had never seen one before.

When Hailey removed the paper and recognized Curly's handwriting, she thought she'd simply found another poem of his. It was only after reading the poem that another possibility hit her.

All the loot that Curly took
He stashed in a secret nook.
This here map will tell you how
To find that place, right now.

[el6]

Start out carefullike, take your gun,
And git your directions from the sun.
Count out the paces real real clost,
And follow the marks on trees and post.

X marks the spot where the treasure's hid,
Dig five feet down, you should hit the lid.
Break open the box and there you'll see,
A king's ransom robbed by old Curly.

10

X MARKS THE SPOT? This poem held directions to the treasure. What about the map? Hailey's hands shook as she turned over the paper and found a roughly drawn map. She had Curly's map!

She couldn't help it. She shrieked with excitement.

A second later the cabin's front door banged open as Cord came rushing inside. "What's wrong?"

"It's real!" She threw herself in his arms. "It's real. He wrote a poem."

"Who? What are you talking about?"

"Cockeyed Curly. And his treasure. I found the map!"

She was so thrilled and wanted to share her discovery with him. She hadn't planned on kissing him. Or having him kiss her. It just happened.

And when it did, something moved within her heart at the unmitigated intensity of his embrace. While he wasn't a man who talked about his emotions, he was a man who felt them deeply, and that came across in the fierceness of his clasp and the sensual thrust of his tongue. Whatever it was he felt for her, he felt it strongly.

Like a match to dry timber, their kiss sparked a conflagration of passion that quickly flared out of control. She had his shirt unbuttoned and tugged out of his jeans almost as quickly as he'd unfastened her powder-blue sweater and tossed it across the room. His gifted hands caressed her bare skin from shoulder to waist. She hadn't worn a bra today and his murmur of appreciation told her how delighted he was at this bit of unexpected daring on her part.

Lowering his head, he lightly teased the rosy crests of her breasts with his mouth until her nipples grew taut and temptingly erect. She tingled, she ached, she wanted.

Turning her so that her back was against the front door, he fumbled with the fastening of her jeans. His mouth returned to hers, their kiss an openmouthed declaration of raw passion. Her hands joined his to shove her jeans down her hips before setting to work on his.

She growled her frustration at her clumsiness in ridding him of his jeans even as she kicked off her shoes and jeans. *Hurry, hurry, hurry* throbbed through her body like a jungle drum, consuming her with its primal call.

"Are you sure?" he whispered huskily against her lips, even as his hands slipped beneath her filmy underwear and sought out her feminine secrets.

"Yes," she whispered back. "Yes!" she cried as he ministered to her body with wickedly creative fingers moving in slow, sensuous circles. "Yes!"

He took her to a staggering peak until she panted helplessly in his arms while surges of fierce pleasure pulsated deep within her, increasing with each knowing move he made. Her body went taut as she reached the zenith. His arms were the only thing keeping her standing. Her knees weren't worth diddly.

She rested her damp forehead against his shoulder. Her quiet but heartfelt "Wow" made him smile. She could feel the upward tilt of his lips as he kissed her ear.

"Yeah, wow," he repeated. "There's more where that came from."

His hand cupped the small of her back, lifting her up to meet him. Wrapping her legs around his waist, she only then realized that he was still wearing jockey shorts. And that they were in danger of bursting from the pressure of his straining arousal.

She kissed him with the confidence of a woman who knew that this was the one man for her, the only one capable of touching her soul when he touched her body. She held nothing back, stroking her hands over his shoulders, moving her body against his.

She felt him tremble and wondered if she was too heavy for him. "Put me down," she whispered self-consciously. "You might hurt yourself."

"I'm used to carrying much heavier loads," he assured her, kissing her nose, her ears, her cheeks, before returning to her lips.

The need was building again. They'd never make it upstairs, she decided, slipping her hands beneath the waistband of his underwear to cup his bare bottom. He almost dropped her. This time she realized the trembling was caused by his hunger for her.

"The rug. By the fireplace." She panted the directions against his mouth.

Seconds later they were both on their knees, then she was on her back on the soft sheepskin rug with him pressed against her. They'd gotten rid of his underwear and hers, but now another problem presented itself.

"Protection," he gasped. "I don't have—"

"I do." Grabbing her backpack, she pulled out an unopened box of condoms she'd bought in Kendall shortly after returning home. She'd kept them in her backpack as part of her fantasy of sweeping Cord off his feet, never believing she would actually need them. "This has your name on it."

"I'm glad to hear that."

Given her clumsiness in the past, she thought it was an incredible sign of his trust in her that he allowed her to put it on him. And she rewarded him with appreciative caresses along the way.

Then the time for waiting was over. He held her teasing hands over her head as he settled against her. The provocative thrusts of his tongue foretold what he planned to do with his body. Freeing one hand, she reached down and guided him home to her. With one powerful surge, she was his and he was hers.

And that was just the beginning. With every undulation of his hips, every rhythmic drive, he built her pleasure. She relished the silken friction as it provided the ultimate delight, taking her higher and higher. Only when she reached her climax did he follow her, his body going taut as he shouted her name.

"WE DIDN'T EVEN MAKE IT to the bed," she murmured in disbelief minutes, or it could have been hours, later. Time seemed to have lost its meaning for her and her body still hummed with the aftermath of bliss.

"Is that a complaint?" Resting against his bare chest the way she was, she felt the rumble of his voice as well as heard it.

"No way." She snuggled closer.

"We could go upstairs and try it in my bed," he suggested, threading his fingers through her hair.

"That's generous of you." She kissed his Adam's apple.

"I have a few things to show you up there."

"I can see them from here," she noted with a saucy look at his arousal. "And a very good-looking thing it is, too."

"You're a wicked woman."

Unrepentant, she said, "Legend has it that the West is full of wicked women."

"Not like you," he murmured, kissing her. "You're a legend in your own right. Come on." He dislodged her by getting to his feet and holding his hand out to help her up. "Come upstairs."

"Race ya," she challenged him.

It was a tie, but only because he scooped her up in his arms as they reached the top of the stairs and triumphantly held her aloft before dumping her on the bed. His bed. She was afraid this was all a dream.

"What's the matter, run out of things to say?" he teased her.

She hadn't run out of them, it was more that she was afraid of saying them, afraid of spilling her love for him.

"That's okay," he murmured. "This time I'll talk."

Was he going to say he loved her? Her heart stood still.

"You're always telling me that you're curious about my work," he said.

She nodded, trying not to be disappointed. Maybe this was his way of introducing the subject of love, through the subject of his work. Something he loved.

"I work best by eye—" He gave her a heated look, his gaze sliding over her like a caress "—and by feel." Now his hands followed the route his eyes had taken, fondling the curve of her bottom lip, the rise of her pert nipples, the indentation of her navel. She sucked in her stomach, more aware of her insecurities with this slow seduction than she had been in their previous encounter. There hadn't been time to think then, only to feel.

"And once I get a feel for the piece I'm working on, I may have to do some measuring," he continued.

Cord measured her with his hands. One hand between her left nipple and her right, his pinkie finger grazing one while his thumb barely brushed the other. She'd always thought he had incredibly creative hands, she'd just had no idea quite how creative until now, as he continued his erotic measuring, this time from her belly button to her feminine core.

"And when I'm ready for the finish work, I have to be careful not to make any mistakes because I'm working with a precious resource." Here he paused to cup her, rubbing against her.

"And when I'm making a chair," he murmured, his voice husky with promise, "I need to make sure everything has a flush fit." He slid into her with a sensual slide that immediately set her off, the powerful ripples holding her and him in their grip until completion was reached by them both.

NOW WHAT? THE THOUGHT KEPT racing in her head as Cord slept beside her. Had he heard her when she'd said she loved him? Okay, when she'd gasped and panted that she loved him.

Had he been listening? Or had it gone right over his head? Was that why he hadn't said anything in return? Because he hadn't heard? Or because he didn't feel the same way?

Sure he'd made love to her—well, that's how she'd describe it, anyway. But maybe to him it was only incredible sex. After all, he'd never given her any indication that his attraction to her went beyond the physical.

Doubt reared its ugly head, stifling her earlier joy and replacing it with fear. She tried concentrating her attention on other things, like the rise and fall of his chest, or even the intricate flow of the tangled branches that formed the headboard he'd no doubt made himself. The construction was solid and complicated, just like him.

Everything, it seemed, led her thoughts back to him. And the more she thought of him, the more convinced she became that she'd made a mistake in confessing her feelings for him. She couldn't help wondering if she'd seen a flash of panic in his eyes at the time. Passion or panic or maybe both?

The once or twice she'd tried to talk about emotions in the past, he'd immediately clammed up. He'd been that way since his mother died. It was as if, with her death, Cord had shut a part of himself off emotionally, making a fortress around himself the way he used to build forts out of branches and logs.

Needing some time alone to think things through, she got dressed and snuck out of Cord's cabin while he was still sleeping.

CORD WAS HAVING A NIGHTMARE. Some part of his brain recognized that, but he still couldn't break the binds that tied him to that place, a place where he was staked out on a hill, naked in body and soul, while the laughter of unseen spectators mocked his anguish.

He woke with a groan. The dream was familiar to him, he'd had it before. But not for years. Why had it come back now?

Hailey. He'd made love to Hailey. Reaching out for her, he was surprised to find the bed empty.

He called her name, expecting her to answer from the bathroom attached to the bedroom here in the loft. It had a big enough tub for both of them. If she was soaking in a hot tub, he'd join her. But she didn't answer.

Getting up, he padded barefoot over to the stairwell and leaned over the peeled pole railing to call her name again. And again there was no reply.

A quick glance out his bedroom window, which faced the front of the cabin, told him that her blue truck was gone. She must have gone home.

Disappointment washed over him. He'd hoped she'd spend the night after they'd made love most of the afternoon and evening.

Tugging on a pair of jeans, he made his way

downstairs, figuring that the world would look better once he had some coffee in his system. The first thing he realized was that the map was gone.

He tried to convince himself he must be mistaken. But a more careful search turned up the same result—both Hailey and the treasure map were gone. This, after she'd sworn that she wouldn't remove any papers from the cabin.

Anger slammed into him. He'd been had. Hailey had made him feel vulnerable, made him want her. But she didn't really want *him*, she wanted the damn map!

How could he have let his guard down this way? Here he'd been worrying about how to tell her that he didn't want any emotional ties, and all along she'd been plotting to get him into bed so she could steal the map.

Her actions only served to reinforce his belief that love twisted your heart and soul and left it a hollow mess. That wasn't going to happen to him. And he wasn't going to let her get away with the treasure map, either!

Without bothering to do more than tug on his boots, he ran outside and hopped into his Bronco to take off after her. The mattress had still retained some of the heat from her body, so she couldn't be that far ahead of him.

Betrayal, that's what he was feeling as he raced down the gravel road leading to the main road. That's why it hurt. He hated being made a fool of. That's all it was.

He almost missed her. It was dusk and the little light remaining made it difficult to see. She'd pulled over to the side of the road between his place and his father's ranch. He saw the flash of uneasiness cross her face even as she slammed the hood down.

She must have had some engine trouble, and that was the only reason he'd been able to catch up with her. Finally, a little luck was going his way.

He left his truck's engine running as he climbed out and stormed toward her. She took a few steps back at his approach.

"I should have known better than to trust you," he growled.

"I'm sorry..." she began, but he cut her off with a slice of his hand.

"Sorry doesn't begin to cover what you've done."

She blinked at him. "I'm sorry you feel that way."

"Feel that way," he mimicked her coldly. "Feelings have nothing to do with it."

She winced as if he'd slapped her, and that only angered him further. She had no right to be looking at him with puppy-dog hurt in her eyes, not when she was the one in the wrong here.

"Your promises clearly aren't worth anything." His voice was curt.

She seemed confused. "What are you talking about?"

"I'm talking about your promise not to take any of my family's papers from the cabin."

"You mean this is all about the map?" she said in disbelief.

"Damn right it is!" he shouted, totally losing his temper now. "You stole it and I want it back. You only had sex with me to get your hands on the map. You could have stolen it when I was gone. But I guess you got to drive your point home more if you stole it after making an even bigger fool of me.''

He didn't care if he didn't exactly make sense. Some part of him still held out a thread of hope that she'd reassure him that he was wrong.

But she didn't. Instead she said, ''You mean this map?'' and reached into her truck's open window to yank it out of her backpack. ''You think I betrayed you for this?''

Hailey then proceeded to rip it to pieces in front of his stunned eyes.

Cord could feel himself pale.

''That was just a symbolic gesture,'' she shouted, now as furious as he'd been. ''The real map is in the safe at your father's ranch. That's where I was. I thought that would be the safest place for it and I didn't want to risk anything happening to it.''

He frowned, scrambling to process what she was saying. He'd been wrong. She hadn't stolen the map after all. She'd taken it to his father's ranch.

He'd messed up big time. He had to tell her that. But how? What could he say?

Instead, she did all the talking, all the yelling. ''I've had it! This is the last straw. That you'd accuse me of having sex with you just to steal the map. I could have walked out with it and never even told you I'd found it. You'd never have known the difference. I did not seduce you to get the map!''

''I'm sorry I made a mistake.'' His admission was delivered with an edge of self-defensiveness. ''Anyone can make a mistake.''

''I sure made one, thinking I was in love with you. But I made a mistake.'' Now she was the one who mimicked him. "I made a mistake *big* time. But I won't be repeating it. Because as of right now, this conversation is over. So is anything else between us. I don't even know what to call what we had. You never called it anything. You never let me know what you were feeling. You probably weren't feeling anything but old-fashioned lust."

"Hailey, wait—"

He reached out for her but she'd already hopped into her truck and gunned it into drive, forcing him to jump aside or get run over.

11

HAILEY DIDN'T KNOW how she made it home in one piece. As it was, she'd had to wipe the tears away as she'd left Cord behind in a cloud of dust while Madonna's song "The Power of Goodbye" prophetically played on her truck's CD player.

Oh, yeah, Cord was definitely the lesson she'd had to learn, but did the learning have to hurt so much? How stupid could she have been? Not as stupid as he was for thinking she'd sleep with him to get the treasure map. If he thought that of her, how little he knew her. How little he cared to know her.

She wiped more tears away as she pulled her truck to a stop in front of her home. She'd come home in tears before, often caused by Cord. But none of those childhood incidents held a candle to the pain she was feeling now. And the anger.

She didn't mean to slam the front door when she stormed in, and she certainly didn't mean to burst into tears the minute she saw the concerned look on her aunt's face.

Ten minutes later the tears had stopped and she and her aunt were ensconced on the living room couch.

"He doesn't want me to love him," Hailey said, dry-eyed once more. "And then there's the fact that he doesn't trust me. Thinking I was stealing his damn map."

"I'd like to tattoo the damn map on his forehead," the older woman tartly said.

"Aunt Alicia!"

"What? I should be nice to the man after he breaks your heart?"

"Tattooing his forehead might be a bit strong."

"Your father would do worse than that," Alicia stated.

"Which is why we won't tell him," Hailey said.

"Won't tell me what?" Tad demanded in his customary loud voice.

"That I'm redecorating the dining room," Alicia quickly lied.

Tad frowned. "You just redid the house."

"I reupholstered the couch, big deal. We need some more changes around here. We're in a rut."

"Speak for yourself. I like things the way they are," he maintained.

"Well, too bad, because things are about to change. That's the problem with you men. You never appreciate when you've got it good." Having said that, she flounced out of the room.

"What was all that about?" Tad asked in a bewildered voice.

Hailey just shrugged. She didn't have it in her to say anything more tonight.

Tad studied her closely and she looked away. She didn't want him seeing her pain and telling her "I told you so" or ranting about how awful the Best family was.

To her surprise he simply gathered her in a big

bear hug, the kind he'd given her as a kid when she'd come home with a skinned knee after some mishap, often a result of her chasing after Cord. "Your dad loves you, y'know," he rumbled in that booming voice of his.

Tears threatened again, but she held them back. "Thanks, Dad. I love you, too."

"Anybody you want me to go beat up?" he asked just as he had in the old days.

She shook her head.

"Well, anytime you want me to have a good talking to that Cord Best, you just say the word."

She nodded, leaning back to give him a slight smile to acknowledge that she recognized this as being the same talk they'd had during her childhood years. "You're the best, you know that?"

"It might not be our surname, but it's our nature," he said with pride.

Which was fine with her. She'd had enough heartache from a man with the Best surname and the worst thoughts of her.

CORD KNEW HE'D SCREWED UP with Hailey. The thought of not being able to fix things with her filled him with dread. And loss. Like a hole in his soul. Dammit, this felt like *love!* Panic was now mixed with the dread.

Did he love Hailey? Was that what was wrong with him? How had this happened? He'd tried to be so careful not to fall prey to the love bug. But Hailey had crawled into his heart anyway. The strange thing was that the idea of not having her in his life anymore was scarier than the thought of loving her.

For the first time in his life he realized that his notion of not wanting to love anyone so that he couldn't be hurt if he lost them had excluded the possibility of loving someone and *keeping* them. If his choices were losing Hailey now or losing her later, his logical, rational side would say losing her now seemed the better choice, but his gut screamed to hang on to her, whatever it took.

An internal light bulb went on in his head as Cord accepted that fear was the true weakness, not love, and he would be a coward if he gave in to it. Love didn't always have to make you vulnerable, it could strengthen you, the way burls could strengthen a tree.

Cord knew he was in a bad way when, instead of burying his emotions as was his norm, he called his older brother for advice. Not even bothering with a greeting, Cord bluntly demanded, "How did you know you were in love with Tracy?"

"Hello to you, too," Zane drawled mockingly.

"I'm serious here. How did you know you were in love with Tracy?"

Something in Cord's voice must have tipped Zane off to his agitated state. "I knew because she told me I was afraid to love her and she was right. What's this about? Something going on with you and Hailey that I should know about?"

"We had a fight," Cord admitted.

"Surprise, surprise."

"So you're telling me that the only way you knew that you were in love with Tracy was because she told you that you were?"

"And because the thought of my life without her in it was worse than—"

"—the fear of loving her," Cord interjected.

"Well, that's one way of putting it, yeah. You know, after my experience with my ex-wife, I wasn't looking to get back in the marriage saddle again, especially with a city girl like Tracy. But she just sorta—"

"—crawled into your heart anyway."

"She told me she loved me, but I didn't believe her at first," Zane said. "Dumb, huh?"

"Idiotically stupid," Cord agreed.

"You'd never do anything that dumb, huh?"

"I already did," Cord admitted gruffly.

"So what are you going to do now?"

"I'm not sure."

"I realize you've never asked me for advice, but if you were to ask me, I'd tell you not to give up. I don't care what it takes. If you have to climb the highest mountain, which in my case was the large cottonwood tree behind the ranch, or crawl over hot coals, which in my case was a jean-eating windowsill, do it."

"I will," Cord vowed. "First thing in the morning. As soon as Hailey calms down. Thanks."

Hanging up the phone, Cord took a deep breath. Waiting until the morning also gave him enough time to figure out how to make it up to her.

Seeing the pain in her eyes when he'd accused her of lying had cut him to the quick. He'd hurt her before, unintentionally, when they'd been kids. But that was nothing compared to the look of a grown woman gazing at him with her heart in her eyes. A broken heart. He felt like he'd led the stampede that had stomped her spirit into the dirt.

Not that she'd shown any lack of spirit when she'd told him to go to the devil.

He couldn't blame her for being furious with him. But she'd come around, because he...he loved her.

And once he told her that, everything would be okay.

But it wasn't that easy as he discovered the next morning when he called her at her father's ranch. Her aunt answered.

"I need to speak to Hailey," he said, his voice gruff with nerves.

"Too bad, because she doesn't need to speak to you," Alicia replied before slamming the phone down.

Okay, so maybe he'd been a little overoptimistic in thinking it would be as easy as a phone call. Clearly this called for a face-to-face meeting. Although confessing his love would have been easier for him to do over the phone, he was willing to tell Hailey to her face that he loved her.

Only problem was that she wouldn't let him see her face, or any other part of her. When he showed up at the Hughes ranch house, Alicia slammed the door in his face.

"I'm a patient man!" he yelled through the door. "I'll just wait out here until Hailey comes out."

But a visit from his brother Reno barely an hour later told him that this plan would have to be dumped, as well.

"Hey, Cord," Reno greeted him as he ambled up the porch steps. "I got a call about an unwelcome presence. It appears that the Hughes family want you off their property. Tad told me that if I don't take you, he'll escort you with a shotgun filled with buckshot."

"He can bring out a cannon for all I care," Cord said. "I'm not moving."

"Come on, don't make me have to arrest another family member this week. Give the lady some time to calm down and then talk to her. Or better yet, call her."

"I tried that," Cord said glumly. "She hung up on me. Or rather her aunt did."

"Keep on trying."

"I aim to." Cord's expression was determined.

"Trying to call," Reno clarified with that good-natured smile he was famous for. "Not camp on their front porch. Or better yet, write her a certified letter. That way she has to sign for it so you know she'll get it."

"I'm not good at that writing stuff," Cord admitted.

Reno slung a brotherly arm around his shoulders and grinned. "I'll help you."

"THE ONLY POETRY SHE LIKES is written by Cock-eyed Curly," Cord told his brother as they both sat on the front porch of Cord's cabin later that afternoon, each nursing a bottle of beer.

"I'm telling you, women love poetry," Reno stated with the confidence of a man who knew what made women happy.

"Hailey isn't like most women."

Reno gave him a speculative look. "She must not be if she's got you tied up in knots."

"You don't have to look so pleased about it," Cord said impatiently.

"Hey, I'm not eager to see you hog-tied and married. That would mean that I'd be the only Best bachelor left, and the workload with the female population might just be too much for me."

"Who said anything about marriage?" Cord asked darkly.

Reno gave him a look.

"Okay, so I want to marry her. You could at least let me say it first instead of telling me what I'm gonna be doing," Cord grumbled.

"I told you, I'm here to help you."

"Then call her and make her speak to me on the phone." Cord's voice reflected his frustration at not being able to contact Hailey now that he knew he loved her.

"I tried that."

Cord eyed him suspiciously. "You're sure you spoke to her directly and not to her aunt?"

"I'm sure," Reno said for the fifth time.

"And you're sure she said no?"

"What she actually said was not in this lifetime."

Cord frowned at this news. "She still sounds mad then, huh?"

"Brilliant deduction." Reno toasted him by lifting his beer bottle.

Cord was not amused. "Then help me write her something good."

"What do you have down so far?"

"Dear Hailey," Cord read and looked at his brother expectantly.

"That's it?"

Cord nodded.

Reno sighed. "I can tell this is going to be a long afternoon."

It took most of that day and half the night, but Cord did manage to write a letter that he could be proud of. And it wasn't filled with the stupid flowery poetry that Reno had recited. It just said things like they were. Well, maybe more than that. Once his brother had left and he'd starting writing, the words had seemed to flow from his heart. Kind of like when he was working and a piece finally flowed, finally revealed its secrets and let him see what the outcome would be.

He'd also reached that point with the commission for Founders Day, and a good thing, too, as it was less than a week away. He still had some things to figure out, but he did know that he was working on the figure of a man kneeling down, most likely prospecting for gold or silver, which had brought many people to this part of the world.

But he had yet to do any of the fine points on the carving. He'd been too distracted by his feelings for Hailey. She was embedded in his mind like a brand into a steer's hide. He just prayed he could get her back again.

When he walked into the post office the next morning, he wasn't prepared for Geraldine's grilling. He should have been, he supposed, but then he hadn't been thinking clearly since he'd made love to Hailey. Not that he was about to tell the nosy postmistress that. But the way she stared at him with those beady eyes of hers when he said he wanted to send a certified letter made him uneasy.

"Before we do that, I've got a package here for you," she told him.

Since Cord frequently got packages, often woodworking supplies or invitations to attend various furniture shows around the country, he didn't think anything about this package until he saw the way Geraldine was squinting at the handwriting on the front of the envelope. "No return address," she noted. "And it's postmarked over in Kendall. Looks like Hailey's handwriting to me."

Cord grabbed it from her before she made any more comments. It was the first time Hailey had ever sent him anything. He couldn't wait, he had to open it. Stepping away from the service booth, he moved to a far corner of the room for some privacy. He needn't have bothered, since Geraldine came from around the counter and followed him. That's why she was standing right beside him when he pulled the white T-shirt he'd lent Hailey after their day up at Oh-Be-Joyful Falls from the mailing envelope.

"Kiss and make out, *awk,*" Geraldine's colorful parrot crowed. "Kiss and make out!"

"Sounds like good advice to me," Geraldine said. "Why is Hailey sending you a T-shirt? It is from Hailey, isn't it?"

"There's no note," he said in a rough voice.

"What about that letter you wanted me to send?" Geraldine asked.

"Forget it," he rasped, crushing the letter he'd stayed up half the night to write in his hand before striding out of the post office.

TWO DAYS LATER, in the dark and smoky interior of the Bliss Bar, Tad Hughes was perched on a bar stool, his glass of Guinness untouched as he drew out his latest fishing yarn. "And I'm thinking to myself, Is this a fish or a freight train I've got ahold of here...?"

"I'd like for you to get ahold of a freight train," Buck growled as he stalked into the bar. "Maybe that will give you an idea of what it'll feel like when I knock your block off."

Further conversation was momentarily delayed as Floyd rang the brass bell. "Take your fight outside, boys!"

Both men ignored Floyd and his bell.

"You told me you had some devilish plan up your sleeve, you and that daughter of yours!" Buck hollered. "You warned me, but I wouldn't listen."

"Plan?" Tad repeated, clearly confused. "What plan?"

"The one you told me about last time we were in here together."

Tad scratched his chin and thought a moment, but his look of confusion remained. "I don't recall any plan."

"Is your memory going as well as your hearing?" Buck taunted.

"I can hear just fine!" Tad bellowed.

"Not a week ago you stood right over there—" Buck jabbed at a spot farther down the polished mahogany bar "—and said that you had some devious plan that was yours to know and mine to worry about. You vowed that the last laugh would be on me and mine. And now you've gone and done that, gone and broken my boy Cord's heart."

"Your boy's heart?" Tad repeated in outrage. "What about my girl's?"

"She's the one who won't see or speak to him," Buck said. "That was part of your plan, right? To get close to Cord to set him up, have him fall for her, and then have her dump him."

"No way!" Tad vehemently denied. "My plan was for her to get close to Cord to set him up so she could steal the...historical item she was searching for," he concluded diplomatically, not wanting to break his word to his daughter by revealing to others the fact that Cockeyed Curly's map had been found.

Buck frowned. "But that didn't happen."

"I know. One small glitch with my plan was that my daughter never agreed to go along with it. I guess you could say it was all in my head."

"I'll give you a good knock on the head if you don't come clean and tell me the truth," Buck said threateningly.

"I am telling you the truth," Tad shouted. "My daughter never agreed, never planned on and never intended to steal—" he lowered his voice to a whisper "—the, well, you know." He jerked his head to indicate the small crowd in the bar, who showed every sign of being avid eavesdroppers. "But your son accused her of doing that and broke her heart."

"So you're saying this is all my son's fault?"

"Dang right I am." Tad's stance was tense, as if he expected Buck to take a swing at him.

Instead Buck slowly sank onto a bar stool and said, "You could be right. My two oldest boys don't exactly have a way with the ladies. Reno, now he's a charmer. But what the other two know about she-folks could fit in the ear of a gnat."

"So what do you aim to do about that?"

"Beats me." Buck gave a perplexed shrug. "Like I tried telling you when we were in the slammer together, Cord hasn't listened to me since his dear mother died when he was teenager. What about your girl? Any chance of getting her to see reason and see Cord again? The boy feels lower than the belly of a snake, and I know things could be made right between them if she'd just see him. Or speak to him, even."

Tad shook his head, his expression regretful. "I've tried to convince her, but she refuses. Says she's bent over backward to show him that she loved him and that he crossed the line when he accused her of stealing."

"What a fine can of worms this is," Buck muttered. "Barkeep," he called out to Floyd, who was wiping down the bar a few feet away, "set us up for a round over here."

"First one's on me," Tad said with an empathetic slap to Buck's back.

By the end of the night they discovered that Floyd knew more bawdy cowboy songs than they did, thereby allowing them to add a few more musical numbers to their repertoire.

"I HAD TO DRIVE YOUR FATHER home from the Bliss Bar last night," Alicia told Hailey the next day. "And I had to drive Buck home, as well."

"You should be pleased then," Hailey noted, keeping her attention firmly focused on the book she was reading about western outlaws. She had her gold wire-rimmed glasses firmly in place again. "I thought you wanted to spend more time with Buck."

"Not with him drunk." Alicia's voice reflected her exasperation.

Hailey sighed, her fingers keeping a tight grip on the book as she looked up. "Don't tell me the two of them were fighting again because of the feud."

"No, it was because of the trouble between you and Cord. And they weren't fighting, they were comrades in arms, it appears."

Hailey frowned. "I don't understand."

"Neither do I," Alicia admitted. "Not exactly. All I know is that the two of them bonded over their mutual inability to relieve their children's suffering."

Hailey firmly pushed her glasses back up the bridge of her nose. "I doubt that Cord is suffering," she said in a no-nonsense voice.

"Buck says he is."

Hailey refused to be swayed. "Buck has a storyteller's habit of stretching the truth."

"Won't you at least talk to Cord?"

"No."

"He called again this morning," Alicia added, her voice softening.

Hailey could tell that her aunt's resolve was wavering, that she was starting to feel sorry for Cord. But Hailey couldn't afford to let herself be open to any more pain at his hands—incredibly talented and sexy as those hands were.

"No, no, no! I don't want to hear this!" Hailey put her own hands over her ears.

Alicia lowered them. "You're not five anymore.

You can't put your hands over your ears and hide your head in the sand."

"I know," Hailey admitted quietly. "That's why I'm leaving Bliss after the Founders Day presentation tomorrow."

"Oh, no." Her aunt's expression was filled with disappointment.

"It's just too painful for me to stay here anymore." Hailey's voice reflected the fact that, while it hadn't been an easy decision for her, her mind was made up.

"But where will you go?" Alicia asked in concern. "Your condo is rented out for the rest of the summer."

"I'll go visit a friend down in Durango. Janet has been asking me to come stay. It's best this way," she assured her aunt. "Best that I get away from the Bests. I was a fool to ever think otherwise."

WHEN TRACY BREEZED into his cabin after a brief knock, Cord knew something was up. His sister-in-law rarely visited him unannounced. Her comment of "I was in the neighborhood" might have worked when she was back in Chicago, but his cabin wasn't in any neighborhood. That's why he liked it.

He wasn't in the best of moods. Work had been progressing slowly on the commission for Founders Day and time was quickly running out. The same was true about Hailey, except that things there weren't progressing at all. He'd tried calling her again today, only to be told she didn't want to speak to him. This time Alicia hadn't hung up on him, but had transmitted the message with what seemed like genuine regret.

But that hadn't gotten him any closer to Hailey. He'd come up with a few wild ideas, including riding over there and kidnapping her like an outlaw of old, the kind she was writing about, but he doubted she'd appreciate the gesture.

The truth was, he didn't know what to do.

Tracy didn't suffer from the same problem. As soon as she was inside, she immediately headed for his kitchen. "I'm parched. I brought a bottle of root bear with me but it's the old-fashioned kind and I need a bottle opener, if you can believe that. Do you have one?" She rattled around in his kitchen drawers until she ran across Hailey's hidden cache of tea. "Earl Grey," she said in delight. "My favorite flavor. I didn't know you drank tea."

"I don't. It's Hailey's." He turned away so she wouldn't see the flash of pain cross his face as he remembered the day Hailey had made tea and flirted with him. He'd asked her if she'd been drinking. She'd sure made him feel intoxicated.

"You know," Tracy said conversationally, "I always thought you were the smart one in the family. Aside from Buck, of course."

He blinked at her. "What are you talking about?"

"You." She took a sip straight from the bottle of root beer she'd just opened. "I always thought you were the smart one."

Cord's laugh was bitter. "Hardly. I struggled through school. Zane is—"

"—a darling, and I love him to bits," she interjected fondly. "But the man is as set in his ways as a rock sometimes."

"Reno, then. He's—"

"—a born charmer," Tracy interrupted again. "But you, Cord, you seemed to be the one that took your time, the one who bothered to study a situation or a piece of wood until you got it right. Turns out that's not what you did with Hailey. Turns out you're more like Zane than I thought. Both of you are filled with preconceived notions about the women you love. Unless you're going to deny that you love Hailey?" The look she gave him was a no-nonsense challenge, daring him to lie to her.

He didn't even try. "No," he said quietly, "I won't deny that."

"See?" Tracy beamed at him. "I told you that you were the smart one in the family. And I have to tell you that I really like Hailey. Even though we didn't have a chance to spend a lot of time together, I felt that we had a connection. Maybe it's the fact that we were both raised by aunts, I don't know. I know that it's a connection Zane and I share, losing mothers much too soon. It's something you and Hailey share, as well."

In all this time, Cord had never thought of that. Instead he'd wasted time focusing on the things that were different about them, the reasons why he shouldn't let her into his heart.

"She won't talk to me, won't see me," he said quietly. "I don't know what to do."

They were interrupted by the ringing of his phone. Could it be Hailey? Each time the phone rang his hopes were raised, only to be dashed, as they were now.

"It's for you," he told Tracy. "That supposedly dumb husband of yours," he added with a slight smile.

She returned the smile and took the phone. "Hello? Calm down, I can't understand what you're...they did what? Oh, I see. Uh-huh. Uh-huh. Sure, I'll leave now."

"What's wrong?"

"It seems the twins used regular dishwashing liquid in the dishwasher instead of the powder you're supposed to use and the kitchen floor is now covered in a sea of bubbles up to your brother's knees."

"You don't sound too upset about it," Cord noted.

"Because I did the same thing myself when I first came to the ranch," she confessed with a grin. "I learned early that when life gives you lemons, you make lemonade. When I get home, the twins and I will use the bubbles to clean the floor and wipe down the walls. Those bubbles will be put to good use in the end. There are times you just have to use what you're given."

That's when it hit Cord. He now knew what had to be done for him to get Hailey back. He only prayed it would work.

12

HAILEY'S SUITCASES WERE already packed in preparation for her departure the next day. Her friend Janet had told her she was welcome to stay as long as she liked.

What Hailey would have *liked* was not to have come home to Bliss at all this summer. Then she wouldn't have seen Cord again, wouldn't have kissed him, wouldn't have fallen in love with him. They said you couldn't go home again, and it was true. Because when you did, you were in for heartbreak. It might sound like something out of a country song, but that's the way she'd been feeling lately. Blue.

She still hadn't decided what to wear for tomorrow's event. She'd only brought one suit with her, the one she'd worn to the Best ranch the first time she'd run into Cord, the one that made her look like a professor. She did have one dress, in a sort of romantic floral design. She'd tossed it into her suitcase at the last minute before leaving Boulder, doubting she'd have an opportunity to wear it.

Maybe if she teamed it with a sweater it would look more down to earth.

Meanwhile she needed to get back to work on her speech. She wasn't happy with her opening hook. "You'd think a town like Bliss would have started with plenty of goodwill, but that wasn't the case. In the beginning, in the beginning..." She paused to nibble on the end of her pencil. She wrote all her speeches in longhand. Usually it helped her to think more clearly. But not today.

Today she was stuck. Couldn't concentrate.

She hadn't had a chance to tell Buck much about the details she'd discovered about Rebecca Best and Rafael Hughes. He'd been too excited to listen to her anyway, once she'd presented him with the map. And not just because of the treasure it might lead to, but also because of the fact that it was made by Curly. Buck had seemed even more excited about the lengthy poem that Curly had written with directions to the treasure than he was with the map itself.

Either way, the map was now secure in the safe in Buck's office. It was actually the ranch office, but she still considered it to be Buck's, what with that stuffed armadillo he was so proud of, holding court from atop the filing cabinet. She didn't know how Tracy could stand having that armadillo around.

She'd run into Tracy in town yesterday afternoon but hadn't stopped to talk to her, fearing the woman would try to convince her to see Cord. She'd heard from members of the planning committee that the details of Cord's commissioned wooden sculpture was still under wraps, with no one quite sure what it looked like. Word was that he was still working on it, right up until the last minute.

Not that she cared. Her interest in Cord was over. Done with. Finito.

Maybe if she told herself that enough, she'd come

to believe it. Meanwhile she had to get back to her speech.

She'd barely written two more sentences when she was interrupted by Alicia.

"I don't know what to wear tomorrow!" the older woman wailed. "This outfit or my red dress? I should never have accepted Buck's invitation to accompany him to the Founders Day."

"Yes, you should. And I think you should wear the outfit you have on now," Hailey replied. Alicia was wearing a denim skirt and vest that she'd made. "I think it would be perfect."

"Thanks, dear." Alicia gave her a quick hug. "I just couldn't decide."

Hugging her in return, Hailey said, "I'm so glad things are working out with you and Buck."

Alicia's face became flushed, her demeanor flustered as she nervously smoothed her skirt. "Yes, well, it's just an invitation to Founders Day, not a proposal of marriage."

"Now you're sounding like me," Hailey couldn't help saying.

"I just don't want to get my hopes up."

Hailey felt the pain jabbing her heart like a thorn that wouldn't come loose. "The way I did, you mean."

"No, I didn't mean that." Alicia looked concerned that her words may have been taken the wrong way.

"It's okay," Hailey reassured her. "I did get my hopes up. Foolishly, as it turned out."

"You won't know that for sure if you don't speak to Cord," Alicia noted.

Hailey shook her head. "I can't go through this

anymore. Cord had his chance to tell me if he had any feelings for me. He didn't. I'm sure he feels badly about accusing me of something I didn't do, but I'm not going to open myself to more hurt just to appease his guilty conscience."

"Well, when you put it that way..."

"I know what I'm doing," Hailey stated. "It's over between Cord and me. I'm finally over him."

"If you say so."

"I do."

"I'd just imagined you wearing a white wedding gown when you said I do," Alicia noted wistfully, "not packing to leave town."

HAILEY TRIED NOT TO FIDGET as she sat on the dais in front of the crowd gathered for Founders Day. Both the weather and the attendance were good.

The event took place in Bliss Park behind the trailer that housed both the sheriff's office and city hall. Next to it was the old Bliss jail, a stone building that had been closed for several years, waiting for renovation. There was a collection box set up today for that project.

Just about everyone in Bliss seemed to be here, which meant that several hundred people were seated in the metal folding chairs festooned with red, white and blue bunting. The raised dais was similarly decorated. Some old-timers, like Floyd and Geraldine, were even dressed in period costume.

Hailey had settled for wearing her floral dress, with cap sleeves and a gently scooped neckline. The skirt was long, falling just shy of her ankles, which she had demurely tucked together the way her aunt had taught her as a young girl. She doubted that her appearance gave any indication that she was a nervous wreck.

She hadn't gotten much sleep last night, worrying about her speech and the possibility of running into Cord at the festivities today. Although she'd seen Reno and Zane, she had yet to see Cord, but then he never came to events like this. After all, he hated crowds. He didn't have to be there as long as his work was.

The commissioned sculpture was here, although it was still shrouded, waiting for the grand unveiling. Until then no one was allowed to peek at it.

"Are you about ready to begin?" Reno asked Hailey. He looked great in his uniform. Why couldn't she have fallen for the charming brother instead of the impossible one?

"As ready as I'll ever be," Hailey replied with a weak grin.

"I meant to tell you that last night we caught a pair of teenage vandals who confessed to breaking into the historical society. We also recovered Curly's portrait before they harmed it."

This time her smile was stronger. "That's good news. Thanks for telling me."

"No problem," Reno said, before wryly adding, "the problems are going to start when my dad begins looking for that treasure. He's already told me he plans on doing so. I told him to stick to fishing instead."

"If you folks will get seated, we'll get this show on the road," Geraldine said into the microphone, which made a loud high-pitched sound that had everyone covering their ears.

Reno, who was doing double duty as town sheriff and soundman, made some adjustment before giving Geraldine a thumbs-up sign.

"Sorry about that," she added, eyeing the microphone as if fearing it might bite her. "As chairwoman of the Founders Day Committee, I want to welcome you all here today. I'm glad to see so many of you. It must mean you took my threats seriously about not passing on your mail if you didn't show up for our festivities."

There were a few hoots and a smattering of laughter and applause, all of which Geraldine took in her stride.

Hailey smiled reassuringly at her aunt, who was sitting in the front row with Buck at her side. Buck was all decked out in black pants and a brilliant white shirt with an old-fashioned string necktie. Next to them sat her dad, beaming at Hailey proudly. In the row behind them was seated the rest of the Best family—Zane, his wife, Tracy, and his twins, Lucky and Rusty. Hailey had to swallow a lump in her throat at the unmistakable look of love that Zane gave his wife.

She'd never been the weepy type before and she hated this sudden weakness on her part. She preferred being angry to being sappy.

She plastered a smile on her face as she listened to Geraldine's rambling oration, which went on for fifteen minutes and covered everything from the Pony Express, which never came through Bliss, to her parrot, Dispatch. It was only when Floyd called out, "Can we get a move on here, Gerry, I don't wanna die up here waiting for you to finish your epic," that she wound things up.

Still no sign of Cord. Hailey had been scanning the crowd for him.

"Next up we have Floyd Bass from the Bliss Bar, who will give us a few of his personal recollections of the history of our town."

It took Floyd almost a minute to get up and make his way to the podium. He had a thick folder with him, which he set on the podium, but he didn't consult it during his brief speech about the good old days and the importance of saloons and bars like his to keep the storytelling going. "Good cheer and great yarns, that's what makes a barkeeper. Plus not watering down your drinks. But mostly it's respecting the past and telling tall tales about it."

"Thank you, Floyd," Geraldine said. "And that leads us directly to our next speaker, a celebrated author who will be speaking about the history of our town. And watch for her new book, which may feature me in it. Here's Hailey Hughes."

"Actually, my new book will cover Colorado outlaws, so I don't think you'd want to be in it," Hailey said into the microphone, and the audience chuckled and settled back in anticipation.

"You'd think a town with a name like Bliss would have started with plenty of goodwill, but that wasn't the case. In the beginning, settlers came here to ranch, but before long conflicts arose between cattlemen and sheepherders." She then went on to give a brief overview of the feud between the Bests and the Hughes and how that conflict had forced Rachel and

Rafael to leave. "This is just one story of the many surrounding the people who came west looking for a new life and new opportunities for themselves, but not for the Utes, who lived and hunted on this land. They were shamefully shoved aside and driven off despite our government's treaties and promises. It was a dark period of our history." Hailey wished she had more time to elaborate but her ten minutes were almost up. "Bliss has seen it all, the good, the bad and the ugly."

"The ugly would be Dispatch," someone in the crowd shouted out.

"Don't you go insulting my bird," Geraldine yelled back. "I know where you live, Con Freeman!"

"Bliss is like a quilt made up of many parts, many stories," Hailey said in conclusion. "I hope you'll take the time to discover your own family's stories and write them down before they become lost forever."

"Like Curly's treasure, you mean?" someone else shouted. "Is it true you found his treasure map?"

She refused to be baited. "As I said, Bliss is full of stories. Thank you."

Given the fact that she was unusually tense, she felt that her presentation went well. Even so, she was glad when it was over and they could move on to the next part of the program. That was, until she realized that next up would be the unveiling of Cord's statue.

There was a momentary pause at the speaker's podium as Geraldine's notes had apparently gone missing. This explained why she was thumbing through

Floyd's girlie magazine, which was in the folder he'd left up at the podium.

During the lull, Hailey did a final quick check of the audience for Cord. He definitely wasn't among those seated. There were a few men standing near the back, but he wasn't there, either. *Relax,* she told herself. *He's not coming. If he was going to show up, he'd be here by now.*

Geraldine apparently found the right page of her notes, because she grabbed the microphone and lowered it to her height. "Okay, folks, we're ready for the grand unveiling now. As most of you know, the Founders Day Committee decided to do something special to commemorate the one hundred and twenty fifth anniversary of the founding of our town. So, knowing how he can make wood talk to you, we twisted Cord Best's arm to do us up a special sculpture." Daintily tugging the tasseled fastener didn't lift the material the way it was supposed to, so Geraldine tried again, this time yanking it so hard the covering almost flew off.

Hailey had a clear view of the sculpture from her seat on the dais. Geraldine was absolutely right in saying that Cord could make wood talk to you. This sculpture did that. It was of a man on his knees, stretching forward for something just out of reach. The wood glowed, the sun shining off it as if giving it life.

Hailey vaguely heard the murmuring of the crowd, echoing her awe and appreciation for the nearly life-size piece. This was not the piece of wood she'd almost burned in his fireplace. He must have changed his mind and decided to create something else. And this piece was definitely something else, something powerful that moved the citizens of Bliss as much as it moved her.

It spoke of a powerful yearning for something just out of reach.

It wasn't until the murmuring became louder that she realized the noise wasn't caused by the sculpture but by the man who'd made it.

Looking neither right nor left, Cord strode directly toward the dais.

Hailey could hear the comments clear up on the dais. *What's he doing here? He never comes to these events. He's a loner. You know how these artistic types are.*

Tongues were certainly wagging.

Then her brain went numb as Cord sought her out with his eyes, those incredibly deep, riveting ultra-blue eyes. He was dressed all in black and as sure-footed as a cat as he ascended the steps to the dais, taking them two at a time.

He was up to something. Did he think he could just show up, look sexy and toss her over his shoulder like some western outlaw? If so, he was in for a big surprise.

Instead, she was the one surprised when he approached her, only to drop to his knees in front of her.

She was even more surprised when his normally wonderful voice trembled as he said her name. Clearing his throat, he began again. "Hailey, I love you and I want you to marry me."

There was a moment of stunned silence.

Then his brother Reno called out, "You can do better than that."

"Give him a chance," her aunt Alicia said.

The rest of the town was spellbound by this drama unfolding before their very eyes. This was even better than watching the main attraction at the Roxie movie theater.

"I screwed up big time and I want to make it up to you," Cord said, his proud voice rough and unsteady. "That's why I did this sculpture. That's me. Reaching for you. For your love. I love you. Will you forgive me?"

Only Hailey could see the fear in his eyes. Knowing him the way she did, she realized that this was a worst-nightmare scenario for him, to bare himself emotionally in front of everyone. But he'd done it for her. Because he loved her. He'd made the sculpture for her. His heart was in that work, there for all to see. The longing, the yearning—it was all for her.

"I don't have the words..." he gruffly began.

"You don't need the words," she murmured, slipping to her own knees. "All I ever wanted was your love." She cupped his face with her trembling hand. "Not fancy words, just your love. And yes, I will marry you."

As she embraced him and he kissed her, the entire hometown crowd started cheering.

Over the din and the fierce beating of her own heart, Hailey heard Buck proudly shouting, "That's my boy!"

"That's my girl!"

Tad shouted just as proudly.

"I'm so happy I'm going to cry!" Alicia declared as the cheers continued.

Geraldine would later claim that there wasn't a dry eye in the park.

As for the unnamed sculpture, it came to be known simply as *Yes.*

The last Best Brother is lassoed by love
in THE LAWMAN GETS LUCKY
Harlequin Duets #26, May 2000.
Turn the page for a sneak preview of
the search for love and
Cockeyed Curly's gold.

1

A LITTLE PEACE and quiet. That's all Reno Best wanted. And a medium-rare cheeseburger with all the toppings. It didn't seem like much to ask for. Not after working an eighteen-hour shift that had included four barroom brawls and two fender benders, one of which had involved a fully loaded chicken truck.

As the town sheriff for Bliss, Colorado, keeping the peace was his job. It was a job that had gotten increasingly harder to do, since word had gotten out last month that there was a fortune in gold buried somewhere around Bliss, hidden by western outlaw Cockeyed Curly Mahoney over a hundred years ago.

Reno still wasn't sure how the secret about Curly's newly discovered treasure map had leaked out. His dad, who had the map locked up in his safe, claimed it wasn't him. Ditto for his two older brothers and their wives.

All Reno knew was that a huge number of treasure hunters had suddenly come crawling out of the woodwork and some days it felt like he was the only sane one left in Bliss.

He was certainly the only one in the recently opened Golden Treasure Diner, allowing him to eat his cheeseburger in peace and quiet. Or at least it was quiet until *she* stormed into the diner. Ignoring the sanctity of his lunch hour, she slid into his booth without an invitation. "What are you going to do about my brother?"

Reno had heard about the new schoolteacher in town—anyone who hadn't lived in Bliss when Eisenhower was elected was considered to be "new" in town. It took him a minute to recall her name...it was something innocent sounding like Annie. *Yes, that was it. Annie Benton.* She'd come west from some small town in Iowa and was very popular with the parents hereabouts, but that didn't give her cause to go interrupting a man's meal.

"Your brother?" he repeated, not having a clue about what she was talking about.

"That's right. My brother. The one who's missing. I called the sheriff's office and left a message this morning for you to call me back. You didn't."

"That could be because I didn't get your message." He swiped his mouth with a paper napkin, silently cursing the fact that his regular secretary and dispatcher, Opal, was home with a head cold. She'd sent her daughter in as a replacement, but the twenty-year-old Sugar had preferred listening to Ricky Martin than writing down phone messages. "If you'd wait until I'm back in my office after lunch, we can discuss this...

"I'm not waiting another second," Annie angrily declared.

This shouldn't have surprised him. Since the discovery of the treasure map, it seemed as if everyone in town was as impatient as a raging bull in a rodeo pen.

She was cute, if you went in for wholesome clean looks and no cleavage. Not that Reno judged a woman by her bra size. No, he liked to think he was more liberated than that. But he did have a weakness for a well-endowed woman. Blondes, redheads, or pony-tailed brunettes like the school teacher here, he loved them all. And to his eternal gratitude they seemed to love him right back.

Not that this woman appeared to be thinking too kindly of him, certainly not judging by the way she was glaring at him. She did have the biggest brown eyes he'd ever seen, though, framed with thick lashes. Her button nose added to her cuteness while her generous mouth hinted at a more passionate nature than he'd detected at first glance. And now that he took a closer look at the curves beneath the baby-blue camisole top she was wearing, he revised his earlier estimation regarding cleavage.

He sent her a friendly smile. "You're the new school teacher in town, right?"

"I'm hardly new," she frostily informed him. "I've been here over three years. But that's irrelevant. I'm here because I need your help in finding my brother. He hasn't checked in with me in two days."

"Has he ever done anything like this before?"

Reno could tell by her hesitation that her brother had. "He promised he wouldn't do it again," she said. "When I called the last place he was staying up in Bozeman, they said he left and didn't say where he was going. His car broke down, he told me he was leaving it there. That was two days ago. He may be hitchhiking. I can't believe you're just sitting there *eating*—" she said the word with utter disdain "—while my brother could be out there someplace needing help."

Her attitude irked him. After not having the time to eat for the past twelve hours, his stomach was just about pinned to his backbone from hunger. And now this schoolmarm had to come storming in, friendly as a diamondback and sore as a boil, to ruin his lunch hour.

He put a hand on his cheeseburger. It was stone cold. So was her glare. His usual patience went out the window. "I'm sorry ma'am, but there's no law that says a man has to check in with his sister every day of the week. I suggest you calm down and stop worrying. He'll call you when he's ready."

ANNIE BENTON wanted to take the cheeseburger—the one he was clearly more interested in than her story—and shove it down the sheriff's throat. Usually she was a calm, quiet and polite person, but where her younger brother was concerned she was like a fierce lioness protecting her cub. She'd had to be. She'd practically raised her brother herself.

And now this laid-back lawman had the nerve to act like she was some kind of overbearing hysterical woman.

She'd heard about Sheriff Reno Best and his womanizing ways. The younger women in town had nicknamed him "Jerry Maguire in a uniform." The older women in town wished they were young enough to chase after him.

She supposed he was handsome. His brown hair was rumpled and he was sporting a sexy stubble on a chin that looked like it could be intractable. He had the kind of chiseled cheekbones that artists and photographers love. His hazel eyes looked like they belonged to a man who found humor in life, judging from the laugh lines at their corners. His hands were gripping his cheeseburger with capable strength while his mouth...

Okay, so the guy was incredibly sexy. Everyone in town was right.

She didn't care. She only wanted the guy to find her brother. "Let me get this clear," she said, using her 'teacher' voice, the one she reserved for perennially misbehaving third-graders. "You're telling me that you're going to sit there on your posterior and not lift a finger to help my brother?"

"I'm going to sit here on my posterior and eat my lunch," he replied, not looking the least bit repentant.

So much for having the sheriff ride to her rescue. She'd wanted his help, but she wasn't going to get what she wanted. She was used to that. She knew the drill. If she wanted something done right, she had to do it herself.

"Fine. You sit there on your posterior."

His golden-hazel eyes gleamed at her humorously as he drawled, "You seem mighty interested in my posterior, ma'am, if you don't mind my saying so."

"I do mind and I'm not interested in you. What I am is concerned about my brother. Clearly I'll have to handle this matter myself."

"Whoa there, ma'am." He reached for her hand, preventing her from sliding out of the booth. "I don't like the sound of that. What do you mean, you'll handle this yourself?"

"I mean that if you won't track down my brother, I will."

He frowned. "I don't think that's a good idea."

"I'm a woman on a mission," she stated, ignoring the flare of awareness his touch had provoked.

He shrugged. "End result is the same. Trouble. And quite frankly, I don't need any more trouble."

"Trouble?" she repeated, yanking her hand away. "You don't know the meaning of the word, but you'll find out if anything has happened to my brother!"

"Give it a few more days and I'll..."

"Forget it. I'm not waiting. And I'm not impressed with your skills as a law enforcement officer," she added for good measure.

"Just with my posterior?" he suggested with a wicked grin.

"It may be the only good thing you have going for you," she retorted. "Trust me, it's *not* enough." Then, she left the diner as abruptly as she'd entered it.

ISABEL SHARPE

The Way We Weren't

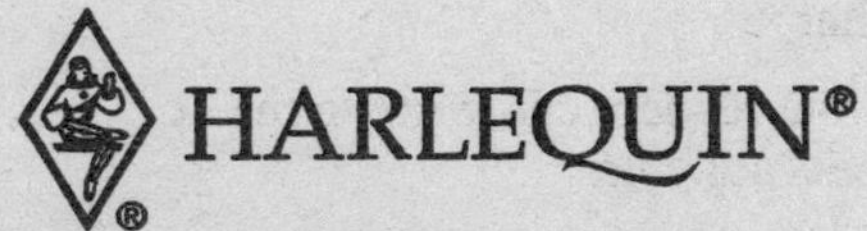

TORONTO • NEW YORK • LONDON
AMSTERDAM • PARIS • SYDNEY • HAMBURG
STOCKHOLM • ATHENS • TOKYO • MILAN • MADRID
PRAGUE • WARSAW • BUDAPEST • AUCKLAND

Dear Reader,

I've been a romantic ever since girlhood when I first fell in love with Batman on TV. In my fantasies, the Caped Crusader and I emerged, unscathed and devoted, from whatever peril he faced in each week's episode. When I grew up and got married, the infatuations stopped (okay, okay, I still get weak in the knees over Harrison Ford), but the stories kept on going inside my head.

I began writing when I left office work to stay at home with my first son, now five. My second son came along in 1998, but I've managed to keep writing, mostly by giving up any and all pretense of housekeeping.

I write romantic comedy because I believe in laughter as a tonic and a weapon against life's inevitable rough spots. Amber's tale grew out of the unfortunate experience of a friend of mine. My comic revenge-gone-awry story is a gift to her—and anyone else who could use a happy ending! I hope you enjoy it.

All the best,

Isabel Sharpe

Isabel Sharpe

P.S. On-line readers can write to me at
IsaSharpe@aol.com

To my brother Philip,
who should have been around to read this.

1

THE MOMENT HAD COME. The diamond ring burned a blistering hole in Lance's pocket. He'd outdone himself to make the occasion special. Fragrant flowers spilled out of a sterling bowl that had belonged to his grandmother. Tall red candles flickered on the spotless white linen tablecloth. He had prepared all Sarah's favorites: smoked salmon, filet mignon, herbed baby vegetables, mesclun salad and Linzertorte. Sarah's blue eyes sparkled at him, reflecting the candle flames over the red roses. Perfect. So why did he have a sudden irrational craving to be on the bleachers at a Red Sox game, wolfing down a chili dog?

"Sarah." Lance took her hand across the table. Her smile gleamed, wide, expectant. She knew what was coming. They'd both known for years, of course, probably even back in graduate school when they started dating five years ago. Five years. A light sweat broke out on Lance's forehead. He took a sip of wine.

"You wanted to ask me something, Lance?" Sarah leaned forward encouragingly. Her smooth blond hair fell neatly over the sides of her headband and exactly framed her pert perfect chin. Her white even teeth glittered in the light.

"Yes, I...yes, I did." He shifted in his chair. *Come on, Lance.* How hard could it be? *Will. You. Marry. Me.* Four little words and the last piece of the life Lance Edwards had been groomed to live would fall inevitably in place.

Never underestimate the importance of a beautiful, well-bred wife to your career, son. His father had spouted the phrase at least fourteen hundred times, embracing Lance's neck with an arm that felt like a noose, gesturing proudly to Lance's mother with his cigar as if she were a prize mare.

Lance ran his finger under his collar. It felt unusually tight, as if his throat were still trapped by his father's domineering arm. He unbuttoned the collar and loosened his tie. God, was he about to follow the very advice he always scoffed at?

He could imagine the call to his parents tomorrow. He, with his arm around Sarah, both of them with game-show-host smiles, the phone to his ear. *Dad, I just wanted to tell you, I have a mare of my own now.* Lance shuddered.

Sarah's expectant smile dimmed. "Are you okay, sweetie?" Her voice dripped pure gold honey, a sure sign she was upset. The madder she got, the less people could tell, unless they knew her. Lance knew her.

"Sure, of course. Maybe a little too much wine." He gulped a little more and tried to take a deep breath. The air must be leaving the room somehow. He glanced around, half-expecting to see some gremlin crouched outside the window, sucking out their precious oxygen with a giant vacuum.

His apartment looked the same as ever, decorated

with impeccable taste by Sarah, no doubt with the understanding she'd share it someday. *Objets d'art* lined the walls and bookshelves: African, Egyptian, Early American—items they'd collected over the years as their respective careers took off. Lance suddenly wanted to put a giant lava lamp in the middle of the antique coffee table, plunk a green velour lounger on the Oriental carpet in front of the entertainment center and watch football for days at a time.

He forced his attention back to Sarah. What the hell was the matter with him? He'd already agreed she could move in next month, as she'd wanted to for so long; it was only right to ask her now. "Is it warm in here or is it me?"

Her smile remained fixed in place. Was the light playing tricks or had her teeth suddenly sharpened into pearly points? "I'm perfectly cool."

He nodded weakly. No surprise there. She made cucumbers seem like hot coals. He glanced at her through his wine glass. She still stared, eyes calm, wide, unblinking, waiting, waiting. "Is that all you wanted to ask me, Lance?"

"No, of course not." He chuckled involuntarily and cleared his throat. "Sarah, will you...will you m-m-m—?" His throat clenched convulsively on the word. Married. To Sarah. Locked in an eternal gavotte of comfortable, predictable sameness. Finally having to give up his dreams of blind love and all-consuming passion.

No. Not yet.

He exhaled breath he didn't know he'd been holding and pointed to his demitasse of espresso. "Will you pass me the sugar?"

LANCE NODDED CURTLY to two teenage girls who squealed admiringly as he passed. *Go pick on someone your own size.* He didn't need puppy love. He needed someone he could really talk to, to try to figure out what was happening to him, why, when his whole life should be coming together, it seemed to be falling apart. He scowled at the sidewalk. Lacking that, he'd have another drink.

A fur-draped mannequin in a nearby shop window swam across his peripheral vision. Newbury Street, lined with one exclusive store after another, was Sarah's idea of shopping heaven. She'd be furious with him for cutting the evening short. He couldn't blame her. But after the fiasco at dinner, he couldn't stand to spend the usual evening in front of her favorite TV shows. So he'd sent her home apologetically, and sneaked out to commune with the alcohol gods.

A tiny dog, or what passed for a dog, came to heel beside him, snuffling at the sidewalk and occasionally peering up through eyes cleared of hair by a blue bow-shaped barrette. A punting dog. Like the cardboard one Sarah bought him for a joke, knowing how much he wanted a real one. She couldn't stand "nasty, drooling beasts."

"Hi, pup, you lost?" The dog wagged its tail and continued on at Lance's side. Lance stared suspiciously. "You're not spying on me, are you?" A withering canine stare came his way. The dog trotted over and anointed a lamppost with lifted leg. Lance sighed with relief. A male. On his side then, in spite of the ridiculous barrette. "I'll call you Spike. Because it doesn't suit you at all."

A chill breeze set last autumn's leaves rattling in tiny tornados against the pavement. Even here, in the heart of Boston's Back Bay, the scent of coming spring made Lance think of his childhood home in Connecticut. He closed his eyes and tipped his head back, inhaling deeply.

His eyes jerked open; his arms flew out to steady himself. *Whoa.* Better turn that last drink into soda water with a twist. He hadn't done anything this stupid since college.

Spike trotted back and nosed his trouser leg; Lance bent to scratch his soft ears. Why did he have to get drunk to notice he'd lived so many of his parents' expectations and so few of his own?

"What happened to that toy company I always dreamed of starting, Spike? What happened to marrying for passion over suitability? What happened to moving out of the city to a house with a yard and trees?"

Spike looked up at him in concern.

Lance dismissed the ideas with a sweeping gesture of contempt. Naive dreams of a spoiled kid who'd been told the world was his oyster. Too late, he learned the family viewed Lance's oyster as permanently out of season.

His entire existence had become a cliché instead. Right down to courting the boss's beautiful daughter and being primed to take over the company. Nothing left to do now but marry Sarah, have two-point-five perfect children and die.

Lance continued down the street with Spike trotting at his heels, absurdly pleased the dog had picked him out for company. He needed company tonight.

"You know, Spike. I've only known you a few minutes, but I feel I can really talk to you." He winked down at the warm brown eyes. Spike stopped and bared his teeth menacingly.

Lance frowned. "Whatsa matter, boy? You think I say that to all the dogs?" Spike advanced, lifted his leg over Lance's Gucci loafers and strolled away down the sidewalk, his stiff derrière the picture of affronted doggyhood.

Lance stared at his damp shoes in disbelief. You couldn't trust anyone these days. He hesitated for only a second outside Daisy Buchanan's before he ducked in. Great bar. Not too crowded on weeknights. Suited his restless mood. One more drink before he went back home to his empty apartment and *objets d'art.*

The edgy, youthful-night-out atmosphere of the bar energized him as he hoped it would. He slid onto a just-vacated bar stool and nodded to the burly man seated next to him. The bartender caught his signal; Lance ordered Jack Daniel's, straight up. To hell with soda water. He slammed his palm on the battered dark wood of the bar. Tomorrow he'd face the idea of becoming engaged. Tomorrow he'd return the yoke to his shoulders and confront the reality of his lost life. Tonight, for one last time before he became a cloned Edwards pussycat, he was a tiger. A savage tiger on the prowl. He growled deep in his throat. The burly man shot him a dirty look and moved away.

Lance shrugged, paid for his bourbon and swiveled on his stool to contemplate the female possibilities in the room. Not that he'd do more than buy her a drink and chat. Even Lance the savage tiger wasn't that sleazy. But she'd represent his last shot at freedom, at really living, in a way she could never understand.

The bourbon slid down his throat in a raw challenge to his manhood. Or was that tigerhood? Anyway, whoever she was, he'd remember her till he took his dying breath. Even though he'd never see her again. No, really.

He narrowed his eyes and concentrated on the task. Plenty of possibilities—the tiger would not go hungry tonight. Tall stacked brunette in the corner…too obvious. Short redhead next to her…giggling—no, thanks. Hopeful-looking woman near the back…attractive, but no soul. He continued his survey: frosted blondes, highlighted brunettes, long legs, short legs, large breasts, small—

The slow turn of his head stopped. Recognition hit him with a stomach-clenching jolt that robbed the alcohol of its power. He hadn't a clue who she was. Nothing to go on but simple certainty he'd found what he'd been looking for.

She leaned across her table talking earnestly. Blond hair, chin length, slightly disarrayed—the style made her look chic and vulnerable at the same time. Her eyes—he squinted through the smoke to see the color and gave up—were slightly anxious; her companion patted her hand as if reassuring her. Casual, plain clothes in muted colors that revealed little of her slender shape, said little about her. Nothing extraordinary. But she drew him, almost as if she were someone he'd known before.

In the biblical sense.

He slapped ten dollars on the bar, big-game adrenaline pumping.

The bartender nodded. "What'll you have?"

"Send over two more of whatever they're drinking." He pointed to the woman's table.

The tiger had found his prey.

"YOU'VE GOT TO LET someone get close to you." Wanda gave Amber's hand a final pat and shook her head. "Poor Fred."

Amber scowled at her friend. A Wanda lecture was brewing, and she wasn't in the mood to hear it. Fred had been a wonderful friend. He'd genuinely upset her when he ended their relationship the day before; the rejection still smarted. But sitting in this smoky pickup joint had been Wanda's idea of a heartache remedy. Amber would just as soon be home with a video.

"If he'd been serious, he would have stayed around."

"The guy was serious personified." Wanda threw up her hands. "Four months and you only let him kiss you a few times. If I were Fred, I'd have been history in a week."

Amber took a defensive sip of her beer; it suddenly tasted watery and sour. Wanda meant well, as always, but she couldn't really understand. For most people, sex and intimacy grew naturally out of the attraction and dating process. For Amber, they grew out of her worst nightmares, like a man-eating fungus.

"I don't like to rush things." The words sounded lame, even to her.

''Rush?'' Wanda yanked at her dark curls as if she wanted to tear them out. ''By the time you'd be ready for him to get it up, he'd be too old to.''

''He wasn't right.''

''Right, schmight. You give me a pain. You're letting one little bad experience in college paralyze your life.''

Amber put down her beer with a thud; a little sloshed over the rim and made a gold bubbled puddle on the table. Wanda had to be really exasperated to bring that up. Amber had only mentioned ''that one little bad experience'' once, years ago on a tipsy confess-all night. No details. She still couldn't bear to tell anyone what really happened.

''The thing is, Amber, you're not the same person you were in college. Look at you. You're thin, blonder, you wear contacts, you have a small cute nose, you changed your name. No one would even recognize you.'' Wanda smacked her plump fist on the table, black eyes intense behind her glasses. ''But you haven't changed *inside.* Outside you may be Amber Jade Daniels, beautiful and fabulously successful. Inside you're still A. J. Kszyckniwicz, pudgy, plain and pitiful. You need to let some guy give you confidence. In the sack and out.''

Amber bristled. ''I don't need a man to—''

''Excuse me, ladies.'' The bartender set fresh foaming beers in front of them.

''We didn't order these.'' Amber frowned and pushed hers away.

''That guy told me to bring 'em over.'' The bartender pointed.

Amber ducked her head so the bartender blocked

her view. She didn't even want to see the guy. She hated this preyed-on feeling. Couldn't he see they were doing fine by themselves? No, of course not. He assumed two women alone were missing something vital: him, of course.

"Thanks, we're not interested."

Wanda squinted, following the bartender's pointing finger. "Hubba, hub-*ba.* Too bad I'm married. A-number-one gorgeous, wealth and success written all over him—your basic mega-catch. You're clearly the target. He's craning around to see your reaction."

"Let's get out of here." Amber slumped down in her seat.

"Wrong reaction. Straighten up, he's coming over."

The bartender moved away. A man's form moved closer. Amber kept her head forward and slid her eyes sideways for a quick glance.

Her eyes snapped back to Wanda in stomach-curdling horror. Her body contracted to hunched stillness. Panic spun up like a roaring waterspout. She forgot to breathe.

Lance Edwards. *Lance.*

"Lighten up, he's a man, not a tiger," Wanda whispered fiercely. "He's not going to bite." She smiled up at Lance and started chatting, occasionally kicking Amber under the table as a signal to join in the conversation.

Amber's eyes refused to leave her friend. She was aware of Lance glancing in her direction now and then. She wouldn't look at him. She didn't need to. One quick glance had Super Glued his image to her eyeballs. Still gorgeous and utterly masculine, hair thick and sandy, perfect corporate image and ultra-patrician features marred only by deep blue sensual eyes that could soften or burn hearts with their intensity. Amber used to tease him that somewhere back along the terribly proper Edwards line, some black sheep did the unthinkable and married a Gypsy.

Eyes notwithstanding, he was still pure Lance Edwards III. A golden boy. One of the privileged. She, tubby, big-nosed, myopic Radcliffe student A. J. Kszyckniwicz, had loved him deeply, and been betrayed more cruelly than she could ever have imagined.

"Hello? Hello?" Wanda snapped her fingers in front of Amber's face. "Sorry...Lance, did you say? She left us for a moment." Another kick under the table, this one vicious.

Amber jumped and forced her eyes to focus. On Wanda.

"Lance was telling me he's a management consultant."

Amber nodded politely. Of course he was. She'd hardly expect him to be teaching special-needs kids.

Lance moved closer and pulled up a chair. Even in Amber's peripheral vision, his familiar natural grace was obvious, as if he choreographed and rehearsed every move. The air in the bar suddenly increased in density.

"Mind if I join you lovely ladies?" His deep voice still sent sympathetic vibrations through her body. Damn him to hell, for all eternity.

"Not at all." Wanda cut off Amber's affirmative answer—and her chance to put an end to this nightmare. Soon she'd have to look at him again. Soon she'd have to speak to him. He was about to ask her something. She recognized the tilt to his head, the angling of his body toward her. He had a way of making people feel they were the only ones in the world worthy of his attention. He should have been a politician. He had the requisite lack of scruples.

"What do you do, Amber?"

She had to answer. *Oh, no, her voice.* She was suddenly back in college. Lance held her between his knees, his arms wrapped tightly around her as they sat together, watching the Charles River flow by. He'd spoken, low and husky against her ear. *You have the sexiest voice. It's like I've died and gone to heaven when you talk.*

What do you do, Amber?

Another kick. She'd have bruises tomorrow.

"I'm a graphic designer." Amber spoke in a high, breathy whisper, like a bimbette on acid. She still wouldn't look at him. Wanda twisted her face to look incredulous, and held out her hands in a shrug that clearly asked what the hell Amber was doing.

"Oh, really?" Lance edged his chair closer. "What a coincidence. I'm thinking of starting my own business—I'll need a graphic designer. Do you have a card?"

"No. I'm out of them." She could tell by the way he very slightly overenunciated that he'd had too much to drink. A little charge of satisfaction swept through her. The old vices hadn't changed.

"I have one." Wanda leaned down and fished exasperatedly through her enormous purse. She handed the card to Lance, ignoring the ferocious scowl Amber sent her. "If you guys'll excuse me, I have to go powder my nose."

Amber's ferocious scowl changed to a plea for mercy. What the hell was she going to do now? She had to get out of there.

Lance stood briefly as Wanda left the table, then settled back in even closer. Amber pretended to find her clenched hands fascinating, feeling as if she were about to become his last meal.

"You'll think this is strange, but when I saw you, I..." He joined her in staring at her hands. She raised her head in amazement. Lance at a loss for words? "It sounds really stupid, but it's like I know you from somewhere."

He raised his head suddenly. Amber jerked back, but was unable to break free of his deep blue, spell-binding stare. Shock crossed his face. She held her breath. He recognized her. Confusion replaced the shock. She inhaled further, daring to hope. He wasn't sure he recognized her. The confusion cleared; he smiled. Amber let out her breath. He didn't recognize her.

Lance glanced at the card in his hand. "Amber Jade Daniels, Daniels Design. You have your own firm?"

Amber nodded, allowing herself to relax a tiny bit. She was proud of that fact and couldn't help enjoying his admiration.

"I was serious about needing a graphic designer. I'm getting really sick of the corporate grind." He shifted restlessly, then snapped his gaze back to her. Amber had to steel herself not to jump. His eyes made Tom Cruise's look bland and unfocused. "You know what I have always really really wanted to do?"

Make toys. She arched her brows as if she couldn't begin to guess.

"Make toys. Ones that are cool enough to be popular, but..." He took a sip of his drink.

But which educate and stimulate.

"...but which educate and stimulate kids' minds at the same time."

"Ah," she commented profoundly. He'd been on about this since college and still done nothing? He'd shown her his drawings, his plans, talked endlessly about how he'd break out of the family mold and make his dreams come true. Blah-blah-blah. The Edwards in him would always beat out the Gypsy.

Lance swirled his drink slowly, seemingly absorbed in the task.

"You know, sometimes it seems like life happens while you're busy doing something else." He spoke without lifting his head. Amber couldn't stop herself from gaping at him. Exactly what had happened to Lance Edwards III that he could be vulnerable?

Whatever it was, she hoped it had been unimaginably horrible.

He jerked his head up abruptly and drained his glass. "Did someone else say that or did I just make it up?"

She shrugged. He fixed his blue stare on her again and leaned closer.

"Look, Amber, I know you're not thrilled to have me barge in on your evening, but I need someone to talk to tonight." His voice got huskier. He leaned back and rubbed his hand across his forehead. "No, more than that. I need to talk to *you.* I can't even explain why, but it's true."

No. Don't do this. I fell for it once already. She glanced at her watch. "I'm sorry. We were just about to leave."

"Can I at least give you a ride somewhere? My car's just down the street."

No doubt a BMW. The yuppie car of choice.

"It's a BMW. Bright red. Very sexy." He leaned forward, eyes boyish and pleading. "What do you say, Amber? I just want to talk. Honest."

Right, talk. And she was Miss America in college. He leaned closer and took her hand. She tensed. Same lines. Same moves. Even his aftershave hadn't changed.

The scent brought back hidden, sensual memories of the times they'd been close like this before—and the times they'd been even closer. Amber jerked her hand away. Hidden memories? More like buried. In a locked safe. With the key in a whale's stomach in the middle of the Atlantic. Where was Wanda?

She stood, unable to take the tension anymore. "I'm sorry, no." She looked desperately around and saw the evil traitoress hovering behind a potted plastic tree, peering at them. Amber beckoned furiously.

Wanda came forward, a disappointed pout on her red lips. "Are we leaving so soon?"

"I was trying to offer you ladies a ride home, but—"

"We'll walk," Amber snapped, and recoiled. She forgot the bimbette whisper.

He didn't appear to notice. "I don't blame you for thinking I'm on the prowl, but I am. That is, I'm not.'' He rolled his eyes and mumbled something under his breath.

''A ride would be divine—it's chilly out there. Thanks very much. We live on Beacon Hill.'' Wanda thumped a tip on the table, collected her things and jerked her head toward the exit. ''Come on, Amber.''

Amber moved close to her. ''He's drunk. We'd be risking our lives.''

''Huh? That guy? He's sober as a judge. Look at his hands. Not a quiver.''

''What if he's an ax murderer? The next Ted Bundy?'' Something had to work. Something had to keep her out of his car.

''A murderer? With those baby-doll eyes? Forget it. You're getting in that car and giving him a chance if I have to drag you in myself. The guy's twenty carats. I have the Wanda Instinct. Never fails.''

Amber stood with her feet rooted in the beer-stained carpet. Her Amber Instinct told her to open her mouth and scream. But with Wanda the bulldozer obviously determined to get her in that car, any successful protest she'd make would probably wake the dead at the same time. There'd be all kinds of questions, maybe Lance himself would start looking more closely. She clenched her fists, feeling as if she were being buried alive. She just couldn't bring herself to give in.

Lance came back toward them, one eyebrow lifted quizzically. ''Ladies? Is there a problem?'' His question attracted the attention of an obviously beer-saturated bar patron who peered at them unsteadily. Amber gritted her teeth. An audience. Hurray.

''Here we come.'' Wanda smiled brightly. ''Come

on, Amber, it's just a ride home.'' Amber shook her head.

''Hey, Amber.'' The drunk slung his arm around Lance and gestured with his beer. ''Give the guy a break.''

Amber tried to vaporize him with her glare. The last thing she needed was more attention to her reluctance.

Lance eyed the intruder with distaste. ''Thanks, but I think I can—''

''Hey, guys, c'mere.'' A group of no-neck, beer-clutching, soft-gutted clones surrounded him instantly. ''My buddy here was nice enough to offer these chicks a ride, and that one won't go.''

A round of Neanderthal tsk-tsking greeted his announcement. Amber groaned. If she hated them enough, would they all go away?

''Let's take a vote,'' the leader bellowed. ''All who think she should go, say 'Beer is king.'''

A mighty chorus of ''Beer is king,'' followed by a ''Go, go, go'' chant was all Amber needed. Lance hadn't taken his eyes off her. That confused don't-I-know-you look was back in place.

She grabbed Wanda. ''Okay,'' she muttered. ''But don't blame me if we end up hacked into pieces at the bottom of the Charles.'' She yanked her things together and stalked out of the bar, the cheers of the Male Drunken Idiots Club ringing in her ears. Thank goodness she and Wanda lived close by.

Ten minutes later they arrived in front of their brick apartment house up at the top of Joy Street. Lance nosed the car into a parking place in front of their building. Amber dove out of the car. Wanda scrambled after her.

So did Lance. "I'll walk you to the door."

"It's three feet away. Not a mugger in sight. Thanks for the ride." Amber marched up to the front door. A bell shrilled behind her. Both women turned and stared at Lance.

"Excuse me, I'm ringing." He took out a cell phone and punched a button. "Hel— Oh, hi. Just a minute." He walked a few yards past Wanda and Amber and continued talking.

"Why are you being like this?" Wanda swung Amber around. "Just because you're mad at me doesn't mean you have to be so rude to him."

"It's him, Wanda."

"Him who?"

"Him *him.*"

"As in college him?"

Amber nodded slowly, eyes narrowed for the full effect.

"So?" Wanda sighed in exasperation. "Whatever happened was years ago. No one's the same as in college. Look at you. He doesn't even recognize you." She gestured at Amber, top to bottom.

"You said I was still the same inside."

"Maybe he's the same outside and different inside. You're being foolish not giving him a chance. He's obviously attracted to you."

"He took advantage of me."

"What guy didn't try something at eighteen?"

"I was eighteen—he was twenty-two. I loved him—he shattered me."

"I'm sure he had no idea."

Amber took a deep breath. "He took my virginity on a bet with his roommate."

Wanda froze; her eyes gleamed behind her glasses. "Kill the bastard."

Amber exhaled in a choked sob that held a touch of relief. Finally she'd told someone who hadn't been there when it happened. Someone she loved and trusted, who didn't laugh at her the way they did in college. The breeze blew early-spring scents past them; a siren howled off in the distance. Amber stood quietly, waiting.

Something was happening. Something that should have happened ten years ago when she first found out about the bet, when Lance's roommate, Chris, first told her, with that laughing sneer on his face, and she'd crumpled: betrayed, humiliated, deflated. It was finally happening.

Amber was starting to get angry. Not annoyed angry. Not fist-waving angry. But red-hot, murderous, crazy-raging angry. "I've spent my whole life emotionally paralyzed by what he did to me. Look at him." She gestured to Lance's broad back. "Management consultant, Brooks Brothers suits, gorgeous town house somewhere, I bet, gorgeous girlfriend somewhere, I'm sure, BMW..."

Amber glared at the car sitting smugly at the curb. She strode over and stood beside it, unable to control her fury and loathing. The red-hot anger turned white. Without even thinking what she could possibly accomplish, she slammed her foot against the fender with all her weight behind it.

To her horror, the car moved. It moved forward and out from the curb, narrowly clearing the bumper in front of it. In a slow, balletic turn, it glanced gently off a car on the other side, straightened and began a sickening, accelerating, driverless descent down the hill toward the traffic on Cambridge Street.

"Oh...my...God." Wanda's voice barely penetrated the fog in Amber's brain.

The car hit the concrete divider bisecting Cambridge Street with a loud splinter of metal and glass. Half a second later another car, screeching to avoid the accident, smashed into the BMW, crumpling one side. The Beemer caromed off from the impact and crashed back into the highway divider on its other side. Crunch.

Silence.

Silence more profound than any Amber could remember since she'd run tearfully to Lance's dorm room for reassurance the whole thing was a ghastly mistake, and some jock friend of Chris's burst in, unaware of Amber's presence, demanding to know if the rumors were true and Lance had won a bet by scoring with some fat chick.

The driver of the second car climbed out and started shouting obscenities at the totaled, empty BMW, searching the small crowd of pedestrians for someone to hold responsible. Amber swung around to see Lance frozen on the sidewalk, his mouth open in shock and disbelief, the phone held limply next to his ear.

And then, through her agony, her mortification, her horror, came joy. Joy so vicious, unbridled and intense in its purity, she could barely keep from shouting it out. Triumph. Victory. And justice for all.

"Thanks for the ride, Lance," she breathed. "See you around."

2

"DELIVERY FOR apartment seventeen." Wanda stood on Amber's doorstep, wrapped in a bathrobe, holding out a thermos and two slices of homemade apricot coffee cake on paper plates. "You ready to talk yet?"

Amber's mouth dropped open. "It's three in the morning. How did you know I was still awake?"

"I live downstairs from you, remember? You've been pacing for over two hours."

"Oh, no, I'm sorry." Amber ushered her in. "You're the best, Wanda. Jerry must think I'm psycho."

"Psycho, schmycho. Jerry could sleep through a nuclear blast."

Wanda spoke with affection and pride that made Amber's stomach clench with envy. Wanda and Jerry had the kind of marriage she wanted someday. Best friends, passionate lovers, devoted parents... She sighed. First things first. Before she worried about marriage, she had to be able to get to second base again. Before she worried about second base, she had to overcome this newly discovered urge to mutilate anything with a high testosterone count.

"Have a sit." Amber gestured to the pillow-decked love seat in the living room and ran to grab mugs and forks from her tiny kitchen, relieved to have someone for company besides her demons.

Wanda looked around and sighed rapturously. "I love being in childless people's homes. They're so calm and uncluttered. Look at this place—it even looks like someone decorated, on purpose. Not so much as a building block on the floor. How can you stand being able to find everything when you need it?"

"I'll trade what's behind door number seventeen for your chaos any day." Amber set the mugs and silver in front of Wanda. True, you had to walk with your head down for fear of stepping on some treasured toy, but the warmth and energy radiating from Wanda's household made Amber's perfect calm seem cheerless and sterile. Some days she lingered there longer than was polite, to soak up as much of the atmosphere as possible.

"You'll have your own chaos someday. Believe me, you'll begin to equate neatness with having some vestige of control over your life—you'll be desperate for it."

Amber smiled, though a little less control over her life sounded pretty enticing at the moment. Her parents had been hippies before being hippies was fashionable. Their lives drifted wherever work and exotic substances took them. Amber figured she became a sober control freak in reaction. Made life easy to manage, but not exactly brimming with spontaneity. That was one thing she'd loved so much about Lance. They'd both been able to—

Amber gritted her teeth, resisting the urge to

growl. Forget it. The whole relationship was a fake. Why couldn't she remember that?

"I brought decaf." Wanda poured two steaming cups. "I figured caffeine in your state would shoot you through the ceiling." She set the thermos down on the glass-topped antique coffee table and picked up her cake. "So, besides the obvious, what's eating you?"

"The obvious." Amber took the plate Wanda handed her, surprised to find herself hungry. All that rage must burn a lot of calories. She took a bite of the rich fruity pastry. "Mmm. Thanks, Wanda. You are the greatest cook. I can't tell you how much I appreciate your coming up to—"

"You going to spit it out or what?"

"The cake?" Amber sent her a mischievous grin. "Of course not—it's delicious."

Wanda rolled her eyes. "Out with it."

"Okay, okay." Amber put her plate down slowly, her momentary lightheartedness draining away. She drew her legs up and stretched the hem of her nightshirt down over her knees. The subject was still painful to talk about. "You'd think after ten years, I could handle seeing Lance."

"No, I wouldn't." Wanda shook her head vigorously. "You spent ten years suppressing everything about him. You couldn't even tell me what had happened—we've been best friends for years."

Amber winced. She felt badly keeping anything from Wanda, but the shame had been so enormous she couldn't bear to tell anyone. Stupidly, she thought she could make the memory go away by ignoring it. Wrong. Major stinking wrong. "You know how shrinks say if you don't express anger, it stays there until you do?''

Wanda nodded. ''I always pictured it black and seething, like oil waiting to be discovered.''

''I thought that was a crock of...fly food.'' Amber unwrapped her knees and leaned forward. ''But when I saw Lance today...'' She shrugged helplessly, unable to admit how it felt to want to maim someone beyond all recognition.

''Up came the bubbling crude.'' Wanda's eyes softened in understanding.

''A regular gusher.'' Amber grabbed her plate and jumped up. ''He won his cute little bet, got the admiration of all his prep-school friends, graduated and probably didn't give me a second thought. Meanwhile, I had to be in school for three more years with my heart shredded, and an entire college of people who knew what happened snickering at me and whistling 'I'm Just a Girl Who Can't Say No.'''

Wanda's fork paused halfway up to her mouth; she lifted her eyebrows.

''Okay,'' Amber admitted, ''not everyone knew. And only one person whistled. But they might as well have printed daily reminders in the *Boston Herald* for how I felt. I haven't trusted a man since. Every time anyone shows an interest, I'm sure he's making fun of me behind my back, even poor Fred. Then, presto, ice maiden, I freeze him off.'' She crammed the last bite of cake into her mouth, her rage rising again, invigorating, glorious and freeing. She shook her fork. ''Well, I'm sick of it. This guy's gone scot-free for too long. And I've spent the whole ten years perfecting the role of victim.''

"Good for you, on behalf of women everywhere." Wanda stood and applauded. "Now, what are you going to do?"

Amber deposited her plate on the table and collapsed onto the sofa. "I have no idea." She might feel like an Amazon warrior, but she didn't have much experience acting like one.

"You need to get this guy out of your system." Wanda held up her hand as Amber started to protest. "I don't mean you still have feelings for him. I mean you have to realize this was not your fault. The guy is a horse's buttock. You are a dynamite chick. These facts have been lost on you—it's time you found them."

"I've spent my whole adult life avoiding this man and this incident." Amber pulled a throw pillow onto her lap. "I never even considered moving to New York because he used to live there. I can't cower in my apartment every day in case I bump into him again. I have to do something." She pummeled the pillow without mercy. "I just don't know what."

"March into his office and confront him." Wanda waved her fist in the air. "Tell him who you are and what he did to you. Show him what you suffered."

Amber bounced off the couch and resumed pacing. "So he can say, 'Lighten up, it was only a joke,' or 'I'm sorry…A.J. who?'" She shuddered dramatically. "I know these people. I know how their shallow little self-absorbed yuppie minds work. Or I should say don't work. I have to think of something better. Something that will really get him. Something underhanded, evil and thoroughly despicable."

"Blackmail?" Wanda suggested hopefully. "Chinese water torture? Dead fish in his mailbox?"

Amber stopped pacing, hardly aware she'd been at it again until she saw Wanda's head turning back and forth to follow her across the room. What were they doing? Instead of thinking in reasonable, psychologically healthy, adult terms, they were considering only forms of revenge. Weren't they being childish? Lowering themselves to Lance's own amoebic level? And how could Amber expect to succeed with this strong-vengeful-woman stuff when she was barely wet behind the ears at being this way?

She smiled and hugged the delicious, unfamiliar feeling of empowerment tightly to herself. Who cared? "When his car crashed into that barrier, once I realized no one was hurt, I felt free and strong like you would not believe. Whoever said revenge wasn't sweet never had that awesome a sugar high." Amber took a deep breath; her hands curled into fists at her sides. "All I could think of was his agony seeing his prized possession reduced to a ball of tin foil. It was exquisite. It was ecstatic. It was ..." She raised an eyebrow meaningfully at Wanda.

Wanda's eyes widened. "Not better..."

Amber nodded somberly. "Better than chocolate."

"Wow. I'd like a piece of that action. How many cars does he have?"

"Exactly." Amber clapped her hands together. "The way I see it, only one thing will work to get me over his foul deed."

"I think I'm going to like this." Wanda lowered her plate, her eyes sparkling. "Do tell."

Amber smacked her fist into her palm. "I, Amber Daniels, dynamite chick, do hereby solemnly swear that I will rest easy only when and if Lance Edwards, horse's buttock, suffers to an excruciating degree." She gave Wanda her best evil grin. "Just like I did."

LANCE STEPPED into his darkened apartment and shut the door behind him, alert for any sign Sarah had come back in the mood for an ambush.

After he'd filled out accident reports, waited for the tow truck and watched his mangled car be towed off to await pronouncement on its fate, his well-deserved hangover had started already. He wasn't quite ready for confrontation. And there was something he had to do. Somewhere in this house, he still had a picture of A.J.

He moved through the living room and peeked into his bedroom, then the guest room. Empty. Guilty relief swept over him. He was free to track down his past undisturbed. He shrugged out of his Burberry raincoat and flung it down over the teak table in the hall. His steps echoed on the hardwood floor, then whispered across the Oriental carpets on the way to his study.

He flipped the light on in his study, kicked off his loafers and loosened his tie. Ahh. His room. The comfortable tacky green leather armchair, the New York Giants lamp, pewter beer stein holding his pens…

"Hi, Rex, did you miss me?" He stooped and patted the ears of the cardboard canine, his first pet since Lucky, the imaginary dog he'd had in childhood. His parents wouldn't tolerate real animals in their house.

"I met another little dog today, but don't worry—it didn't work out."

He crossed to his closet and pushed his way to the back. The picture had to be in there somewhere. He rummaged through the mess of never-unpacked boxes containing his college notes, textbooks and memorabilia. Halfway through the third box, he grinned triumphantly and pulled out his senior yearbook. Bingo. He brought the book out into the room and flipped impatiently through the pages.

"Where is the damn thing?" Lance turned the book over in exasperation and shook it. A picture fell out. He grabbed it and brought it closer to the lamp. She was dozens of pounds thinner now, but lots of people slimmed down after they went off the pizza-and-beer college diet. Her nose was no longer the "wondrous honker," as she used to call it, but didn't she always joke about Uncle Charlie the plastic surgeon whose hands itched every time he saw her? The other changes were superficial, the voice an obvious fake.

He ran his hand over the glossy photo. "Her eyes are the same," he whispered to Rex. Heart-piercing blue, with vulnerability and strength in equal measure. And the way Lance reacted to her hadn't changed, either. In a bar crowded with appealing women, she'd drawn him inevitably. Her subtle scent and the curious tilt of her head sent the same old messages—straight to his groin.

It had to be her.

He slammed the book shut. No wonder she looked so panicked when he said he thought he knew her. No wonder she wanted nothing to do with him. No wonder she seemed so fiercely happy when his car mysteriously rolled down the hill to its doom. "She still detests me, Rex."

Rex did not seem to find that particularly poignant. The dog definitely lacked something as a companion.

"God, what I must have done to her." If only he'd had the balls ten years ago to break down her door and make her listen after she found out about the idiotic bet. Make her understand he really loved her.

Faced with her icy refusal to see him and his own shame, he gave up much too soon.

The bet had been his roommate's idea, cooked up at some college bash. Lance had agreed only jokingly, blitzed to near dysfunction at the time. Chris had led him across the room and introduced him to A.J. Told her Lance wanted to ask her out, but was too shy. She was suspicious, to say the least. Lance had stood there like a low-life invertebrate, grinning foolishly, while Chris sweet-talked her. For some reason she'd agreed to a date.

That date started at six o'clock on a Thursday, with burgers and onion rings at Mr. Bartley's Burgers, and ended at three in the morning in her room, when exhaustion finally overtook their conversation. That date changed his life.

Lance chucked the yearbook back in the box, still clutching the photo. No, it didn't. It should have. It did for a while.

He'd fallen for A.J. hard. He'd never felt like that about any woman before or since. She was the only person he'd been able to talk to about absolutely anything, the only person who really understood what he said. Being around A.J. made the world a new and energizing place.

With her, he saw keenly how the cloned existence he was heading for would suffocate him. How he was no more full of life than poor old two-dimensional Rex. She gave him hope he could ditch the expectations people had of him, and follow his own dreams. He stopped drinking. Began to get turned on by his studies. Began to get very turned on by A.J. When they finally made incredible, soul-shattering love, his mind was too full of her to have room for the slightest thought of the bet.

Lance tossed the picture on his desk. But he'd been a contemptible coward. Chris assumed Lance's increasing involvement with A.J. was merely an attempt to win the bet. Lance had been too much of a chicken to disabuse him. God forbid he admit he was falling in love with her. God forbid he bring home that type of mare to his parents. After all, Big Men on Campus didn't fall for fat, big-nosed, ugly chicks.

He groaned and hung his head. A.J. was never any of those things to him. "Why didn't I have the guts to shout it to the world?" He stared at Rex, misery and regret squeezing his breath. Rex sat placidly, propped permanently on his triangular cardboard support, tongue lolling out from between his tiny teeth in an idiotic doggy grin. "Rex, you mutt, you don't even care."

He pulled out A.J.'s card from his suit pocket and fingered the edges gently. Amber Jade. In college she laughingly put him off every time he asked her what "A.J." stood for, telling him the name didn't suit her. He couldn't imagine why she thought so. It was the most beautiful name he'd ever heard.

Adrenaline fired through his body. He'd let this wrong go for too long. It wasn't too late to try and make it right. He'd call her and apologize. Find some way to make her listen this time. He grabbed the phone. Right now.

He squinted at the number. His fingers shook over the keypad. One ring…two rings…

"Hello?" She answered tentatively, as if not quite sure whether she was awake yet, her voice low and thick with sleep. Tenderness washed over Lance as he pictured her struggling to clear her head. Did she still sleep in the nude?

He suppressed a groan of longing. "A.J., it's Lance. I…know it was you tonight. I know you're angry, but…I really loved you, A.J. You showed me a part of me I never thought I—"

"Who the hell is this?" A man's voice boomed across the line. Lance stopped cold. She wasn't alone. Why didn't it occur to him A.J. could be involved with someone? A knockout like her would have men prostrating themselves wherever she went.

"This is— Where's A.J.—Amber? I just talked to her." He cursed under his breath. He sounded like a complete fool.

"This is Bud. You spoke to my lovely wife, Kristen, who is trying to get back to sleep." Bud's polite tone dripped sarcasm. "We'd love to chat, but we don't talk to freaks. Have a pleasant evening, and *get lost.*" The phone slammed down.

Lance sighed and hung up the receiver. *Nice dialing, cowboy.* Okay, so it wasn't a great time to call.

He'd wait until morning. His brain would be awake and thoroughly deboozed by then. He'd have a slightly better chance of not screwing it up.

He yawned and peered at the battered clock on his desk. Three in the morning on a school night. Bed now, change his life tomorrow. Suddenly stupefied by exhaustion, he dragged himself to the bathroom, brushed his teeth, then flung his clothes onto the floor of his room and passed out on the bed.

AMBER GROANED and dragged herself up to unwilling consciousness. Who the hell was calling in the middle of the night? She squinted at the clock and shot bolt upright. *Seven-thirty.* She absolutely never overslept, even when she'd been up late. A bad beginning to the day.

The phone rang again; the machine picked up. Amber swung her legs out of bed, grabbed a robe to ward off the chill on her naked skin and stumbled to the hallway, grimacing. Her throat felt like a desert full of spiderwebs. She'd see who was calling, then decide if she could stand answering.

The machine clicked on. "Amber, Lance Edwards." The smooth, businesslike voice filled the hall. Amber froze, gaping at the machine as if it were a hand grenade with the pin pulled out. "I'm sorry I didn't catch you before you left for work. I wonder if you'd be free for lunch one day next week."

Amber took a hasty step back. A rain forest of butterflies descended, uninvited, into her stomach.

"I want to talk about my new business and see if I can interest you in designing some promotional materials. Let me know what day would suit you. I'll be tied up in meetings today, but you can leave word with my secretary.'' He rattled off his number and hung up.

Amber blinked at the machine. The red message light blinked back. Hello? Was she still asleep or did Lance Edwards just call and invite her to lunch? Anger curled her stomach and sent the butterflies panicking back to the tropics. She gathered the hem of her robe into tight fists. Maybe she wasn't quite rude enough last night. Maybe turning his car into a pile of junk metal was a little too subtle. Maybe he didn't get the message that she'd rather cuddle rats than ever see him again.

Her fists uncurled. Her eyebrow lifted. Unless...by seeing him again she could better find a way to put her plan in action.

She rubbed her head to try to clear the fog. Reality check. How could she even consider having lunch with him? Sit across the table and chat as if they'd just met? Giggle at his jokes? Pretend to find him delightful company, all the while wanting to skewer and roast his innards?

Amber shook her head. Whatever power she felt last night, she wasn't tough enough to endure that kind of torture, no matter how much she wanted revenge. What could she possibly do to make someone like Lance Edwards suffer, anyway? His actions in college made it clear other people meant nothing to him. In the heat of battle last night, revenge sounded like a noble goal. But she was hardly that kind of woman....

She smiled. Except when she watched his BMW meet its glorious and timely death.

Amber grabbed her keys from next to the phone, barreled out her front door and down the stairs. She needed help with this one. Wanda answered the door, two-year-old Rudy clinging to her ankle, howling in fury.

"Oh, boy." Wanda ushered Amber in. "Looks like you're not much happier than Rudy here. Come on in." She walked stiff-legged back into the apartment, hauling the child along with her. Halfway to the kitchen, Rudy started to giggle, obviously delighted by his new mode of transportation.

Amber grinned at him weakly, her brain still reacting to Lance's call. If his new business was so important, why did he want to hire a stranger? Especially after the way she behaved toward him last night. Could he really be that clueless? Or was it another example of Lance completely oblivious to anything but what he wanted? She wrinkled her nose. More likely his famous inability to deal with rejection. Her blunt rudeness probably made her enticing in some twisted way. Not that he really wanted her. But heaven forbid any woman develop resistance to the Edwards charm.

"Are we still replaying last night? Or have we moved on to new horrors?" Wanda pulled up an extra chair to the table where four-year-old Angelo and six-year-old Stephanie were finishing their cereal.

"New horrors." Amber sat and greeted the kids absently. "Lance just—"

"Auntie Amber!" Angelo yelled. "Watch this!" He stuck two fingers up his nostrils and waggled his head from side to side with his tongue hanging out. Amber stared. Even on a clearheaded day she'd have no idea how to react to that one. Parents were amazing beings.

Wanda rolled her eyes. "Am I the only mother in the country who hopes her child will *not* become president someday? Angelo, go upstairs and brush your teeth or you'll miss your bus."

Angelo gave a dramatic sigh. "O-kaaay."

"Go on, Amber." Wanda set a cup of coffee in front of her. "What did Mr. Nightmare do now?"

"He called me this morning and—"

"You look a little ugly today, Auntie Amber." Stephanie regarded her solemnly. "Your hair sticks out, and your eyes are all small and red. I think maybe you're sick and have to go to the hospital and die, like my kitty."

"Stephanie, please—"

Amber held up her hand to cut Wanda off. Out of the mouths of babes... "I'm feeling a little sad this morning, Stephanie."

"Why?"

"Because a man I don't like very much invited me to have lunch with him next week."

"What?" Wanda's face wrinkled up in outrage. "Stephanie, go brush your teeth."

"O-kaaay." Stephanie stomped out of the room, clearly insulted not to be considered part of the grown-up conversation.

Amber slumped back in her chair. "He wants me to design promos for this new business he's starting."

"What did you say?" Wanda passed the box of cornflakes and a bowl, wide eyes riveted on Amber.

"He left a message. I overslept so I didn't pick

up, thank goodness.'' Very few things could have been worse than having to respond to that deep voice with her head still cloudy from sleep.

''What are you going to do? Go to lunch and poison his soup?''

''I wish. I'm tempted just to ignore him.''

''Ignore him! What happened to Amazon Amber? What happened to making him suffer the way you did?''

Amber stabbed her spoon into the bowl, pulverizing several innocent flakes in the process. ''For ten years I've accepted the humiliation, done nothing about this. One night isn't going to change who I am.''

''I beg to differ. If they could invent a drug with a high like the one you were on last night, the entire world would be addicted.'' Wanda put her hands to her temples. ''Clo-o-ose your eyes and think of that car hurtling down Joy Street.''

Amber managed a giggle. ''It was pretty great.''

''Did he mention the accident?''

''Not a word.'' Amber reached for the milk and sloshed it on her cereal. ''But I know it hurt. He looked like a man whose anatomy had just been permanently altered.'' She ground cornflakes between her teeth, reliving the glorious crunching sound of car against concrete. For someone like Lance, a Beemer meant more than transportation. Amber had destroyed part of his status.

She swallowed and put down her spoon with a thunk. Status meant everything to a man like Lance. In college he avoided popular hangouts once he and Amber became a couple, opting instead for quiet clubs and restaurants outside Cambridge, like that one on the North Shore he liked so much. Heaven forbid he'd be seen sharing a kiss with anyone who wasn't centerfold material. Amber tightened her lips to a sneer. The thirst for revenge came flooding back. He'd treated her like litter box material. He deserved whatever she could manage to dish out.

A glow of fantastic inspiration began to heat up her imagination. What if the car was only the beginning? What if Amber could manage to sabotage Lance's entire life-style?

She sat bolt upright. "Wanda," she whispered. "I've got it."

"What, what?" Wanda scooted to the edge of her seat.

"Men like that—"

"Good morning." Jerry came into the kitchen and poured himself a cup of coffee.

"Daaaaaddy." Rudy rushed into the room and head-butted his dad midthigh.

Jerry flinched and grunted. "A couple more inches on you and you'll be the last kid for sure. What's up, Amber?"

Wanda sighed. "Go away—we're having a girl talk."

Jerry shuddered and grabbed a doughnut from an open box on the counter. "I'm out of here. C'mon buddy." He scooped up Rudy in one hand and left the kitchen, doughnut clenched between his teeth, coffee cup in his free hand, the picture of comfortable fatherhood. Amber stared wistfully after him. He represented everything she'd thought Lance was: kind, responsible, loving, trustworthy....

"Go on, Amber."

Amber pushed away her cereal, embracing the cold resolve that crushed her useless slide into nostalgia. "Men like Lance are the sum total of their trappings—Beemer, condo, designer clothes, beautiful girlfriend, promising career." She counted on her fingers. "Take those away and what do you have?"

"Jerry?" Wanda smiled affectionately at the door he'd passed through.

"You have nothing." Amber leaned forward. "Take their life-styles away and they shrivel and dry up, like a slug in salt."

Wanda recoiled. "Nice image."

"It's perfect." Amber pulled her bowl back and attacked her cereal. "He took away my confidence, my self-esteem. What better way to return the favor than destroy what matters most to him?"

"Excuse me." Wanda put her hands together to form a Tee. "Time out. Exactly how are you going to accomplish all that and stay out of jail?"

"I managed the car, didn't I?" Amber jumped up and paced the kitchen, gesturing wildly. "I'll booby-trap his apartment, get him fired, drive some wedge between him and whoever Ms. Romantic Perfection is at the moment."

"Assuming there is one."

"There has to be." Amber smacked her hand on the table. "Lance wouldn't even get a haircut without suitable female decoration."

"I don't know, Amber. Sounds a little dangerous. Wouldn't a nice simple punch in the nose do the trick?"

"Too crude, too obviously prosecutable." Amber

pretended to pick up a phone. "'Lunch next week sounds divine, Lance. I'm so, so interested in your little project.'" She indulged in a surge of excitement at the prospect of seeing him again, this time with the power on her side.

"What if he recognizes you? What if he already did?"

Amber dropped the pretend phone. Confronting Lance as Amazon Amber was one thing. Quite another to relate to him again as A. J. Kszyckniwicz. All those old feelings...

She gritted her teeth. What old feelings? They'd succumbed to noble rot years ago. "I'm sure he didn't recognize me last night. If he does during lunch, I'll act as if he barely made it into my long-term memory banks. A completely insignificant blip on the vast radar screen of my love life."

"I don't know, Amber—"

"I'll be fine. At the very least I can keep telling him how sorry I am about his car and watch him writhe."

Wanda laughed. "That much I approve of. Just be careful. Make sure he's the one doing all the suffering."

"Worry not. From now on, I call the shots." She aimed an imaginary revolver. "Lance Edwards's smooth climb up Yuppie Mountain is about to encounter an Amber avalanche."

3

LANCE STRODE DOWN Exeter Street toward TGI Friday's where A.J. suggested they meet for lunch. Not quite the intimate table at Maison Robert he envisioned, but he couldn't risk any of his actions seeming unprofessional. He had no leeway with A.J. for mistakes. If he had to apologize over burgers and fries instead of *steak haché* and *pommes frites*, so be it.

He pulled open the restaurant door and braced himself for the sight of her. Would she dress up for him or make herself deliberately dowdy? Would she be waiting nervously, or with the cool calculation of a professional assassin? Would she smile in greeting or immediately pull out an Uzi?

He surveyed the crowd. Not here yet. The overly made-up hostess took his name, and he found a clear space of wall to lean against, eyes glued to the door. He still couldn't believe A.J. accepted his invitation. Granted, she thought he wanted to hire her for this brilliant new business he was supposedly starting. Last week, when he first met her again under the influence of his friend Jack Daniel's, the plan to drop out of management consulting and devote himself to BrainToys had been genuinely all-consuming. Back on sober ground, of course, the idea was ludicrous fantasy. There was absolutely nothing wrong with his life; his golden future beckoned, exactly as planned. Whatever nagging doubts he had that evening were the product of his childish overindulgence, and typical male panic over getting engaged.

But what harm could there be in playing the role of entrepreneur for a short while, as long as his ultimate goal was good? Once he apologized for the incident in college and A.J. forgave him, his conscience would be clear. They could bury the past, shake hands and part company the best of friends.

Lance grinned. Brilliant plan. The whole thing would be a piece of cake.

The restaurant door opened. A.J. burst through, cheeks ruddy, hair tumbled. The soft scent of still-chilly spring breezes surrounded her, making Lance acutely aware of the stale inside smell he'd become part of. An aura of wholesome freshness that had nothing to do with the breeze radiated from her and punched him with startling aphrodisiac effect. He swallowed. A piece of cake? It wouldn't even be a crumb from a moldy *biscotti*.

She spotted him immediately and advanced, eyes clear and direct, full mouth in a burgundy half-smile. He took in a long breath. If they were meeting for the first time, without the overweight baggage of their past, he'd have her in his bedroom within the—

Lance gave himself a mental smack. Bedroom? With a two-carat diamond sparkling away in a velvet box in his nightstand, and a partner of five years who felt understandably entitled? Time to reconnect with reality. He had come here to "recognize her," apologize and go back to the life he belonged in.

"Mr. Edwards, nice to see you again." She extended her hand and squeezed his in a killer grip.

"Please, call me Lance. I'm glad you came." He spoke smoothly, smiled politely and felt shaken like a martini. She looked so confident, self-assured. Not at all like the A.J. he knew ten years ago.

The hostess called his name and led them to their table. A.J. sat down, shrugged off her suede jacket and unwound a bright scarf from around her neck, tossing her hair to free it. The familiar gesture made Lance's insides contract with unexpected tenderness. How many times had he sat across from her and watched—?

"I'm very interested in hearing about this business, Mr.—Lance." She gave a low chuckle that made him wish she'd drop the fake breathy voice and use her own. "Mr. Lance. Shall I call you that?"

"As you wish." Lance could feel the awkward grin on his face. He'd faced furious boardrooms that were less daunting than this altered vision from his past. How had he handled them? He mentally reviewed the procedure. *Rule one: direct, unwavering eye contact. Rule two: make sure…*

The rest of rule two vanished under the direct, unwavering eye contact of Ms. Amber Jade.

"I hope you had good news about your car."

"I'm afraid not." He searched her stare but failed to locate anything but sincerity. If he hadn't seen her vicious pleasure when his car crashed, he'd take her concern as a hopeful sign his apology would be well-received. "The insurance company says it's a dead loss."

"Oh! What a *shame.*" She leaned forward, sympathy and regret etched into her features. "You must have really loved that car."

He smiled. At least he could put her anxiety to rest on that score. "To be honest, I hated the damn thing. My dad bought it for me—his idea of what 'successful' men drive. I always wanted a nice unpretentious dark-colored Honda."

Her polite regret froze. "A Honda."

"As far as I can tell, I left the emergency brake off and the car went AWOL. Clumsy, but ironic." He smiled harder. Why didn't she seem reassured? "I ended up doing myself a favor."

"A favor." A.J. registered what might have looked like dismay on a face less tightly controlled.

"Not to mention the fact that I was in no shape to drive. The accident probably saved my life."

"Saved...your...life." She spoke through clenched teeth.

Lance's by-now-enormous smile slid down his face and ended up dangling upside down above his chin. Had the earth just started revolving the other way? Wasn't she touchingly concerned for him a second ago? Right now he'd swear she wished *she'd* pushed the damn car. A.J. didn't have a vengeful bone in her body. But what did he know of Amber Jade, except that her nose had shrunk? She seemed sorry he wasn't killed. He drummed his fingers on the table and developed an absorption in looking for the waitress. Getting this apology over with suddenly seemed a task of Herculean proportions.

The beaming waitress arrived on cue and asked for their lunch choice as if she cared deeply about little else. A.J. chose grilled knockwurst and sauerkraut; Lance ordered soup and mushroom quiche. His mom made superb quiche, and he needed comfort food at the moment.

A.J.'s mischievous grin flashed for a second before she squelched it. Lance remembered too late: "real men" didn't eat the stuff. When had he felt like such a bumbler? Handling people was his specialty. He pulled himself up straighter. Time he put his talent to good use. *Rule two: make sure you ask the questions.*

"How long have you lived in Boston, Amber?"

"Since graduate school, four years ago. I went to Rhode Island School of Design."

"An excellent school." He was impressed. Also smug. They were talking about schools. The perfect place for a segue into his plan. "Where did you do your undergraduate work?"

Her eyes dropped. She picked up a spoon and flipped it over and over. "Here in Massachusetts."

He nodded politely. Cambridge to be exact. "I was Harvard, class of '87. Maybe we were here at the same time."

"Wouldn't that be...something." Her eyes shifted side to side. Up. Then down. Lance waited while she examined every atom in the restaurant except those belonging to him. He couldn't help being a little pleased. About time she did some of the flustered duty.

The waitress brought their drinks; A.J. seized her iced tea with a grateful smile and busied herself guzzling. Lance watched patiently, sipping his seltzer. *Rule three: never back down but occasionally let them think you might.*

A.J. put her empty glass carefully back on the table and shot him the look of the condemned to the executioner.

"I'm interested in seeing your portfolio." Lance took a pen and notepad out of his jacket pocket. "And I'll show you a few of the toys I'm thinking of."

A.J. nodded, obviously relieved, and dug out an oversized binder. "I put together some pieces you might find relevant. We haven't done toys before, but we did the design specs and marketing collateral for a line of children's clothing. I've also included some of our other retail projects."

He accepted the binder and leafed through the pages, poring over each picture as if his appetite were increasing. She was good. She was incredibly good. Especially the work on the kids' clothes. The logos were jaunty and fun, the marketing pieces brightly colored and eye-catching, bold and uncluttered. Excitement pounded through his system. Just what he wanted. A perfect fit for the products he had in mind. He reached the end, shut the book and raised his head.

A.J. was watching him with the peculiar defiant vulnerability of someone having her work judged. Lance nodded. "These are terrific, Amber. You're very talented." He couldn't make his voice sound as hearty and detachedly professional as he wanted. Wasn't that rule number four? At the moment he didn't care. Across the table sat the link to making his dreams a marketplace reality.

He passed the book back to her. How ironic that the link existed in the form of the only woman who ever believed in those dreams, and at a time when fulfillment was a virtual impossibility. BrainToys was doomed to remain a fantasy.

Lance drew two quick sketches on his pad. "I'm interested in two toys to start. SpySam, undercover agent by day, single dad by night. To give boys the idea that fatherhood is macho, too."

"Diapers and detective work?" She laughed. "I like it. Kind of James Bond meets Mr. Mom."

"The other is a trivia game which I haven't named yet. It's a board game for preteens with a slime-spouting monster. If you answer the questions wrong, you get slimed." He grinned at her skeptical face. "Trust me. It's like candy-coating spinach. You have the gross-out aspect, and kids won't notice they're learning."

"We could have a field day with that one." A.J. framed her hands as if envisioning headlines. "Goo For The Gusto, or Ooze It Or Lose It."

Lance chuckled. "How about Slime Is A Terrible Thing To Waste?"

Their laughter died down into awkward silence. They reached for the same water glass; their fingers touched. A.J. yanked her hand back and jerked her head up to meet his eyes. Immediately the room narrowed and focused until it became only A.J., trapping him in a gaze he couldn't break if he wanted to. Her skin glowed warmth; her lips opened to speak, then released only a soft sigh.

Lance's brain ground to a testosterone-induced halt. He ached to pull her up over the table, bend her back into his arms, cover her mouth with long, hot—

"Theeere you are, lover! Chris told me he saw you on the way here." Sarah's syrupy voice acted like a glass of ice water in his lap. His brain screeched back into activity, spinning in panic. What the hell could he say? Sarah would have a fit if he so much as mentioned the bogus plan of starting his own business. Where would that leave her plans of him running Daddy's Empire?

Sarah turned to A.J. "Naughty boy. He told me he was eating lunch in his office today and here I find him out with a beautiful woman." She beamed, jealousy skillfully hidden behind the all-important projection of sole ownership.

A.J. narrowed her eyes and directed a look of intense disgust across the table. Lance winced. Did that look come out of the same eyes he'd just been lost in? He made a mental note to strangle Chris.

The silence stretched. Lance loosened his tie. What the hell rule covered this? "I bumped into Amber on my way to do some errands. We, uh, went to college together."

Amber's narrowed eyes shot wide open. She gulped audibly.

"College!" Sarah entered the wide-eyes contest and won. "Imagine that—*what* a coincidence. Well, I certainly don't want to butt in. How nice to meet you, Amber. We should have lunch sometime. I really want to get to know *all* of Lance's old friends. Do you have a card?"

"Right here." Amber handed one to Sarah with a smile that froze solid when it turned in Lance's direction. "Lunch sounds great. I'm sure we have lots of stories to share."

Lance grinned weakly.

"Super." Sarah's lips remained determinedly stretched over blinding white teeth. "I'll call you next week. Bye, honey.'' She gave Lance an icy peck on the cheek and glided out of the restaurant.

A.J. stared after Sarah, then slid her eyes back to Lance without turning her head, her expression clearly apprehensive.

''I'm sorry, A.J.''

She drew in a sharp breath. ''You recognized me. I thought maybe the college line was a coincidence.''

Her voice had dropped back to the low, rich tone he remembered. He could have cheered. ''I should have said something sooner, but I couldn't figure out how to broach the subject after all this time. I wanted to...'' His brain dangled a billion or so possible phrases. None satisfied him. ''That is, I feel so badly...'' He tried to reroute his synapses with no success. How could he have arrived at this moment so unprepared? ''It's only right I should...'' Damn, damn, *damn.* He couldn't tell her now, mere minutes into their reunion, in a crowded restaurant, that Chris hadn't known what he was talking about, that Lance hadn't meant to hurt her, that he'd loved her deeply. Ridiculous. ''Chris, my roommate, was—''

''Are you talking about the bet?'' A.J. picked up her knife and began toying with it.

''Yeah.'' He sent her a sheepish grin, keeping a watchful eye on the serrated instrument in her hand. ''I'm sorry.''

''Oh goodness, Lance.'' She made a dismissive gesture. ''That was a million years ago. A little college prank. I barely remembered until you brought it up.'' She gritted her teeth together in what was apparently supposed to be a smile; her fingers clenched around the knife.

Lance sighed. He'd guess this did not count as a

good time to tell her how he'd really felt about her. In her mind he lured virgins into his bed as a "prank" and then met them for lunch ten years later behind his girlfriend's back. No wonder she thought he was a jerk. He felt like one at the moment.

"As for Sarah, I haven't told her about my business ideas yet, which is why she didn't know I was meeting you today. I work for her father, and until I know the new company is going to fly, I don't want to risk rocking the family boat."

"I see." She looked as if all she could see was his funeral. "You've put me in a difficult position on that score."

"I didn't intend to. I had no idea Sarah would find me here."

The waitress delivered their plates. A.J. looked down at her large pink knockwurst and raised her head with a sudden sweet grin. Lance instantly went on guard. In his experience unexplained mood swings in the female of the species boded no good for the male.

"I guess I do understand. This must have been very awkward for you." A.J. slathered her knockwurst with mustard, stabbed it with a fork and lifted it off the plate whole. "I doubt secrecy will be a problem. Whether you hire Daniels Design or not, I doubt I'll see much of...Sarah, was it?" She brought the knockwurst up to her mouth. "It'll be our little secret." Her lips formed an O, then closed slowly around the huge sausage. Without breaking eye contact, she sucked mustard leisurely off the tip.

Lance nearly choked on his quiche. A.J.? She couldn't be...she mustn't realize what... Oh, man.

She smiled at him. Sweetly, without the faintest

trace of awareness of what she was doing. "Mmm. Delicious."

The knockwurst made another slow trip to heaven and back. Lance swallowed hard. If he were a cartoon character, his eyeballs would be sproinging across the table by now. Wanting to kiss her before didn't begin to compare to what he wanted to do to her now. Or what he wanted her to do to—

In a sudden swift movement, A.J. bared her teeth and gave the knockwurst a vicious bite. Lance jumped and instinctively covered his lap, barely stifling a yelp. Message sent. Message received. At this rate his confession would have to wait until they colonized Mars.

Still smiling, A.J. chewed the bite thoroughly. "Now," she cooed, "shall we get down to business?"

"YOU WHAT?" Wanda could scarcely speak for laughing. Tears rolled down her cheeks, and she gasped for breath. "You *what?*"

Amber shrugged, still giggling madly, and passed Wanda a bowl of fudge-twirl ice cream. She still couldn't believe it herself. "Honestly, I don't know what got into me. But I was furious when I couldn't gloat over his car, and even more furious when I found out Sarah didn't know we were having lunch. The poor woman. She tried not to let on, but I know she was crushed." Amber had noticed Sarah an instant before Sarah spotted her and Lance together, and saw the hurt and surprise on her face before she carefully hid them behind her perfect smile.

"Who wouldn't be crushed?" Wanda wiped her eyes. "I take it Sarah is the unlucky woman?"

Amber nodded and put the ice cream back in her freezer. Unlucky was an understatement. "Why a class act like her would hang around the sleaze of the century is beyond me. She didn't even know he wants to start a new business. He's probably got a thousand mistresses already lined up for married life, starting on their wedding night." Amber sat down again. Better conveniently forget the twinge of jealousy when she found out Lance was seeing someone. Nothing unexpected—she'd predicted as much. Just her competitive spirit surfacing in an irrational place. Nothing too mysterious about that.

"After that bit with the knockwurst, he'll think twice about adding you to his mistress list."

"You should have seen his face." Amber collapsed over her ice cream into another spasm of laughter. "He felt true kinship with that sausage, I'll tell you."

She tried to forget the image of his face immediately before her teeth met the mark, when her lips were doing their work. After his initial shock, his gaze had narrowed, darkened, increased in intensity; his features had taken on a potent, predatory cast.

The unfamiliar thrill of discovering her seductive power replayed its shiver through her insides. Amber extracted a vein of fudge and slid it around her mouth, hoping to cool her heated cheeks. Nothing wrong with discovering seductive power. As long as she never applied that power to Lance again.

"I should think you'd feel like you got a bit of your own back anyway." Wanda fanned herself with her hand. "Whew, I haven't laughed like that since Jerry announced he was giving up junk food for a macrobiotic diet. So, how far are you going to go pretending you'll work for him?"

"As long as it takes." Amber thudded her fist on the tiny kitchen table and made their bowls jump. "I can spend a few hours here and there and pull together something fairly believable. It shouldn't be too hard. Might even be fun. I hate to admit it, but he's got some great concepts. If he weren't Satan himself, I'd root for him to give this business his best shot."

Amber grinned at Wanda's shocked expression. She'd been surprised herself at how the toy ideas appealed to her. All it took to bring her back to reality was the episode with Sarah. "As it is, I'm only too happy to escort Mr. Satan back to hell. The world needs to be safe from Lance Edwards—he must be stopped before innocent children buy SpySam and that trivia game to line his evil pockets."

"So what's next?"

"Aha, the million-dollar question! Remember those yuppie essentials?" Amber reached for the phone pad and a pen. "Car, condo, wardrobe, gorgeous girlfriend and successful career." She wrote a neat list.

"Car's done." Wanda wiped her hands with a satisfied smack. "Check it off, woman."

Amber put a huge check mark next to "Car." "Which means condo is next."

"What are you going to do, blow the place up?" Wanda gave a dubious frown. "Society takes a pretty dim view of that kind of stuff, even for people like Lance."

"It doesn't have to be so drastic. Maybe just something that will make the place uninhabitable."

She waggled her eyebrows at Wanda. "Like a gross of roaches under the door."

"Not bad, not bad. I like the under-the-door stuff. A little more subtle than the A-bomb approach I expected you to—" Wanda jumped up. "Amber! I've got it."

"Better than roaches?" Amber smiled expectantly.

Wanda folded her arms across her chest. "Roaches, schmoaches. Listen to this. Take an economy-sized bottle of garlic powder and a fan, and blow the granules under his door. His entire apartment will smell unbearably like bad breath for weeks."

Amber twisted her face skeptically. "Sounds more like a prank out of *Animal House* than the noble revenge of Amazon Amber."

"You're close. My frat boyfriend pulled the stunt in college, in retaliation for having his underwear soaked and put in the freezer."

"I don't know..." Amber stared at the table, considering. A vision poked its evil head into her consciousness. On their second date Lance took her to a downtown Chinese restaurant. Over soup and Tsing Tao beer, she argued passionately her probably half-baked ideas on James Joyce's *Ulysses*. Partway through her earnest speech, she realized Lance was no longer listening. A tiny smile curved his lips, his gaze narrowed intently on her. His eyes emitted warmth, pleasure and charged sensual energy in a breath-stealing combination she never encountered in anyone else. The effect mesmerized her. She broke off, blushing and flustered.

He took her tightly clenched hand in his, looking

for all the world as if he were about to proposition her. No man had ever looked at A. J. Kszyckniwicz that way. She held her breath, fascinated and half-afraid.

Lance leaned forward. His lips parted. "I hope you'll try some of my spicy garlic chicken."

She deflated, absurdly disappointed. So much for a proposition. "Uh, yeah, sure."

He took her other hand, the tiny smile spreading into a slow, sexy grin. "Because if we both have some, you won't mind."

"Won't mind?" She was idiotically baffled.

"When I kiss you later tonight, A.J." His low, rich voice sent throbbing resonance directly through her body to where no man had ever touched her....

Amber thrust the memory back under the slime-covered rock in her subconscious where it belonged. She had to give it to him; he'd been good, the bastard. And what a ridiculously easy target she had made. Like a little lamb, frisking happily all the way to the slaughterhouse.

She tightened her mouth and nodded firmly to Wanda, rage seething again through her veins. "I'll do it."

"Atta girl." Wanda saluted with her spoon. "He'll never know what hit him."

"I'll need a couple of weeks to put together some designs before I perform the nasty deed. Then, a nice friendly phone call to tell Lance the drawings are ready, and an oh-so-polite question about how he and Sarah passed the evening..."

She and Wanda dissolved into giggles. So the car hadn't quite worked. Lance still had plenty in store.

4

LANCE STRODE ACROSS the overly ornate pink marble lobby of 125 High Street, grimacing at the modern building's vain effort to look old and elegant. He joined a group of suited employees waiting for the elevator and exchanged brief greetings with a few familiar faces. The elevator doors slid open, and he followed the group on, mentally going over his schedule for the day. Meetings this morning, lunch with Bob Tucker, Sarah's father, to discuss the Davis account, more meetings this afternoon to—

He became suddenly aware of bodies shuffling away.

"Whew," someone muttered behind him. Lance rolled his eyes. Damn smell must have gotten into his coat; he couldn't tell anymore. Thank God his bedroom door had been closed so his clothes were safe. The rest of his apartment was downright toxic. He smiled uneasily at his fellow passengers and made a mental note to order concrete shoes for his landlord if he hadn't fixed the problem by the time Lance got home. Some animal must have died in the heating system. Strange that the building superintendent had gotten no other complaints.

The elevator doors discharged him on his floor, no doubt to the relief of the other riders. Lance removed his coat and crumpled it under his arm. He turned the corner and greeted his secretary, who held up a folder.

"These letters need your signature, and Mr. Tucker wants you to call as soon as you are ready for lunch."

"Thanks, Darla." He nodded and walked into his corner office. The immediate city view was not exactly scintillating, but farther out he could see a bit of Boston Harbor. And the light coming through the wall-wide windows made the space energetic and productive on all but the gloomiest days.

The phone rang; he grabbed the receiver, trying not to hope it was A.J. Two weeks had gone by since they'd had lunch. She said she'd call when preliminary designs were ready. How much longer could it take? He still had to find a way to get that whole mess off his conscience, though after the fiasco at their lunch together, leading up to an explanation would be rough going.

"It's your Sarah-bear."

"Sarah." He smothered the guilty stab of disappointment. Maybe he had a little crush on A.J., so what? Sarah would be his wife someday. "Why don't we have dinner at Bertucci's tonight?"

"We're going to Chip's surprise party, honey. You didn't forget, did you?"

"Of course not." Of course he did. Damn. Dull people, dull conversation. His college roommate Chris ogling Sarah and putting him down. So damn predictable.

"I'm dying to see what Martha will wear this time. Not to mention how she'll react when she sees Chip and Bootsie together. After the barbecue last summer, I'm surprised she's even willing to be in the same room.''

Lance put himself on autofiancé and arranged the notes for his morning meeting in a neat pile. Over the years he'd perfected the art of tuning out Sarah's gossip. He could review data for his meeting with the majority of his brain, and let his subconscious interject perfectly timed chuckles or tsk-tsks based on the tone of her voice. Just one of the things he'd learned to live with. A lot more to a successful marriage than being thrilled by your spouse's every word.

He tried not to think of his endless talks with A.J. Passionate, furious arguments...tender, halting confessions...long, painful analyses of their childhoods and dreams...

''Sarah.'' He interrupted her monologue before he'd even thought out what he wanted to say. ''Let's...blow off the party and drive up to the North Shore for some seafood. Somewhere we can be alone and talk.''

''Oh, honey, we're committed to Chip. Besides, they'll be buzzing over Annie's engagement, and I'm dying to see the ring. Oh, and I can't believe I forgot to tell you! Listen to this.''

She went off on another catalog of domestic crises. Lance went back to his notes. Stupid suggestion anyway. His and Sarah's schedules didn't allow for that kind of spontaneity. Even if the little restaurant on the water still existed, he couldn't quite imagine himself there with Sarah. He and A.J. had piled into his car one evening and just started to drive. He loved taking her to places where he could have her all to himself, away from the stifling sameness of the college social scene.

Lance shook his head. He was wildly overromanticizing the relationship. He and A.J. probably had nothing left in common. Whereas he and Sarah had grown together over the past five years into a solid, mature partnership. The future held no ugly surprises for them. How many couples could be so sure of that?

He pulled himself to the present to keep from wondering why that didn't sound as satisfying as usual. Sarah had just asked him a question. He searched his short-term memory. Something about seven o'clock at her place. "Sure, sounds great. See you tonight."

Lance replaced the receiver, unable to shake the uneasiness that began with his disappointment on hearing Sarah's voice. He looked at his watch. Better get going to the meeting. He liked to get there first, to project the all-important image of calm control as his intended victims shuffled in. Exactly the image he hadn't been able to keep hold of at lunch with A.J. He winced. Her teeth in the knockwurst had made it clear who got to play victim in that round.

Faced with that degree of castrating hostility, how could he explain without making the whole situation worse? She'd come to the lunch nursing a ten-year-old grudge, a grudge he'd compounded by lying to his girlfriend in front of her. The only reception he'd get from an attempted clarification at this point would be flying lead. Maybe he should shelve the whole idea. She'd detested him for one decade; what harm if she detested him for a few more?

He leaned back heavily in his chair and folded his hands behind his head, staring at the high gray ceiling. A.J.'s face flashed into his mind, glowing triumphantly at the devastation wreaked on his car. He shook his head. Call it fairness, call it justice, call it massive ego, call it anything else a shrink could come up with. He just couldn't bear to have her think badly of him when it wasn't deserved. Ten years ago he hadn't had the guts to make sure she knew he wasn't playing games. He had to make her see the truth now.

Lance lifted his feet and sat up in exasperation. Which left him exactly where he started. With an apology doomed to be rammed back down his throat. He'd have to turn into Sir Galahad even to get her to smile pleasantly at him. Maybe he should try showing up at her apartment in full armor, offering a white rose.

He grabbed up his papers and tapped them sharply on the desk until they were perfectly aligned. In order for him to have any chance of being forgiven, A.J. had to trust him again. That could take some serious time.

Lance stiffened. Of course. He whacked himself on the forehead. *Rule five: when the direct assault doesn't work, resort to the long siege.* He'd have to continue the distasteful charade of having her do design work for a company that didn't exist. But sooner or later she'd see he wasn't such a bad guy. Sooner or later she'd start doubting her conclusions from what happened in college. Just at the right moment, the real version would confirm a picture of wonderful, misunderstood Lance. He'd be forgiven. All his plan needed was enough time to spend with her.

Lance filed his notes into a new black folder and sharpened three pencils to needle points. The idea of making peace with his past must be what made his blood suddenly warm. Nothing to do with the thought of spending more time with A.J. He patted his pocket to make sure his gold pen waited at the ready, then stood abruptly and headed for the door. All aspects were in order; his course of action was clear.

The intercom buzzed behind him. "I know you're on your way out, Mr. Edwards, but there's a Ms. Amber Daniels on line one. She says you're expecting her call."

Lance swung around. A surge of jittery excitement threatened his calm. He thought of the meeting room, due to start filling up any second. If he took the call now, he'd lose his advantage, betray one of the Edwards golden rules that got him where he was. He'd better deal with Amber later. In any case it wouldn't hurt to be unavailable. No sense panting like a puppy dog whenever she beckoned.

"Do you want me to take a message, sir?"

Of course. Take a message, Darla. Lance was never, ever late to meetings.

"I...I'll talk to her." He sighed. Woof.

AMBER MARCHED UP the uneven winding stairs of 55 Hereford Street, the old brownstone she rented for her firm's offices, trying to keep her mind on what she had to accomplish today—besides calling Lance to find out if he enjoyed life in a Dumpster. He should not be the focus of her day. Nor should he have been the focus of yesterday, the day after the crime. But she'd decided to wait to contact him, just in case he could possibly make a connection between her call and the disaster.

She replied in kind to the warm greetings from Bob, Alec and Liz, who comprised her design staff; she'd worked hard to be a fair and loyal boss, as well as a demanding one, and was proud of her hard-working team and the pleasant pull-together atmosphere that resulted.

She crossed the main workroom, between the computers and cluttered drafting tables, and walked into her office, once the master bedroom for the apartment on that floor. Not much of a view, but spacious enough, and with the door closed, quiet. She placed her armful of drawings precisely in the center of her desk blotter, steadying the considerable pile with a careful hand before she sat.

"Knock, knock!" Her assistant, Steve, infallibly cheerful, entered the room waving a handful of pink message slips. "Good morning. The Z.A.B., Inc., people are wetting themselves wondering when the revisions will be done, Doug from the Burrell Companies is drooling all over you to do their fall product release, ditto John from Bartson, etc., etc., and I am leaving at noon today."

Steve smiled his dazzling even-toothed smile. He was a gem. Blond curls, dynamite blue eyes behind wire-rimmed glasses—the kind of guy that made her wish she had a little sister to sic him on.

"Check." Amber held out her hand for the messages. "How was your date last night?"

"Terrible." Steve shook his head. "I took her to a Japanese place, and she spent the whole night crying into her sushi about the last jerk who dumped her. I thought I had a sure thing."

"All that buildup for one cold fish and a plate of damp ones." Amber clucked sympathetically. "Wish I knew some hot babes for you, but all the women I know are gay, married, bitter or all three."

"I'd take bitter over freshly maimed any day. Got their numbers with you?"

She laughed. "Out of my office, Romeo. And close the door, I have to make a call."

"Ooh, what's his name?"

"Out!" Amber flung a freshly sharpened pencil at him, and picked another one out of her drawer. She liked her pencils sharp enough to wound.

She flipped through the pile of designs on her desk, and pulled out the drawings for BrainToys. For a slapdash effort, they were pretty good. She'd spent the last two weeks grabbing whatever time she could to work on a logo and marketing pieces.

The logo she'd done in bright primary colors, letters slightly askew, as if slapped on the paper with a loaded paintbrush. BrainToys, Inc. Then underneath, in a descending line of third-grade-teacher perfect printing: Smart Choices For Cool Kids. The slogan had come in a bizarre moment of inspiration. She didn't usually involve herself in that side of the creative process, but the phrase seemed too good not to suggest to him at least. The marketing pieces were sketched in, but until she could see a prototype or at least a photograph of one of the products, there wasn't much more she could do.

The toughest job had been remembering why she was designing the pieces, and for whom. Every time she forgot, her creativity and the spark the ideas lit threatened to make the work enjoyable. Enjoyment and Lance Edwards must stay in distinctly separate categories for her plan to work.

Her satisfied smile widened. Now for the call to Lance. Now for the blazing triumph of good over evil, of wrongee over wronger. Now for the chance to gloat over his suffering. Maybe he'd already had to rent a room at the YMCA. She wrinkled her nose. More likely the Ritz. Still, he'd be out of familiar surroundings. Enough to make anyone miserable.

Her hand faltered on the phone. Was she really up to hearing his voice? To actually interacting again? *Chin up, Amazon. You've got the power.* She dialed and asked his secretary to put her through.

"Amber! Great to hear from you. Great." Lance sounded edgy and distracted. Maybe she'd interrupted his call to an air-freshener company. Her confidence grew. What had she been so worried about? The enemy showed weakness after all.

"Hello, Lance. I have some preliminary drawings ready, which I can bring by anytime."

"Great, great, though you probably better not come by my office here. Sounds great, though."

"Of course not." Maybe he could say "great" one more time. She'd rarely encountered Lance Edwards off balance. Perhaps the smell in his apartment had shorted out some brain cells? She grinned and prepared her voice to sound as casually innocent as possible.

"How about *your* place some evening? Or is Sarah

there every night? I realize you don't want her to know about BrainToys yet..." She crossed her fingers. If her plot had worked, Sarah would undoubtedly not be around for a while.

"Sarah? Well, actually, she won't be around for a while."

Amber suppressed a giggle. All signs pointed to success. "Oh? Is she traveling?"

"No, she's...no." He started and halted several sentences. Amber pressed the muting button on her handset to stifle her laughter. Tears squeezed out of the corners of her eyes. The prank had worked. Completely juvenile, totally ridiculous, but it had worked. The familiar victorious surge of adrenaline rose up through her system. Lord, she was wicked. And she felt great. "The truth is, Amber, this horrible...smell has invaded my apartment." He laughed nervously.

She let the silence last just a touch longer than polite. "A smell."

"Yes, can you believe it?" He gave another mortified chuckle. "Like some creature with bad breath has been panting through the heating ducts."

"Ah," Amber managed to say before succumbing again. *The Lance Edwards Story: Life in Halitosis Hell.* She snorted and gasped behind her hand, trying to bring herself under control long enough to break the lengthening silence. She failed.

"You know, Amber, I just had a thought." His voice became suddenly cheerful and hearty. Amber's giggles all but died out. He didn't sound nearly miserable enough. "It's incredibly ironic, but this might be a godsend for us."

"A...godsend." Her smile grew stale. A strong

sense of foreboding threatened to upset her position in the universe. What could there possibly be about a stench-filled apartment that would have him crediting the Almighty?

"Sarah refuses to set foot in the place, so we won't have to worry about being discovered. We can meet there as often as we want to discuss BrainToys until the problem is fixed."

"You mean, with the...smell?" How could he possibly want to meet there? The one sniff she'd taken lingered in her scent memory with revolting clarity. She listened incredulously for his answer. With her luck he owned a pair of gas masks.

"You won't believe it, but there is one room the smell didn't reach." He was obviously enthusiastic. Amber let her head drop into her hands, picturing herself perched on the commode, passing her drawings to him in the bathtub. "As a matter of fact, I was thinking before this happened that you might like to have dinner with me, a celebration of our new partnership. This would be the perfect opportunity, as long as you don't mind—" he hesitated long enough to make Amber's warning bells reach a deafening pitch "—meeting in my bedroom."

Amber's entire body became a block of concrete. She couldn't speak, couldn't breathe beyond an outraged wheeze. She thought she'd pulled off the caper of the century, sure to reduce the snide snake to a quivering mass of mortification, and now he was cheerfully inviting her to have an intimate celebration dinner. In his bedroom.

"A.J.? Are you still there? Hello?"

The concrete loosened just enough for words to grind out. "I'm here."

"Look, I know what you're thinking." His voice became softer; he cleared his throat. "It does sound a little...unprofessional, especially given our history. But you met Sarah—she and I are practically engaged. I'm not planning anything but business." *And the pope is not Catholic.* "I'll get some takeout. There's a great Chinese place across the street. We can look at the drawings leisurely and get to know each other again in the process." *Everything I need to know I learned in college.* "What do you say?"

Amber's mouth worked like a dying goldfish, but nothing came into her brain that she could say and maintain a PG rating. A sick lump of disappointment swelled in her stomach. Her bubble had been well and truly burst. It was supposed to be his turn this time.

Steve knocked and waved frantically outside her office window; he pointed to his watch. Amber nodded in immense relief. "I'm sorry, my nine-o'clock staff meeting has already started. I'll have to call you back."

"Nine o'clock!" He swore. "I'm late, I don't believe— Yes, call me back."

Amber hung up the phone, the concrete slowly being replaced by leaden misery. Curses! Foiled again.

Steve stuck his head in the door. "Everyone's waiting. We've got a loaded agenda today." He frowned. "What happened to you?"

Amber looked at him numbly. "You want to go out for sushi at lunch?"

"Sushi again? Well, sure, why?"

"I could use something to cry into."

THE ENTIRE DAY had been a waste. Amber had made it through her morning meeting, but her staff surely suspected her of some oncoming mental illness. Instead of displaying her usual ability to retain a staggering number of details, she'd botched clients' names, forgotten the date and asked for progress on projects completed the previous week.

All afternoon she'd sat in her office, tapping a pencil against her keyboard, her insides engaged in an enormous war over what to do. At the end of the day there were no prisoners, no survivors and no solution. She'd dragged herself home and gone through the motions of settling down to enjoy an evening she had no intention of enjoying.

How could Lance possibly benefit from an apartment that smelled like a hangover? Utterly preposterous. The man deserved pain; he deserved anguish. Instead, Amber had made their getting together obstacle free, secret and exciting. A meeting in his bedroom for a get-to-know-each-other-again dinner his girlfriend wouldn't know about. Not the way it was supposed to happen. Not what Amber wanted at all.

She wanted him humbled, outcast, the adult equivalent of the kid who always got picked last in gym class. But how to go on from here? The last time she'd been alone with a man in his bedroom, the man had been Lance. Not as if she had dozens of other memories to confuse with the experience. How could she possibly sit through an intimate evening with Mr. Edwards, Chinese takeout and a giant mattress?

So far, remaining on the sidelines with her rage

for company had been easy. Cheerfully attempting to sabotage his very existence had been delightful. But spend social time with him? Time where they would have to talk and interact? Time where his charm would shine through, where memories would be triggered? The lunch they had together proved he could still rattle her, knockwurst notwithstanding. And at that restaurant they'd been surrounded by other people, not perched on a bed with only egg rolls between them. That, she couldn't do.

Amber gave a frustrated moan. *Someone* was a wreck over Lance Edwards.

Again. Why did she even try to fight him? He made Teflon look like Super Glue.

Wanda's quick patter of knocks sounded at her door, and Amber rushed to open it. Wanda was considerably more objective; she could help make the path clear.

"I'm doomed." Wanda slumped into Amber's apartment in a dramatic collapse. "Doomed!" She reached for Amber's legs and clawed her way halfway to standing. "Must...have...chocolate."

"Uh, Wanda?" Amber stared down at her friend's contorted features.

"He's done it."

"Who? What?"

Wanda stood abruptly and drew herself to her full five feet two inches. "Jerry has gone macrobiotic. Worse, he requests that I join him."

"What did you say?" Amber shook her head. She couldn't imagine the Lewis household without junk food.

"I'm his other half, what could I do? He said the diet is supposed to make you feel wonderful."

"Except while you're eating." Amber patted Wanda's shoulder. "Are you allowed to sneak up here and cheat?"

Wanda breathed a sigh of relief and nodded briskly. "Whadya got?"

"Let's see." Amber led the way to the kitchen. "There's a half plate of everything I've had for dinner this week, ice cream, a few miniature chocolate bars, pound cake and some cookies."

"Sounds fine. Dish it up." Wanda watched Amber closely. "Something's bugging you. I do not sense triumph in this room. Did our hero's stench bath not come to fruition?"

Amber plopped some ice cream onto a slab of pound cake and broke a chocolate bar into pieces for the final garnish. "Yes and no." She told Wanda the gory details of the dinner invitation.

"Yer not sherioush." Wanda's words barely emerged from a mouthful of cake and mint chocolate chip.

"Yesh, I am." Amber couldn't help smiling at her friend's obvious bliss. "Would you like a shovel?"

"No, thanks." Wanda swallowed and sighed happily. "Though a small garden trowel might come in handy for my next helping. So did you tell him where to...shovel it?"

"No, we were interrupted. The outcome is still undecided." Amber plunked her chin into her hands. "This might be too much for me. The whole thing is turning out to be more than I—"

"Excuse me, do I sense that Amazon Amber is on

vacation and has left Jelly-Knees Jade to replace her?''

''Wanda, I can't go through with the dinner. I can't spend that kind of intimate time with him. I can't walk into his bedroom and pretend—''

'''I think I can, I think I can, I think I can.' I read that story to Rudy last night to inspire him to undecorate his room with my panty hose.'' Wanda took another bite and closed her eyes. ''Mmm. You should have some of this. I think lack of food is clouding your thinking.''

''Maybe you're right.'' Amber managed a smile. The world always seemed a little brighter through Wanda's rosy lenses. For some reason Amber had been uncharacteristically lonely in the past couple of weeks. Having a comrade in arms at her side tonight helped a bit. She retrieved leftover lasagna from the fridge, thinking it might help bolster her spirits a little.

''Why not suggest a restaurant instead?'' Wanda asked.

''He wants to look at the drawings—we'll need the space to study them properly. We can't meet in his office because they don't know about his new company. We can't meet in my office because I'm doing this on the side and I should be spending every waking minute helping my staff with the Jacobson account....'' She shrugged helplessly. ''I'm trapped. He's always gotten everything he wanted. Why should that change now?''

''Exactly why he needs you to take him down, woman.'' Wanda shook her spoon emphatically. ''Did you forget what he did to you? Forget what he deserves? By whose hand is the destruction better wrought? Trust me. What's next on your list?"

"His wardrobe."

"What better chance to gain access to his clothes than during dinner in his bedroom?"

Amber chased the last bite of lasagna around her plate with a fork. Easy for Wanda to say—*she'd* be home, cozied up with the man of her dreams, eating kasha and seaweed.

"Listen, woman." Wanda leaned forward and pounded her fist on the table. "Think vixen, not victim. You are not going to his bedroom to be seduced again. You are going to create mass destruction. These two scenarios have nothing in common. Get it straight."

Amber laughed. "I knew you'd turn this back to black and white. After this morning's call the whole world seemed to have gone gray."

Wanda touched her still-black curls. "Tell me about it. If Jerry keeps this diet up, by the end of the month I'll go completely salt-and-pepper."

Amber laughed again and went to the sink to wash their plates, her brain tumbling thoughts around like a lottery-ball machine. Wanda was right. Amber had been thinking like a victim again, though vixen might be a bit of a stretch. Woman warrior fit her new personality better. Amber turned off the water, her excitement slowly reawakening. With a slight shift in attitude, she could still pull this off.

"You know, Wanda dear—" she turned and blinked innocently "—I hear Chinese food stains something awful."

"That's my girl." Wanda gave a thumbs-up sign.

"Yes, it does. And that pesky *moo shu* pork has a tendency to fly across the room when you least expect it."

"Or..." Amber threw the dish towel across her shoulder, an Amazon regirded and ready to do battle again. "He proposed a celebration dinner, in honor of our new partnership." She bestowed an oh-so-sweet smile on Wanda. "What's a celebration dinner without champagne?"

Wanda frowned. "I don't follow you."

"I'd have to be very careful that the bottle didn't get shaken up."

"Ha." Wanda's eyes gleamed. "No, indeed, you wouldn't want that. Nor would you want to open this bottle too near his closet full of suits."

"Think of the mess." Amber shook her head.

"I'm thinking, I'm thinking." Wanda's body began to shake from her giggles. "Wait until my priest gets an earful of this one. We really are awful, aren't we?"

Amber lifted an imaginary glass in a toast. "Here's to us. Here's to awful." She narrowed her eyes, hoping she looked like a tigress with a buck by the throat. "And here's to victory at any cost!"

5

AMBER CHARGED UP the steps to Lance's front entranceway, champagne bottle clutched in one hand, portfolio of drawings in the other. She pulled the front door open and went straight to the hallway panel housing the apartments' doorbells. Edwards, Apt. 3. She punched the button and closed her eyes, taking deep breaths. No sense letting him glimpse her excitement. He'd misinterpret the cause. Heaven forbid he thought she'd worked herself up over the ecstatic pleasure of seeing him again.

The buzzer blared unpleasantly. Amber jumped, and grabbed open the heavy door. Infiltration successful. Weapon ready. Now to track down her prey. She stepped into the familiar elevator and prayed to the patron saint of devious and unholy revenge that this time her ploy would exact the kind of misery Lance Edwards deserved.

The elevator doors opened. Amber emerged, grateful for the long hallway and the tiny chance that distance gave her to calm her crackling nerves. Two steps into the pursuit of extra tranquillity, Lance's door swung open. He strode out to greet her, dressed in a dark wool suit that fit his unfairly flawless build with unabashed perfection and emphasized his height and graceful stride. He advanced, head tipped slightly to one side, a warm and somewhat mischievous welcome in his eyes and smile. Amber fought the urge to throw the champagne bottle at his head and run away, screaming. What right did he have to be able to take her breath away after all these years?

His eyes flicked over the bottle in her hand and widened in surprise. She regained enough confidence to return his smile. *Think the bottle surprises you now, Lance? Just you wait.*

"You said the dinner was to be a celebration." She held up the champagne. "I thought I'd make it official."

His smile spread. He took the bottle. "I'm delighted. Come on in." He touched her arm with the barest of pressure and gestured her to precede him. "Don't be embarrassed if you need to hold your nose."

She needed to. The smell in the apartment transcended unpleasant, achieving the title Truly Unbearable. Amber hid her smug grin under the hand holding her nose. She owed one to Wanda's fraternity friend. Lance took her elbow and hurried her through a richly furnished living room, and down a narrow hallway. He opened a door on the right, pushed her gently through and slammed the door behind them.

Amber stood awkwardly and surveyed the premises, feeling decidedly inexperienced in bedroom-business-dinner etiquette. The room's furnishings, an eclectic combination of antique and modern pieces, worked together to create a luxurious comfortable space. He'd set up a card table for their dinner with china, silver and a small bowl of white roses. Amber's eyebrows rose along with her apprehension.

Looked like he expected a date, not a colleague. If he had any doubts about which she was, she'd soon put them to rest.

She glanced around again. Target sighted. The double door to her right must be the closet.

"Feel free to breathe in here." Lance smiled at her for several endless seconds while Amber wondered whether she could still change her mind about coming here tonight. "Can I take your coat?"

"Sure, thanks." She shrugged one arm out of her light jacket. Lance moved behind her. His hands brushed across her shoulders. The intimacy of being alone with him in his bedroom closed over her in a suffocating cloud more oppressive than the smell outside. Amber stepped forward and jerked her other arm out of its sleeve, thankful she hadn't worn anything too feminine. She had come here as Warrior Woman; her navy suit made appropriate armor.

Lance laid her coat on the bed and held up the champagne. "Shall I open this now?"

"*No!*" She caught herself and moderated her voice to a more normal decibel level. "Why don't we wait until after dinner? We can look over the drawings first."

"Sounds great." He put the bottle on the table and indicated the bed. "I'm afraid that's the only flat place in the room."

Amber nodded and approached the queen-size bed, which suddenly loomed enormous, as if it were the only piece of furniture in the room. Lance stood close beside her, his presence so tangible she was tempted to elbow him in the stomach to break the tension and save herself from the god-awful weak-kneed attraction she still had to fight.

She yanked open the zipper on her portfolio and dumped her drawings onto the dark blue bedspread. At least she had confidence in her professional capacity even Lance couldn't shatter. She stacked the boards neatly, willing her emotions to organize themselves in a similar fashion.

"I've added to your logo." She handed him the design. "I don't normally take that kind of liberty, but the phrase came to me in a vision so I thought I'd try it out on you. I think the change makes your statement stronger."

Lance studied the logo carefully. "Smart Choices For Cool Kids." He chuckled in what sounded like genuine delight. "I couldn't come up with anything half that good. This will appeal to parents and their kids. That's important to me. Kids today have more money at an earlier age than we did. They're not going to 'waste' their cash on a toy they think their teachers and parents would approve of."

"My friend Wanda constantly complains she can only find 'smash and maim' toys for her older boy, and everything for girls amounts to training to become Little Miss Shopping Mall." Amber kept her eyes on the logo, careful to keep a slight distance between her body and Lance's arm.

Lance nodded enthusiastically. "That's what BrainToys is all about. One man's attempt to save the youth of America from becoming violent shopaholics." He flipped through the rest of the drawings, expressing occasional approval. "Just what I was looking for, Amber. I'm impressed."

Amber squelched the thrill of pleasure at his admiration. He'd always been able to use flattery like a weapon. "Until I see prototypes of SpySam and the trivia game, there's not much more I can do on the marketing pieces.''

''No. Of course not. I understand.'' He spoke slowly, examining the logo again. ''I'm negotiating with a company in California that manufactures prototypes. And...a friend of mine, Randy Andrews, of J.C.S. Marketing fame, is...''

Is...what? Amber dared a glance up at his face, surprised at the breakdown of his usual smooth-running chitchat. He looked remote, pensive, almost wistful. She twisted her face in disgust. What possible reason would Lance have to look wistful? Not as if he'd ever had the misfortune to go without the slightest thing he wanted.

''These make it so real,'' he said unexpectedly. ''As if BrainToys is really going to happen.''

Amber peered at him. *Hello? Are we not down from orbit yet?* ''Isn't that the general idea?''

''Of course.'' He broke off his perusal of the drawing and grinned at her. ''Just the culmination of a lifelong dream—it's still hard to believe. The drawings are wonderful, A.J. I'm lucky to have found you again.''

Amber's next sarcastic reply clenched in her throat. He was gazing at her with a warm, thoughtful expression that made her extremely uncomfortable. What happened to the infinitely detestable smooth finish he always had in place? He seemed truly moved by her work and what it represented. Amber shook her brain free of the thought and turned away from his stare. The implications of Lance experiencing genuine human emotions were too huge to grasp.

A bell rang distantly outside the bedroom. Lance set her designs almost reverently back on the bed.

"The food's here. Time to wade through the city dump again." He took a deep breath, like a diver ready to go under without oxygen, and disappeared into the hall.

Amber waited a beat, then crossed quickly to the double door she'd noticed earlier, and peeked inside. A satisfied chuckle rose in her throat. Perfect. She fingered the elegant materials inside. *Lance, Lance, how does your garden grow? With leather belts and silken ties and pretty suits all in a row.* Just waiting for a nice champagne rain shower. She only had to chat sweetly through dinner to allay any possible suspicion, and lure him over to the closet to open the bottle. She rubbed her hands together, sneering her best bad-guy sneer. Wanda was right to convince her to come tonight. She'd have been a fool to waste this opportunity.

Footsteps sounded hurrying along the hallway. Amber scurried back next to the bedful of drawings. Lance burst into the room and let out a long exhale, arms full of white cardboard containers and a six-pack of Tsing Tao beer.

"I made it." He deposited the food on the table. "Maybe not the best Chinese food in the city, but they deliver. I hope you like what I ordered." He began opening containers on the table. "Steamed dumplings, *kung pao* shrimp medium hot—" His hand stopped on the next open container; his eyes widened in apparent surprise and confusion. "I...don't remember ordering this."

Amber rolled her eyes. Having his car totaled and his apartment rendered uninhabitable didn't faze him in the least. Getting the wrong entrée from a Chinese takeout completely flustered him. Maybe she was on the wrong track. Maybe she should hang out in the Tucker and Company cafeteria and mess with his food.

"What did they send?" The aroma wafted across the room, making Amber's mouth water. Something smelled vaguely familiar....

He frowned. "Spicy garlic chicken."

Amber's confidence experienced a sudden and complete meltdown. *Spicy garlic chicken.* The same freaking dish they'd shared the night of their first kiss.

"I can't believe... They've never made a mistake before." Lance chuckled awkwardly, then shrugged. "We'll have to make the best of it. Are you game?"

Amber swallowed and tried to force her determination back on-line. "Sure." She sounded as if she'd never been sure of anything in her life. A horrible suspicion robbed her of her bearings on planet earth. Did he remember the first time they'd shared the dish? Was he baiting her to see if she remembered? Or did one of the Fates have a particularly sick sense of humor?

She had to find out.

"Have you had the chicken before?" Amber cringed. In her strained voice, the simple question sounded absurdly unnatural.

Lance glanced up at her, then back to the carton. If she'd been looking at an emotionally functional human being, she would have thought she glimpsed hurt and surprise in his eyes. "Yes. About ten years ago. But not since."

"Was it that bad?" *He did remember.* Amber's heart started a marathon hammering session. Thank goodness she'd made him think she didn't. Having to take that unbearably awkward dead end trip down memory lane right now would have doomed her mood for the rest of time.

"Not at all. Just some… memories attached to the evening. Nothing that concerns us tonight." He laughed humorlessly.

Amber made an attempt to echo his laughter and ended up sounding like a candidate for the Heimlich Maneuver. His stare at the container held a touch of sentimentality she wouldn't have thought him capable of. Could he possibly have felt something for her after all?

Amber forced an abrupt end to her musings. Needless torture. If he'd had any real feelings for her in college, he wouldn't have turned tail when the story of the bet came out. Any power Lance Edwards had over her now, she gave him. She had only to reassign it to herself.

She banished the remaining worry from her brain. It was only Chinese food. He was only a man. Just because he remembered eating the dish before didn't mean he attached any importance to the evening. He'd probably been staring at the box trying to remember which mega-babe he'd been with that night.

Amber smiled and walked over to occupy the chair Lance held for her, managing not to flinch as he bent to push it back in and a wave of male warmth tinged with aftershave teased her nose. She inhaled deeply over the food to push his scent away with the restorative power of ginger and garlic. On to playing the role of the charming dinner companion.

"This all looks delicious." She helped herself and stabbed up a large forkful of garlic chicken, determined to replace bitter memories with smug thoughts of the loaded champagne bottle. *Here's to new spicy garlic memories, Lance dear.* She popped the bite into her mouth and chewed ferociously. Seconds later the bite bit her back with sizzling chili heat.

"Whew." Amber reached for her beer, eyes streaming. "They ought to market that as a decongestant."

Lance fanned at his mouth with his hand before he, too, reached for his beer. "Probably keeps vampires away, as well." He contemplated the food mischievously. "I might be able to use this stuff."

"You know people who qualify as vampires?" She made herself smile at him. "In your business or personal life?"

He chuckled. "Good question. In my life the two often overlap—in fact, more than I'd like. I miss having friends who are just friends."

Amber nodded. "If it weren't for Wanda, I'd be calling information for someone to talk to." She winced internally. *Go ahead, Amber. Admit you're a wallflower dweeb to the man who made you that way.*

"You're not...seeing anyone?"

"Oh, not at the moment." Amber wiped away a fresh batch of spicy garlic tears, hoping she sounded like someone who had stopped to take a breather from the steady stream of suitors.

Lance retrieved a box of tissues from his nightstand and held one out to her. "Been a long time since I made a lady cry over dinner." He grinned, then his face fell. "That sounded horrible. I hope you know I was kidding."

"I'm sure you've crushed a few hearts in your time." Amber's voice supplied a healthy dose of unintentional acid before her brain could censor it out.

She had to keep him believing the incident in college had barely even scratched her pride.

"None I'm proud of." His expression remained serious. "At least one I wish I never had."

Amber felt a sudden need to examine each grain of rice on her plate. If she didn't know him better, she'd think he was sincere. In any case A. J. Kszyckniwicz doubtless didn't rate as his regretted love. Probably some woman who'd gone on to become a supermodel. Think what a delightful *accoutrement* she'd make now. Must keep him awake at night.

"So what made you decide to risk starting BrainToys? Seems like you've got it made." She gestured around the room at the elegant furnishings, genuinely curious, as well as desperate to change the subject.

"I suppose I do have it made, outwardly at any rate. But management consulting doesn't exactly feed the soul. You go to work, you have meetings. Then you have meetings on the last meeting and meetings to strategize the next meeting. You go to client companies, talk to workers, ask for their 'valuable feedback' and return to more meetings with the recommendation their job should be cut."

"Sounds dismal." *Sounds right up your alley.*

"I exaggerate, of course. We do good work that helps companies do better over the long term. But with what I've learned, I could run my own company in a healthy and productive atmosphere, doing something that matters to me personally."

"How long have you been with Tucker and Company?"

"Almost ten years." He grinned. "You're about to accuse me of having a thirty-something crisis."

"Me?" Amber opened her eyes innocently wide. "Never. Anyone who prefers a Honda to a BMW can't be too mired in midlife crisis yet. And Sarah hardly seems to be the voluptuous airhead half your age you're supposed to take up with."

"True." He gave a huge regretful sigh, then laughed at Amber's daggered expression.

Amber smiled teasingly and congratulated herself. They were finally at ease together. She could pull this off, and he wouldn't suspect a thing. The rest of the meal passed equally pleasantly. If she allowed herself to be honest, she would almost admit to enjoying herself in his company. Good thing honesty played no part in the chosen path of Warrior Woman.

Lance pushed his plate away with a contented sigh and drained the last of his beer. "I love this food. At our house salt and pepper were the big adventure in seasoning. My right-wing parents probably thought flavor was a Communist plot."

Amber gave a genuine shout of laughter. "Not in my house. I got sent to school with pesto-and-goat-cheese sandwiches way before they were fashionable. When it came to trading food, I was the lunchroom leper."

He smiled, a mixture of sympathy and understanding that set Amber's teeth on edge. He was so much easier to deal with when he bragged about breaking hearts. "As I remember, we both felt a little out of step back then. Though at first you thought I was a shoo-in for alpha male." He chuckled. "I always wondered if that was a compliment."

She smiled brightly. *Not in the least.*

"I've been good at understanding the game and following the rules," Lance said. "But I envy people who understood the game, then followed their hearts instead. You always struck me as one of those people."

Amber shrugged. "I've managed to do what I wanted for the most part."

"I admire you. You probably remember me talking about my plans to do the same. But somehow I ended up doing what other people wanted, instead." He leaned forward, paralyzing her with his intense blue gaze. "That's why BrainToys is so important to me. You of all people know how much."

Amber drew in a breath that didn't seem to want to stop. If he was playing the game now, he was doing it so well he had her fooled. For one horrible moment, she had glimpsed the passion and unpolished cut of the man she loved in college. This would never do.

She opened her mouth, unsure of what would emerge. But something had to break this endless, silent deadlock of their eyes.

"How about that champagne?" She accompanied the words with a sweet smile, equilibrium returning. Her crushed heart could look forward to getting some shape back soon.

"Great." He picked up the champagne bottle and pulled at the foil top. "I have some wine glasses in here somewhere. I keep essentials in the stink-free zone for when I have time to eat at home."

Amber stood and wandered apparently aimlessly toward her target. "What a lovely room. Is this the closet behind here? It's huge. You should see the size of mine." She peeked back at him. He'd retrieved the glasses from his dresser and had the foil cap off the bottle.

"I lived around the corner from you on Beacon Hill when I first moved to Boston," Lance said. "Those old apartments have closets too small for hangers."

"No kidding. I'm lucky if I get two blouses in mine." She patted the door and faked demure hesitation. "May I peek? Out of pure envy?"

"Help yourself." He untwisted the wire cage on the cork. She had to work fast. The door opened easily and revealed the dense row of dark suits, probably representing more money than she made in a year. "What luxury, to have all your clothes in one place." She moved quickly to one side and studied a painting on the wall, a jumble of lines and fragmented images.

"I've been admiring this print. It's so—" Her brain searched for a word. Art criticism was not her strong point. "—involving."

"You could say that." He gave a short laugh. "Sarah's father gave it to me. He's an art collector, among other things."

"How nice. Is this a little boat, right here?" She pointed to a vaguely boat-shaped splotch in the corner of the painting nearest the closet, hoping he'd come over and look.

He did. He stood right next to her, craning his neck toward the picture, angling his body away toward the closet while he worked the wire cage off. Amber braced herself. Victory was at hand. "Yes, I think—whoa," he muttered suddenly. "This cork has quite a pull to it. I should have—"

The cork shot out with a tremendous bang, and ricocheted off the ceiling. Champagne exploded out of the bottle in a huge wet wave of glorious bubbly destruction, defying gravity in a rocketing trip up and out into the air, then landed with a sodden splat...everywhere.

Amber gaped, too astonished at the incredible power of the blast to do more. She'd bull's-eye-hit her targets beyond her wildest hopes. Even the ceiling was liberally spattered. A burst of victorious energy shot through her. Amazon Amber had done herself proud.

Lance stared along with her, first down at his soaked suit and tie, then at the closet full of damp, wino-scented wool. What must he be thinking? She wished she could crawl inside his mind, hear the battle for control over rage at the devastation. What would he have to pay to get this all dry-cleaned? What could he wear to work the next day? And on top of what happened to his car and apartment! Oh, what a cursed life he must lead!

"Lance, I'm so sorry. I can't imagine what happened. The bottle must have been shaken up at the shop. I handled it like fine china." Except when she did the dance of the seven banshees around her apartment, waving it over her head.

Lance blinked champagne out of his eyes and shrugged. "Guess we got a live one." He held up the bottle. "I'm more concerned about whether there's enough left to toast our future success than I am about the damage."

"You are?" Surely he was being polite. Men like Lance couldn't possibly brush off such a potential blow to their vanity, however temporary. He'd just carefully hidden his dismay. That had to be it.

He crossed the room and set the bottle down on

the table. "I hope you don't mind if I change into something dry."

If you have anything left. "No, I don't mind at—"

Amber froze. Lance had taken off his jacket and loosened his tie. He was going to undress right here? In front of her? She gave a panicked glance around, hoping to see a bathroom off his room where he intended to disappear. Nothing.

He began unbuttoning his shirt. "Sorry for the Chippendale routine, but frankly, I'd rather not go out there again until I have to." He began a smile and stopped unbuttoning when he saw what must be horror on her face. "I'm making you uncomfortable."

"No, no, of course not. I'll just turn around." Amber backed away, eyes fastened on the undershirt-covered torso that emerged from his soaked clothes. She only had to turn away. She only had to look somewhere else.

She could only stare, at the familiar chest and abdomen that emerged from the undershirt, at the powerful arms that tossed the clothes on a nearby chair. She'd been intimate with every square inch. She knew the taste of his skin, the rough, sexy feel of the coarse hair on his chest. He looked in even better shape than in college, not pumped and artificial, but muscles well-defined and perfectly proportioned. He turned away to his dresser and bent to the bottom drawer. His skin was naturally deep golden, his back smooth, the strong planes shifted as he stood again and—

He caught her frank stare and held it, his own gaze at first slightly amused, then questioning. Amber's breath tried to back up her trachea. Her brain vainly sent a barrage of messages to her eyes to look away. A new expression came over his face. Amber's breath came out in a tumbled rush. *The Look.* The look that had finally undone her in college. The look of a man who intended to drag his woman back to his cave and ravish her until she could no longer stand. Only Amber was, too conveniently, already in his cave. She shrank back slightly, as if trying to resist the pull he exerted, electric shivers skittering through her body.

He broke the eye contact and glanced down at the pair of jeans he'd extracted from the drawer as if he had no idea how they got into his hands. Amber's stomach contracted in horror. Was he planning to take his pants off right here? After what had just passed between them?

He threw the jeans over his shoulder and strode to the door. "Back in a minute."

Amber sank onto the bed, still staring at the door he'd closed behind him. A breathless warmth had invaded her body and rendered her joints unable to support her. She put her hand to her forehead. Maybe she was coming down with something. Maybe inhaling garlic powder brought on some deadly illness that affected her brain. Wasn't she here to do *him* damage? *She* shouldn't be feeling shattered.

Amber jumped up. She had to get out of here. Now, before it was too late. His charm, she could handle; his physical presence, she could handle. But when it came to The Look, she had just proved herself as lamblike and vulnerable as in college. She moved to the bed and bundled up her drawings. Maybe she could escape while he was still out of the room.

Lance came back in, chest still bare, jeans hugging his lean shape in a way that made Amber afraid she'd break out in stress hives. "Sorry about that."

Amber managed a response that sounded like "Ohsaright." *Pull yourself together, woman. You're ten years older and wiser.*

He went back to the dresser and pulled on a clean T-shirt, then bent again to rummage in another drawer. With his Greek-god build somewhat covered, Amber's trachea gave up its boycott; air began circulating a bit more normally through her system. Her panic receded. Downgrade "red alert" to "caution." She might not be quite back to warrior status, but as long as he kept his clothes on, she'd manage until she could regain her emotional footing.

"That's better." Lance turned and pulled on a sweater. Amber swallowed hard. Her somewhat strengthened joints turned watery again. Ivory fisherman's sweater. She'd bought the yarn direct from Scotland ten years ago, knit the intricate cable pattern on nights when they weren't together and succeeded in surprising Lance for his birthday in February. He'd been so touched, so pleased, so tender and sincere in his compliments and gratitude. She'd never have expected him to keep it all these years.

"Remember this sweater?" He ran his hands over the wool. "It's still one of my favorites."

"Hmm...yeah." Amber cursed him under her breath. How the hell could she regain her emotional footing when he kept the ground shifting like that?

"Now for the champagne and that toast to our partnership." He poured out what remained in the bottle and deposited a glass in her hands, lifting his own in salute. "I'm glad you came here tonight. I'm thrilled with what you've done so far and have every expectation of future success. And—" he came too close and clinked his glass gently to hers "—I'm glad to know you again, Amber. Here's to us and the future of BrainToys." His voice had gotten lower, soft and husky.

Amber lifted her glass. The bubbles churning crazily in the gold liquid had nothing on the crazy churning in her brain. She sipped the cool wine carefully and raised her head to find Lance still standing too close, hypnotic blue eyes watching her in an intent, purposeful way that made the bubbles in her brain erase any further hope of coherent thought. *He was going to kiss her.*

"A.J." The room blurred into a picture of his face bending down toward her. Her senses dwindled to the sudden, gentle pressure of his mouth on hers. *This can't be happening.* She closed her eyes, lost in the exhilarating familiarity of the moment. He felt the same; he tasted the same; the memories flooded back in a sensual assault on her control. She responded simply because she was incapable of doing otherwise.

He ended the kiss and looked down at her, his breathing uneven, his eyes showing equal measures of desire and uncertainty. Then, in their mesmerizing blue depths, came a flicker of smug satisfaction.

Amber recoiled. What had she just done? What happened to reassigning power back to herself? Had she unwittingly set the scene for another seduction plot when she booby-trapped his apartment?

He opened his mouth to speak. Amber braced herself. He was about to tell her she could expect her design fee to be paid with sexual favors. *How about a hay-roll for payroll?... Care to examine my antique sheet collection?... Like a crash course in Lance polishing?*

"I apologize. That was way out of line." The smug look had been replaced. He appeared concerned and off balance. "Rest assured it won't happen again."

Amber nodded mutely. She hadn't expected contrition. Something that would have felt like disappointment had she given it any notice sank like a boulder into her stomach.

"Though I was just thinking..."

Amber's eyes widened. The unacknowledged weight in her stomach rose slightly.

He smiled a trifle sheepishly. "It's a good thing we both had the spicy garlic chicken."

6

"GOOD NIGHT, AMBER." Lance kept his lips stretched in a smile until the elevator doors slid shut to hide A.J.'s stony face. His smile sagged. *What the hell had he been thinking to kiss her like that?* He leaned forward and thumped his head against the hard metal doors. He hadn't been thinking; that was the whole problem. He'd just been feeling, from the moment she arrived in his hallway, cheeks flushed, eyes brilliant, ill-fated champagne clutched in her hand.

They'd talked almost immediately about things that mattered. He'd gone on and on about BrainToys, as if he really intended to go through with the start-up. He'd talked disparagingly about his career at Tucker and Company. Meetings, meetings and more meetings. What kind of strange spell did this woman cast over him? He loved meetings. The tenser, the more overcrowded, the hotter the room and the tempers, the better. In those situations the power and fire and skill that were Lance Edwards III shone brightest.

So what was it about sitting at a card table, eating sinus-clearing chicken with someone he hadn't laid eyes on in a decade that made his whole life feel like a bad play, with a cast of stuffed shirts?

Lance whirled around and dragged moodily down

the hall and through his stinking apartment to his bedroom. He needed to talk to someone. He pushed into the damp closet and retrieved Rex from his hiding place. Bad enough inviting A.J. over when his place smelled like a swamp; a cardboard pet would make him seem like a complete alien.

He set Rex back up in his new corner and frowned. The shower of champagne had puckered and marred the dog's glossy finish. A single drip still hesitated above his lolling tongue, as if waiting for him to lick it up.

"What am I going to do about this woman?" Lance sank on the bed and looked down at Rex. "Tonight I planned to show her what a nice, trustworthy guy I am. Instead, I lure her into my bedroom under what she's got to believe now were false pretenses. Strike one. Then, like a bumbling idiot, I proceed to order dish number twenty-five instead of twenty-six, the one food guaranteed to remind her what a fake she thinks I am. Strike two. Pursuant to which, I act like some lowlife who tries to get into a woman's pants before he knows her last name. Strike three, and I am outta there. She has to think I planned the whole evening to seduce her."

Any satisfaction he'd gotten from her response to his kiss had disappeared into a quicksand of agony the minute he realized what she must be thinking. He doubted his apology had done much to change her low opinion of him.

Lance sank his forehead onto his hand and shook his head. The drawings had been a bad start. Seeing his dreams come true on paper had transported him back to his early twenties, when he'd been so sure he'd break out of the Edwards mold and follow his heart. Talking to A.J. had been worse: a reminder of what his life lacked. But the damn spicy garlic had been the clincher. The pungent aroma evoked so many memories. It was a miracle he hadn't attacked her the second he smelled it.

He gave a moan of frustration. Kissing A.J. ranked about as far away from the crude idea of attacking a woman as he did from being in her good graces. There had only been one thing on his mind when he held her, and it wasn't getting her into bed. The tantalizing, perfect way their lips fit together, the sweet taste of her mouth, the thrilling, terrifying sensation had begun something that could easily swallow him whole—the kiss had been so much like their first, he'd been startled when he pulled back. Instead of A.J.'s shy, surprised pleasure, he saw Amber Jade, whose expression screamed only, "Dial 911, the jerk is at it again."

Lance raised his head. He might be a lot of things, but a jerk wasn't one of them. That much he still had to prove to her. Hauling out the sweater she made him had scored a minuscule point, judging by the pleased surprise in her eyes, but minuscule wasn't nearly enough.

He jumped to his feet. *Rule six: when everything seems hopeless, don't look for a way out—look for a solution.*

The phone rang. He strode over to answer it, his nerves suddenly alive. For some reason, he knew the call was from A.J.

"It's your Saaarah-bear." She giggled.

Sick disappointment weighted his head and stomach. Sarah. Tipsy by the sound of it.

"Hi, Sarah." He heard his flat voice as if it belonged to someone else. Five years and she suddenly seemed a stranger.

"Chris got another promotion! We're all going to Top of the Hub to celebrate." A male voice boomed in the background; she squealed and giggled. "Chris, stop it! Lance, sweetie, we'll be at the bar in a half-hour. Look for us, okaaay?"

The breathless singsong voice he used to find seductive grated on his nerves. Seeing that crowd after his evening with A.J., however disastrously the dinner had ended, would be like following a fine French meal with vending-machine candy bars.

"I think I'll stay in tonight."

"Oh, pooh." He could hear the infamous S. Tucker pout beginning in her voice. "Since when did you become such an old—" Her voice faded off into more giggles as someone apparently grabbed the phone from her hands.

"Stay where you are—she's mine tonight." A growl followed Chris's yell, then another round of squealing. Lance hung up. Speaking of jerks, his college roommate had the title all sewn up.

He bent his head forward and let it hang, shoulders tight and aching. He'd spent the evening feeling connected to someone. For the first time in ten years, he'd talked about what he wanted, what he felt, and someone had listened, and understood. Whenever he tried to voice his fears to Sarah, she seemed to develop a hearing problem. Sarah didn't want troubles. Sarah wanted success.

"What's going on, Rex? How can this much of my life have changed in one month?" He turned to his cardboard confidant. The champagne had dissolved the glue holding Rex to his backing. The upper half of his head had peeled away, and hung down in a dismal droop. Lance walked over and stood looking down at him, hands on his hips.

The answer rose up from his subconscious and smacked him between the eyes. Nothing had changed. He was just coming alive. Like Rex, the two-dimensional picture of life he'd pasted over his true self had started to peel away. For the second time, A.J. had shown him who he really was, and what he really wanted.

Lance passed his hands over his face, suddenly exhausted. Enough earth-shaking revelations for one evening. Too much to take in all at once. *Rule seven: when you see a possible solution, don't rush to implement it. Check all angles and ease into the change slowly.* He couldn't trash a five-year relationship based on the bad feeling from a couple of evenings. The next few weeks would tell whether he and Sarah were meant to be together.

As for A.J., he'd planned all along to regain her trust and explain his true motivation for pursuing her in college. Even with old feelings reawakened tonight, that tack could still go along on course. He'd start with small changes, let some time go by and see how the world looked through this new emotional filter. Maybe he'd even give his friend Randy a call, send him Amber's designs and his own sketches to see how they flew.

He bent to pat Rex's damp paper back, thinking of his childhood imaginary pet, Lucky. "Rex, old pal, I think it might finally be time to get a real dog."

AMBER CHECKED her makeup in the bathroom mirror. She was due for Saturday brunch with Sarah in a half hour and she wanted to look cool and elegant. What better way to appear innocent when dropping a mega-ton bomb? She attempted a cool and elegant smile, which changed rapidly to a grimace. Maybe she'd settle for looking decent.

She climbed on the bathtub rim and tried to catch a full-length view of her pants and cotton sweater. Her grimace changed to a scowl. Okay, so in spite of her total transformation since college, she still didn't rank as a clotheshorse. Her lunch date would doubtless show up in pearls and unwrinkled linen. Amber sighed. Maybe Sarah could take her shopping....

She jumped off the tub and headed out the door. Shopping? What had gotten into her? She wasn't out to snare an image. Her appearance suited her fine. Endless worried primping was for women on the man trail, a road Amber decidedly did not care to travel. One kiss by a certain odious con artist had been plenty to remind her of that fact. One long, burning, mind-blowing—

She snatched her purse from her bed and yanked on her jacket. She'd been telling herself for three days *not* to think about that kiss anymore. When would she listen? Thank goodness Lance hadn't contacted her in the meantime. He must be waiting for her next move. Amber smirked. Consider it made this morning.

Wanda's knock sounded at her front door. Amber grabbed a package of chocolate sandwich cookies wrapped in plain brown paper off the hallway table and opened the door.

"Whew, I caught you in," Wanda panted.

"Jerry's out for a few minutes so I ran up to get the goods."

"Here's the stuff." Amber thrust the package into Wanda's outstretched hands. "What's on the menu today?"

"Oat-flake soup for lunch." Wanda made a desperate face. "Brown rice balls with *nituke* vegetables for dinner. Dandelion coffee this morning. Honestly, Amber, you're saving my life. At least the kids can get decent junk at school. Keep a tab—I'll pay you at the end of the month."

"No problem." Amber zipped up her jacket.

"You're really going through with this?" Wanda leaned her plump form against the doorjamb and patted her chest to calm her breathing.

"Of course." Amber looked at her friend in surprise. "Why on earth should I change my mind?"

"I don't know, Amber. Meddling in someone's relationship..."

"Meddling?" Amber bristled. They'd agreed on this plan. Amazon Amber depended on Wanda's support. "I'm doing Sarah a favor. She wanted to have lunch with me anyway. I'll just casually let slip that her boyfriend is a philandering monster who is starting a business behind her back."

"Uh-huh."

Amber scrutinized her friend closely, apprehension churning through her body. She didn't care for that skeptical I-see-something-you-don't look Wanda wore. "Do I sense a sudden lack of enthusiasm for this revenge plot? What happened to you?"

"What happened is that I saw your face when you came home from dinner in his bedroom on Wednesday. All the rage and bluster in the universe couldn't cover the stars in your eyes."

"Stars? Are you out of your mind?" Amber's voice rose to a sputtering shriek. "The guy is a complete—"

"I've heard the party line, Amber. But if you ask me, half your wild-tigress fury that night was directed at yourself, for wanting to go back and finish what he started."

Amber's mouth couldn't possibly open any wider. She heard herself making little gasping sounds of female outrage. The William Shakespeare line floated through her brain: *"The lady doth protest too much, methinks."*

Amber shut her mouth and told Billy S. where to go. "After everything I—"

"On top of that, all of a sudden you're awfully anxious to break him up with his girlfriend. See what I mean?"

Amber planted her hands on her hips, prepared to blast her friend out of the apartment with a few well-chosen words. Wanda backed away, hands held up. "Oh, no. Save your fangs for Mr. Wonderful. I wouldn't be a good friend if I didn't keep you up-to-date on the Wanda Instinct."

Amber glared at her. "Enjoy your cookies."

"Be careful, Amber. I believe you think you're doing the right thing. I just don't want to see you get hurt over this guy again." Wanda walked down the hall, tenderly cradling her package, and disappeared through the stair door.

Amber listened for Wanda's footsteps going down, then yanked her apartment door shut and followed on the stairs; she had too much energy to stand still in an elevator. How could Wanda possibly think the kiss meant anything to her?

She jumped down the last two steps and thumped onto the landing of the second floor. Okay, so the kiss had been nice. Okay, really nice. Big deal. A kiss was a kiss was a kiss. She could completely separate the physical enjoyment from the person doing the kissing. Just because you loved getting your scalp massaged by your hairdresser didn't mean you wanted anything more lasting than a hair wash. Lance was attractive, no question. But deep down she had no feelings for him but those that would earn her a ticket straight to hell.

Amber banged through her building's front door and struck out on Cambridge Street toward Quincy Market. The warming April air and her energetic walk gradually cooled her anger and lifted her spirits. Wanda had been trying to protect her. She didn't understand that Amber was in no danger of falling for Lance again.

By the time she reached Houlihan's Restaurant opposite Faneuil Hall and spotted Sarah, Amber had managed to pull out a cheerful mood.

"Hello!" Sarah's sweet smile was warm. "We're lucky to have beat the tourist crowd. I was worried. Jack here has a lovely table for us. Jaaack?" The eager-looking host bounded right over. "We're ready, Jack. My friend has arrived."

"Yes, ma'am. This way."

Amber followed in Sarah's wake, wondering if queens from around the world came to her for coaching. Sarah sat and beamed at Jack, who assured her, all but drooling, that their waiter would be right over.

Amber slid into the seat opposite, convinced she'd become invisible.

"I'm glad we're getting the chance to know each other. Lance is very closemouthed about you." Sarah took off her jacket and smoothed her linen top. "He must have a crush on you."

Amber's water glass mysteriously discharged half its contents onto the table. "Oh. Well. No." She mopped at the spill. "I doubt—"

Sarah laid her hand on Amber's arm. "I'm teasing, honey. Lance and I have no jealousy between us. We've known each other so long and are *so* sure."

For an instant before the serene smile swept again across Sarah's face, the lovely features seemed to harden; the hand on Amber's arm felt like a claw. Just for an instant.

Amber shook off the impression. Poor Sarah. She'd be heartbroken when Amber told her what kind of man Lance really was. Amber knew all too well how it felt to think you knew someone inside out and then find your world turned upside down.

"Now." Sarah patted her arm. "We'll order and then get down to chatting. I'm absolutely starved for something greasy and fattening, aren't you?" She picked up her menu.

Amber nodded and studied the menu distractedly, emotions bouncing off each other like little bumper cars. In order to save her own sanity, she had to see justice done. In order to expose Lance and rescue Sarah, she had to kill Sarah's dreams of happily-ever-after. Pretty heavy stuff for someone who avoided any relationship more complicated than a quick good-night at the door.

The waiter arrived to take their order.

"Thank goodness you're here." Sarah sent him a dazzling view of her perfect teeth. "We're practically at death's door. Amber, you first."

"I'll have...cream-of-broccoli soup, and a medium-rare cheeseburger with fries."

"Oh, does that sound good! You'll enjoy that." Sarah beamed at Amber and addressed the waiter. "I'll have a dinner salad with a squeeze of lemon, and an iced tea."

Amber sucked in her breath. What happened to greasy and fattening? The bare beginnings of antagonism scratched at her friendly intentions. Nothing made her feel more like A. J. Kszyckniwicz than sitting down to lunch with a smug bunny rabbit. Sarah had pulled the ultimate female betrayal.

The antagonism scratched harder as Sarah led the conversation through a wide range of pleasant chitchat topics. Apparently nothing went on in Boston, politically, culturally or socially that Sarah Tucker didn't know everything about. And apparently Sarah Tucker couldn't help experiencing tremendous surprise when Amber hadn't heard any single piece of this terribly vital information. Amber had to hand it to her; the ugly game of one-upmanship had never had such a lovely coating. The idea of bursting Sarah's bubble became a trifle more palatable.

"Now, Amber, you must tell me what Lance was like in college."

Amber mentally gathered her forces. Her turn. She instructed her features not to appear too eager. "Sarah, I didn't just bump into Lance that day you saw us at lunch—he invited me."

"Oh?" One slightly quirked eyebrow formed the extent of Sarah's reaction. Amber might as well have told her she had spinach in her teeth. The scratching antagonism intensified.

"He hired me to do graphic design for a new company he's starting, producing children's toys." She waited, trying not to look smug. That information would certainly get a rise.

"Ah." Sarah pushed the last bite of lettuce onto her fork and chewed daintily. "Children's toys. I see. What made you decide to impart this little tidbit?"

Amber leaned forward. By now, she relished dropping the next bombshell. No normal woman could possibly hear her beloved had wandered and react as if her manicure had just been postponed. "Because the other night something happened that I'd want to know if I were you."

"Mmm?" Sarah clasped her hands under her chin and regarded Amber calmly. Amber had to suppress the urge to smack her.

"Lance invited me to have dinner at his apartment, ostensibly to discuss business matters." A blush crept up Amber's face. She gritted her teeth. So much for cool and elegant. "After dinner—"

"Don't tell me, let me guess." Only Sarah's lips moved, still curved in an unconcerned half-smile. Her voice had lowered to a gentle purr. "You were supposed to be dessert."

Amber stared across the table, utterly dumbfounded. What was with this chick? She'd make an ice princess shiver. Didn't she care that the love of her life had been licking lips other than hers?

The waiter appeared at their table and grinned foolishly at Sarah. "Would you ladies care for dessert?"

"Just more tea, please." Sarah sparkled at him,

then returned her placid gaze to Amber. "I hate to disappoint you, but you are undoubtedly not the first, and you undoubtedly won't be the last. What Lance does on his own time is not my business, nor is what I do on mine his. As for his toy company, do you have any concrete proof other than his word?"

The doubt had been skillfully planted. Panic welled up in Amber's stomach. No. He couldn't be lying about that, too. BrainToys meant so much to him.

The waiter brought a full glass of iced tea and removed Sarah's plate. Sarah took a tiny sip and set the glass on the table in front of her. She leaned back, idly winding her pearls around a long slender finger.

"When my father retires, Lance stands to inherit one of the largest consulting firms in the country. Do you really think he'd throw that all away to make wetsy dolls and toy trucks?" Her sweet laughter rolled across the table in a sickening wave. "If you ask me, it was an elaborate setup to get you in bed. Believe me, Lance can be very creative. Chris told me in college, Lance convinced some fat girl he was in love with her, then he— Oh!"

Sarah stared down in disbelief at the iced tea spreading its brown stain over the dry-clean-only perfection of her linen ensemble. Amber removed her hands from under the table's edge, and jumped up, fierce satisfaction flooding her. One tiny jerk had done the trick.

"Sarah, how clumsy of me. I was reaching for my purse. Here, let me help." She picked up a napkin, sodden from the spilled liquid, and dabbed at Sarah's outfit.

"I think you've done quite enough." Sarah

snatched the wet napkin away from Amber's hand. "Sit down."

Amber ignored the tense shaking of her limbs and prayed she could pull the rest of this off. She drifted back to her seat and sat as gracefully as she could, curving her lips in a sweetly concerned smile. "I'd be happy to pay for any damage."

"To hell with the blouse." Sarah threw the napkin on the table, where it landed with a soggy splash. "I've got news for you, missy."

"Oh?" Amber quirked her eyebrow slightly.

"I know what game you're playing here. You can't pull one over on Sarah Tucker."

"Ah." Amber rested her chin on her clasped hands and gave a tiny smooth nod. "And when did you decide to impart this little tidbit?"

Sarah stood up, her face an unbecoming shade of red. "Lance and I have our whole lives worked out together. If you think you can cause trouble between us, you are sorely mistaken, is that understood?"

Amber bestowed her sweetest smile. "Mmm."

Sarah yanked up her belongings and stalked out of the restaurant, trailed by a swarm of concerned male wait staff proffering towels. Amber slumped back in her seat, drained by the cost of her victory.

She let her head fall back and contemplated the ceiling, frustration building. This was supposed to be *her* game, not his. BrainToys couldn't be just a ploy. She couldn't have been that much of an idiot again. But what proof did she have that Lance was serious? He'd mumbled something about a prototype company in California and a friend at J.C.S. Marketing, but proof? No.

Amber flung down a too large bill and fled the

suffocating restaurant for the cool outside air to ease the steam pressure building between her ears. Monday morning she'd call J.C.S. Marketing and ask to speak to the contact Lance had mentioned, Randy Andrews. If he confirmed what Sarah seemed so sure of, that BrainToys amounted to nothing more than a cheap bid for Amber's seduction, she'd be paying Mr. Lance Edwards an early Monday visit.

And it wouldn't be pretty.

AMBER STORMED INTO Lance's reception area Monday morning. "Is Mr. Edwards in? I'm Amber Daniels."

Something of her savage mood must have shown on her face because the secretary jumped up and hurried into Lance's office. Amber paced across the thick carpet in quick, jerky steps, battling fury's bid for domination of her emotions. She had to remain controlled. No one took a shrieking female seriously. If she wanted to impress on Lance that his child-producing days on earth were numbered, she'd make more of an impact with deadly calm than hysteria.

First thing that morning, she'd called J.C.S. Marketing. Of course the receptionist had never heard of Randy Andrews. Granted, the guy sounded as if he'd never heard the world was round, either, but even the lowliest village idiot would know the names of the big guys he worked for, however far up the food chain they might be.

Amber pumped her fist in anticipated triumph. This time she had Lance where she wanted him. The penultimate nail in the plain pine box had been carefully placed. And Amber had brought her hammer.

"Mr. Edwards will see you now."

Amber swept by his secretary, giving Warrior Woman's best attempt at a haughty nod of thanks.

"Amber, what a nice surprise." Lance's smile died on his lips at the sight of her face. "Uh, what can I do for—?"

"I was in the neighborhood and thought I'd drop by. I have some free time coming up and I'm anxious to finish the marketing pieces for BrainToys before the rush hits again. I wondered when the prototype toys would be finished." She forced her voice to stay steady against the rage that wanted it to shake.

"Ah. The prototypes." He leaned back in his chair. "I called the company this morning. They should have them ready in a week or so."

"I see." She wanted to kick his potted plants over and grind the dirt into the Oriental rugs underneath them. How dare he sit there so calmly and spew garbage in her face? She already regretted her attempt to cause trouble between him and Sarah. They deserved each other. "And the contact you mentioned at J.C.S. Marketing? What did he think of the designs?"

"I met with Randy on Friday. He was very enthusiastic."

Like hell. "So he's agreed to market your line?"

"Yes."

"How nice." She itched to fling heavy office equipment at his head. Cold-blooded deception had always come easily to him. Why should she be surprised he hadn't changed? More to the point, why did she still let it hurt?

"Amber, you are shooting off enough hostility to scatter a pack of wolves." Lance looked at her in concern. "Is this about what happened in my bedroom?"

A gasp came clearly through the open door of his office. Lance swore and went over to shut it. "Great, now Darla thinks I'm a sex addict."

Amber's control became a thing of the past. "She wouldn't be far off."

Lance turned and faced her, surprise and disbelief on his face. "I apologized for Wednesday night. I assure you, I'm not in the habit of making passes at colleagues, even colleagues who are old girlfriends. But you're about six times angrier now than you were then. Either you're on a delayed fuse or something else has happened."

"You set me up. This whole thing has been one long attempt to lure me into your bed again, from the moment you bought me the drink at Daisy Buchanan's to last Wednesday's supposed climactic moment on your tasteful blue bedspread." Her brain hurled the accusations down to her tongue before she knew what she was saying. It felt great.

"Wait a second, Amber. That's unfair. I hired you for BrainToys because—"

"BrainToys, my rear end. You'd give up your mother's life before you'd give up this little empire you're in line for."

"Where the hell is this coming from?"

Amber drew herself up in an attempt to look taller than she was and took in a long breath. Sarah must have kept quiet about the lunch or he'd know exactly where her anger came from. "All I've seen is two sketches on a notepad, which you scribbled out at the restaurant. After that scene in your bedroom, I got suspicious, so I called J.C.S. Marketing myself.

They've never heard of Randy Andrews. Either you show me some proof right now, or I'm suing you." She held herself rigid, exuding maximum righteous indignation, hoping he didn't have a legal background. There might not be anything she could sue him for.

"I don't blame you for being angry." He crossed back to his desk and fumbled distractedly in a drawer. Amber's eyes narrowed; a vicious thrill pulsed through her veins. She had him now, a fat fish struggling in vain on her skillfully cast line. See him try to wiggle out of this one.

"I admit it..." He rummaged some more. "Where the hell is that card?"

"You admit it?" Amber's mouth dropped open. An unexpected weight of disappointment pulled on her shoulders. She hadn't realized until now how much a tiny rebellious part of her still wanted to believe in him.

"Aha! Here." He waved a business card triumphantly. "I admit BrainToys has been slow in starting. This is a huge step for me, as you rightly pointed out. I've been groomed for this job at Tucker and Company for ten years. I can't throw away a career overnight. But I am committed to BrainToys, Amber. You've spurred me on to realize the extent of that commitment. I'll always thank you for that."

Amber fought against confusion and her deflating anger. "What about Randy Andrews?"

"Randy left J.C.S. to start his own company last spring." Lance walked over and handed her the card. "Whoever answered the phone when you called must have been brand-new."

Amber stared at the card in her hands. Randy Andrews: Marketing Specialist. The address was impressive. Clearly he had done well for himself. She looked up at Lance in disbelief.

"I don't blame you for being suspicious. I can give you the name of the company in California if you want to check me out there, too. They're working on SpySam and the trivia game as we speak."

Amber shook her head and glared down at the card. Her anger balloon began reinflating. The stinking fish had jerked away from her line to swim away scot-free, leaving her empty-handed once more.

She determinedly mustered a new attack. There was one more baited hook in her boat. "I'm sorry I doubted you, Lance." She made herself smile up at him. "But you have to admit, the bedroom setup was pretty suspicious."

He nodded, a relieved grin curving his mouth. "Guilty of appearances, Your Honor. You should have seen me smacking my head on the wall after you left. I still can't believe I kissed you. I have no idea what came over me."

Amber smiled into his eyes and stepped forward until barely a foot separated them. Her gaze dropped to his lips. "Lance." She pitched her voice low, aiming for husky and alluring.

He took in a sharp breath. "Yes?"

"May I tell you something?"

"Of...course." He swallowed. Amber suppressed the insane desire to giggle. He sounded as if not enough blood could get to his brain.

"You know, I really had such a nice time..." She smiled wider, stepped closer.

"You did?" His eyes darkened; he bent toward her.

She parted her lips invitingly. "...with Sarah on Saturday."

Lance jerked back. "You saw Sarah?"

"Yes, we had lunch. We found sooo many things to talk about."

"Really?" He made a strangled noise in his throat. "Like what?"

Amber looked at her watch. "Oh, my gosh, would you look at the time. I really have got to run. Be sure and let me know when you have more work for me. See you later."

She sent a syrupy Sarah smile at his eye-popping panicked expression and let herself gracefully out, triumphant laughter bubbling up through her chest. Outside his office she leaped up for the imaginary game-winning three-pointer. Swish. Right through the basket.

She gave the astonished Darla a thumbs-up sign. At long last a win for the home team.

7

NOTHING WAS COMING OUT right today. Amber frowned at her computer screen. Her images were plebeian, color choices blah, fresh ideas worse than nonexistent. The Jacobson account provided good income for Daniels Design, but making funeral-home catalogs enticing required a good deal of effort and ingenuity. Amber didn't need another reminder of how much she enjoyed working on Lance's toys.

She clicked her computer mouse to rescue a white-satin-lined casket from an unattractive angle on the catalog page and placed it back into a worse one. She grimaced at her uncharacteristic ineptitude.

Something was definitely eating at her. If she were hung upside down by her toenails and subjected to extensive torture, she might confess that after she learned of Lance's genuine commitment to starting BrainToys, she was finding it a trifle harder to summon the necessary hatred to continue her plan. Worse, being able to cause a strong sensual reaction in him by simply lowering her voice and stepping close had produced a giddy thrill that still cavorted traitorously through her veins.

Amber leaned back in her chair and closed her eyes. For A. J. Kszyckniwicz to feel attractive and desirable, after spending ten years convinced she resembled a female Frankenstein…well, it was probably what caterpillars felt like when they'd served their cocoon time and emerged, bewinged and beautiful.

Amber opened her eyes and jerked forward to renew her computer battle with the stubborn casket. *Steady, woman. These feelings are fine as long as you keep them under control.* She needed to keep telling herself the reaction had nothing to do with Lance in particular. A.J. had simply started to shed her cocoon at last. Sexual confidence represented the final stage of her rebirth as Amber Jade.

As for hating Lance less, neither A.J. nor Amber Jade had yet gone beyond wanting to cause a few small but uncomfortable hiccups in his relationship. After seeing Sarah's true colors, Amber was starting to think an eternity with that woman would be nearly punishment enough for what Lance did in college. Going so far as to cause serious or permanent trouble between them would only work against such a perfect life sentence.

But in order to get those small hiccups started, she needed to find a way to follow up on her minor victory in his office this morning. To take the anxiety seedling she'd planted by mentioning lunch with Sarah, and nurture it into a towering redwood of neuroses.

If Sarah still hadn't told him about the date with Amber two days later, she probably wasn't going to. Amber would be willing to bet Lance hadn't made plans to rush to the phone and ask Sarah about their conversation either. As long as his beloved snake-woman hadn't come after him with fangs extended by now, he'd think himself safe and leave well enough alone.

So, to make his suffering complete, Amber must confess in total, abject, utterly insincere shame, that in a moment of petty weakness, she'd told Sarah about BrainToys and the kiss, in revenge for what she misinterpreted as a seduction plot last Wednesday in his bedroom. *And oh, my! She felt so so sorry now and saw the error of her ways and hoped so sincerely that no damage had been done yes indeed she did.*

Amber grinned a warrior grin. Knowing his secret had been leaked, Lance would be forced to tell Sarah the truth about BrainToys. They'd have a few gruesome battles, then settle back into their comfortable pairing of mutual distrust and betrayal, and live unhappily ever after. Amber couldn't have planned this part of her revenge better.

Only one hitch remained: where to enact this nearly tearful confession. To be able to manipulate her manly marionette with the greatest of ease, Amber required the perfect setting: quiet enough to set a serious mood and avoid the intrusion of crowds, but not so intimate as to suggest she hankered after a repeat of the bedroom scene. Dinner in an elegant restaurant or her apartment, ideal for distraction-free maneuvering, reeked of unnecessary coziness. There had to be something better.

"Knock, knock." Steve poked his head into Amber's office. "Happy Monday. I see you're enjoying a cheerful romp through Coffins-R-Us."

Amber swung her chair around, glad for the excuse to give her aching eyes a rest from the computer screen. She gave Steve a glare of mock severity. "Good afternoon, young man. I trust your morning off had no connection to the date with Ms. Perfect last night?"

"No such luck. I had a dentist appointment." He rolled his eyes. "As for last night, disaster struck again."

"Another sushi sobber?"

Steve dumped a pile of mail in her in basket. "This time it was me."

"You cried in your food?" Amber shook her head. "Really, Steve. Isn't that taking the sensitive-guy thing too far?"

"I didn't cry, but I wanted to. I invited her to my place for dinner. I figured what could be more romantic than a bottle of wine and Steve's famous meat loaf?"

"Nothing, I'm sure. What happened?"

"I forgot to set the oven timer, and got distracted by a *Lost in Space* rerun. The meat didn't look so bad. I figured it would be okay with enough ketchup." He gave an agonized sigh and swiped a hand through his blond curls. "There just isn't enough ketchup. Not in the entire country."

"Ouch." Amber winced. "Not a happy scene."

"I figured I'd make up for it with dessert. I'd made this fancy heart-shaped French-cream thing my mom used to make. To unmold it you just had to dip the pan in hot water for a few seconds. Only I got distracted."

"*Lost in Space* again?"

"Uh. No. She was leaning over to—" He shook his head. "Never mind. Anyway, I took the mold out of the hot water when I recovered, turned it over a plate and shook it, just like the directions said. Nothing happened at first, then the whole thing slid out with this horrible sucking sound, and made a giant gooey puddle all over the table."

"Oh, Steve." Amber wiped the tears of laughter out of her eyes. "Any decent woman would have fallen in love on the spot."

"She was not amused." He wrinkled his brow mournfully. "You wouldn't think a little thing like food could ruin a whole evening for someone, would you? Well, it can. I lived it." He slumped into a chair and began cleaning his glasses despondently.

Food could ruin someone's evening. A siren and flashing lights went off in Amber's brain. She straightened in her seat, spirits buoyed by her inspiration. The perfect means to keeping intimacy out of dinner at her apartment. She could accomplish all her goals at once.

Amber smacked her fist on her desk. "Steve, you're brilliant! You just solved my most pressing problem."

"Which is...?"

"Which is none of your business. Thanks for the mail. Now get out of here."

"Yes, boss." He hauled himself out of the chair and turned to leave, looking utterly dejected. "Glad I could do something right."

Amber's heart softened. Poor Steve—he deserved a Ms. Wonderful soon. "Ahem." She grinned at his miserable face. "The right one will come along, I promise. When you least—"

"I know, when I least expect it. Why does everyone say that? It's ridiculous."

Amber shrugged and waved him out, grimacing at the irony of her words. If not expecting Mr. Right were the best criteria for finding him, she should have met seven or eight perfect candidates by now. Luckily she had something better: the chance to show Mr. Wrong how decidedly wrong he'd been.

LANCE CHARGED UP the steps behind Lucky, grocery bag full of dog necessities bumping his leg, feeling like the kid who'd been given the candy store. After a lifetime of longing, he finally had the dog he wanted.

His new pet, part retriever, part collie, part mystery, bounded eagerly ahead of him, straining at his leash, as if he knew he was coming home. The decision to buy him had been settled the minute Lance stepped inside the animal shelter and saw those intelligent eyes pleading for rescue.

He'd originally hoped to find a Great Dane, from a devilish desire to see Sarah's face when the "nasty, drooling beast" greeted her, but who knew how long before he could sell his place and find the house of his dreams? Keeping a dog that size in his apartment would be cruel.

Lance opened his door and released the chain around Lucky's neck. "Welcome home, boy. Feel free to drool and shed as much as you want. We'll be sharing a bachelor pad by midnight."

He laughed at his own exhilarating words. After tonight he'd be a free man. A.J.'s visit to his office three days ago had put all doubts out of his mind.

Any woman who could make his heart and loins do jumping jacks just by standing close made taking a chance worth it. Though he dreaded hurting Sarah, spending any more of his life with her seemed like selling out.

He liked Sarah; he respected her. They had a lot in common on the surface. But the new and improved Lance Edwards extended way below that surface now. In the next few weeks he had a feeling he'd discover how much he wanted to share that deep part of himself with A.J. again.

Lance dropped on the couch and gave Lucky an energetic rubdown, sending the dog into wriggling ecstasy. He just had to get through this evening. Then his life would really begin. The call from Sarah this morning had not been entirely unexpected. Instead of going out for their regular Thursday-night restaurant date, she wanted to eat in. She had something to discuss.

Her warm, loving tone had tipped him off immediately. Discuss? No. She intended to grind his bones for her bread machine. Why, he wasn't sure, but he suspected the reason had something to do with her lunch with A.J. Sarah must have wormed something out of her about BrainToys. A.J. was a self-confessed lousy liar, and no match for a world-class manipulatrix.

Lance got Lucky food and water, shut him in the kitchen and took a quick shower, singing raucous songs from his rugby days. Still whistling, he pulled on a cotton shirt, keeping one eye on the clock. Six fifty-nine. Sarah would arrive in precisely one minute. Lance would miss a lot of things, but her insistence on a rigid schedule wasn't one of them. He paused outside the kitchen door and shook his head. Better keep Lucky locked away for now. One shock for his soon-to-be-ex at a time.

Sarah's key turned in the lock. "Helloooo, I'm heeeeere. Anybody home?" She sniffed suspiciously and breathed a sigh of relief. "Thank goodness the place doesn't smell anymore."

"Hi, Sarah. Come on in." He tried to quell his elation when he realized this was the last time he'd have to endure one of Sarah's scheduled "discussions." After five years, a little sadness and regret were in order.

He bent to peck the cold cheek she offered, hiding a wince at her cloying perfume. Sarah knew how he felt about that particular scent. The stuff could be used for biological warfare. She'd probably sprayed it extra thick tonight, like a knight putting on chain mail before a battle.

"I brought over some dinner from Balducci's." Sarah held up the bag. "They have such excellent *charcuterie.*"

Deli salads, Sarah. He took the food from her and set it on the dining table. "I've already set the table out here. Would you like a glass of wine?" He started to open the bottle, hoping he was acting even remotely normal. Sarah deserved a lot more than this eagerness to be rid of her. He'd be ashamed of himself if he weren't so busy being impatient.

"Mmm, thanks." She drifted to the center of the living room and picked up a crystal paperweight from the coffee table. "Laaance?"

"Yes?" He stifled a groan. He hadn't expected the

full frontal attack before dinner. She was definitely furious.

"I had lunch with an old friend of yours on Saturday." She peeked at him coyly over her shoulder.

Rule eight: when they've got you cornered, surprise them with honesty. "Yes, she mentioned it." Lance punctuated his casual statement with a loud pop of the cork.

"Oh, you've seen her since then?" Sarah turned gracefully. Her smile widened, became a gentle, radiant sunbeam.

He nodded and smiled back. Scratch furious. She was murderous. Maybe she'd even initiate the split and save him the trouble. "She's working for me, on a—"

"*Working* for you?" The confectionery voice would give a diabetic sugar shock. He wished she'd put down the paperweight; it could do serious damage to his skull.

He crossed over and held out a glass of wine which she ignored. Apparently she'd prefer his confession to an aperitif. He set the glass down on the coffee table and took a deep breath. "I wanted to find out if the project was feasible before I told you. I've decided to start my own company making children's toys." His voice came out choked—not with guilt, but with pride. When was the last time an Edwards had risked more than an illegal parking ticket?

Sarah tipped her head slowly to one side. Her eyes blinked carefully. Twice. "You mean you're not just trying to sleep with her?"

Lance nearly spit his wine back into the glass. "No, of course not."

"Because that I'd understand."

Lance stared. His giddy mood began to evaporate. She must have injected some mind-altering drug into the wine. He couldn't possibly have heard her correctly. "Excuse me?"

"I said, I'd understand." She put on her best maternally indulgent expression. "No one person can be everything to another. I respect you—we're good friends. Those things last a lot longer than passion. I haven't ever asked you any questions, and...you haven't asked me."

Lance set his glass down slowly, waiting for the flood of rage and jealousy people were supposed to feel when their lovers revealed they had been cheating. Instead, he felt a mild shock similar to the first time he saw Sarah without makeup. Still Sarah, but with all the imperfections revealed. Maybe he even knew subconsciously she'd been unfaithful, and chose to ignore the information. Now, with some kind of future with A.J. to hope for, he was almost past caring. Her little bombshell only made his own a lot easier to drop.

"Frankly it didn't occur to me to ask questions."

Her features hardened. "Don't play Saint Edwards with me. Whatever I've done, I'm sure you've done double."

"An eye for an eye?" He gave a humorless laugh. "The irony is I haven't been with anyone else."

Sarah's mouth fell open, then closed. An unattractive flush rose up to mottle her face. "Ha! You tried to put the make on Little Orphan Amber the other day."

A flash flood of rage threatened to mobilize

Lance's best right hook. Immediately he invoked the powerful control he relied on at work. He was not in the habit of socking people, however much they deserved it. "I kissed her once. End of story. I take it your confession would last a little longer."

"What I do when we're not together is my business." Sarah gulped the contents of her wine glass, and began to pace the room. Lance folded his arms and watched her. Whatever his feelings for Sarah had been, contempt was taking over now, and looked to be settling in for a long stay.

She whirled to face him. "What's more my business is that without consulting me, you decided to junk everything we planned for our lives together for some flash-in-the-pan venture."

"Maybe we should change the plan." He spoke softly, wanting her and her perfect teeth not only out of his life, but also out of his sight as soon as possible.

"Change you inheriting Tucker and Company?"

Lance smiled like the hero in an action movie would, right before he pulled the trigger. "I was thinking more about changing the part where we spend our lives together."

"I see." Sarah stepped back. Her blotchy face turned blotchier. She took a deep breath and held it.

Lance watched in fascination, feeling like a scientist studying an active volcano. Would she erupt? Or cut her losses and steam out the door? For the sake of whatever they'd been to each other, he hoped she'd bow out gracefully. Instinct, however, told him Sarah Tucker wouldn't take rejection lying down.

"You've changed, Lance. I suppose Ms. Amber

has you believing in true love.'' Sarah's shoulders twitched, belying her smooth tone. ''Can Santa Claus be far behind?''

He shrugged. ''At least I believe in something.''

''Such virtue. I am awed to be in your presence.'' Her eyes narrowed. ''But you'll have to kiss your little kiddie-company idea goodbye. Daddy will never allow it.''

Lance sighed wearily. So much for a mature, amicable parting. Hell had no fury like Sarah scorned. '''Daddy' doesn't have anything to say about it, Sarah.''

''The hell he—'' She caught herself, smoothed her contorted features with obvious effort and oozed toward him, barely blanketed hostility radiating from every peaches and cream pore. ''Well, Lance. This has been fun for you to spring on me tonight, I'm sure.''

He shook his head. ''No, Sarah, it hasn't. I don't want—''

She held up her hand to stop him. ''As it happens, I have a surprise for *you* now. Chris and I are lovers. I'm sure he'll be delighted to find me free.''

Lance couldn't help the twinge of pain. He should have known, but the news managed to hurt anyway. He widened his smile, mimicking her favorite trick, and began to move toward the kitchen. It was time to introduce Sarah to Lucky. ''I wish you every happiness. Of all the people I know on this good earth, Chris deserves you the most.''

The barb hit. Sarah swept past him and gathered up her groceries. ''I hate to spoil your fun, but I really must go. Or do you have any more surprises? It *is* your turn.''

''Only one.'' He opened the door to the kitchen. A rocket-propelled beast exploded through and welcomed Sarah with saliva-rich canine passion, covering the floor with spilled *charcuterie* in the process.

Lucky's performance was more than Lance could have hoped for. By the time Sarah had extricated herself and huffed out the door, he could barely control his laughter. He hugged the dog tightly, his coiled nerves relaxing into immense relief. ''You couldn't have done better, Lucky. I actually bought that vulture a diamond.''

He shuddered. The male population of Boston must have benefited considerably from his blind idiocy. She probably had a take-a-number machine by her bed. What a fool he'd been.

He changed into sweats and returned to the living room, where he poured himself a celebratory bourbon. He was surprised to feel no regret, except for the wasted, comatose years he'd spent being Sarah's perfect mate. He'd done the right thing tonight.

The phone rang; he slouched onto the sofa and reached over Lucky's head for the receiver.

''Lance, Amber Daniels.''

''Amber.'' At the sound of her voice, full understanding of the change in his situation hit him, sending heat through his body. A.J. was no longer off-limits. He sat up and put down his drink, picturing her holding the phone to her cheek. He could go about the business of seduction honestly. Not of her body yet, but of her mind. As much as he desired her physically, he'd wait until he knew exactly how she felt. He glanced at his suddenly tightened sweatpants. Although the delay might kill him. "I'm glad you called."

"Oh? Have there been any new developments?"

"You might say that." He grinned and winked at Lucky, who dropped down to invite play, then went dashing off down the hall. "I'm expecting models of SpySam and the trivia game next week. When can we meet?"

"I was going to offer my apartment for dinner. It's not as spacious as yours, but it does have the distinct advantage of not stinking. We can take our time over business."

Lance pushed to the edge of the sofa, adrenaline racing through his system. Dinner? At her place? He'd expect her to suggest Park Street Station after their last few encounters. A very interesting and, frankly, tantalizing development. "Sounds great. We'd better choose a date the week after next to be sure I can get the samples. I'll call the company again in the morning."

They arranged to meet at her apartment a week from Monday. Lance hung up the phone, practically winded by the frenetic pace of change in his life. How many short weeks ago had he sat in this very room trying to make himself propose to Sarah? Thank God he'd listened to his doubts. That same night he'd stumbled over A.J. again. She precipitated the chain of events that led to his current rebirth. She made this new high of being alive possible. She was his good-luck charm. He'd have to remember to tell her so. Maybe she'd even be pleased.

A low whining growl emanated from down the

hall. *Lucky.* Lance lunged off the sofa and barreled toward his bedroom, apprehensively going over a mental list of chewable valuables. He rounded the corner and stopped short. "Oh, Lucky."

His new pet sat on the carpet, blissfully wagging his tail, surrounded by the sodden chewed cardboard bits of what had once been Rex.

AMBER PUT A POT of bouillon on the stove and added aromatic vegetables to make a simmering liquid for the evening's main course: calf brains. Before that, she'd serve a nice bowlful of pasta with squid and anchovies. The combination would set the proper awkward tone for the evening, allowing her plenty of opportunity to keep Lance off balance while she sprung her news about the "slips" to Sarah.

She lowered the flame under the broth and danced into her bedroom to change, still savoring the fantasy. Poor Lance. She almost felt sorry for him. Imagine his dismay when he realized Sarah knew all about BrainToys and his little indiscretion in the bedroom. Ms. Tucker might have decided to remain silent until now, but Lance would have to bring the subjects up when he found out Sarah knew. In doing so, he faced certain sugarcoated torture.

She pulled out the red figure-hugging, near shameless dress she'd bought on an impulse over the weekend, and stepped into it. She hadn't bought the dress to impress Lance. Not exactly. Just to celebrate her mood and the changes in her life. If he responded appreciatively...okay, sexually...so much the better. After all, though he fared questionably on most aspects of humanity, biologically speaking, he definitely ranked as a man. And she was a woman, becoming more definite all the time.

She approved her reflection in the mirror, did a last check on the table and settled down with a magazine, determined to remain cool and composed. Roughly eight fidgety seconds later, she decided to see if frantic pacing could be done in a cool and composed manner.

After six turns back and forth in the room, the doorbell rang. A battalion of jitters swarmed through her body, making war on her resolve to waft unconcerned through the evening. She forced herself to appear calm and went to answer the door. As Lance came into view, the battalion became a massive raging army. Could he have gotten ten times better looking in the past week? Or was she merely going out of her mind?

Lance smiled and gave her and the red dress a brief once-over. He held out a bottle of wine, eyes warm and appreciative, the mischievous light strong in his gaze. "I brought the bottle this time, but I thought with our track record, I'd leave out the bubbles. It's white—I hope it goes with what you're serving for dinner."

"Perfect, come on in." Amber gestured inside, suppressing a giggle. When he saw dinner, he'd be wishing he'd brought a bottle of antacids instead. "Would you like a glass now?"

"Sounds great." He walked into the apartment behind her. She could sense his presence filling the room and, if her female radar wasn't malfunctioning, his eyes on her derrière. She pivoted quickly to catch him midinvestigation, expecting her condemning stare to freeze him into mumbling apologies.

Instead, he continued his calm inspection until his eyes wandered back up to hers. "That is a great dress. I've never seen you in anything like it." He put his hands to his hips, pushing back his jacket, and continued to stare appreciatively.

Amber spun back to the wine and mumbled something about spring fever, feeling sexy, feminine and extremely flustered all at once. *Hello, Amber? Isn't this the biology you bought the dress for? Lighten up.* She forced herself to defluster, opened the wine, and poured with a steady hand. This evening was her show. She picked up the glasses and turned to find him seated on the couch, digging packages out of his briefcase.

"I brought the models with me. They arrived Friday."

"I'm dying to see them." Amber carried the wine over and sat beside him, her curiosity genuinely piqued.

"Voilà, SpySam." He began unwrapping a small bundle. His expression was controlled, but his voice betrayed contagious excitement. Amber leaned toward him and peered into the paper.

SpySam emerged, a magnificently muscled superhero male, with dark hair, bronzed skin and not a stitch on his anatomically modified body.

"Hubba, hub-*ba.*" Amber quoted Wanda's favorite male-appreciation phrase. "Make sure you take him home with you tonight. I can't be responsible for my actions with a man like that in the house."

He sent her a brief surprised look and burst out

laughing. "I'm glad you approve. I may have to tone the physique down somewhat. Girls have suffered long enough over impossible body standards. I don't want to continue the trend with boys."

Amber nodded, amazed he would be sensitive to such a topic. Not as if he grew up with anything but ten-point-zero looks. She, however, wrote the book on that kind of suffering in her youth. "Good thought. I got a little carried away."

He grinned and raised an eyebrow. "Maybe that dress has made a wild woman out of you."

His low suggestive voice made Amber's body temperature soar. His flattery exhilarated her—no denying that. She'd certainly asked for it with her comment about SpySam. Something had made her a little reckless tonight. Flip of a coin whether the dress was the cause or merely a symptom.

She tried to shrug casually. "What else do you have for him?"

"Here comes the cool stuff." He ripped the paper off a black-belt martial-arts outfit, a dark suit complete with trench coat, and a jeans-and-sweater outfit. Then came a dazzling array of secret-agent gadgets disguised to look like ordinary objects. "There'll be a line of undercover disguises eventually. These gizmos are just models for photographing, but you get the idea of what they'll be like when the working ones are produced."

Amber picked the toys up one at a time. "These are really fantastic. Makes me want to get down on the floor and play right now."

"I won't touch that one except to say that red is definitely your color." He grinned at her. Amber fought to keep her face from matching her dress. She'd meant the comment innocently; she wasn't *that* reckless.

Lance unwrapped the final package from the set and held out a toy. "SpySam's son, B.J."

B.J? Amber glanced at him suspiciously, but his face showed no unusual reaction. Add paranoid to reckless. If C.J. and D.J. showed up in one of those bundles, then she'd wonder.

She took the little boy doll in her hand. He was about nine years old, still a child, but with a face full of determination and toughness that reflected his father's.

Lance touched the boy's head tenderly. "His mom was killed by some super-bad guy or other. We'll manufacture him someday so SpySam can dedicate himself to seeking revenge. B.J.'s a great kid—his dad takes good care of him. I want this close father-son relationship to be a big part of the marketing. The human aspect is what sets SpySam apart from your basic search-and-destroy superhero, what makes him more powerful, and more vulnerable."

Amber stared at the boyish features in her palm, inexplicably moved by what he represented. She turned to Lance, not bothering to hide what she felt about the toy. How could an amoral bottom-feeder come up with such a beautiful, touching idea like this?

He smiled gently. "Crazy, isn't it, how he gets you? I got all choked up when the models arrived. I'm glad you feel that way, too. It's important that whoever works with me doesn't view the project as just another way to make a buck."

Amber picked up her wine and took a healthy swallow. Who was responsible for turning her neat black and white world back into disorienting shades of gray? Maybe alcohol, instead of further muddling her head, would cancel the confusion out and bring her back to comforting odious reality. Something had to.

"Now, from the sublime to the ridiculous—the trivia game, which I am still not sure what to call, but which I've got to decide so we can move ahead." Lance opened a flat square bundle. A fairly standard board game emerged, with colored squares along a path from start to winner boxes. He then unwrapped a loathsome bulbous creature who fit into slots carved in a corner of the board. "Behold, the beast of slime. Every player gets a little colored bucket to move around the board. If he answers a question wrong, he has to put his bucket here." He indicated a notch in the monster's hideous wart-ridden face. "The monster's head will ooze a blob of green slime into it. If your bucket gets full, you lose automatically and can't continue."

Amber made a face. "I can see why you can't think of a name. The ones you and I came up with before wouldn't exactly make the game sound appealing."

"I don't want appealing—the name should be truly disgusting. Kids will go nuts for it and they won't realize they're learning. I've racked my brain, but my ideas are either too juvenile or not juvenile enough. The whole thing is driving me nuts."

"I'm sure something will come to you." She relinquished B.J. as Lance began rewrapping the models. "The toys will be really fun to work on, Lance."

He turned and smiled, a smile of genuine pleasure that lit his eyes in a heart-lurching manner. "Thanks, A.J. That means a lot to me."

Their eyes held for several endless seconds. Amber felt as if she were slowly dissolving under his gaze. For the first time since she'd met him again, there were no artificial barriers between them. Their open, honest communication came from the heart, as it had immediately when they started dating in college.

She blinked and looked down at her wine glass. *Good job, Amber, fall for his lines again.* The good Lance might giveth, but the good Lance surely knew how to taketh away, without a second thought for the consequences to anyone but himself. She couldn't forget what he'd done to her, and probably countless others. Like SpySam, she had to remain an agent for revenge.

She stood. "I'll go and get dinner ready."

"Anything I can do?"

"No, thanks." *You've done plenty already.* She gave her best Sarah-smile and ambled toward the kitchen, where the dinner of devastation awaited him.

8

"AMBER, THAT WAS a great meal." Lance pushed back from the table and smiled.

Amber sat opposite him, slumped in utter defeat. The dinner had been delicious. The squid was tender and crisp in its bread-crumb coating, salty and enticing with the rich, subtle flavor of anchovies and garlic. The brains had been supremely fresh, delicately flavored and were complemented perfectly by the brown-butter-and-caper sauce. Lance had exclaimed over every bite, praising her skill as a cook and her sophisticated menu planning. Not since Paris had he had a meal of such exquisite, unusual flavors. Had she ever thought of starting her own restaurant?

She'd held her head up gamely, absorbing the failure of the initial phase of her plan with as much tight-lipped dignity as she could muster. The close intimacy they'd achieved early in the evening had long since vanished under her slow burn. Something, *something* she planned had to work to her advantage. Admittedly, finding some measure of success against him had become an obsession.

"I'm so glad you enjoyed it. Not everyone can wax so poetic over squid and brains."

"Not everyone can make poetry out of squid and brains." He bowed gallantly and addressed an imaginary audience. "'Squid and Brains,' a sonnet by Amber Ja—" He jumped up and threw his napkin down on the table. "That's it!"

Amber eyed him warily. "What's it?"

"Squidbrain! The perfect name for the trivia monster game." He practically leaped down the length of the table and pulled her to her feet. "You, Amber Jade Daniels, are my Queen Midas—everything you touch turns to gold. If I could even begin to tell you the good you have brought into my life..." He stood there, holding her hands, his breath coming fast, his face alive with electric intensity.

At that moment Amber decided she had to hate him. With all her soul and as never before. His Queen Midas? After all her efforts to bring him doom? That did it. He was about to find out her "golden touch" could produce lead, too.

"Lance, I'm glad you think I've helped you. But I have to tell you..." She cast her eyes down, and willed her lower lip to pout out to the perfect degree.

"What is it?" He lifted her face with a gentle finger under her chin, his expression one of deep concern.

"At lunch with Sarah, I..." She trailed off, much as she was dying to let him have it. Make him think the words had to struggle to come out. "I let slip about BrainToys. I know you didn't want her to know yet. I just feel awful."

"It's okay, Amber. I had to tell her sooner or later."

What the hell did he mean it was okay? "There's more. I...I was angry about that scene in your bedroom, when you kissed me." She hurried over the last words. He stood too close for her to want to dwell on the picture. In a matter of inches, he could be kissing her again. "I told Sarah you made a pass at me." She dropped her head to hide her smug pleasure. *Take that, golden boy.*

He lifted her face again, this time with his hand cupping her chin and cheek. "Amber, it doesn't matter."

Amber's smug pleasure froze into apprehension. "It doesn't?"

He shook his head. She considered becoming hysterical and hurling leftover squid around the room. Something had gone seriously awry here. He should be registering panic, confusion, cold betrayal. Anything but warm, almost possessive intimacy. He should be stepping back, gesticulating, shouting at her, or speaking with low, icy rage. Anything but moving closer, grasping her shoulders, making her look at him.

"Sarah told me the week before last. We had a pretty nasty fight. I found out some things about her I'd begun to suspect, but you helped me see more clearly."

"Me," Amber mumbled. Sarah had stolen her thunder. Worse, an awful suspicion crowded into her brain as to where this little unwelcome speech of Lance's was leading. She had to get away from this deep-eyed eel who had so easily slithered away from punishment for his sins. Better still, get away from this planet altogether.

"The bottom line is, I broke up with her."

"Broke up with her." Amber gaped at him in horror. *Another* plan backfired! Could she have no power against this man? How could the gods smile so repeatedly on such a loathsome specimen?

"The truth is, Amber, I'd been thinking about ending the relationship for a while. Actually—" his voice dropped to a husky whisper "—since you came back into my life."

"Since I—" Amber bit her tongue. She had apparently lost the capacity to form her own phrases. Her mind screamed at him to stop talking. She knew what he was going to say next as if she were going to say the words herself. Why couldn't he stop looking at her so openly and earnestly? What happened to the arrogant sleazeball she'd seen in the bar that first night? He was so much easier to loathe.

"I hope we can spend more time together. Not just as business partners..."

Amber gritted her teeth. If he said "But as man and woman," she'd stomp on his foot.

He leaned down until his lips were just short of brushing her own. "But as man and woman."

Her foot raised for the promised stomp, and lowered ineffectually back down to the ground as his mouth moved onto hers. She meant to pull back, but his arms slid around her, he increased the pressure of his lips and Amber found her muscles completely unwilling to respond to anything but his kiss.

His touch was glorious, all fiery heat and passion, sinking into her bones and burning through her body until she went completely crazy with longing for him. All of him. In every way. Naked. Now.

He pulled back and traced the line of her lips with his finger. "I know a relationship could be complicated by us working together. I don't want to rush you into anything before you've had a chance to think about it.''

Amber nodded mechanically, still overwhelmed by the rush of emotion and her desperate, urgent need to drag him off to her bedroom. After one kiss. If he ever touched her more intimately, she'd probably drop to the floor and beg for it then and there. *Nice show of strength, Amazon.*

He smiled and kissed her once more, briefly. ''Thanks again for dinner. I'll call you soon.''

Amber showed him out, certain she'd turned into a zombie from *Night of the Living Dead,* cleaned up from dinner, and got ready for bed, not allowing herself to feel anything.

She lay down and drew up the covers, fists clenched, face tight with the effort to keep her emotions at bay. Three hours later, exhausted and near tears, she relaxed a tiny bit. Realization sprang immediately into her consciousness, as if waiting for the inevitable weakness.

She was in serious danger of falling for Lance Edwards. Again.

AMBER CLUTCHED her cotton bathrobe tightly around her and stared at the nearly completed list on her kitchen table. The first three items sported bold black check marks: ''Car,'' ''Condo'' and ''Wardrobe.'' She added a pencil line next to ''Gorgeous Girlfriend.'' Some victory. Instead of sending Lance to the Sing Sing of relationships for life, she'd helped liberate him to hunt once again. And lo and behold, she got to play the dainty doe nibbling grass in the clearing, already fixed in his sights.

Her pencil moved down to the last target on the list, "Successful Career," and tapped a few times. That one wouldn't be too difficult. Sarah's father would already be upset with Lance for dumping his little girl; he could probably be pushed further into rage that would carry over into the workplace. One well-chosen straw, and the camel would be making an emergency trip to the chiropractor.

Amber's pencil tapped harder. If Mr. Tucker got angry enough so that Lance's effortless rise through the Tucker empire appeared endangered, Lance might just realize how much he was risking. Amber would bet the farm the cowardly Edwards in him would win out in the end. BrainToys would end up once again in the faded-dreams file.

She dropped her pencil and scrubbed her fingers through her hair. Nice logic, all of it. But nothing covered the fact that she couldn't quite summon her usual level of eagerness to execute the master plan. Being around Lance stirred up so many old feelings that the entire project was becoming hazardous to her sanity.

For the past ten years when anyone kissed her, she'd been hard-pressed not to haul out sharp kitchen implements to defend herself. When Lance kissed her last night, she'd been engulfed in enough passion and longing to heat the city of Boston through four winters. She could go on claiming to herself A. J. Kszyckniwicz was just experiencing the final transition into the full glory of womanhood, but the fact could no longer be ignored: something about *this* man made him able to coax her deepest soul from its hiding place.

Amber jumped up from the table, dumped her breakfast dishes in the sink and fled to the bathroom for the comfort of her morning routine. The steaming water in the shower cascaded over her body, and she scrubbed mechanically, trying to ignore the sensual awareness and memories Lance had stirred. In spite of her best efforts, the picture she'd tried most to forget fought its way into her consciousness.

How could she not remember? The night they made love ten years ago had been one of the happiest and most fulfilling of her life. Lance's strength had been utterly controlled to sweet tenderness, his caresses tantalizing, seductive and supremely patient. When he'd urged her to cross the final barrier, his words had been soft, steady, cherishing. "Let me please you, A.J. Let me love you. Let me be the only one."

Amber let out a Warrior Woman roar and twisted the faucet off so hard she hurt her wrist. If she had any doubt about her continued lust for revenge, that particular memory just beat it to a pulp. The two-faced, shallow, lying bastard.

She dragged a towel over her body, practically taking off a layer of skin in the process. So he wanted to spend more time with her? How much more? Just until his relationship alarm went off? *I'm sorry, your time is up. Thank you for being you. Next.* Sarah hadn't even made the grade after five years.

Amber sped through the rest of her preparations, scooped up the latest junk-food delivery for Wanda and ran down the stairs. She'd need reinforcements for this last phase of the plan.

At her signal Wanda opened the door cautiously.

"Jerry's still here. He's working on our toilet right now," she whispered. "Little Rudy is our resident plumbing terrorist. Come on in, but be careful." She pulled Amber in and grabbed the package. "Mmm. What is it today?"

"Marshmallow Fluff and those pink-frosted cake-ball things. I don't know how you can eat that stuff. I get a sugar buzz just holding the package."

"I thank you, my stomach thanks you, my marriage thanks you." Wanda took the wrapped bundle into the kitchen and stuffed it away in a high cupboard. "So what's on your mind? Not my sweet-tooth fix by the look of it."

Amber grinned wryly. Wanda could read her like a book. Unfortunately that often included back chapters Amber wanted to keep hidden. This morning she'd have to be extra careful. "I need your help."

"Part of your scheme, eh? How did dinner go last night?"

Amber told her, leaving out the kiss and her reaction to the toys. Some things had to remain off-limits.

"It's eerie how everything keeps blowing up in your face." Wanda gave her a thoughtful look. "Maybe you're being sent a message—time to pack it in."

"With only one item left to go?" Amber bristled. She needed Wanda's encouragement, not her common sense. "Not on your life. I'll see this through if I go completely off my rocker in the process."

"He kissed you again, didn't he?"

"No!" Amber stiffened. She sounded like a

screech owl. Wanda wouldn't be fooled for a second. "No, of course not. Nothing like—"

"I thought he did." Wanda folded her arms across her chest and gave Amber her best schoolmarm frown. Finally she sighed. "Okay, what are you planning to do next?"

Amber hugged her friend, relieved to have support, however lukewarm. "Lunch with me sometime this week at the Tucker and Company building. That's all I ask."

Wanda's eyebrows shot up. "Lunch? What am I missing?"

"Lunch at a table next to Mr. Tucker, who won't be able to help overhearing our conversation. We'll have fascinating things to say, trust me. When Lance notices things are getting rough at work, he'll ditch BrainToys in a flash to save his precious skin."

Wanda shook her head and laid a friendly hand on Amber's shoulder. "I wish you'd quit while you're behind."

"No." Amazon Amber had set out to destroy the enemy and she would finish. "I'm not quitting."

"Okay, it's your funeral." Wanda raised her hands in surrender. "I'll help because I said I would, but—"

"Wanda." Jerry walked into the kitchen, wearing Rudy and a look of exasperation. "Can you keep this young primate away from the bathroom?" He pried the youngster's hands off his leg.

"Are you helping Daddy too much?" Wanda lifted the child away.

Rudy pouted and shook his head. "Daddy close door. I want to watch."

"Ah. Top secret repairs?" Wanda smiled at Jerry, rocking Rudy on her hip. Suddenly she froze. "*What* is that on your upper lip?"

Jerry's eyes widened as far as hers had narrowed. He wiped desperately at his mouth and missed the brown smudge completely.

"It looks like *chocolate.*" Wanda put Rudy down and advanced on her husband. Her hand shot out; she lifted a crumb off and examined it. "Chocolate *cake.* Why, you sneaky little—"

"Excuse me, I think I hear destiny calling me." Amber let herself out of the apartment, glad for the chance to escape. Wanda's famed Instinct had gotten a little too close to concepts Amber wasn't in the mood to face.

Her friend's shrill voice cut through the heavy apartment door. Amber giggled. Jerry was really in for it. Maybe someday she'd tell him about the hidden packages, just to even the score.

She ran down the stairs and out into the warm May air. In the meantime she had a score of her own to settle.

WANDA AND AMBER PRESSED close to the wall of the lobby restaurant at 125 High Street, home of Tucker and Company.

"There he is." Amber jerked her head at the suited figure moving briskly toward the restaurant entrance. She recognized Mr. Tucker immediately from a copy of the company's annual report. He wore impeccably fitting clothes on his round figure and a decided the-world-owes-me-big-time attitude. "The lone diner, just as his secretary let slip. Poor woman,

I had her completely confused. She had no idea what she let him in for."

Mr. Tucker nodded curtly to the hostess and strode over to a table off to one side. Amber pushed Wanda forward. "Let's go."

They approached the hostess and asked for the table next to him. Mr. Tucker gave them a brief glare as they were seated, and pulled his chair farther away.

Amber grinned at Wanda. First hurdle overcome. They were in target range. He'd soon be lost in his *Boston Globe* and double martini and forget they were there. Until they let him have it. She crossed her fingers. *Please let this work.*

They finished their meal as the waitress served Mr. Tucker his third martini. Amber winked at Wanda and nodded.

"So are you still dating that dishy guy? The one with all the dough?" Amber adopted a thick Boston accent and raised her voice. Mr. Tucker looked up and frowned, then snapped his paper up to cover his face.

"I don't know if you'd call it dating, exactly." Wanda picked up her cue immediately and spoke in a throaty, suggestive tone. "But we're certainly...getting together, if you know what I mean." They both laughed too loudly. The newspaper gave an irritated shake.

"I'll tell you, he is one talented hombre. That four-hour 'lunch break' the three of us spent together was the pinnacle of my experience." Amber sat back languorously. "And I have had a *lot* of experience."

The newspaper lowered slightly. Wanda opened

her eyes meaningfully and tipped her head slightly toward it. Amber smiled and nodded. They'd hooked their prey.

"Wasn't it awesome?" Wanda gave a wistful moan. "The guy never stops. He has some fancy girlfriend somewhere, too."

"No kidding! Lucky lady." Amber sighed loudly. "Think he uses the harness and chains on her?"

The newspaper fell to the table. Mr. Tucker grabbed his martini and took a huge gulp.

"Naw." Wanda stretched and yawned. "Ms. Fancypants probably wouldn't go for it."

"Well, you can keep Mr. Gere and Mr. Gibson." Amber leaned across the table as if wanting to keep her words confidential. Mr. Tucker leaned closer and took another gulp of liquor. "I'll take Mr. Edwards III any day."

The swallow of martini erupted in a fine spray across the table. Mr. Tucker leaped to his feet, face beet-red.

"I'm with you," Wanda said smoothly, "They don't call him 'the Lance' for nothing."

Mr. Tucker threw down a bill on the table and stalked out of the restaurant as if he were the leader of a posse.

Amber watched him go, heat flooding her face. Instead of the expected swell of triumph, a wave of shaky sickness curled up in her stomach as if it intended to remain there forever. They'd executed the plan that couldn't fail to perfection. Mr. Tucker would read Lance the riot act. The golden boy's days of no accountability were over. This was to be Amber's moment of supreme, exquisite victory. So why did she feel ugly and small? Why did she suddenly wish she could take back what just happened?

She put her hand to her churning stomach. Even if her plan worked, it had already backfired.

"Well, you got exactly what you asked for." Wanda patted her hand, not bothering to suppress an irritatingly smug smile. "By the look on your face, I'll spare you the I-told-you-so. Has it occurred to you yet that you're still in love with the guy?"

"What?" Amber recoiled as if Wanda had thrown a brick at her head. "In love with that...that..." Her brain went dry of suitably insulting epithets.

"Yeah, yeah, I've heard his nicknames before. But I've watched you through this whole thing. Right now you are operating under a seriously strong emotion, and it ain't hatred anymore."

"How could I be in love with someone capable of what he did to me?" Amber struggled to control her indignation, and struggled harder to avoid noticing Wanda's words struck a chord that rang suspiciously true.

"Love isn't always logical." Wanda shrugged. "Or I would have married the next Bill Gates. But tell me this. In college, after Chris told you about the bet, did you ever confront His Royal Weaselness snout to snout?"

Amber nodded. "His face said it all—guilty as charged."

"Did he ever come after you, try to talk to you?"

"I wouldn't listen." Amber pretended fascination with her napkin to avoid meeting Wanda's eyes. At the time, her hurt had blinded her to anything but the need to protect herself. In the retelling, it did sound as if she had cheated Lance out of a fair chance to explain. "Right before his graduation, he sent me a note asking me to meet him at Radcliffe Yard so he could explain everything."

"And?"

"And nothing. If I wanted to hear lies, I could turn on the government channel. He graduated, went off on his requisite European summer vacation, and I didn't hear from him again."

"So let me get this straight," Wanda said. "The version of this story you base all your venom on came from Chris, who even according to you makes Lance look like the second coming?"

"I guess so." The sick feeling grew in Amber's stomach.

"Give the guy a chance, Amber. Stop kidding yourself about how you feel about him and give him one little measly chance." Wanda looked at her watch. "End of lecture. I have to pick the kids up from school. Think about it, please?" She stuffed some bills into Amber's hand, gave her a hug and rushed out of the building, loose jacket flapping around her plump figure.

Amber sat in the near-deserted restaurant, feeling as if her world had been turned upside down, inside out and moved to another galaxy. Give the man who'd almost destroyed her a chance? A chance to what, start an honest, committed relationship or make a fool out of her again?

She blew out a breath, sending sandwich crumbs shooting off the table. She couldn't risk reliving that kind of heartbreak. Better just to end the whole ridiculous episode now. Lance would soon be out of her life anyway, when he dropped BrainToys to make sure he had time to keep Mr. Tucker happy.

Amber groaned and put her head in her hands. Which would accomplish a grand total of—nothing. Wanda was right. In order to resolve her feelings, she had to confront them. She had to come clean about her revenge plots, bring up what happened in the past and this time give him a chance to tell his side. If Lance was all he seemed to have become, she owed it to him and to herself to explore her emotions honestly. Starting now.

"Amber?"

Amber jerked her head up. Lance came across the restaurant toward her, eyes warm and electric with excitement. Her insides began a credible impression of an out-of-control Ferris wheel. "Starting now" had just assumed an immediacy she hadn't exactly planned on. Had Lance spoken to Mr. Tucker yet? He didn't look as if he'd been recently raked over hot coals. What if Lance made the connection to her presence here today when the rake did come out? Just when she was finally ready to give him a chance, he'd want to give her a one-way ticket to eternal damnation.

Amber hid a silent whimper of panic under her smile. Too much to hope that Queen Midas had worked her previously unwelcome magic again, and the plan would somehow backfire. He'd caught her with her pants down.

And not even the way she'd intended him to.

9

LANCE PULLED UP a restaurant chair and sat opposite A.J., unable to control the foolish grin on his face. He'd worried when he didn't hear from her after his proposal early in the week that they spend more time together. She must have come here to see him. He wanted to hear her say the words. "What brings you to this neck of the woods?"

"I, uh, came to see you." She moved uncomfortably and studied her clenched hands.

Lance's grin surpassed foolishness to become embarrassingly goofy. Her confession delighted him, much as she was obviously shy about admitting her motives. "I'm glad you did. I got the prints of the prototypes back from the photographers. They came out great. I can't wait to show them to you."

She lifted her head and smiled wanly. He studied her. Not quite the hoped-for glow of a woman halfway to being in love. She looked almost guilty about something. He took her hand. "I have a surprise for you."

"Oh?"

"I've decided to work full-time on BrainToys. I just quit my job with Tucker and Company." He waited for her reaction. Imagine Lance Edwards III leaving the safe highway for the rocky path to true happiness. She'd practically go into cardiac arrest.

A.J.'s eyelids zoomed up. Her chin almost dropped onto the table. Lance laughed, elated. She must realize by now he wasn't the cloned sheep she thought. "Didn't think I had it in me? I woke up one day last week and said, 'Who am I kidding?' BrainToys is where my heart is." He squeezed her hand. "At least part of it. I gave notice to Mr. Tucker when he got back from lunch."

Amber's hand jerked in his. "How did he take the news?"

"Terribly," Lance said cheerfully. "I think he might put out a contract on me. Other than that, pretty well. Sarah must have fed him some pretty ridiculous stories, though. You wouldn't believe the things he accused me of."

"No, I'm sure I wouldn't."

She examined the table again, as if searching for flaws in the plastic top. Lance's elation sagged. What was the matter with her? He'd made up his mind when he decided to quit Tucker and Company: he had to come clean with A.J., explain about the bet and her part in getting BrainToys started. After the dinner in her apartment when she'd kissed him like a woman possessed, he had every confidence she'd forgive him.

Now, with her guilty reluctance to meet his eyes, he was starting to wonder if she'd come by to tell him to get lost. His heart hammered.

She couldn't. Not when everything in his life was coming together so well. So much of his future plan depended on her.

"Amber, you have no idea how happy this has made me. The rest of my life is suddenly stretching out in front of me like a wide blank canvas, instead of a paint-by-number scene. I owe so much of this to you."

She opened her mouth, no doubt to protest. He held up his hand. "I know what you're going to say—you didn't plan any of what happened to me." Her hand jerked again. Lance sighed. When would she be able to relax around him? The sooner all secrets were out between them, the better. "You helped free me from the yuppie straitjacket I didn't even know I was wearing." His voice dropped to a husky whisper. "I'll never be able to thank you enough."

A.J. lifted her head and met his eyes full on, hers wide and tinged with uncertainty. She bit her lip. His heart accelerated from merely hammering to splintering his ribs. She couldn't drop a bomb on him now. He loved her. As truly and deeply as he always imagined love should be. How could he possibly have pretended anything else all those years ago, and all these past weeks? He gripped her hand. They had so much to offer each other for the rest of their lives. She had to see that.

A.J.'s lips slowly curved into a smile. She covered his hand with her free one. Her expression gradually opened, and became confident.

"I'm glad I helped you, Lance." She laughed, her eyes warm. "I really am."

He couldn't decide whether to collapse on the table or run laps around the restaurant from the sheer joy and relief. Whatever her hesitation, she'd gotten over it. He could barely control the urge to lean across the table and kiss her. She was so beautiful. She'd always been beautiful to him.

"Do you have the prototype prints with you?" Her leg brushed his under the table and rested against him. He tensed. An accident?

"No, we'd have to go to my apartment."

"Got anything better to do right now?" She gave a slightly provocative smile that made his blood race.

He stood and pulled her to her feet. "Let's go."

Lance drove like a wild man back to his condo. A.J. sat with her head back, legs slightly apart, skirt hiked well above her knees, legs smooth and firm. He could barely keep his hands on the wheel. The promise in her eyes tantalized him. If he read her correctly, she'd given him the chance to spend the next several hours getting right what he'd blown so badly ten years ago.

They arrived at his building, hurried into the waiting elevator, down the hallway and burst into his apartment. Lance shut the door behind him and leaned against the cool wood for a second, wanting to memorize forever the way A.J. looked at this moment: happy, flushed, eyes brilliant and shining. Lucky gave a barely audible whine from the kitchen. Lance sent a pleading look to the closed door. *Not now, please not now.*

A.J. turned to him, smiling in shy invitation. He took one step toward her and whacked his head into the brick wall of his conscience. Every instinct in his body yelled at him to take her in his arms, take her into the bedroom, take her on his bed. Now. Before his groin exploded off his body.

But how could he risk making the same mistake

he'd made in college? He couldn't make love to this woman again without being totally honest. This time *before* disaster struck. He had to tell her about BrainToys—that the company hadn't existed until she'd inspired him to follow his dream. He had to explain about the bet—tell her making love to her in college had nothing to do with pranks.

He put his arm around her shoulders and drew her over to the couch. The new Lance Edwards wouldn't let cowardice get in the way of doing the right thing again, no matter how great the short-term rewards.

Amber sat next to him and turned her face up close to his, lips parted, eyes half-closed. This time he couldn't resist the invitation and bent his head down to her. Once couldn't hurt. She returned his kiss with a sweetness that made him ache with savage tenderness. He deepened the pressure, savoring the warm, willing contact.

A.J. made a soft, desperate sound in her throat and pushed her hands into his hair to clutch him closer, as if a wild sensual part of her had suddenly broken free. Her mouth against his became hot with erotic abandon. Lance stifled a moan. *Great* wouldn't even begin to describe the short-term rewards; the experience would probably shatter him. He forced himself to draw back. He couldn't lose sight of the big picture.

"Amber, I have a story to tell you."

She gave him an incredulous look. "Now?"

"Now." He laughed at the face she made. "Then if you still want me, I'll be only too desperate to oblige you." He gave her tempting mouth a painfully brief kiss.

A.J. wound her arm around his neck and kept the kiss going until he had no choice but to reach for her. Her leg, all but bared of skirt, reached across him to straddle his lap. "Let's save story time for after recess," she whispered, and wriggled close against him. Her hands unbuttoned his collar; her lips made soft contact with the skin at the base of his neck.

Serious trouble.

"Amber," Lance groaned, "you're making this extremely hard for me."

She drew her lips in a warm line up the column of his throat to his mouth. "That's the general idea."

He summoned every micron of control he had left and lifted her away from him. "Not yet. I have to do this now."

Amber lay back against the couch and let her head loll sideways to look at him. "Okay, okay, story time before recess." She inhaled deeply and let her breath out in a resigned sigh.

Lance moved on the couch to try to find the more comfortable position his tight pants were making elusive. From the kitchen came the faint sound of a cage being rattled, its occupant obviously wondering why he was being ignored. A.J. didn't appear to notice. Lance cleared his throat. Five minutes, then he'd get Lucky…if all went as planned, in more ways than one.

He suppressed a smile. "It's an Edwards fairy tale, starring a princess who thinks her prince is really a frog."

"I see." A.J. raised her brows. "And have we had our medication renewed recently?"

"Just give me five minutes. If you still doubt my sanity, you can run out to the pharmacy yourself."

He searched his brain for how he'd planned to begin. The whole thing seemed so easy when he rehearsed all week. He'd begin his explanation disguised as a fable, she'd catch on, become overcome with emotion and forgive him. Then they'd ride off together into the smoggy city sunset. "Once upon a time there existed a well-meaning but occasionally cowardly prince—"

"That would be you?"

He nodded, pleased. She'd figure out his intentions in no time. "Who, years before, had met a beautiful and noble princess."

"Beautiful? That would be Sarah."

"No, actually it wouldn't."

"Oh." Her brows drew down. Lance's confidence suffered a small setback. In his rehearsal she always looked up with eyes full of hope at that part. Lucky gave a forlorn yelp from his crate in the kitchen. A.J. half-turned toward the sound. "Is that her? No offense, but she sounds like a dog."

He grinned and shook his head. "Let me get through this, then I'll introduce you. The beautiful princess rescued the prince from the nasty prison of his existence. She showed him life could be dreams-come-true and anything-is-possible."

"Well, she sounds like quite the super gal." A.J.'s voice dripped acid.

Lance frowned. At that point she was supposed to say, "Oh, Lance, darling, did I really? I had no idea you felt that way." Maybe he'd been watching too many old movies. Lucky gave a heart-wrenching howl. Lance gritted his teeth.

"But the prince, through his cowardice and certain intervention by a staggeringly evil sorcerer, did not treat her as she deserved, and eventually lost her. She—"

"Can I interrupt here?"

He sighed. That didn't sound like "I love you, Lance, take me now, make me yours forever." He'd definitely been watching too many old movies.

"Go ahead."

A.J. stood up. "I may be off base here, but in my book of etiquette, it's a tiny bit tacky, when one woman has just made herself available, to go mooning on about another one."

He stared. How could she possibly think he meant anyone else? Did she really have so little idea of his feelings for her ten years ago? "What other one?"

"Princess Perfect." A regular series of thuds came from the kitchen as Lucky began throwing his body against the side of his cage. A.J. folded her arms and glared at Lance. "Your dog and I both want out."

"For crying out loud, you haven't heard a word I've said since we met."

"Believe me, I've heard plenty." She turned away and took one step toward the door.

He caught her in two strides. "I am not letting you get away again. This time you'll listen to—"

A splintering crash echoed from the kitchen, followed by a yelp of doggy pain. Lance ran to the kitchen and flung open the door. Lucky had managed to turn his crate on its side, smashing two decorative glass bottles Sarah kept under the table. Lance yanked open the cage door and bent to examine him. Not a scratch. Good. Back to A.J. She better still be there.

He dashed back out into the living room, Lucky close on his heels.

"Is he all right?" A.J. stood where he'd left her, her face anxious. Lucky jumped up to embrace her, and almost knocked her over. She laughed drily. "Apparently no serious injury."

Lance almost passed out from the high of his relief. She'd stayed. She was laughing. "He's got skin like a rhinoceros. A.J., meet Lucky."

"I didn't know you'd gotten a dog." She spoke stiffly, but patted Lucky's chestnut hide, sending him into immediate puppy frenzy.

"At the risk of sounding trite, there's a lot you don't know about me." He grinned at the sight of the two of them. Lucky had saved the moment. Lance still had a chance to get his guilt off his chest and A.J. into his life permanently. Things still looked hopeful.

A key sounded in the apartment's front lock. Lance froze. *Oh, lord, not Sarah, not now.* He'd forgotten to get his key back from her. He glanced at Amber, who stared at the door apprehensively. Erase all previous hopefulness. Certain doom approached.

"Oh, Mr. Edwards, I didn't know you were home." Edith, the girl he'd hired to walk Lucky, stood shyly in the doorway.

Lance almost hugged her. Certain doom receded rapidly. Perfect. Perfect. Now he'd convince her to walk Lucky all the way to Vermont and back, and he'd have uninterrupted time to settle things with

A.J. and make mad, delirious love to her. He almost ran for his wallet.

"Could you keep him the rest of the afternoon?" He slipped some bills into Edith's hand, probably too many, but he was a desperate man. "I have some business to do here."

"Wow! I mean, sure, Mr. Edwards, no problem. I'll keep him all week for that."

Lance handed Lucky over, thanked her and walked back to A.J., who was surveying the damage in the kitchen. He came up behind her and took her shoulders.

"I'll clear up the mess later. Right now there's something more important to set right." He turned her toward him. He had to make sure she understood *she* played the starring role in his fable. A.J. stared up at him, eyes vulnerable, hair mussed, lips smudged burgundy from his kisses. Whatever adventures he had planned next for the cowardly prince and the noble princess were overcome by the depth of his feelings for the woman in front of him.

"Amber, I...love you." He could say nothing else. The words released a ten-year-old tension inside him, like a bunch of balloons cut from their straining strings to float away, all lightness and freedom.

"You what?" Her look of shock and confusion temporarily interrupted the balloons' romantic maiden voyage.

"I love you. That's what this whole story was leading to." He bent to kiss her stiff, surprised mouth.

"I can't believe I'm hearing this." She sounded overcome, awed...or maybe only dumbfounded.

He'd have to proceed with caution, letting her know how he felt from the beginning.

He kissed her again, starved for the taste and feel of her, coaxing her lips to relax and respond. He could finally allow himself hope for the kind of love he always knew existed. The chance he thought he'd lost forever ten years ago, when he couldn't convince A.J. he hadn't betrayed her.

"God, A.J., we've wasted so much time."

She gave a strained smile. "Our lives aren't quite over yet."

"Thanks to you, mine is just beginning." He slid his hands down over her hips and pulled her slender body tight against him, wanting her to feel the effect she had on him, wanting to feel her passion break through the control she'd regained.

A.J. drew back. "There's something I need to tell you."

Lance groaned in frustration. "No. No more words. What's here between us now is what matters. We have the chance to put ten years of loneliness and misunderstanding to rest." He scooped her impatiently into his arms and headed for the bedroom. "Whatever you need to tell me can wait. I've wanted this moment too long to put it off now."

She giggled nervously, the strained look back on her face. "Lance, I think you've been watching too many old movies."

10

HE LOVED HER. Lance Edwards loved her. Amber leaned back into his arms, her body tense, her mind reduced to a chaotic whirl of thoughts and emotions. His eyes held hers, his intent clear: to ravish her until she could no longer stand. The idea made breathing a practical impossibility.

She'd been so sure the story about the beautiful princess would lead up to a typical male disclaimer: "I'll never find a woman like that again, so don't expect more from me than my body." That would have made his position clear. Instead, he'd broadsided her with his soul-baring declaration and put her heart at risk again.

Lance set her on the bed and stretched out beside her up on one elbow, leisurely stroking her hair, outlining her features, tracing her mouth. Amber lay stiffly, a mass of conflict and indecision. Sex, she'd expected as the next logical step in their relationship. But this reverent tenderness from a man who said he loved her could shatter defenses she hadn't yet been able to reinforce. She needed more time to understand how she felt, to trust him again. She hadn't even come clean about her revenge plans. How could she make love to him with that kind of deception unmasked?

"Lance, I need to tell you—"

"Shh." He laid his finger across her lips. "Nothing you say can change this." He kissed her over and over, exploring the line and shape of her mouth with his lips and tongue, over and over, soft, gentle kisses. Not at all the carnal assault she expected. Memories flooded back of the first and only time they were together like this. He'd been patient then, too, lingering over each kiss as if he'd be allowed only one, making no attempt to increase the passion, as if he could ask for nothing more than to taste her mouth again and again.

Amber slowly relaxed to a degree she hadn't thought possible, her thoughts and objections stilled by the drugging sweetness of his kisses, her physical self reduced to a state of tranquillity, a secure, sensuous place Lance brought her to. Conscious awareness of her body, his body, the room around them, dissolved into deep peace and calm, as if he had found the undisturbed core of her being and brought it to the surface.

In the midst of this trance, the ten-year-old tangle in Amber's mind cleared. She loved him. She loved him as surely and deeply as he kissed her, as surely and deeply as she'd ever known anything to be true. With this awareness came strength and freedom that made any she'd known under the cheap mask of triumphant revenge seem weak and forlorn. She loved him.

Amber brought herself back, out of the stillness and peace, to an entirely different awareness of the man beside her. Lance's mouth changed from a comforting presence to a teasing, tantalizing instrument of torture. A glow of erotic heat began low in her body. She gave a soft moan. She wanted more; she wanted all of him.

She pulled him closer, opened her mouth to him, twisted her body to lie facing his. He responded immediately, sliding his hand over the curve of her hip and pressing her close until his hardness strained against her.

Too many clothes. She wrapped her leg over him to lock them together and began feverishly unbuttoning his shirt. She needed to feel him, to taste the skin she'd glimpsed in this bedroom weeks ago, the skin she'd tasted once before. She explored his chest with her hands, mouth and tongue, reclaiming possession of the only male body she'd ever known so intimately. Lance groaned and rolled on his back, pulling her on top of him. Amber rid herself of her blouse and bra, eager to bare herself to his touch, thrilling in the fulfillment of her feminine power. He cupped the weight of her breasts in his hands, drew her down and suckled them, his mouth hot and demanding.

"Lance." She could scarcely think, scarcely speak, but she had to say the words. "I love you."

He lifted his head from her breast, held her face between his hands, his own expression frozen. "Say it again."

"I love you." She felt as if the entire world had just rolled off her shoulders. Lance took a deep breath and closed his eyes. When he opened them, whatever glimpse she thought she'd had of the real Lance Edwards up until now paled in comparison to this sight of him. Fierce, possessive joy lit his face, bold and proud like the warrior she'd only tried to be.

He undid her skirt and rolled her over on her back to slide it off. "Let me see you," he whispered. "Let me see all of you, Amber, love."

She lay before him, naked, unselfconscious, burning with the need to join with him. He gazed at her with something like awe, then touched her as if she belonged to him, as if her body were more his than hers. His warm, masterful hands and mouth stroked her inner thighs, pushed her legs wider, explored the hungry heat between them until she thought she'd go mad wanting him inside her.

"Please." Her breath came in small panting gasps; her body writhed in an agony of desire. "Now."

Lance shed the rest of his clothes and reached into his nightstand for protection before he rolled over on top of her. He gathered her close, said her name, then slowly pushed in an inch at a time, his eyes locked with hers, until she became near crazed with impatience. She thrust her hips up to take him all in, crying out at the glorious feel of him filling her completely. He began to rock inside her, his fingers and lips gentle on her face and neck. Suddenly she no longer lay with him at that moment, but back ten years ago, discovering for the first time what it meant to merge into someone.

"Let me please you, A.J. Let me love you," he whispered against her mouth. "Let me be the only one."

He moved slowly, then more urgently, building in her a momentum of rising ecstasy that grew from a fierce pinpoint of light to a sensation-screaming suspension of time, before she finally shattered into pulsing release. He said her name again, pushed faster, harder, until he tensed, gave a low hoarse groan, and his own climax contracted inside her.

Their breathing slowed together; the room gradually took shape again, not a cluttered Harvard dorm room, but Lance's elegant condominium. Amber gave a dreamy, satisfied chuckle.

Lance lifted his head and grinned. "What exactly do you find so amusing?"

"Let's just say you took me somewhere else for a while." She ran her fingers through his sandy hair, then stopped. Her fingers clenched. Unreasoning fear swept away her chance for afterglow. Her déjà vu moment had brought back the horrible sequel to their first intimacy.

"Ouch!" He removed her hands and rolled off her. "You mind telling me why you're trying to induce premature balding?"

"What did you say to me while we were making love?"

"When?" He searched her face warily. "I didn't think to write anything down."

"You said, 'Let me please you, A.J. Let me love you.'" She could barely get the words to exit her voice box.

"That's what I said to you last time we made love. Did you remember?" He smiled and stroked her cheek.

"Yes." She tried not to pull away from his hand. Panic clawed at her insides. She remembered too much. She remembered how much the words meant to her the first time. Words. Just words. Followed by his betrayal. How could she know he wasn't ready to call Chris the minute she left his apartment tonight? *You won't believe it, Chris. She fell for it again.* Wouldn't that be a hoot? A real thigh-slapper.

She shook her head. No. He couldn't deceive her twice.

"A.J., what is it? You look like you've swallowed poison."

She clutched his shoulder in a death grip. "I need you to tell me this isn't part of another gag."

"What?" His eyes narrowed incredulously. "How could you think that after—?"

"Just tell me."

He groaned. "A.J., darling, sweetheart, this is not part of a gag. Do you think I say 'I love you' to every woman I...date?"

"It's possible." She attempted a light tone and achieved a paranoid screech instead. What if he did? How would she know? *Calm down, Amber.*

"A.J., I think I've loved you since the night we met."

She tried to smile. The fear swelled. What normal sincere person actually used a line like that? "Which night we met? Both times you were too drunk to remember your own name."

Lance frowned. "I guess you have a point. Okay, I'll never forget our second date." He touched her lips with his thumb. "When I kissed you after the spicy garlic chicken."

"Recently or ten years ago?" She struggled to regain her equanimity. Someone was chatting calmly to Lance about their past. Whoever she was, she was doing a bang-up job covering for Amber while she had a complete mental breakdown. ''I guess something about Chinese chicken makes you very amorous.''

Lance laughed. ''Something about *you* makes me very amorous.''

All the right lines. All the right moves. Had he really changed? Could she ever trust him again? She smiled somewhat desperately, feeling disoriented, as if she'd been given nitrous oxide by an invisible dentist. ''So you didn't really invite me into your bedroom that night to talk about toy designs?''

''Did I use that as an excuse?'' He frowned. ''Barely a step above the proverbial etchings. All I remember is how much I hoped Chris was out for the evening. I couldn't wait to kiss you.''

''Not in college. I meant recently, in your apartment.'' The parallels slapped her in the face. *That was then, this is then, too.* They'd gone through practically the identical sequence of events ten years apart. Could she have been stupid enough to make the same mistake again?

''Oh, *recently.* I couldn't wait to kiss you then, either.'' He raised himself on one elbow. ''A.J., I don't blame you for being furious with me. I should have made you hear me out. When you wouldn't listen, I didn't fight for you. I can't tell you how I wish I had.''

Amber laughed uneasily. Why was he making such a big deal out of the kiss in his apartment? She could swear he had something on his mind he wasn't saying. If she could get her brain to behave according to normal physical principles, she might have a shot at figuring it out. ''That night didn't mean life or death for anyone. Nature took its course between us. The rest—just circumstance.''

He brought her limp hand to his lips for a kiss. ''Your forgiveness means a lot to me, A.J. A lesser woman would have been out for my anatomy with a cleaver.'' He took in a breath as if to speak, then cleared his throat awkwardly instead. Amber braced herself. Here it comes.

''While we're on the topic of forgiveness...I have a confession.''

Amber stared at him as if he could suddenly turn back into the slime monster from the deep. ''I don't know if I want to hear this.''

''It's about BrainToys. The company didn't really exist until shortly before I quit my job at Tucker and Company.''

Amber's mouth dropped. ''What? What did you...what?'' She slipped away from him and crouched naked on the edge of the bed like a cornered animal ready to flee. A cold shiver broke over her skin. More deception. More lies. Could Lance Edwards ever operate without them?

''I made the whole thing up to get close to you again.'' His eyes were dark, full of the appropriate amount of regret. ''I'm sorry.''

Amber stood and stared at him. The enormity of his confession hadn't hit her yet. She watched the pain approach, like a cartoon character staring at the boulder hurtling down from the cliff above. He'd won again. The whole time she thought she played master of the game, he'd been pulling his own strings. Hiring her, having her come up with designs, inviting her to his bedroom for that bogus business dinner to review them. No wonder he'd overapologized for kissing her that night. Her instinct that he'd been hiding something was right on.

"I'm sure you enjoyed making a fool of me again. You've certainly become the consummate professional." She made a grab for her clothes, too late. He snatched them up and shoved them behind him.

"A.J., we are going to have this out here. You won't run away from me again. Not after what just happened between us."

"What happened between us was just sex. Everybody does it. Birds, bees, educated fleas, the whole universe." Amber moved around the bed, trying to get at her clothes. Maybe he lied when he told her he loved her, too. Sarah said he could be very creative getting women in the sack. Her instinct told her he'd been telling the truth, but her fury didn't want to listen. In any case the truth wouldn't wipe away his other lies.

Lance shook his head and kept her clothes out of reach. "You can't tell me that was 'just sex' for either of us."

"That's all it could be. My turn to get what I wanted from you and walk out, just like you did to me." She began pacing the room, trying to gain control of the ugly need to hurt him.

"Bull." He narrowed his eyes. "You could never stoop that low, A.J. You said you loved me. You've always been a lousy liar. I would have known if you didn't mean it."

She lost the battle for control. "Well, I learned how to lie. I had an excellent teacher, Mr. Edwards.

As for stooping low, I think I've proved I can do that, too."

"What do you mean?"

She spun around and stared at his bewildered expression. He had no idea of Amazon Amber's efforts to destroy him. Her desire to hurt him had found the perfect outlet. "What do you think really happened to your car? Your apartment? Did that champagne shake itself? And, oh my, I feel so badly about letting slip to Sarah about BrainToys and that sleazy pass you made." She clutched her heart, then stabbed a vicious finger at him. "Last but not least, why don't you check with Mr. Tucker where he heard those rumors about your lunchtime activities?"

Lance pushed himself off the bed, his eyes bitingly cold. "Is that why you agreed to come to work for me? Just so you could hurt me? God, Amber, I'd never have thought you had that much spite in you."

Amber tried to chill her eyes to the same degree, on some level aware his indignation claimed more solid ground than hers. She drowned the feeling in a flood of self-righteous wrath. "I'd gladly rewind and replay the whole plot for what you did to me."

He turned, swept up her clothes and launched them at her. "I've tried too many times to explain about the damn bet. Let me know when you're ready to listen." He grabbed up his pants and walked to the door. "You can find your own way out."

AMBER STARED AT HER SCREEN, trying to find design inspiration from Quazor, Death Master of the Underground, a computer game for Z.A.B. Companies, Inc. She hadn't found much inspiration in anything since the blowout with Lance three weeks ago. Even summer fever, usually a raging disease by early June, passed her by this year. Her dealings with Mr. Edwards since that horrible afternoon had been professional to the point of sterility; most contact between them took place by fax or mail.

Her marketing pieces for BrainToys had been produced; a manufacturing company in New Jersey had scheduled Squidbrain and SpySam for production over the summer. Major toy and department chains throughout the country would feature the toys in the fall. Randy Andrews, marketing magician, predicted a huge rush over the holiday season.

Amber arranged the ludicrously overarmed death master in a more menacing pose. Life had progressed from agony to ecstasy and back, leaving her emotions locked in paralyzing limbo. Twice over ten years the Fates brought her and Lance together, and twice she thought they'd found something special. Both times he'd eventually proved himself untrustworthy. Amber wanted an open, straightforward relationship, not one based on lies and manipulation.

She rolled her eyes. To be fair she hadn't exactly distinguished herself in the lies and manipulation category, either. But didn't that provide all the more proof she and Lance couldn't approach each other honestly? She sighed. Too much damn water under the damn dam.

Her phone rang. "Hi, it's Wanda. Jerry and I are taking you and the kids out for banana splits tonight. Since you refuse to get high on love, at least try fat and sugar."

"I have a date tonight." Amber shuddered at the

thought. Why had she ever thought going out would help?

"Date schmate. Unless you're with Lance, it doesn't count."

"It's Steve's new girlfriend's cousin. He's supposed to be great. We're all going out for Thai food." She sounded as if she were announcing the hour of her own hanging.

"Okay, but do me a favor. Notice carefully what a complete drip he is compared to Lance, come home, exhausted from the strain of being pleasant to a wienie dog all evening, pick up the phone, call Mr. Edwards III and patch things up. Okay?"

"Sure, Wanda. Then I'll just sit back and wait for him to expose his next little deception. 'Gee, Amber, did I forget to mention my six wives in the commune? And the three others who died from mysterious jungle diseases moments after they displeased me?'"

"Listen, woman. At the beginning we were operating under the assumption Lance needed to see a surgeon for maturity implants. Now I'm starting to wonder if I should call Mass General to schedule you in."

Amber bristled. "What does this have to do with my maturity?"

"Let's face it. That revenge business we were so excited about ranks right down there with what you thought he did to you in college. Now, you're—"

"What do you mean what I *thought* he did? You sound like you're on his side. I gave him the measly chance you told me to, and all I discovered were more lies."

"Did you ever stop to think he's been trying like hell to win you back? I bet he's been in love with you all these years. The guy is obviously a wild romantic. Do you know how many wildly romantic guys there are on this planet? My two-year-old can count that high."

"If he'd loved me in college, he would have—"

"Fought for you, I know. But you said yourself you didn't give him much of a chance. And how do you know he doesn't regret letting you go to this day?"

Wanda's words triggered an immediate picture of Lance, after he and Amber made love. *I should have made you hear me out. When you wouldn't listen, I didn't fight for you. I can't tell you how I wish I had.*

An eerie, disorienting shiver ran from the bottom of her feet up to the top of her bad hair day. She'd assumed Lance referred, somewhat overdramatically, to the pass he made the night the garlic powder trapped them in his bedroom. Had he actually been trying to explain about the bet? Had he really loved A. J. Kszyckniwicz ten years ago?

Amber shook her head. Nice story. She wanted to believe in happy endings. But too much pain lay between them now. "I've given him everything I have, Wanda. Twice. I can't get hurt like that again."

Wanda sighed. "Okay, okay. I think you're making a mega-mistake, but I hear you. Listen, if you need to vent after your evening with Deputy Droopalong, my door's open."

Amber thanked her and hung up the phone, more tired than she'd ever felt in her life. Maybe Wanda was right. Maybe her fear and pride were standing in the way of a lifetime of real happiness. Or maybe they were protecting her from a lifetime of paranoia and mistrust. Could she take that kind of chance? She let her head bonk down on the edge of the desk. Taking chances took energy. She was fresh out.

"Knock, knock, speedy delivery. Package for Ms. Amber Jade Daniels." Steve's grinning head poked through the door. "You psyched for tonight?"

"Come in, Steve. Yes, I'm psyched." She tried to force some "psych" into her tone and failed miserably.

"Yeah...you really sound on fire." He looked at her in concern and deposited a box on her desk.

Amber saw the return address on the package: BrainToys, Inc. Her heart gave a pathetic flutter.

"Amber, you'll love Chester. He just got back from a Star Trek convention and has a great two-hour slide show he says you'll die for."

Amber's eyes froze open in horror. "You can't be—"

"Kidding, kidding." Steve laughed heartily and smacked his thigh. "The guy's cool, I promise. We'll be by your place at seven."

Amber rolled her eyes. "Guess I walked right into that one."

"Live long and prosper." Steve let himself out, still chuckling.

Amber regarded the package on her desk doubtfully. What could Lance possibly want to send her? A gift? An apology? An explosive device? She grabbed a pair of scissors and attacked the packing tape. Three wrapped bundles and a note inside. She grabbed the note; the pathetic flutter in her heart increased to a wild flapping. Maybe this was a sign. Maybe he'd written something that would clear her brain of confused stagnation. Something that could even push her into action. She had to admit she was teetering. An apology, a tender word, a hint of affection, even "Love, Lance..."

Dear Amber,

I thought you should have these. Thanks for your hard work.

Sincerely,
Lance

Amber twisted her lip; disappointment delivered a vicious jab to her insides. So much for a sign. So much for Mr. Wild Romantic. She unwrapped the bundles miserably. Squidbrain emerged from the first, with a canister of slime to insert in his warty body. Amber grimaced and put him aside. Wanda's children could enjoy that one.

The next two bundles contained SpySam and B.J., noble and handsome father and son, dressed in matching martial-arts suits, ready to battle the forces of evil in the universe. Amber turned them over and over, her throat full. She loved these toys. A tiny slip of paper protruded from B.J.'s white jacket. She unrolled it and recognized Lance's writing.

I never told you, but I should have. I named B.J. nine years ago, after a woman I loved who embodied everything the world ever did right.

Amber stared at the note, then read the words over at least thirteen times. *Nine years ago…a woman I loved.*

Joy lifted through her like a just-launched rocket. She put her head back down on her desk and started to sob. Lance loved A. J. Kszyckniwicz. He'd rediscovered her as Amber Jade and he'd loved her again. Maybe he still did.

"Knock, knock, are you okay?"

Amber held up B.J., her eyes streaming. "Doll. This one is named me. I'm it. He loves me." She hiccuped.

Steve's eyebrows shot up. "That's…great news, Amber. Being loved by your dolly is very important."

Amber burst into slightly hysterical laughter. "Steve, Steve, I can't make it tonight. I have a date with my destiny."

"Ah. Your destiny. That would be the, um…" He pointed to B.J.

"Go away." Amber sank back rapturously in her chair and clutched B.J. to her heart. "We want to be alone."

11

LANCE STARED AT the envelope in his hands.

"I said, could you sign here." The messenger thrust his clipboard impatiently under Lance's nose.

Lance signed absently. He barely noticed the messenger leaving, mumbling unflattering things about executives' brain capacities. He couldn't take his eyes off the letter. From Daniels Design. Amber must have gotten the note inside B.J.'s jacket. In his hands he held her answer.

He swallowed. Lance Edwards wasn't used to having his happiness decided by someone else. But Lance Edwards had never cared about anything quite as much as what a certain beautiful, sexy, exasperating woman wanted from his future. Any anger he'd felt over her attempts to avenge herself had long since fled. Who could blame her after what he must have put her through? All he wanted from her now was a happy ending.

He tore open the envelope, and another fell out, this one addressed to her. A letter he'd sent her in college, well-worn, crumpled, as if it had lain in the back of a closet for the past ten years, which it undoubtedly had. Hope rose inside him like a giant hot-air balloon. She'd kept something of him with her. He removed the letter inside.

Dear A.J.,

Graduation is in two days. I can't leave here without one more attempt to explain. I'll be at Radcliffe Yard at 5:00 tomorrow. Please be there.

Lance

Lance read the note over at least thirteen times, reliving the agony of desperation he'd suffered writing the original. He grimaced in disgust. What a typically cowardly Edwards way of operating. He'd been boiling over with passion and pain and had written a note that sounded as if he wanted to explain about a missing sock. No wonder she hadn't taken him seriously.

He turned the paper over to see if she'd made any comment. Nothing. What did she mean by returning the letter now? Did she send a message of hope or doom? The letter was dated June fifth; the meeting would have taken place on the sixth, if she'd ever shown up. God knows he'd waited long enough for her, thinking up every possible reason she might have been delayed, and then every impossible one, before he finally accepted in despair that she wasn't coming and reluctantly put her out of his life.

June sixth. Lance yanked his desk calendar closer. Adrenaline bolted through his system. Today was the fourth. He leaned back in his chair and exhaled deeply to quiet his jumping nerves. If he read her right, and if he could manage to live another two days under this kind of strain, he'd be waiting for her again.

AMBER WALKED DOWN Brattle Street toward the entrance to Radcliffe Yard, placing each foot carefully in front of the other, trying to gain some measure of solidity and comfort by concentrating on the simple action of walking. That much her brain could handle. To contemplate her goal for meeting Lance today required too much mental anguish. Just because he'd confessed to loving her ten years ago didn't mean he'd forgiven her for the recent past. Would he come? Would they finally have the chance to be together? Or would he forever consign her to the trash heap of his heart?

Amber reached the appointed bench in the yard and stopped. No one there. The sweet scent of mowed grass teased her nose, bringing back memories of that awful first spring before Lance's graduation. She glanced at her watch. Three minutes early. She'd been ready for the past two hours, but had delayed coming, knowing how much she'd hate having to wait.

She began pacing, calculating how long before she wore a trench in the walkway. For once the beautiful green calm of the yard had no effect on her. Had Lance waited this anxiously ten years ago? Her heart ached. If nothing else, if he'd felt even a tenth of this tension, she owed him a few crates of retroactive antacids.

"Amber."

She spun around, elated at the sound of his voice, took two steps toward him, then stopped. The crazy rush to fling herself into his arms had been instinctive. For all she knew he'd come to pump her full of lead.

He walked up and stopped two paces away. "I got your invitation. Or rather, my invitation." He smiled, his eyes questioning.

"I'm glad you came." Her answering smile stuck on her face in what probably looked like a death mask. Glad he came? She was ecstatic. But why had he come? Did he want her? In his bed? In his life? For now? Forever? How did one politely phrase these questions?

The silence between them became more potent than the smell of cut grass. Amber cleared her throat. First the apology, then the small matter of their entire future. "I wanted to tell you a story."

"By any chance involving a prince and princess?" He chuckled.

She shook her head. "This one is about an ugly duckling."

"Who grew up to be a beautiful swan." He took a step closer.

Amber shook her head again. "I'm not sure this ugly duckling grew up at all." She took a deep breath. "Lance, I owe you an apology for—"

"If anyone should apologize, it's—"

"I never gave you the chance to explain about—"

"If I'd had any guts, the whole thing never—"

"I should have told you a long time—"

"Amber." He stepped forward and grabbed her shoulders. "I think we've beaten ourselves up adequately. Can we stop now?"

"As long as we understand one another."

"Seeing as how we haven't finished a single complete sentence, it should be unlikely. But somehow I think we do."

Amber nodded and cracked her death mask with a genuine smile. The hope she'd beaten into submission for fear of disappointment sprang to life. She didn't have him forever after yet, but she wouldn't need to worry about dodging bullets. Lance's eyes had lost the guarded look and come alive—deep, warm, intense.

The Look.

Sensual lightning crackled through her system. She stepped closer, close enough for her breasts to touch his chest if she let them. She didn't. There was more to clear up than whether they were still attracted to each other.

He moved his fingers up and down her arms in a skin-tingling caress. "The way I see it, we have two options for the immediate future. We can hire lawyers and begin a long battle over every nuance of our questionably sane past, from day one in college up until now..."

Amber grimaced. "Or?"

"Or we can go back to my apartment and, uh—" he moved forward until his chest took over the contact she'd delayed "—plan our future."

His low, husky voice and the touch of his body removed most of Amber's ability to function. The majority of her brain was busy keeping track of the erotic explosion zinging through her system. She determinedly held on to the gray cells left her. "What kind of future did you have in mind?"

He snapped unexpectedly into business mode, with a hint of mischief peeking through his yuppie demeanor. "I'm offering you the position of social hostess and primary concubine, assuming, of course, after a probationary period, you fulfill your duties in a satisfactory—ouch!'' He removed his foot from under her vicious stomp, grinning. ''I take it that means I shouldn't bother preparing the contract?''

''Unless you want it delicately thrust down your trachea.'' Amber laughed.

He slid his hands down her arms, clasped her fingers and brought them to his heart. His expression grew serious. ''Would you like to live outside the city, Amber? In a renovated farmhouse? With Lucky and me?''

His heart beat strong and fast under her curled fingers, but not half as strong and fast as her own. What did he mean?

''As primary concubine?'' She tried to make her voice light, but the last word broke at least an octave.

''No, Amber, as my wife.'' He kissed each of her hands, his eyes passionate and slightly vulnerable. ''All my life I was told marriage equaled a career move. All my life, deep down, I suspected it could mean more. But I never dreamed, until I met you again, how much more, and how desperately I could want someone to share my life.''

Amber inhaled endlessly. A curtain of delirium fell over her senses. He wanted to marry her. She was the one.

He bent his head down until his lips were inches from hers. ''The minute I saw you at Daisy's, I fell in love with you all over again.''

''I don't think I ever fell out.'' She eliminated the inches to his mouth until only one remained. ''Yes, I'll marry you, Lance.''

He moved his mouth down as hers moved up. For

the first time in ten years, Amber gave herself over to kissing him without reservation, without fear, without worries over distrust and deception. She wound her arms around his neck and pressed her body to his in a slow rhythmic expression of her desire.

Lance's arms tightened around her, then he drew back slightly, blue eyes dark, his breathing uneven. "I seem to want to get you to my apartment immediately."

She pressed her lips to his throat, thrilling in his response.

He swallowed hard. "There's a bottle of champagne in my refrigerator to celebrate our engagement."

"Unshaken?" Amber blinked innocently.

He grinned. "Then I want to take you out to Maison Robert for dinner. About time I treated you right."

Amber half-closed her eyes and leaned her upper body back to aim a seductive gaze at the man who would become her husband.

"I'd rather stay home—" her hands wandered down his chest and stomach, teasingly close to the fly of his jeans "—and make hot—" she moved forward to trace his lips with her tongue "—steamy..."

He gave a weak moan of protest. Happiness ricocheted off Amber's every internal surface. This was hers. For the rest of her life. She smiled into his eyes and pursed her lips to whisper against his waiting mouth, "...spicy garlic chicken."

It's NOW OR NEVER

For three women who find themselves in danger...because of the men they love.

Award-winning author

brings you three heart-stopping stories about intrigue, danger and the mysteries of falling in love.

Now or Never by Anne Stuart,
coming to a bookstore near you
in November 1999.

Available wherever Harlequin and Silhouette books are sold.

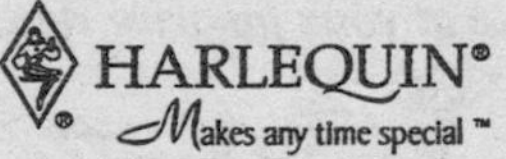

Visit us at www.romance.net

PSBR31199